STEP SOFTLY ON THE BEAVER

STEP SOFTLY ON THE BEAVER

FRANK HARRISON

WALKER AND COMPANY,
NEW YORK

c./

First published in the United States of America in 1971 by the Walker Publishing Company, Inc.

DEC 14 '71

ISBN: 0-8027-0354-2

BL

Library of Congress Catalog Card Number: 77-161101

Printed in the United States of America from type set in the United Kingdom.

To Beth Black and Jim Davies

PROLOGUE

Up in the North country when the earth first quickens and stretches in its spring pangs, the bush, quiet and chaste for so long under the white yoke, becomes abandoned and wanton.

From everywhere flows the water, in widening pools from the melting snows—seeping out of the ice-locked land, and pouring in an unbroken stream from the skies.

The whole land weeps with freedom, until the creeks and rivers, swollen beyond bearing, belch out over the prairies, sweeping the rubbish of fall in careless tide-lines across the pastures. The overflow sinks down into the topsoil, helping to sweat out the frost, and the crust crumbles and dissolves into a glutinous red slush that clings high on the thigh of man or beast.

In the vast, brooding bush a single tree becomes a green torch. Soon there are a dozen, then a score, and at last the whole forest, straining at its roots, gives a great push and in an exultation of colour, the land is reborn.

The people of the bush who have stubbornly shared its long silence, rejoice in its delivery. All the pain and weariness of winter dies with the first warm wind from the south. They breathe in the new scents, and are touched by the exhilaration. Through the early days they call to each other, their voices filter across the clearings and through the poplar stands. The dogs join in, starting a message that circles in ever-widening ripples, till it touches the foothills, and even the far-off Bay. In the muskeg, the frogs take up the chorus in a never-ending throbble, and across the high skies the snow geese echo it, far north to the tundra.

> Winter is dead.
> Winter is dead.
> We are alive! Alive! Alive!

*

Fat Mary Littleleaf, child of the bush, heard the song of spring and in her belly was born an answering throb, that grew with the waters of the creek and ran wild, sap-like, through and through her.

She knew this feeling. She had had it before, and she knew to

3

what it would lead—but that was for the next days, and the bush folk live only for today.

Eat while the meat is hot.

There was so much wildness in this quiet-looking woman. She was very, very hot. She was spring-hot.

'Hey you kids, go camp the old lady,' she called to her children and they scampered away through the bush, like a bunch of prairie chickens, the dogs yapping and jumping at their legs.

That's them fixed for sure, she thought. They would stay around the old lady's place, eat her meat and bannock, split logs for her, bring water and share the floor at nights with a dozen other grandchildren.

There was nothing else for her to worry about. Fat Mary was not married and had no ties, no animals either to have to tend. She was a walk-away woman, and it was time for her to walk. She scooped up two handfuls of earth from beside the lower logs and carried it into the house where she threw it over the fire ash. Then she wrapped a strip of moose meat in an old skirt, tied the parcel at both ends and looped the string over one of her big shoulders. She went out to the woodpile and rolled a stump from it, nudged it with her foot over against the door.

'Goddam dogs,' she said. After a final look-around, she pushed through the willow wands behind the cabin and took the trail to the lake. She was a large woman, heavily thighed, and as she walked, her buttocks rolled under the restricting cloth. Mud sausages squeezed up between her toes and she gave an occasional kick to scatter this slush.

After a quarter of a mile the trees began to thin out, and she came on to the grassy slope above the lake. She walked along the lakeside until she reached the mouth of a creek. Here in the bush, on the near side of the gully, was old Henry's cabin, and it was a pretty good bet that some of the guys would be in there with the cards.

The old man's shack was small: a square of logs, mud and moss-packed, a broad roof sagging out in front. Fishing nets hung like giant webs from the boards, reaching down to the woodpile and its carpet of chips. The undergrowth had reclaimed most of the original clearing, and grew close around the sides and back of the building, as if propping it against the winds that pressed constantly on it from the lake.

Mary stopped to take a breath and saw a thin smoke-wisp wandering upwards from the roof pipe. A wagon stood at the front of the cabin, and she recognized the team as being Pete Crow's.

4

That wasn't good. She didn't like the breed, he was crazy and bad medicine. He was older than Mary but she knew all about him from Band talk. She stood watching his cropping horses, and remembered what was said of him. How he'd gotten the devil inside his head, the devil that crooked his eyes up, so you didn't know which one to look at. He grew his hair long and wore it in tails like the old ways, but he didn't belong in the Band on account he wasn't Treaty. Pete Crow was Frenchy Alex's brother. Pupped by old Jerry Crow, the both of them—Pete out of a white woman who shacked up a while with Jerry, and Frenchy out of Jerry's real wife.

When the white woman ran herself into the lake, Jerry Crow moved back in with his wife and took the breed boy with him. The people said Jerry should have left the kid out for the coyotes, but Jerry didn't have no other boy child then.

'Them coyotes too damn smart take this guy, anyways,' he'd laughed. So Pete stayed around Jerry all the time, trailing after him like a dragging lodgepole. Then Frenchy got born and Pete switched his trailing to Frenchy, and those two guys always were together.

They grew up like that—least Frenchy grew up, but Pete always stayed short-assed. Frenchy got big, real big like Jerry, and he was noisy like Jerry too, always making people laugh. He'd say, 'Jeez, this little breed, he okay-o. He got his head full of worms, that's all. Ain't that right, Pete?'

Around the reserve Frenchy was the boss, but it was different in the bush. Folks said that Pete belonged in the bush like fleas in the hairs of a dog. He sniffed out old moose and shot him down, and then Frenchy put the quarters up on his big back and packed them out to the trails. And they said about Pete, that when he went into the bush, he didn't ever take more than two, three shells 'cause he never wasted a shot. And that was a strange thing to understand, how he could shoot with his eyes all twisted up like that, because you sure don't shoot from the smell of things.

Now Frenchy was over in the Fort since New Year's, for cutting the ear off one of the Lake Indians. The breed must have moved in on Old Henry. Hell! She didn't want nothing with that crazy guy—she didn't want his worms going right up inside her, till they reached up and twisted her eyes around. While she hesitated the door opened and Pete came outside. He walked over to the wagon and opening his trousers he began to water against its wheel.

They stood like this, throwing shadows across the same stretch

5

of grass, but he gave no sign that he had seen her. He finished what he was doing, shook himself, fastened up, kicked up the hay pile, and went back inside the cabin. But he left the door open.

Mary walked up to the cabin, stepping carefully in her bare feet over the scattered wood chips, and went through the doorway, and saw to her surprise that Frenchy Alex was there.

There were others too, but Frenchy was the first one she saw. He was telling a story but he stopped and jumped up when he saw her.

'Hey! It's that Mary! How you been doin' these days, you little wolf woman? Who you been keepin' warmed up, eh?'

They gripped hands, and he stood huge-bulked and open-legged in front of her, his man smell close and warm.

Mary's belly began to throb again, and the hot song of spring was strong, so strong.

'Hey! You big man Alex! When you come down from there, uh?'

'Jeez, them guys figured I eat too much. They say I got a gut like a horse. Pretty soon they got no meat left in there, so they turn me loose to catch my own. Hey you, Pete, where that bottle? You give Mary drink!'

Pete reached under some rags and brought out a bottle. He pulled the cork and gave it to Frenchy, who swallowed and then passed it on to the woman.

'You take damn good drink, Mary. That's hell-of-a-good stuff. Old Pete here, he make it special. He sure make damn fine liquor, Pete boy!'

Mary leaned back her head and drank deeply. The first shock of the liquor caught in her throat and she gagged it back out, over her chin and down her neck. The men roared, but she ignored them and took another long drink. This time the liquid got through and she felt it, scraping like needles in her chest. Then Frenchy took the bottle from her and drank, and sent it along round.

The men crouched back down and Frenchy resumed his story, 'So I say to this guy——'

Mary sat out of the group, listening to their talk and watching the men. She saw Pete, scratching at the floor with his knife, keeping his twisted eyes away from her; the old man, his face grey and filled with year-lines, and snuff juice on his chin; he was chewing at the end of a stick and spitting out the bits. She saw Solomon, her father's brother's boy, and Sammy Painted Rock, young

6

bucks making it up big with Frenchy, laughing loud at his jokes, and all of them drinking hard except Pete. When the bottle reached the breed, he took a quick swallow or allowed it to pass by him.

'What's with you, Pete? You sick, you can't drink?'

'He sure scared to drink his own piss, that's it.'

The breed got up and went out, and they heard him unhitching his horses and turning them loose into the bush. And Frenchy told his stories, and the boys laughed more and the old man began to sing.

So the day went, sliding away, like the sun dropping behind the far side of the lake, while the bottle tipped and tilted, was emptied and replaced.

Mary squatted silently behind the men. She knew that with her coming, the party had taken on a new purpose. She was savouring the harlot-making importance of being essential to a man group. Soon they would fight over her and Frenchy Alex would win.

Good! She waited with belly-tingling anticipation for that to happen. Meanwhile she drank.

The wine—wet on her face and hot in her blood. The old man singing to himself. Frenchy talking and boasting, and swelling himself up like a big frog for the two boys, and Pete scratching away silently at the floor with his knife.

'And when I die, I die.'

'Old man, you ain't gonna die—you old folks all the same—you all die in winter when that earth too damn frozen for diggin'—ain't that it, Pete?'

Laughter from the boys—silence from Pete.

Wine from the bottle. Wine in her head, singing like the old man; wine in her legs so she couldn't stand; wine in her belly making her rumble. Now all of them rocking on their haunches, singing,

'And when I die, I die.'

'Hey! Hey! Hey!'

'When I die.'

Fire smoke, tobacco smoke, smoke from the lamp, twisting and turning, fogging-up the faces, everything black or shiny.

'Hey! Hey! Hey!

Ho! Ho! Ho!

Hot! Hot! Hot!'

She tore open the neck of her dress and her breasts, deep cleft, dark nippled, swung free.

7

The young buck, Sammy, winter sprouted and liquored into desire, reached across and gripped her flesh. She knocked his hand down and rolled away across the floor as he tried to sprawl on her. Coming to her knees she screamed at him, 'You get the hell away from me, you goddam pup! You got nothin' for this woman! You got nothin' big enough for me!'

'Hey Mary, how's about this guy? He big enough for you?' Frenchy got up from the floor and came between them. He crouched, pushing out his behind and spreading his arms. Then he began to stump around the room, lifting his feet high and snorting, 'Ho! See this old moose! He ain't no baby! He feelin' damn good, boy! This moose he gonna make one real calf this time, for sure!'

There was a howl of laughter. Mary joined in, her unfettered breasts shaking with the violence.

The noise grew into a roar as they all got to their feet and began to stamp around her, animal-like, bellowing, snorting and shouting. Sammy came to her again and grabbed her hair.

'Hey, look at this goddam moose gonna make one calf for you.' He dragged her over into a corner and they fell together onto the boards.

Now they lay quiet around her, like dropped animals. All except Pete Crow who still sat, who still scratched at the earth with his knife. Mary turned her head towards the breed. He got to his feet and came across to her and looked into her face. Then he drove the knife into the ground and lay down on her, and she was soon filled with a passion that was beyond bearing.

The old man was singing again and someone was snoring, but the woman was holding tight, tight, and never wanting to let go, until relief sobbed its way out of her.

The breed got up, showing no more concern than if he had been fastening a moccasin, and went around collecting the bottles. He poured all the dregs into one and stopped this up with a rag. Then he put the bottle inside his shirt, and without speaking, he walked away into the night.

Mary pulled herself up and staggered after him. The old man was still singing and his voice followed after them into the thick, dark bush. They went in deep till they could hear him no more, until all that came to them from the shack was the smell of spruce smoke, sweet and thin on the night air.

They went on until the bush was too thick even to push through. There Pete stopped, and scraped some leaves together with his moccasins.

8

Then he turned to her and she squatted down.

*

Two days later Mary came out of the bush alone. Great streaks of dried mud scarred her clothes and tangled her hair. Sometime during those hours she had been beaten, and she carried the marks of this on her face.

Her stomach ached with foulness and hunger. She felt sick and old. She staggered over to a thick spruce and crouched with her back against the tree, heaving and shuddering.

'Oh Jesus! Oh Jesus!'

Around her the land still throbbed but she no longer shared in its exultation. Her eyes were dead and in her body only a dirge remained where the song had thrilled. She crouched against the spruce and heaved.

This was how the children found her when they came back to check on the cabin. The three little ones began chasing each other in and out of a new stream, slapping the water with willow wands and screaming with delight at the splashing. The boy, Francis Littleleaf, came up and squatted down near to her. After a few moments he moved even nearer, till he could almost touch her. His big black eyes were puzzled and unhappy. He wanted her to shout at him, or run him through the bush, but she paid him no heed, and so he just sat with her. The two of them sat in sadness, while the frogs warbled and the warm breezes ruffled out the new leaves.

The bush tolerates its children but it is not kind to them.

AUTUMN

An English schoolteacher spending a year on an Indian reservation in northern Canada, comes to understand the people and their culture through the help and personal concern of one man for whom the forest was life itself.

When the kids go back to school it's goodbye summer. Me too, next week I'll be in the city and summer sure is drifting away. Saw a red-leafed tree along the road this morning, by Tom Henry's turn-off. Soon be frosting up at nights, guess the lake will be all frozen over next time I see her. Farmers are sweating it out on the land, never saw so many birds waiting for grub. Told Henry Holtz that the hawks must get a real good look at this beautiful land from up there. 'Boy,' he said, 'they're too busy scouting out the shadows to see the sunny places.' Dust is high over the combines, they sure tear up the earth, those guys.

> *Big Red Massey Harris*
> *Charging over my land,*
> *Dusting up my sky.*
> *Stopping putting on the dog,*
> *The hens will dirty you*
> *By and by.*

The above extract, like the others which head each chapter, has been taken from a journal which belonged to Francis Littleleaf of the Big Fish Band of Cree Indians. This journal is now in the possession of Ruth Lancaster.

It had been a hot and thirsty summer. Day after day the high-climbing sun had soared and seared, crusting the mud in the creek bottoms, baking the green out of the grass, drawing to it all moisture, even the vapour from the deep forest. The few thunderheads that had built up in the afternoons exploded late in the evening so that their bounty was soon soaked up, the roads were dried out and dusty long before the following midday. Ditches cracked apart like slabs of old chocolate, and over them hovered clouds of mosquitoes, humming in fury at unlaid eggs.

A man can get as thirsty and as dry as any ditch but he doesn't have to wait for Heaven's gentle rain—not when Redville and its beer parlours are but a pace down the road. He can easily find an excuse for an afternoon trip to town and follow up the five minutes at the bank or in the store with a couple of hours in the hotel. Farmers' trucks get a better servicing in hot summers than during cold winters.

The long bar at the Western had served them well, extra hands had been taken on to keep the beer flowing and to stop empties from cluttering up the tables. Friday afternoons were the busiest times. On this day, the usual floppy-capped farmers' gathering took on a more cosmopolitan hue, conversations embraced a wider, less rude range. Drillers, pipe-layers and construction gangs, *en route* for their city homes and still crowned with ochred helmets, met the week-enders who were fleeing from that same city and its heat, its white concrete and blinding glass—breaking the journey to the lake cottage while patient wives and less patient children fretted in the big, boat-towing cars out front.

Here was fertile soil for the dollar-growers, the city-suited gentlemen.

Insurance? New car? Big deal, boy. Just sign here, Frank, Pete or whatever your name happens to be, they'll know it by the bottoming of the first glass. 'Four more over here, waiter!'

And also for the locals, the regulars: the quicker-talking partner from the garage on Main Street hawking his special in tyres; the chain-store manager splitting the trip between his store at this end of the street and the Royal Bank at the other; the ex-school bus, ex-store owner, down now to the last few dollars he had raised on his ex-wife's fancy shot-gun, and of course the old man with the empty glass but hopeful look in streaked and rheumy eyes. Friday afternoon saw all of them temporary brothers in alcoholic haze, jostling and crowding the little tables.

Spread fingers raised high were a demand and the waiters scurried in answer, carrying their trays through the throng and short-changing the well oiled with the same deceptive ease. King Edwards and Tennysons blued and thickened the air, their discarded plastic holders crunched beneath the feet, forming a common litter with screwed-up Old Dutch packets and bits of pickled egg.

Such a Friday this day had been, a summer laggard, for the corn heads were golden and August was dying. The high tide of the afternoon had flowed and ebbed and its flotsam, lingering before the final clear-out that would send it blinking and peering on to the sidewalks, tried to extend the decreasing minutes.

The ash-trays on the tables were over-full and the old local, unlucky in the beer stakes, began to move among the tables, emptying their rubbish into a tin box. When he had finished this unbidden chore he found a brush and bucket and disappeared into the men's room, making as much noise as he could. The young man behind the bar grinned and shrugged his shoulders—

what the hell! It was worth a beer, some guy might have been sick in there.

Tommy Tyler, little, grey mouse-man, chatterer of the town took out and consulted his watch, said, 'Five minutes!', and rose. He picked up his chair and carried it over to the window, the other men remaining in the room followed his example. They made a half ring looking out on the street below, resettled their buttocks and stretched out their feet so that their boots rested on the sill. It was close to five o'clock, and on that hour the North-star came through town and paused on its long haul north. They waited for the daily distraction much as folks do the world over when there is chance of something new, some different face.

Their chatter was the same as on a dozen previous afternoons, their quips also.

'Betcha she's late.'

'Betcha.'

'That's Jimmy Mather's dog.'

'Got worms, I reckon.'

'The dog or Jimmy?'

'Not him. He's too mean to keep a wife even.'

'This goddam beer's warm, Fritz.'

'So's my ass.'

'Ain't payin' for that, Fritz.'

Tyler was the talker, words tripping from his mouth like a chorus line-up, his tongue always in a hurry to speed them on, always ready with a fresh supply. His listeners included a few farmers, Louis the Traveller, George LaPlante and Flanagan. Louis had been everywhere, at Government expense, through four war years. If there was to be a rival to Tyler then it would be Louis, but he preferred to be complementary, jam on the butter George LaPlante, town bully-boy, was on the fringe of the group, his chair a little back of the rest. He was a man of big frame and lazy bones. He saw himself totally occupied in going through the motions of life, eating, moving, keeping his hat on and his pants up and of course, drinking. But the time had long passed when these men would subsidize his companionship and his was a lonely chair.

Flanagan was quiet, half-listening, half-dreaming. He had driven over to meet a passenger from the bus, and now that the meeting was imminent the worry it was causing him was at its highest. First the worry, then the depression, there was a pattern to be followed, he would help it along with a little beer. Of course the girl could be okay, he could have given himself a tight belly for nothing. But she could as easily be a whole year's misery to him, and the longer his wait the more likely this seemed. He heard Tyler repeat a remark, realized that the others were watching him.

'Them Indians, Matt. I said how is that bunch of goddam chicken-stealers coming along?'

'They're still eatin'.'

'And drinkin' too?'

'You bet!'

'Never did meet nobody could drink like them Indians,' Louis said. 'Them Indians in Paris, France, they just as bad too.'

'Is that right? Hey, that was some teacher they had up there one time, that Charlie Gibbs. You 'member him, fellas?'

They remembered but Tyler reminded them just the same. 'One time I was over that way to a wedding. Powers' girl it was, yeah, it was Powers' kid. Aw, what the hell! Anyways I got this jug of wine under the seat and I'm driving over the reserve, I think maybe I'll stop by at the school and give Charlie a drink out of this wine. Well, I goes in there, he chases all them goddam little kids home. "Go on, kids!" he says. "It's too hot for work." So we drink the bottle, sure, and we go into his house. Holy Christ! He's got more beer in that house than Fritzy here got. Man! I leave him sleepin' on the floor. He's still there next day when the Indian kids come to school. Damn if they don't finish off all the beer he has left.'

'What happened with that guy, Matt?' somebody asked. Flanagan shook his head. He had heard stories of the man but of his going or his whereabouts he knew nothing.

Fritz came around the end of the bar carrying a last on-the-house round. LaPlante was not included. He pushed his chair farther back and stared hard through the windows, full of hate for Redville and all its people. This goddam town! This hogs-ass of a town! I'd like to bust this goddam town to little pieces and tramp them in the shit. I'd like to burn it and everybody in it. Goddam, goddam bums!

Then the bus hooter sounded to end his purgatory. The feet came down from the sill and the men lifted themselves in the chairs.

'You picked it wrong, Tommy. She's late.'

'One minute, man! That's not costing me a beer, not one minute isn't.'

The bus change-over was a quick operation performed immediately below them. City editions were thrown off, passengers got down and collected their bags, new travellers climbed up and sought seats on the sun-starved side. The driver took a thermos and a packet of sandwiches from one of the restaurant girls, and then the bus was on its way again, a long blast of its horn farewelling the town and its erstwhile cargo.

'Just lookit that old bus wagging her ass at this town,' Tyler said, as the Northstar rolled over the rutted main street. 'Every night I see her wagging that goddam ass, someday she's goin' to drop a load on the street right outside the bank. That's gonna be some deposit, uh?'

They all laughed except Flanagan. He was giving his attention to the disembarked passengers. Only one was making no move away from the hotel front. This was a girl, a tall, slim girl dressed in a grey suit. Her dark hair was lifted from her neck and topped with a little hat, also grey. She looked hot, her suit was creased and she pulled at its skirt as if to ease some hidden constriction.

'Hey, wait on honey, I'll be right out there to help you,' Tyler said. His words could not have carried to her, but the laughter they caused did. She looked up at the ring of faces. For a moment she held their stares, then without hurry she bent and picked up her travelling bag and moved closer to the hotel and thus from their view.

'You should have kept your mouth shut, Tommy. You've scared that little chicken.'

'She's not little, she wasn't scared, neither. I figured she was going to spit up in my eye.'

Flanagan got up and walked over to the bar. If this girl was his passenger then he was not in a great hurry to meet her. Tall men were bad enough, tall women were even worse, an emphasizing of his shortness. He had difficulty in conversing with them, he was uncomfortable in their presence, he avoided them. But if she was the one he had come to meet there would be no avoiding her, she would be living on his doorstep for a whole year. The prospect was not pleasing, he would most certainly have to drink on it. He reached for the beer list. 'I'll take a couple of crates, Fritz.'

'Carling's Black?'

'They'll do.'

He signed the list, paid, and carried the crates toward the door. As he passed the group, Tyler was asking, 'Now who do you figure a real dinky dolly like that could be waiting to meet?'

'Me,' he said and went out.

The laughter he caused died and one of the farmers asked, 'Who is that guy, anyways?'

'He's the teacher down there on the Big Fish.'

'I knowed I'd seen him someplace, must have been when I was over there fishing last fall, must have been then.'

'Fritz!'

'No! No more, you guys. You've had it all you're goin' to get. Go home! Go milk your cows!'

'Hey, you callin' my old lady a cow? Is that right?'

'Man, you should know. Now why don't you guys go home so I can catch me something to eat.'

The girl was waiting, standing beside her case in the shade of the veranda. He walked over to her and as he approached she straightened herself. He saw a gloved hand—Christ! he thought, gloves in this heat!—reach up to recapture and return wayward strands of hair. He doubted she would find any, her whole appearance, apart from the creased skirt, was of a controlled neatness. He did not think her the kind of woman to have untidy hair. As he feared he had to look up when he spoke to her. He saw well-spaced grey eyes below strong brows, the nose was slender and straight, the mouth wide and its lips were well shaped. Her make-up was very sparing, a touch of darkening at the brows, an emphasis of the lips. And there were no stray hairs.

'Would you be Miss Lancaster?'

'Yes. Are you Mr Flanagan?'

'That's right.'

'Good! They said you would meet me but you never know with this kind of arrangement. I was beginning to worry.'

Her voice surprised him, it was well modulated, the words were given full value, they were free from drawl, there was no laziness in their production, yet this was accomplished with ease, it was natural to her. He had heard such a voice before, for a moment he was baffled, then he remembered those old T.V. movies. Judas Priest! he told himself, she's a Limey!

There was the slightest quiver of the slender nose and she moved her head. It was a barely perceptible movement but he knew that she had caught the smell of his breath. He said, 'Well I'm here anyways.'

'I am pleased to meet you, Mr Flanagan.'

'Me too.' He did not offer his hand, both were occupied with the crates, but he nodded. Depression was going at him again, he wished he could put back the clock and eradicate this meeting, return to the security of the morning. But there was no chance of that, he could not banish this tall woman, he could not make her disappear. He said, 'Is that all the baggage you've got?'

'I have a trunk but it's coming later.'

'We'd as well go then.'

He tucked one of the crates under his arm, picked up her case and walked around the side of the hotel to its cindered park. His Pontiac was the only car there, he opened its rear door and pitched in the case. Then he put the crates on the floor and turned to her, but she spoke first, 'I would like to eat before we leave. I haven't had anything for hours.'

'There's a restaurant in the hotel.'

'In there?'

'That's right.'

'You don't mind waiting for me, do you?'

'I don't mind it.'

He showed her into the restaurant and then tried the beer parlour door but Fritz had prevailed, its doors were locked against him. There was a drug store down the street with a magazine rack; he decided to pass the time there and had reached the hotel door when she came out of the dining-room and called to him.

'You finished already?'

'I've changed my mind. I have decided to wait.'

'Suit yourself. We can go then?'

'Yes, please.'

He slid behind the wheel and started the engine. Then he made a quarter circle that brought them on to the street and followed this to where the highway sliced through it. Here he turned without pausing and she was caught off balance. There was a flash from pale knees but she covered these and pulled down the skirt.

'I didn't thank you for meeting me.'

'That's okay, I was coming in for the beer anyways.'

'Were you in the hotel when I arrived?'

'I was,' he answered and waited, but she made no comment.

A silence began and grew. She sensed the reserve building up in him and knowing how tense she was herself she made no attempt to intrude. She tried to relax but found herself smoothing her skirt again. 'Oh, for Heaven's sake!' she told herself and turned her attention to the scenery.

The highway was of recent construction. It unrolled before them, straight, smooth and dark, but scant inches beyond its hardtop lay a jungle, a packed tangle of thin-stemmed trees and competing bushes. She found its colours and textures exciting and soon lost herself to them forgetting her silent companion and the stickiness of her clothes.

Undergrowth spilled out from the forest into the ditch and emerged from this, ceasing only where a black fringe spoke of controlled burning. Masses of red and gold rose from the ground to explode among the cooler green and yellow leaf-growth above. Occasional breaks in the bush gave glimpses of cleared acres where the earth had been scraped to a golden fuzz or where piles of bulldozed trees awaited the torch. Sometimes she saw buildings of straight up and down boards that had never known paint, their windows were dark eyes, sad in their isolation—the surrounding threat seemed too great for their survival.

Along the highway itself yellow and black signs demanded notice, their geometrical exactness and economy of colour alien, but successful in the surrounding profusion.

> No Parking on Highway
> Watch for Break in Pavement
> Soft Shoulder

. . . for this hard road to rest on, she mused, and she cringed as a fly spattered into a yellow star on the windscreen.

'Cigarette?' Flanagan asked, fumbling at his shirt.

'No, thank you. I don't smoke.'

He shook out a cigarette, put it between his lips and lit it. His first inhalation was deep and then smoke clouded around them. Her mind seized on this, made too much of it and it became very important that she open a window. But she did not, the car had begun to lose speed and she heard its indicator ticking. A sign approached on the left of the road bearing the legend *Muskrat Lake* and she saw a break in the forest. Flanagan moved the car over to the centre and made the turn, and there was immediate change. The sun was cut out, the forest closed in, seeming almost to touch the car. There were ruts too, the car jerked and the bottles rattled in their crates. It seemed to her that they had entered a tunnel and she did not like it.

'Is this the only road?'

'It is from the north. You're on the Big Fish now. The reserve begins where we left the highway.'

'It's very rough, isn't it?'

'You'll see it rougher. When she gets a little rain on she's a real bitch.' He was concentrating too much to notice her reaction, he repeated his words, 'She's sure a bitch then.'

The car climbed, up and around the bends of two hills and raced down their far flanks. 'Tophills,' he said, and as twin stretches of water gleamed through the growth on each side of the track, 'That's Good Lake, that one over there. The one on this side is Bad Lake.'

From the latter a finger of water reached towards them, ending against a small, tree-covered bank. The bush had been cleared a little and she saw a log hut. He didn't slow and all she caught was an impression—of flaked, whitening dark roof and broken windows that had been stuffed with rags. Flanagan raised a hand from the wheel and a man rose from the foot of a tree and waved in answer. She saw that he was dark-skinned and that his hair was very long and then they were past.

'Is he an Indian?'

'Johnny Painted Rock, that's his place.'

'Painted Rock? Is that really his name?'

He was surprised at her surprise. 'Sure, why not? We got lots of Painted Rocks. It's a Band name. Littleleafs, Falltimes, Painted Rocks, they're all Band names.'

Rocks and leaves, she thought, things of nature. Important to them, important enough to become a part of them, an identification with, and of, them. And no wonder, if they have to live in there, it's dreadful.

They were forced to go slower now, the ruts were so deep, their rims so narrow that driving had become a balancing act, with twists and curves to add sophistication to the art. The bordering growth, above and about, was thick, untrammelled and challenging. For a wild moment she imagined it closing in on them, blocking the road ahead, preventing retreat, stranding, surrounding and finally overgrowing them.

Claustrophobia, she told herself. I didn't know I suffered from that. No, it's my imagination again. But this is getting worse, it must be leading us to some dreadful place, some core of thorn and darkness. We will never get out of it.

Flanagan seemed to know neither fear nor care, his hand was quick and decisive on the gear shift, a strong, brown hand, a practised, man's hand. She looked at her own, hidden in their cloth covering, but saw them white and long-fingered. They would never grip a wheel with such assurance or move with violent suddenness as did his. It is their hands, she thought, not the rest of them. Their hands are so different, so impatient— tools of their own impatience, capable, eager tools, whatever their work. Even as these thoughts lingered the hands they encompassed were at work, synchronizing, matching movement of feet, bursting the car out of the jungle to a stretch of open land. There was water in front and shining sun again, and sharp light and sky.

'Muskrat Lake,' Flanagan explained with laconic indifference to the familiar. He stopped the car and lit another cigarette and she stared at this lake. Here was no core of thorns but a vast circle, open to the sky and bearing wide waters. It was grassed and peopled, tents grew, tall mushrooms in the grass and there was movement among these of human figures and dogs and smoke wreaths.

The lake itself astonished her. That such a place could exist, lost in this land of forest, a sparkling diamond unseen by all except the natives along its banks. She moved her head slowly, seeing the differences between this and her own well-loved lakes, remembering their rain-washed, blue-and-green poster beauty. There was nothing of that here, where the violence of colours, clashed in the twisting, turning movements of life.

They were facing a neck in the lake where two large surfaces came together, at a point no wider than a hundred yards across. Over this narrow strip, the trees, distant and hazy around the opposite shores, crowded together to plume above the lake; a magnificent red and gold head-dress staring into its own reflection, a forest lady checking her appearance and watching for the first touches of age.

'It is beautiful,' she said, 'yes, it is beautiful.'

Then for a third time she said, 'It is very beautiful but it is wild, it is a wild beauty.'

He nodded towards a stand of spruce trees, 'There's the school.'

She saw a large, white building with a green roof. Close by this was a lower, log building.

'That small house was the old school. Now I live there. You will be sharing the main teacherage with Marjorie.'

'Who is she?'

'Marjorie? She's the third teacher, Marjorie Golding. Her old man runs the store at Upcreek. I guess she will stay over there mostly, so you should have the house to yourself.'

'Is Upcreek nearer than Redville?'

'Hell, yes! Redville's twenty, twenty-five miles. Upcreek's only two miles across the neck.'

'But you can't drive across it.'

'You can for half the year. Rest of the time you go south around the lake. It's maybe ten miles that way, no more. Or you wait for the ferry and that could take up to an hour. I drive round.'

'And there isn't anywhere else nearer than Redville?'

'No, except there's Smallhill up the highway a piece. It's no bigger than Upcreek but it has a beer parlour.'

'Where are the nearest people?'

'White people, you mean?'

'People like us, yes.'

'Upcreek. 'Cept there's the odd farm across the lake.'

He started the engine again, rolled the car gently forward into a scooped ditch and up its other side and drove across the prairie to the school. Here was no definite road, but a criss-crossing of car tracks told its own story. He followed one set and it brought them to the buildings he had indicated. The school was bigger than it had seemed, the sun bouncing bright from its white boards dazzled her eyes. There were tufts of grass at its corners but they were straw sticks with no juice left in them. Many feet had trampled mud during a recent rain and this had baked into a patchwork of concrete footprints. They led in all directions, a composition in arrested movement and an indication that this was a much-visited place.

Flanagan took her case and she followed him up the steps to a flat-roofed block that extended from the rear of the main school building. He put down her case and opened the door. 'You should find it okay. The Peters have cleaned it through. If they haven't stripped the place you should find what you need in the way of pans and that. The heat's on too, there should be water. I'm going across to Upcreek now, if you want anything from the store let me know so I can bring it.'

'I haven't got any groceries. I thought that we would be near to a store. I didn't realize that we would be so far away from anyplace.'

'Better make out a list then. I'll come by for it.'

'I'm not sure what to ask for. I don't know your names, the things to get.'

'Look, why don't I ask Marjorie to figure out what you'll need to keep goin' a few days. I'll bring it. Is that okay?'

'Yes. Would you, please. But what about money, how much should I give you?'

'You don't have to worry about that. She'll charge it and you can work it out between you.'

'I'm sorry to be such a trouble. I hope it won't be for long.'

'They pay me,' he said.

It was very quiet in the house. She left her case in a bedroom and made a first exploration. The Peters, whoever they might be, had done a good job. The floors were polished, the walls had been washed down. But they were bare. There were no pictures, no other trivia to speak of habitation—the rooms were devoid of personality, their late owners had left no ghosts. She checked her

23

appearance in a dressing-table mirror and thought that she saw dust on her face. She felt again the stickiness of skin and restriction of her clothes and had a sudden urge to feel warm water around her body. She went through to the bathroom and tested the water. As Flanagan had promised it was hot. She opened the, faucet and left the water running while she returned to the bedroom. Its windows were uncurtained so she took out a towel, a pair of shorts and a blouse and carried these into the corridor. She slipped off her skirt and pulled down the punishing girdle. Its marks were red across stomach and hips. She massaged these and as she did, the thought came quickly—Ted would have made a crack about those. He wouldn't have missed a chance like that. The tiles were cool against her feet. It was good to be like this after the close confinement of the last several hours. She found the remnants of a hair shampoo and poured this into the water. 'I hope this Marjorie person remembers soap,' she said, as the bubbles soared upward.

When she stepped into the bath the foam covered her calves, and it rose to meet her as she knelt and shut off the faucet. She lay, and let the water work its way into her, its curiosity penetrating, drawing out the tiredness. An iceberg of foam sailed up the channel between her knees and came to rest against her breast. Its bubbles popped on her throat.

With relaxation came thought, and this, descending through its usual spirals, settled upon herself as its target. I don't think Flanagan likes me very much. He must have sensed danger. There's one man that doesn't need to worry, he's quite safe, the little shrimp. What was it he said, 'You will have the house all to yourself.' He doesn't know how good that sounded to me. All to myself, that's what I want. That door stays locked and this time there'll be no handing out of keys. I never did get that key back. I should have asked him for it. I should have asked him in the staff room in front of them all. That would have stood their ears up. I should have said, 'Oh Ted, your Little Tits would like to have her key back, now that you have stopped using it.' She remembered the final embarrassment. She would never forget that. She would never live a moment when that memory would not chill her skin. She splashed water over herself. 'Little Tits!' she said. Tears began to slide down her face and mingle with the sweat at the corners of her mouth. 'Oh, for God's sake!' she said, and there was anger in her voice.

After her bath she made a more thorough search of the teacherage and fixed its layout firmly in her mind. She discovered stocks of books in a classroom and took a selection of these out to the seat on the porch. She settled herself and began to inspect the books— she felt cooler now, the faintest of breezes touched her, bringing scents from the near-by forest. It was pleasant, quiet, and peaceful. After a time she put the books aside. She must have dozed, as a sudden noise disturbed her. She turned her head and saw that she had an audience. Three little girls were watching her from the foot of the porch steps. They wore long dresses that were waistless and reached almost to the ankles; their feet and legs were bare. The faces were a pale brown, the colour of willow bark, and their eyes were still and dark, below thick fringes of the blackest hair she had ever seen. One had a small boy by the hand, his only garment was a jersey that stopped short of his navel. Below it swelled a stomach caked with dried mud. They were all very dirty.

They stood for only a few seconds after they were discovered and then one fled. The others broke after her, their bare soles flashing as they sped to the spike grass at the fringe of the forest. Here they crouched, she could see them easily for the bright rags on their bodies defied concealment.

'Teacher!' one of them called.

She heard giggling.

'Teacher!'

'Teacher!'

2

It's sure hot and awful dry. Henry Holtz told me there won't be grain enough to fill a sack, there's so many hoppers. The flies are bothersome to the horses, going for the wet in the eyes and mouth, maybe laying eggs in there.

> *The wheat is thirsty.*
> *White cloud,*
> *Package of rain*
> *Proud sky woman.*
> *Squeeze a tit*
> *Over the wheat*
> *The thirsty wheat.*

It was close to seven when Flanagan drove into Upcreek. The town was suffering a hangover from the heat of the afternoon, not many of its people watched him steer the Pontiac through the ruts to the coke-top patterned earth in front of the store. Among the few who did were some high-schoolers who were squatting on the board steps of the store. They stopped their conversation as he approached and spoke, 'Hi kids!'

'Hi, Mr Flanagan!' one or two of the girls answered, lifting their sun-drenched faces towards him, and staring at the man in him, with the unintended insolence of their age. He picked his way between them and opened the screen door and walked into the store. After the heat of the street the cooler air in the high-roofed room was a welcome relief. The building was in its third life. It had been put up long ago as a village hall during days of high hope when it was logical for folks to go west around the lake on the long trek to the north. The local pioneers had made a double project out of its erection, seeing in their shared sweat and labour the rising of a community fabric. But the town had never grown beyond the one-street stage. When the promised highway took the right fork to the east of the lake Upcreek's hopes of becoming a staging town died, and Redville's were confirmed. The pioneers cut their losses by converting the hall into a school. Its walls remained as a scarred history of the origins of the homesteading families, Bronski, Wentzel, Dziubinskis, McGregor, Fritz Muller in capitals with a dotted u, and in a newer, neater style Herman

26

Miller—Old Fritz's grandson who had changed a letter in deference to racial consciousness before leaving to conquer the cities of the south.

Then Redville struck again. A new all-grade school was opened in that town and its yellow buses began to fish the country roads, hooting at each quarter section and creeping always nearer to Upcreek. A few of the sterner spirits continued to send their children to the old school but this could not last. The kids themselves had none of that 'we put it up ourselves' spirit. They were too eager to get on to the yellow band-wagon and have fun with the other boys and girls. Ukes who would have held out for ever against those goddam Frenchies in Redville, capitulated to their own children. The old school shut its doors, its walls suffered no more. After this desertion the building remained empty for many months, and there was talk of pulling it down on account of all the mice that were homing there. Then the Goldings moved in and opened it up as a store. Upcreek people helped them—here was promise of independence from Redville, they were glad to help. Sun-rotted and cracked boards were pulled down and burned together with the curled shingles in big bonfires. While the children roasted potatoes or corn, or danced around the fires, their fathers put a new roof on the building in which they had learned to read, and sometimes even write, the new language of a new land.

Somehow the store survived the gloom of the thirties when stock markets rocked and the nation shivered, when there was no money to borrow from frightened banks, when soil was worthless and jobs as scarce as hen's teeth; when food was for filling hungry not choosy, bellies. Farmers grew thin and desperate and old too soon. They became bitter about crops grown on land they had cleared with their own hands, crops that they could not sell to a world full of hunger. They ate their own seeds and cursed the government, as men the world over curse the man in striped pants: 'Those goddam fellas over there in the east!'

But the Goldings and their store survived. Helmut, the strong giant who could heave and hold sacks higher than any man around, and Sarah, his wife and harvester of the rewards of his work, giver to each nickel of the loving care a farmer has for his grain. Hiring was cheap in those days, a man did a day's work for a supper for his family. Helmut used a lot of that kind of labour and financed it with his otherwise unsaleable stock. Men, who had helped him unload his stuff in the early days, now put up shelving and built a porch and a sidewalk and added rooms. At the end of each day they stood in line and Sarah doled out to them the equivalent of their labour in dried beans, peas, or corn.

It was during those years that the old friendliness that had characterized the store eroded and the gatherings that had been held around its fat stove fell away. The men began to meet instead in the waiting-room at the station, for you can owe a man money and pay the interest due on it, but you can't laugh and joke with him while you are doing this. A friend has got to be as poor as you are in hard times.

Marjorie was born in the early forties and the experience was unhappy for Sarah. She resented the time spent away from the store, and she suffered from her late and primitive delivery. When she had recovered she begrudged Helmut her favours, and so, in his prime, and strong and lusting now that his physical work was easing, he grew morose and sullen like a bull in musk. Until one day the store door opened and an Indian girl entered, a girl who was young and hungry and whose eyes did not turn from his. After that he found what he wanted on the Big Fish, and Sarah was left in peace to bring up the child and balance the books.

Such was the history of the store, and much of it was also the history of the town and the west.

The storekeeper was touching sixty now, still big but saggy, his stomach bulging on both sides of its bisecting belt. Long hours spent in the lamplit gloom before the front windows had been cut in had worn away his sight, so that he must use spectacles. Most of the time he kept his head lowered and peered over them. he did so now as Flanagan approached. You look like an old owl, Helmut, he thought, I guess you speak like one too, could we understand them.

The man's voice was deep as befitted such a deep belly and his words still bore foreign inflections.

'Hullo, Matt. Gosh ain't this heat somethin'!'

'It sure is. Judas Priest! You could fry an egg out there.'

'We gotta get rain some days.'

'I guess. Some years we are in mud to here, then again other years all we got is dust.'

'That's how it goes, Matt. Never does what folks want, always keeps us hoppin'.'

'Marjorie home?'

'In the house. Go through.'

'Sure, say there's a new teacher come in. I brought her this afternoon. I thought Marjorie could fix her up with some stuff, enough to keep her going so I don't have to feed her.'

'That's okay, Matt.'

He called after Flanagan, 'Where did you say this teacher come from?'

'The old country. Not yours, not mine. You know—*the* old country.'

'Is that right? She come all that way?'

Flanagan went through into the house where he found Marjorie and her mother looking in on a T.V. quiz show. He sat and watched them, seeing the girl lively and bright, well rounded, and wondered as he had done so often how she could ever have been born out of the stiff, ungiving figure across from her.

When the programme was ended she went back to the store with him and gathered an order together.

'What is she like, Matt?'

'Like the same as the first time you asked.'

'I'm dying to see her and hear her talk. Does she really talk that way?'

'She does. Don't fill this box too full, could be we're bringing it all back by morning.'

'Why? She won't quit, will she? Do you think she might quit?'

'With this kind who knows what she's gonna do. What has she come out here for anyways? Who does she think she's gonna be teaching? Hiawatha? All that heap big chief and white maiden crap. Wait till she gets her first stink of an Indian. That's something I sure want to see.'

'Matt!'

'Ah! You should have seen her nose when she smelt me out of the beer parlour. And that's it! No more! I'm goin'.'

He picked up the box and carried it to the car. The kids had scattered, only a couple of girls remained. One of these spoke to him as he put the groceries on the back seat of the car. 'You comin' to the dance, Mr Flanagan?'

'You bet I am. You too?'

'Sure am. You savin' me a dance?'

'Uhuh!' Then he said to Marjorie. 'Are you comin' across?'

'Yes, I've got to see her. Will you bring me back or do I walk it?'

'You could use the walk, but I guess I'll have to fetch you.'

'Little Moise' Montpelier came to the open door of his garage to see who was going by. He did this whenever he was not on his back beneath a vehicle, his constant curiosity had worn a groove in the earth floor. It deepened into a hole at his observation point behind the post. He recognized Matt's car and raised his hand and Marjorie waved in answer.

'Bet you guys are up to somethin' too,' he said as he returned to the darkness of his shed. 'That Marjorie she's not bad either, not bad at all.' He crawled back under the Ford, this was one car he loved to service. It set up his special Friday hour, and that made bearable all the oil-stinking drudgery of the rest of his week.

She would come in and ask after the car, and he would tell her it was running fine and the tyres were good. Then he would ask how was it in the city, and she would say it was the same as usual and that it didn't ever change. They would lean against the fender and she would be wearing a smart city dress and he would be able to tell just where her nipples came. She would be that close, and she would keep looking at him and laughing with him all the time. When she bent her head to light a cigarette he would fill his lungs with that clean sweet smell of her hair—Christ, that was a marvellous smell!

The last time or two he'd about said something, some words born of the excitement she started up in him, some special phrase that had nothing to do with cars or with the city. But there was a touch of fear spicing the excitement—a remark taken wrongly would finish it all. He had to be sure. A rebuff would be final.

'She must want something, though,' he told himself often, especially on Fridays. 'She don't come down here lookin' like she does and standing around like that and not want somethin'. Why don't I come right out and ask for it? Why don't I do that?'

He finished working on the car and walked once more to the door. The road that was Upcreek continued past the store and a few frame houses and finished up against the dull red of the elevator. He saw movement of something white near the dark building and guessed that it was she, she was coming for her car. He walked back into the garage and waited.

Down the street Joan McKenzie, daughter of the grain-elevator manager, lit a cigarette and inhaled deeply. Then she began to walk, not hurrying—there was no need for that now that she had paid her weekly tribute, eaten at the family table, laughed at her father's jokes, endured his observances.

She would pick up the car, chat up the Frenchman, funny how even she thought of him as this—the outsider—though he was the only man in town with whom she liked to talk. She would drive the car up and down the highway and perhaps pull over for a cigarette, then she would go home and retire to her bedroom where she would pass the hours with one of those books. When she returned to the city she would give it to Peter and he would read it in his bedroom before sending it around the class. A lot of kids around Redville could thank her for their thrills; a lot of Mommas and Poppas would swallow their tonsils if they knew.

Poor Peter, still years to go before he escaped the family vice. She smiled as she remembered how she still stopped outside the town each Friday to take off most of her lipstick. She was twenty-three years old, she had been working in the city for five years and had never yet missed coming home on a Friday.

She walked on past the store and turned away her head as she always did, as she had done ever since she had caught Old Golding bending down to look up her legs. And that was funny too, because Pete reckoned that Little Moise had the dirtiest picture gallery of any garage he had ever been in, stuck up on the back wall of his shed. But he didn't bother her like Golding did. Perhaps it was because he was young, he had a right to look at things if he was young, but that old goat in the store, he had no right to anything, not even a look. Sometime, she thought, I'm going to ask Little Moise can I look at those pictures. He'd sure be embarrassed then, I guess.

She reached the dark entrance to the garage and stepped inside.

Little Moise was not the only one to show interest in Flanagan's car. Ivor Jones, town postman, also watched, pausing on the way in from the well. He had time for a quick glance only but he recognized the white car and scowled.

'What in hell's wrong with Matt, he couldn't stop by? My beer no good no more?'

He went on to the house carrying his cold pack of butter and the screen door slammed behind him.

It's going to be lonesome days in the city without Julie. I wish she didn't quit. I know why she did it.

> *Down the deep city*
> *Glass walls have shaded eyes.*
> *But in Old Folk's town*
> *My houses*
> *Wink, bloodshot, to the skies.*

Flanagan and Marjorie Golding came around the western loop of the lake, driving slowly over a track that was hardly wide enough, but whose holes were deep, and often, and spring-testing. They had passed several shacks and were approaching another when an Indian stepped on to the road and thumbed them. Flanagan stopped the car, reached behind and opened the rear door. The Indian slid inside and shut the door with a bang. Flanagan asked, 'How far, George?'

'Oh, just along by the school will be fine. I'm goin' to catch the ball game.'

'I didn't hear there was a game.'

'Sure, Marjorie. We're in with the Roughies tonight. Say, Matt, you wouldn't have a cigarette, would you? I'm right out. Gee, thanks Matt.'

They drove into the open pasture where they could see the crowd at the ball game diamond and hear the shouting.

'Get him, boy!'

'Go after him, Joe!'

Clear above the noisy tumult the voice of the umpire rose like that of a bullfrog over the throbbling of his harem.

'Strike!'

And the roar of approval told them of a home-team break-through. The Indian grinned as they got out of the car.

'Hey Matt, you couldn't let me have five bucks for a day or two, could you? Jeez, I got me some coming in the morning, I could sure pay you back then.'

'You're right, I couldn't.'

'Could you make it a couple then, Matt? I got a pair of pants for surety, damn good pants those, too.'

'Go and watch the game, George.'

'You ain't gonna lend, then, Matt?'

'That's right, if you want money, go and earn it.'

'Okay, Matt. Thanks anyways.'

'You're welcome.'

Ruth Lancaster was still on the porch when they arrived and she got up as they approached. Marjorie stopped at the foot of the steps with Flanagan, box in arms, behind her. She said, 'Well hi! It's sure nice meeting you.'

'You're Marjorie aren't you?'

'That's right.'

'I'm very pleased to meet you. My name is Ruth, Ruth Lancaster.'

'Did you have a nice trip?'

'Yes, thank you.'

'I guess you're tired.'

'I am, rather.'

'This box is goddam heavy.'

'Sorry, Matt. Say, can we unload this guy?'

'Of course. Come in, I should have asked you to. It was very good of you to go to so much trouble.'

'That's all right, it was no trouble, was it, Matt? I'm sure glad you got down here, I was beginning to see myself all alone next year. I wouldn't like that, I'll tell you. You think you're going to like it here?'

'I don't have much choice now, do I?'

'No, I suppose not. But you'll soon get used to this place, it's kind of nice, especially in the fall. You'll like it then. It's peaceful, too. I think you'll like it when you've got settled in. It's hard to start over somewhere new, I guess.'

'I wouldn't know. This is the first time I've done this. I haven't seen much of the place yet. I haven't been beyond the porch. It *is* different though. I didn't think it would be like this.'

She realized that they were both waiting, both watching her. 'It's wilder than I expected.' Marjorie said, 'Oh, you don't have to worry about that. There's Matt and there's me. If you want anything you have to shout. We'll come running, won't we, Matt?'

'Why don't you clam up, kid? There's a ball game out there and I want to catch a bit of it.'

'Is that what all the shouting is about?'

'Uhuh. Ball-crazy, these guys.'

Flanagan went to the door. He stopped there, remembering his Indian passenger. 'Say, I should tell you. Keep your money in

33

your purse if any of these guys come around. They've got the best collection of hand-me-out you'll ever hear. When word gets around they'll be comin' knockin'. That's when you've gotta be deaf. That's when you keep your purse shut.'

After he had gone, Marjorie said, 'He's right, too. He really is. Nobody knows these people like Matt does—you have to be careful when they are on the make. They don't bother me though, they know me too well, I guess. If you live in a store, you learn quick.'

'They don't seem very pleasant people.'

'I wouldn't say that. No, I wouldn't say that. Lots of them are real nice guys, it's just a few. It's the same isn't it? With us, I mean. You can't say they're all no good, can you? Not about anybody.'

'I suppose not. Can I pay for these. I'd rather pay now.'

'If that's what you want, or you can charge it. Are you coming to the game?'

'I hadn't thought about it, but I don't see why not. It would be the quickest way of meeting these people. It would get it done with, wouldn't it? Yes, I'll come. So far I've seen four children, that's all. And they didn't ask for anything.'

'They won't. It's their daddies.'

'They like other people's money?'

'It's the way they live. They share, you know—pass things around. Like their wives too, some of them.'

'Their wives! That can't be true.'

'Don't count on it, some of them do. They're a mite easier than whites about it, but you'll find that out. You'll learn quick on on the Big Fish.'

Ruth didn't answer. She was thinking how funny that last remark was. I knew all about that kind of thing before I ever heard of the Big Fish, she could have said. I know all about husbands who have alternative arrangements. I have served my apprenticeship at that trade, I didn't need to travel so far to learn about it.

'Shall we go then?' the girl was asking. She could become a nuisance; she never stopped talking. Talking first, and then would come the asking. Here's a girl who's going to have to be kept guessing, Ruth thought. She said, 'All right, but I'll have to put a skirt on first.'

'Yes, you'd better do that. We got the hungriest mosquitoes in the west right here on the Big Fish. They'll chew you all to pieces if you go out like that.'

'Do you have mosquitoes in the old country?' she called into

34

the bedroom. Ruth paused with the skirt round her shoulders. She smiled to herself and did not answer.

The last innings was coming up and the Big Fish Feathers were in the lead. A cacophonic climax was in the making and the small area between the safety fence and the line of battered cars was crowded with a hooting mass of Indians. They were venting scorn on one lone bat-upraised figure. He chewed slowly and without perturbation.

'Get him Joey; get him this time!'

'This guy he no good, he can't bat for nothin'.'

'You walk him, Joey, I give you a beer!'

'Hell, Joey! Me I give you something too.'

'Better than a beer she'll give you, you bet!'

The pitcher stretched his moment of glory. He stamped on the mound, swung his arm, and rubbed his shoulder so that they might know how much their triumph was costing him; so that they would remember the work he had already done this night and the faces would turn towards him and he might hear sweet words in its later hours. Then a quick roll in the dust for the ball, a pull-down of the cap peak to keep out a sun long gone from a bloodied sky, a reaching to the same sky of the left knee; and at last, over and down came the arm, and the ball zoomed and zigged on and through. The bullfrog roared, 'Ball!' and the crowd around the girl erupted.

'Ball, hell!' The catcher, face caged and chest corseted, flung his cap into the dust and howled at the umpire. Mask to mask like fencers without swords, they fought with words and the crowd joined in, hurling abuse and reaching through car windows to sound the horns. Even Marjorie was incensed. 'Did you see that? Why, that doggoned ball was right over. Isn't he ever a nut!'

'Play ball!' challenged the umpire.

'Play ball!' answered the catcher, picking up his cap and beating the dust from it against his rump.

'Play ball!' chanted the crowd. 'Play ball!'

Ruth regarded these people with whom she was to live. They made a collective picture that was beyond anything she had experienced or could have imagined. There was a lush mixing of primary colours—in the men's shirts and caps, in the flower-patterned dresses of the huge, cucumber-breasted older women, in the bright uniforms worn by the players—and this was heightened by the teen-age girls with their slacks, black hair and dark spectacles, whose only concession to colour was the brilliant glare of lips or occasional scarf. The dust, the baked mud earth, the heat and noise all complemented the canvas, as did the shine of sweat on brown temple, the white flash of a smile.

Children crowded like roosting hens on the rails, clinging, shrieking, and sometimes falling to the dust, to jump up and fight again for a place; or run, hopping barefoot through the sharp stubble after an escaping ball. Four old men sat cross-legged in the dirt playing cards, their ears shut to noise. A younger man in a red shirt strummed a guitar and walked endlessly, hiplessly, taking his music to everyone and giving it to no one but himself. Babies were everywhere, howling in the cars, clinging to mothers' backs, creeping along the ground, being walked by not much older sisters, some even hanging on to the nipples, impervious to dust or shout or buzzing fly in search of body sweat. The indifference of this exposure surprised Ruth more than its reality. No one cared, no man stared, young boys close by ignored it, it had importance only for herself—the stranger, the outsider.

Little girls came around them, long-skirted and barefoot, and discovering her, stared with great eyes. Some came close behind and she felt small fingers touch her, tentative and curious, and she moved away from them afraid that her light skirt might be soiled. Older girls wandered by, dangling transistors on long straps and they stared openly at her, their faces showing nothing of their thoughts. Their slacks and shirts contained beautiful and natural bodies. They sauntered about as if they were unaware of this. She thought that she had never seen such figures nor such a casual ownership.

One girl especially held her attention. Perhaps it was because she did not wear the dark glasses of her friends, perhaps it was the red ribbon tied low across her brow. More probably it was the girl's thrusting vitality. She spoke to Marjorie about her.

'Oh, her! That's Julie Redstone. She's Tom's daughter, Tom Redstone. She's just quit school; made Grade eleven, she did and then quit cold.'

'Was she at school here?'

'Gee, no! We only go to Grade six. She was at school in the city—she lived in there. We had a couple from the reserve doing that. There was Julie and Francis Littleleaf. Now there's only Francis, but he's different. He'll go through, Francis will.'

'She's lovely.'

'Julie? Yes, I suppose you could say that. I hadn't thought about it though. I don't see much of her since she's been in the city.'

'How old is she?'

'She'll be about eighteen, I guess. Yes, she'll be eighteen.'

36

Eighteen years old, Ruth thought. I am ten years older than she. Ten years! What have I done with them? She has all that time before she is like me. She is a beautiful thing. I wonder if she ever weeps. A beautiful thing like that won't have to. It will be choosing for her, choosing all the way. She won't need dreams to make things easier for her. She will be too busy. She'll make those years work. She won't be hiding herself at the end of them.

She watched the girl under cover of the surrounding disorder. There was fascination in the unaffected use of her body. Every movement that Julie made emphasized her femaleness, and yet no conscious effort was made towards this. It was compounded of many things, of flesh smoothed over bone, of curve and hollow, and indolence and slow lift of hip, of opened mouth and shining hair. Ruth told herself,

'I could never do that. I could never just be animal like that. My mind would have to be empty, I would have to forget too much. We stop being women when we start to think. It's one thing or the other for us, bitch or neurotic. I messed up the bitch part. I had to dream.'

Julie Redstone. That is a good name for you. An Indian ruby. When you are polished, your fire will burn very deep. And you are eighteen!

She watched the girl stop to lean against a post, her bare arms crooked themselves around it, her legs enfolded it. An Indian came between Julie and herself. He sauntered up to the post, a tall man in a leather jacket, a dark man with long arms and big hands. He placed one arm over the post and the other on the girl's shoulder. Julie looked up at him and smiled. Then, as if they were alone, as if there were no other eyes to see, as if the shouting pack did not exist for them, he moved his hand, brought it slowly down her back, fingers spreading and feeling, right to the hollow and over the swelling cheek beneath. Ruth watched it rest there, cupping the round buttock, and then Julie looked up at the man and smiled again. The hand moved on, disappeared beneath the buttock and the girl looked into his face and Ruth saw the shine of her teeth. You could put back your head and howl, she thought, and she turned away. When next she looked, the pair had parted. The man still leaned against the post but Julie was sauntering away, her pants tight against rump and calves. You walk like a satisfied cat, Ruth thought, you have had your cream and you are purring. She looked at the man again. His hand that had been used so casually was now scratching the thick hair of his neck in just as casual a movement. He dropped it to the post and it hung there. She stared at it. It was so easy to imagine, it was almost like remembering. She stared at the hand and imagined it thrusting between her own legs. It was so easy she could feel pain down there, pain waiting to become joy. 'For God's sake, not that!' She snapped at herself and forced her eyes away. When she had calmed enough she asked Marjorie, 'Who is that man over there?'

'He's John Blood. He's a breed. There's a bunch of those guys living on the road allowance by Upcreek. They've a regular camp there, but they're always around the reserve some place.'

'You called him a breed.'

'Yeah, that's right. You know, half-Indian—the mamma-half. John there, and the guy he's talking to, they're both breeds. I guess half the men on the team are, too.'

'Why the mamma-half?'

'Why, that's how it is. If the woman marries a white she loses her Treaty rights. Her kids are breeds. But if an Indian marries a white woman then his kids are still Treaty. It doesn't seem fair to me, but don't men always have it made? Take John there, he never does any work unless he has to, but his wife, does she have to work!'

'He is married?'

'John? Sure, he's married. Why do you ask that, Ruth?'

'I thought he was Julie's boyfriend. They were together a few minutes ago.'

'Julie, she doesn't have a boyfriend. Anything in pants is her boyfriend. And John—he has four kids of his own.'

A great shout as a dropping ball homed into a waiting glove signified the end of the game. The crowd began to break up and Flanagan left the players' bench and walked across to the girls. 'You look at all this energy, you'd figure some of those guys could maybe do a little work sometimes.' Ruth asked, 'Don't any of them work?'

'Huh! Only work some of those guys do is put in their curlers at nights.'

'Don't they think at all about the future?'

'They don't have a future. They never did. They don't think past tomorrow.'

'They can't live long like that.'

'They've managed a thousand years like it.'

'But times have changed.'

'All that much? Drop one bomb and we're back in the bush with them.'

'Don't take him too seriously, Ruth. He's a pessimist, Matt is.

He barks worse than an Indian dog but he doesn't bite, not really. It was him started the team in the first place.'

Flanagan walked away from them. They followed him slowly, the younger girl still talking, 'He's nice when you get to know him. But he gets mad easy. He's done a lot down here, he's worked hard for these people. You know what, he's been here for three years.'

'He must like it.'

'He used to be married. His wife walked out on him.'

'Oh!'

'Oh, he's not like that, Ruth. He's not bitter about it. He never speaks about her and I sure don't ever talk about it. He's probably a bit off, you know, on account of the way you talk and that. He's perhaps finding it a bit hard to get used to you. But you'll see, he's okay.'

'I don't understand how people can exist like this in the middle of the twentieth century. How can they live in huts and tents, right inside a modern society? How can you let them?'

'Us? Let them? It's not that way at all. It's how they want it. You try pushing these people off here, you'd soon see. They don't want to leave, they're happy here. They couldn't live in a city. They'd die there. Ask me why they're like this and I'll tell you, you'd get a dozen answers. Everybody in Upcreek could give you the answer to that, and each one is different and each one a little bit right. As for me, I think it's living so long in that bush. I think it affects them, it brings out the animal in them. We've got it too. Look what happens in New York and that's a bush, I guess. Look at the animals, how they behave in a place like that.'

'You're of the environmental school.'

'Uh?'

'You blame their faults on their environment.'

'I sure do. Take a look at that bush. That's where they live, all their lives they spend in it. All their lives! I think it's bad on them. I think there is a lot of evil in there. See how it makes them. Matt doesn't think that though. He says it isn't the bush.'

'And what does he say it is?'

'He says it's us. He says all they have to fear is us.'

When Flanagan drove Marjorie home later that night they spoke about the newcomer.

'What do you think? Can you live with it?'

'She's all right, Matt. She's different from us, but you have to expect that. She's quiet, but she thinks a lot. And she doesn't put it on like you told me. Doesn't she talk cute?'

'Is that it? Cute?'

'Don't get nasty with her, Matt. She'll get with us. She's going to need friends and she only has us. Besides, I don't want to be third man in the ring all the time.'

'I'll go back and shine up her shoes.'

'How old would you say she is?'

'Thirty, I guess. Or forty.'

'She's no more than twenty-five. Twenty-four or five.'

'Okay, she's twenty-five.'

'Did you see her dreamy legs?'

'I saw.'

'If I had legs like that!'

'If you had who'd see them? You never wear anything else but slacks. And here's it, out you get.'

'Aren't you coming up for supper?'

'Not tonight. I have another call to make.'

'Ivor Jones?'

'That's right.'

Ivor Jones brought in two bottles and holding each in turn between his knees, flipped away their tops. Then he sat down across the table from Flanagan and they began to drink.

'Saw you early on, Matt. Figured you wasn't comin' in, I did, the way you went past.'

'I was at the store getting some things for the new teacher. Say, she's from your old country too.'

'Man, you don't say! Then you gotta bring her up here. You do it right away, Matt. She's gonna make a real change from all the two-faced she-coyotes I have to look at all day.'

'I'll do that. Maybe in the morning, let her hear how good you are at cussing. She'll sure enjoy that, oh, she will too!'

'I don't cuss when there's ladies present. Trouble is with me, there never is no ladies present and in this goddam place there never is gonna be, neither. But you can fetch her, Matt, and I'll watch it.'

'Hey, this bottle is empty already.'

'Matt, how much longer are you gonna be wastin' yourself down there? Time you was out of it, man. You been too long already. You don't watch out you'll go all Indian yourself— finish up with a squaw.'

'No sir, no squaw for Flanagan, not brown nor white. I have it figured to do this one more year and then go over east for a spell. Lot of country over there to see.'

'You ain't gettin' married again?'

'Far as I know I'm married right now.'

'You didn't hear nothin' yet?'

'Nope! Not for months, not in a year. Anyways, I don't think I'm the marryin' man any more. I guess you have it figured right, Ivor: cook your own supper, pay your own bills—if you ever pay the goddam things, which I doubt. No, it comes easy to some folks, but we had it hard from the first. Harder we tried worse it got, till all we were doin' was tryin' and there wasn't anythin' else left. Then one day we quit pretending and off she went. That's all there was to it, nobody wrong, nobody right, just a goddam mistake and she had the guts to straighten it out. No, I didn't hear from her, I hope she's okay wherever she is.'

'Do you ever miss her?'

'All I miss is the goddam fighting we used to do.'

'I'll tell you, Matt, fightin' is better than nothin'. It is so. If you don't watch it man, you'll finish up like me, nobody to fight with but your own self. That's when you find out how mean you are, when you get to fightin' with your own self.

'Say, I'll tell you about women, Matt. I've often figured this about women. They're just like the roads you see around here. And a man, he takes after one like he'd go down a road, not knowing how it ends up. When he takes a shine to her it's like she never had no beginnin', like she was always there, stretched out in front. He's sure he knows all about her then, nobody can't teach him nothin' and she's straight as is. Then he hits the first bend; 'fore he knows where he is, it's in the ditch. They can be straight as the highway and then get all twisted up worse even than a hill trail. They can get iced up or all muddied, they can be smooth as hardtop, or rough as gravel. Knew a fella once, he used to say if you wanted right of way on a woman then you'd got to do first grading of her. I wouldn't know.'

'You're drunk, Ivor.'

'Not yet I'm not, but I'm workin' on it. I'm sure workin' on it.'

Ruth Lancaster stood at the window and gazed through its wire screen. It was dark beyond—an earth-hugging gloom that would hide the stars, the heat of a day seeping out of the soil, and adding velvet to the night. Smells of this night strained through the mesh; these were not the familiar scents of honeysuckle or moorland, there was tinge of burning wood on the air . . . there was forest too, crushed cones and needles, mouldering bark and leaf. She heard clanking noises; there were horses out there, hobbled horses that must hop like kangaroos, shaking the stones in the cans on their bridles.

Beyond this close gloom lay the bush, a dark mass now; Marjorie's source of evil, home of a people who owned no tomorrow. It was from here that the scents came—from the wilderness of thorn that put bad into people. It seemed to her, standing like this, remote from it and out of communication with it, that the bush was waiting, that the night itself was waiting. There was a hush of expectancy, the air was a waiting mood.

She thought of a people, noisy beings of the ball game but quiet now, in there with their night. 'It is your imagination, this expectancy,' she told herself. 'How often you have been told about your imagination. How often you have enjoyed compliments about it.' She was glad of the horses, thankful for their clinking cans. They were company, living things that she could not see but who sent their message of life for her to hear. They would ask nothing in return. They would hop around the periphery of her consciousness, she would count them into sleep. She listened to them for a long time, seeing all the while the pale-bellied fluttering of moths against the screen. There was so much movement, so much noise, but all were hushed beneath night's muting veil. At last she switched off the light and slipped out of her skirt, shook her hair loose and brushed it. Then she stretched herself on the bed. Her day had been long and tiring but stimulation from its experiences lingered. Her nerves were agitated and she knew that sleep would not come easily.

Imagination, she thought, is not a talent. There is a difference between imagination and inventiveness. Behind one lies hope, but the other is of the will. That was my talent: the willing, the wishing, the invented dreams. There never was hope in it.

She closed her eyes but sleep was elusive. Bitterness came to turn down the corners of the mouth of her night. I am eroding into spinsterhood, my dreams are blowing away. I am becoming a thin stack. It is a private thing, this—the acceptance of withering. It is taken in the silence of a bedroom, in the loneliness of a meal. These are the sounds of the erosion. They are not for sharing. It is only yourself who knows the terror of waste.

Then all at once she thought of John Blood. She saw the man quite clearly, as if he stood above her, as if his long hands dangled inches from her. Her mind spoke for her. 'John Blood the feeler. I had a man who did your kind of things to me. I brought him to it. I built him up, piece by piece, dream by dream. Oh, it was so easy! You put in the first piece when he gives you the first smile and you add another when he says, "Good morning" the first time, and you put in a great big one when he stands back and holds the door for you, because that shows he has seen the woman in you. That's how you do it. It's so damned easy, John. Why, before you know where you are, you are undressed. That's when the foolishness begins. You tell yourself that you are unique. You think that you invented sex, that you, only you, could suffice for the man. You start to change dreams into plans until you find that you are the only one who's playing that game. You don't find out at once. You make yourself blind. That's when you put shutters over your eyes so you can't see what everybody else is laughing at. Oh yes, I had a man like you, a feeling man. But he didn't do it in front of everybody, he wasn't honest like you. It had to be in the dark for him. Have you ever tried it in the back seat of an Austin? You'd know what cramp is then. But no, you wouldn't, would you? I mean it wouldn't be you on the rack.'

Her hands had risen to her breasts. Then she lifted them to her face, and smoothed the wet from her cheeks. The ache she had felt in the evening returned and with it came a wild thought:

> *Ted Swift's body lies a-mouldering in his semi*
> *But his soul goes marching on.*

It is marching on down there. Damn it! Damn him! It will always be down there, now.

Suddenly, into the night sprang a beating, a gentle drumming of far-away thuds on a tight skin, spreading, rising and falling, spreading and falling, spreading and telling. Dogs barked. A voice wailed.

I was right, she thought. There was expectancy. She knew that it had been herself, not the night, that had waited, for all at once she was in communion with it. I can hear a night beating, I can smell a night burning. An Indian night, Julie's night, John Blood's night; John Blood who has hands that stroke and search: dark man with possessive hands who makes a search of beauty as if by right of his strong hand. Men's hands ... how I hate them!

Her own stirred, began to touch herself. She turned her head to one side and quickly to the other. There were tears on her cheek, they fell from face to pillow.

The drumming rose and fell and spread, and became thin as it travelled with the smoke through the trees.

4

I could take a stick of grass from any other place and put it on our land in the Big Fish and that grass would grow up into a flower.

On the second morning after her arrival there should have been a wedding. She had noticed a gathering crowd at the neck and a lot of noise had been coming from that direction. When Marjorie arrived to take her to Upcreek she asked what was happening.

'Rosie Littleleaf is getting married to Leonard Peters. I guess they're all going across on the ferry.'

'I'd like to see that. Could we?'

'Sure. If that's what you want. You could get a surprise though.'

'How?'

'I think I'd best let you see for yourself. That way you'll learn quicker.'

'I've been to weddings before.'

'Not like this one.'

She saw quickly enough. A pick-up was parked at the side of the track overlooking the landing stage. It had been decorated with pink and blue streamers. The wedding party was sitting, stolid and silent, and squeezed into the back of the truck. One of them, a girl who was obviously the bride, claimed and held the attention. She was dressed in shining blue satin and her hair was decked with flowers and ribbons. She was many months pregnant, and she was weeping. Tears came without aid of sobs, collected on her chin and nose and hung there before falling to the damp satin.

'See what I mean?' Marjorie said.

'Yes. She's in a state, isn't she?'

'It's not because she's like that. They don't get upset over that. There's something else bothering her; I guess I'll get out and see.'

She came back and said, 'They're out one bridegroom. Leonard is missing. He took off into the bush with some of the boys last night. They went on a stag and they're still in there some place. She's going to have to wait till they find him and that could take all day. When they do find him he could be too bad to get it done. She might have to stay a Miss for another couple of nights.'

'What a sordid mess, and it's only the beginning for her. Why doesn't she go home and forget him. She's sitting up there like a sacrifice.'

'She won't do that. She wants to get married. She'll sit here till somebody finds him. I told you about that bush, this shows you doesn't it? Some day we'll get rid of all that bush and then these people will start to live, because they're not going to do any proper living while it's here and they're in it.'

On the journey to Upcreek, Ruth said, 'You mentioned that name before—Littleleaf, I mean.'

'That would be Francis, I guess.'

'Yes it was. We were speaking about Julie Redstone.'

'And I said about her quitting school and all and how Francis was keeping on. You have a good memory for names, haven't you? Well, he's cousin to this girl. We have a lot of Littleleafs, it's a Band name like Peters and Falltime and Painted Rock. I guess they're all cousins at that. Francis, he's great, and you know what? His mother—phew! But he's okay, he's still at school and everybody's counting on him being the first to make it to University. What do you think of that?'

'He is at school in the city?'

'That's right. Julie was with him too. They reckon she was smart enough but they say she has chickened out. Hey! Look who's here! Talk of the devil and it's sure to show.'

Two people, a man and a girl had stepped out of the bush. The girl lifted a lazy arm, one knee leaned in against the other, there was no mistaking her. Marjorie pulled up and they got into the car. 'Hi, Julie!' Marjorie said.

'Hi, Marjorie! How you been doin'?'

'Okay thanks. I hear you quit.'

'That's right, too. Me, I got enough of that city. I keep gettin' lonesome for the reserve so I figure I'd just as well stay home.'

'Francis is still there?'

'Sure. He's not like me, he's got brain, that guy. He hits the grades good—me, I'm always in with the Counsellor. I guess he's gonna be a genius yet. You know what? We walked around that city and Francis used to tell me poetry, right there on Mountain Avenue! He wrote that stuff himself. What kind of guy is that, anyways? Did you read any of his poetry, Marjorie?'

'No. I never did read any but Matt told me about it. He thinks Francis writes good stuff.'

'He likes that kid too.'

'He sure does. Say, what was it about, Julie, that poetry?'

'Oh, it was lots, it was different too. Kinda nice though. Everything is shiny for that Francis boy. I guess he's lucky too.

No, I couldn't figure a lot of what he was sayin' but you know, the way he said it, that made the reserve seem closer. Even there in the city!'

'And what are you going to do now you've quit?'

'I ain't figured anythin' yet. Maybe I'll just better get married.' They all laughed. Marjorie asked, 'Do you have anybody in mind?'

'Not yet I don't, but I'm working on it. There's five or six could-be's. I'm going to do me some figurin' first.'

While they were talking Ruth shifted in her seat so that she could see the Indian girl. Julie leaned forward, her arm stretched along the back of Marjorie's seat, her chin resting on it. At such close range the face was plumper, its skin smooth and unblemished. The eyes were large, the pupils very dark. The brows had been well shaped and the mouth also, its paint glistened. Julie had not wasted her time in the city. The lips were full and curved. You have a generous mouth, Ruth thought, it is the mouth of a cupid, of a brown angel. But you couldn't be that, not with your body. Angels are sexless. You are living, breathing, walking sex. Still as you are right now, you fill the car with sex. Maybe you'd better just get married! And you could, as easy as that, you could.

Julie moved her head. Her throat showed, strong and supple, leading to supple body within the shirt. Ruth stared at the throat, its flesh was so young, in its very thrust she saw a challenge. I could hate you, she thought. I could easily hate you, Julie.

The man did not say a word. He was elderly, thin and morose. Julie did the thanking for both of them when they got out at the store. She followed him up its steps but Marjorie took Ruth across to the Post Office. 'That's Julie Redstone,' she said.

'I remember her. She isn't someone to forget.'

'The man is her daddy, Tom Redstone.'

'He hasn't much to say for himself.'

'Not with Julie around. She knows what she wants, Julie does.'

The Post Office was a boarded-up front room of a one-storey frame house. There were several notices pasted on the boarding, framing an opening which had been cut into it. One gave Christmas posting dates, another was a warning against tossing cigarettes into underbrush. A third was more original and scripted in ballpoint:

DON'T WASTE MY TIME AND YOUR OWN
IN HERE AND DON'T SPIT ON MY FLOOR,
SAVE IT FOR YOUR OWN. THANK YOU.

They were laughing at this when a whiskered, gnomish face appeared at the opening.

'Hee, hee! How do you like that, Marjorie? Ain't it good? That'll show the bastards not to come in here like this was a goddam beer-parlour. Hey! Who's this you got with you?'

'This is our new teacher, Ivor, Miss Lancaster, all the way from England and she must be disgusted at your talking that way.'

'What for? What I said? Ah, don't pay no heed to what I say. I get so het-up with this no-good bunch comes in here. And you're the new teacher, is that so? Say, Matt was telling me about you, doggone I'm happy to see you. Marjorie, what in heck are you doin' in there? Come round back and visit awhile and bring the lady with you, and don't you ever go in there again. I told you that a hundert times already.'

Tom Redstone walked slowly back and forward between shelf and counter, never carrying more than a single packet or can. Julie stayed beside the Coke machine, watching him and occasionally glancing across at the storekeeper. They were the only ones in the store and Golding waited patiently behind the counter. He knew better than to try to hurry them. Long experience had taught him that nothing would hurry an Indian. So he waited, calculating as was his habit each time a new article joined the pile on the counter. Apart from one glance when they had first arrived he paid no attention to the girl. Then he looked at her and caught her stare, full on himself. She turned her head away but that one moment began a kindling; ashes flickered that had lain quiet for too long, old excitements stirred. He looked her over, noted the hips and the swelling bust, and the excitement became appetite. An idea was birthed. When the Indian next approached he remarked, 'Tom, I hear your girl quit school.'

'She quit.'

'What she gonna do now? What she gonna do for work?'

'I guess she'll work someplace.'

'Ain't that many jobs around these days, 'specially not for Indian girls. Too many white kids there is, looking for work.'

The Indian made no answer. He moved along the shelf, picked up a boxed cake, added this to the pile.

'You know something, Tom. Maybe, yeah, maybe I can help, too. Mrs Golding, she's wanting a girl around the place. You know—do the chores. If Julie's wantin' I could fix for her to take that job.'

Again the Indian did not reply, but this time he looked at his daughter. She turned from the window, took a Coke, fitted it to the slot and jerked the cap. She lifted back her head and her throat swelled as she drank. Golding watched the smooth skin move with each swallow and there was movement, swelling, within him also. 'Could pay her maybe couple dollars a day, leavin' out Sunday and Monday. All she does is get dishes and clean up house.'

The Indian pushed his collection across the counter.

'You check these, Helmut. I get the mail.'

'Sure, Tom.'

The thick fingers began to hammer at the adding keys. Tom Redstone walked out of the store and his daughter followed after him. She was still carrying the Coke. Golding watched them through the window, they were standing in the street, talking. Once the girl looked back at the store and laughed. Then she swung her arm and the bottle soared. He heard it strike the lower boards, and he pressed himself against the counter, he was so hard from sight and thoughts of her. His heart began a familiar thumping as the man turned and walked back in, alone. A fly which had been circling came down suddenly on the storekeeper's face and as he brushed it away he felt the sweat on his hand.

'Julie, she been in with city folks.'

'I know that, Tom.'

'She awful goddam clean, that girl.'

'She sure is. She's clean for sure. That why I figure her for the job.'

'Julie thinks two dollars ain't much. Maybe four more better. Jesus Christ! She work real good, that girl.'

'Hell, Tom, I can't pay her no four bucks. Old Lady won't let her come she knows it costin' all that.'

'That's what Julie say.'

'What you say, Tom? She's your girl.'

'Maybe three bucks, eh?'

'That's okay with me then. I tell Old Lady she's comin' in the mornin'. You fix that with Julie. How's that?'

'I'll sure fix it. She don't work good, you give her a lickin'! You gonna charge these things against her pay?'

'Okay, Tom. But you be sure she comes or you get nothin' else here, and I'll fix it so you get nothin' else no place.'

'She'll come.'

Golding stood at the window and watched the Indian who was waiting for his daughter. She must have been on the corner or watching the kids pitching, because she soon came and again they stood close together. Then, to his surprise she walked across to the store, opened the door and stood just inside it. For the first time she spoke directly to him. 'About that job then, there's one thing, Mr Golding.'

'You comin', or ain't you?'

'Maybe I'm comin' but——'

'What is it?'

'I get the money, not my old man. That's what. I get it, else I don't come.'

'You get it. I'll treat you good, Julie.'

'Okay! I guess I'll see you, then.'

She went out and walked away down the street. Her father had already disappeared. In a moment she had gone also but she would be back. It made him hard again just to think that. He stood for a long time at the store window, his thoughts carrying him into the past, to the lost-for-ever years. He remembered the horse rides through the mud, the hot, impetuous, lusting man, strong with youthful vigour. How pleasing he had been to them at the end of those rides, taking them against a tree, or lying on a blanket, always under the stars. It was so much better like that, under the stars. How cunning he had been on his return, scraping the mud from his clothes with a skinning knife before he came in, standing out there in the hut and cleaning himself and then kidding Sarah about where he had been. Man! those were the days, and this girl, she was good as any of them, she was better—she was ripe, like a melon ready to burst.

'I'll burst that bitch!' he promised himself. 'By Christ! I'm gonna burst her all over.'

After a time, he heard the house door open and Sarah called down to him, 'Helmut! Are you there, Helmut?'

'I'm here, Sarah. What is it you want then?'

'I want for to go over and visit with Mrs McKenzie. Marjorie's brought the car back. Will you shut store and run me over?'

'Can't Marjorie do that?'

'She's not come in. She's out on the street someplace.'

'With that Jones, I bet. I wish she didn't go in that place, he always filling her with tales. I take you then, go on down, I'll be out front.'

In the car he broached the subject that was uppermost in his mind. 'Sarah, I been thinkin' about you. Maybe it's time we had somebody come in, help you with those chores. All these years you been workin' hard, maybe it's time you got a rest, too. With Marjorie ain't home to work, it's gonna throw it all on you again. I don't figure that's right. What you think?'

'I don't know, Helmut. Not sure I'm wanting anybody comin'

into my house. 'Sides, who was you figurin' on? No women round here would come scrubbing floors that I know of.'

'I was figurin' maybe I'd send word down to the reserve, ask one of those kids down there to come. Must be some of those kids could do okay for you. Jeez, that would rile up Mrs McKenzie too, that would set her cluckin' if you had a help-girl.'

'Helmut! You shouldn't say that about her. She's my friend. She ain't like that, and you know it.'

'Well I'm gonna do it, anyways. Any Indian comes in tonight, I'll ask him to find one for you. I'll tell him you want a real good, clean girl. How's that?'

'I suppose! I could sure use some help, too.'

'That's so, you'd go right on workin' yourself into that grave. I ain't lettin' you do that. I'm gonna send word down there. In the mornin' you'll have your own girl to do chores.'

Young Pete McKenzie looked in on his mother and Sarah Golding, said, 'Hi!' and told his mother he was going over to pitch for a while.

'Okay honey, but mind you're back by nine-thirty. You know your father doesn't like you being out too late.'

'Aw, come on Mom. Nine-thirty, that's baby's bed-time.'

'You heard me, Mister. Nine-thirty!'

'Gee, parents!'

He went out of the house carrying his mitt and walked to the diamond. It wasn't a proper diamond, only a cindered corner between the garage and the railway track. The boys gathered here and sat on a pile of old railroad ties, chatting in between turns at pitching. Grass grew high around and between the ties, it was heavy-headed and good to chew while you waited your turn. A lot of boys had chewed grass on those ties; a lot who were now men had chewed grass on those ties; a lot who were now men had talked wars and want, and politics and girls on those ties; a lot of young rumps had picked up slivers there.

Two boys were already working out, so he sat down next to Henry Ramsey who was in the same grade at Redville.

'You comin' to the picnic, Pete?'

'I guess so, if you've got room for me.'

'We got room. There's four of us and you—we got room for one more. Any ideas?'

'Who's comin'?'

'Miller boys, they're driving; and Tommy K, and you and me.'

'No dames this trip.'

'Not going. Maybe, comin' back. I hope so, we could go one in the back. Susie'd be okay wouldn't she?'

'She sure would. Wouldn't be safe for none of us guys though. You know Susie, Old Wandering Hands.'

'I sure do. Damned near pulled mine off once. She did too, Pete, honest! Hey, there's somethin' else, all the guys are bringin' a bottle. You know, to liven' it up a bit.'

'Jeez! I don't know about that. You know my old man, he's death on that stuff. We don't keep any around the house, not even on Christmas. I don't see how I'd get any of it.'

'I thought I'd tell you anyways. I know you wouldn't be wantin' to drink other guys' beer and not have any of your own for passin'.'

'Well, thanks anyhow, Henry. Maybe I'll get hold of somethin'. I'll look around.'

'Why don't you call your sister? She could bring some from the city.'

'Yeah! Maybe I'll do that. Hey! Let's go pitch.'

5

Soon be fall time. I could sure like the fall if I didn't know winter was on its tail. One time I was out root picking with Fritz de Brunner, we took his pick-up for an oil change and we ate hamburgers in the snack counter. That was the first meal I ate off the reserve. A bunch of girls were in, they were playing this record, Jim Reeves it was. Fritz went for a beer and I sat in the cab. I waited a long time till I went looking for him. There was a paper on the door: 'Dogs and minors not allowed'. Somebody had put 'Indians' between those two. Whenever I smell onions frying I hear Jim Reeves. You don't smell nothing in the city except burning gasoline.

The opening of the school brought a surprise to Ruth. The children, whom she had seen in tatters and unkempt during the few days she had been on the reserve, arrived in new dresses, fancy shirts and creased jeans. Hair no longer danced freely and wind-fussed but had been disciplined and ribboned. Feet were hidden in white socks and strap-overs. The boys were also shined up and sported new caps, bright red for the most part though some were black, and one bore the proud boast, 'THE YANKEES.'

She spoke about this to Marjorie. 'They are dressed to kill this morning, aren't they?'

'They sure are, but don't count on it lasting too long. Give them a chance and they'll be right back at first base.'

'At least they make a good start.'

'It's a ritual. School has become part of the reserve life, they set their calendars by it. Opening day is big, the women want to send their kids looking real good. They've been in the store all week buying clothes against their next allowances. It's one time they don't let the fellas get hold of the money.'

'I don't think you like the men.'

'Is that how I sound? Well I didn't mean it that way. They are Indians: all they want to do is live from one old car to the next. They make those things go too! They shift bits from one to another, that's why you see so many wrecks around the houses. Only an Indian can do that, you know—improvise like that. They're the world's best improvisers. In between cars they break the monotony by getting hooched up and beating heck out of their wives. Come to that, I think a lot of these women like their husbands to beat them up, they like to go around with a shiner.

It shows their old man still has an interest in them. They were slaves in the old days, the women were, did you know that? I guess it dies hard that kind of tradition.'

'Last night Mr Flanagan implied that these men do no work. Now you say the same. Is it really true?'

'Some of them work. A lot go on trap lines through the winter and I guess that's as hard as any work can come, living up there in the bush in the snows. That's enough to send anybody crazy. Maybe that's why they spend all summer drinking, so they can forget winter in the bush.'

'Don't they care about their children?'

'They sure do. They're crazy about their kids. Like when any kids are in hospital they can't wait to get them back home. And they don't ever hit their kids. I know guys who beat up their wives all the time but I never yet saw a beat-up Indian kid.'

'They are a strange people.'

'I suppose. It's not surprising. Their grand-daddies were chasing buffalo around and hitting each other with stone axes. We forget that too easily. They've picked up a lot of ideas from us, but get an Indian hooched, and he jumps back a thousand years. That's why they aren't allowed buy it. That again is why they make their own and make it out of anything they can get.'

'They are children of Adam.'

'What?'

'Didn't he get hungry when he couldn't eat?'

'Yes—that's true isn't it? I guess we're all like that, we're supposed to be, aren't we? They must be a little closer to Adam than we are, that's all.'

'Their children look happy.'

'They sure do.'

Flanagan came out of his house and a lot of the younger children crowded round him. He must have greeted them with some quip because they heard delighted shouts from his audience.

'They seem to like him.'

'They do. They know he's a good guy. Kids can tell a thing like that, it's instinctive with them. They all love Matt.'

And you do yourself, Ruth thought, learning this at that moment.

The morning was used for registration and at noon the children went home. There were to be three classes, Marjorie taking the children in the first two grades, herself the middle two, and Flanagan the seniors. Ruth found herself with a class of thirty, the majority of whom were girls. She was working her way through the register taking particulars from each child, when she came to a fat little boy whose hair was thick and curled over his shoulder. He stood silent before her, his eyes looking fixedly at the desk.

'What is your name?'

'Peter.'

She wrote this, becoming aware once more of the strong smell of burned wood that came from these children. It was the smell of her vigil, the tinge of the bush and of its people. She moved her head so that she did not have to breathe it, it was not pleasant at such close range.

'What is your father's name, Peter?'

'Golding.'

She had bent to enter the name when its implications struck her. So far the list had been composed of Birds, Peters, Littleleafs and Falltimes. To suddenly hear Marjorie's name gave her a shock.

'Did you say Golding?'

He nodded, his face expressionless, mouth slightly open, eyes dark and without message. He looked beyond her, into the space above her shoulder. She experienced a strong curiosity and asked,

'Who is your father?'

Now he grinned but still would not look at her, nor did he answer her question. Some girls were giggling behind hiding hands. One of these crept forward and whispered to her, a confidence of pink tongue and white teeth, huge eyes and smoke smell.

'Teacher, his mamma her name Lucy Peters, his dadda his name Goldin'.' She smiled again, beautiful with the pleasure of helping. Then she added, 'He's the guy at the store.' and Peter nodded in support of this and he was looking at her now, and the girls were laughing openly, happy because she understood and there was no more tension.

She did not go immediately to Flanagan, she was not sure how to tell him. When she did speak to him she was as direct as she could be. 'There is a boy in my class who says his father is Mr Golding, Marjorie's father. What can I do about it?' He was equally to the point.

'Which kid?'

'Peter. His mother is Lucy Peters.'

'Then put him down as Peters. Call him that. In no time the kids'll do the same. Marjorie won't be taking him for anything, maybe it'll pass her by.'

'Thank you. I'll do that.'

'That's okay. Say, don't think too much about it yourself. Lucy, she's tryin' it on. That kid could have his pick of a dozen different fathers, she's been under the blanket with any amount of guys.'

She returned to her desk, but as she continued through the long morning and as the heat and stuffiness of the room increased, restlessness grew in her. And then quite suprisingly she found herself thinking about a man. She dismissed him at once from her mind, but he returned and with him came phrases that she had heard.

'They like their husbands to beat them up. Jump back a thousand years. Him! He has four kids of his own. Under the blanket.'

The memory of the man became as strong as if he sat across from her, as if these bush smells were coming from him, as if the dark eyes were his and looking upon her, as if the white teeth were his and grinning at her, as if he were making a mystery of himself for her to solve. The great lake; the bush, dark behind that light fringe, its heat, its colours, its life and death, its cruelty and its knowledge—these were all part of his mystery, so were its sounds and its scents. The rest of it was his manhood, greatest of all mysteries because whatever solution she discovered to this would be the creation of a female mind, of female glands. 'Stop it!' she told herself. 'This is daytime, you are at work. Stop being so damned silly!' The children passed before her and she spoke to them and listened to their shy voices but all the time thoughts of him nagged, giving her no peace. Finally she put down her pen, sent away a waiting child and rested her head between her hands. She concentrated all her mind on ending this problem. At last she could speak as if to him: 'Go to hell, Mr Blood! I don't want to be bothered. I don't want to dream about your dirty hand. I don't want you in my mind, not now, not at night, not at any time.' She heard a child's voice. She looked up into a worried face.

'You sick, Teacher?'

Flanagan finished checking over the register and drew up a list for the Bureau to send on to the Family Allowance Board. This showed the school population to be up on the previous year by eighteen, bringing the total to over a hundred. The Vanishing Indian, he thought. Put up Family Allowance another buck a head and they'll come oftener than gophers. What the hell! They pay for my beer, why should I complain. He went out through the rear of the house to a big barrel of water and unhooking a string from the branch above it, he fished out a bottle of beer. He placed the lid of the bottle against the barrel's rim and with a sharp blow of the base of his wrist sent the lid plopping down into the water.

'Here's how!' he wished the trees around him, and lifting the bottle he drank deeply. Then he returned to the house, sat down and put his feet up on the table. He finished off the bottle, drinking slowly. While he drank he considered the many things around the school that he wanted to do, and how he could best fit the two girls into his schemes. He wondered about the English girl. He had got over his first fears about her; she seemed to be settling in without a lot of belly-aching and she hadn't bothered him at all. She's not dumb either, he thought. She's taking her time figuring us all out. She was quick, too, spotting that Golding kid. Goddam old goat, that storekeeper! 'I wonder which one he's shacking up with now?' he asked himself. He opened a cupboard and took out some crackers and a packet of cheese. He sliced off a piece and put back the rest. Then he filled his pockets with crackers and went out to his car. Two or three children were standing by the school swings and they called to him, making sure that he saw them. 'Hi, Mr Flanagan!'

'Hi kids! Hey, ain't your mammas got no jobs for you guys? No wood splittin' to do?'

'Already! Already!' they chanted and laughed at him and he grinned back. Then he drove away from the house and the children ran after him, but they soon fell behind and he came on to the road and turned north to the highway. He bit off some cheese and followed it up with a cracker. The sun was low but the trees still held down the heat and he drove with arm bent out of the window. Dust followed the car, swirling up and away to coat the yellowing leaves overhead. This is a fine night for a bottle of beer, he thought and then, taking in the dying undergrowth, gonna be an early winter. I'll get her winterised before the end of the month.

When he reached the highway he turned west away from Redville and drove until a branching sign showed the town of Smallhill. He took this road and drew up in front of the hotel. This was a square-fronted building that had been pink-washed and glowed in the lowering sunbeams as if it had been sprayed with giant strawberry shakes. He parked the car and went into the beer parlour. It was early hours yet and only a few customers were in the room. He knew one of them and went over to join him. Bill Bruchk was a small-time farmer who had been cutting an acreage into virgin bushland to the south-west of the reserve. He also had the road-grading contract for the township and this brought him to the reserve several times a year. It was on these grading trips they had met. Flanagan liked him. He knew the farmer had lost his wife some years ago and that there was a younger daughter who helped him keep house. Flanagan didn't often see him in the beer parlours so this meeting was an unexpected pleasure.

'Hi there, Bruchk!' he kidded. 'Don't you have anything better to do than sit in beer parlours?'

'Hi, Matt! Sit down then. No, I'm just loafin'. A real loafer, that's me.'

'Yeah? Since when? Don't see you often enough in here.' He emptied his pocket, put the cheese and crackers on the table. 'Have a bite of supper.'

'Thanks. You know how it is, Matt, I don't like leaving Christine home by herself. She's staying in Redville tonight. Leaves me free to do some chores in town here.'

'Like emptying glasses. Empty yours so I can get them filled.'

'Like emptying glasses. I done a few other things too.' They finished off the cheese and lit cigarettes. Flanagan asked, 'Christine back to school today?'

'Yeah. And you too?'

'Uhuh! More kids than ever. How those women keep it up I don't know. If this goes on the school's gonna be bustin' out of its jeans.'

'Who do you have teaching down there this year?'

'We got Marjorie Goldin' and a new kid.'

'Marjorie is okay. She's real grown up these days.'

'Yeah. You should see the other one. Straight from the old country. Guess she can't help how she talks at that, but you should hear it. I guess she has us figured for a bunch of pioneers. You should come visit, Bill, show her a real old pioneer.'

'How's your roads?'

'Rough! Lost half my undercarriage coming out today. When are you gonna come down there?'

'Township don't like me doing those reserve roads. Scared I might bust a blade on them. But I'll try to get out if I can manage to, later this week.'

'Thanks anyways. Say Bill, I gotta go now, pick up this girl I was tellin' you about at Marjorie's place. Why don't you come up here on Saturday evening. Have an hour, it won't hurt. Never hurt me.'

'Won't you be at the picnic?'

'Judas Priest! I'd forgotten that. I guess I'll have to go. It means catching a drink in Redville then. Maybe you can make it to the Western.'

'I guess I could.'

'And I'll buy you a beer for grading that road.'
'When I get to it. I said I'd try, that's all I said.'

It was night time and Ruth stood again by the window listening to the horses. The world beyond was a noisy place. Its multitude of small sounds fitted together into an unceasing tumult. But this ceased at the screen. On her side was only her breathing. There would be nothing except that, or her unheard voice through all the night. This was what she had sought, it was her choice.

> Land of opportunity
> Blue skies
> Mountains and Mounties
> Brochured beauty

and peace. This was her choice, a place where she could be alone, where her licking of wounds would not be a public spectacle. But now that she was here there was emptiness where pain should have been. She could not feel the wounds. She had been surprised by that. She discovered that such wounds belonged to the place of infliction, they would bleed again at the moment of return there, but had no existence here. There were no watching friends, there was not a bed that had been shared, no hooting of an Austin horn, no records, no contraceptives to be cleared away. There was no room that must be entered each morning with steeled stomach. There were no wounds here; only pride pained, and the womb that must now get used to hunger. What had she said to Marjorie? We get hungry when we cannot eat.

This was why the memory of John Blood had been so disturbing, because he was a reminder of the hunger. It was not that he was attractive, not because of himself at all, but because of what he could be. Food for her hunger. All men could be that to all women, but some were more immediate, more positive. They did not hide the rod. Women recognized them and were afraid of them. Or was it pretended fear? Did fascination lie as close as love is to hate? I could wish him here, she thought. I could take him and twist him and shape him into an answer to my hunger. I could bend him to my will. I could use him and discard him, all within the darkness of this room. And he would be no danger because he would never escape from it. I could own him and his rod in here. She used her voice now, 'Listen to the horses. Hear them shake their stones, telling where they are; saying that they are lonely too. Lonely horses, lonely house, lonely me who does not have to be alone. Come to bed, spinster.'

She said the word almost gently, without bitterness, as if in experimentation. But before she slid between the sheets she dropped her nightdress to the floor. It was a pale patch in the dark. She stood above it for a moment, delaying the dream which had begun at its shedding. Then she lay naked beneath the sheet and accepted the smells of the night. When he came, as she knew he would, as she had known all day, this dream man who was more than a dream, who was alive somewhere out there in the shelter of his bush; when he came he stood on that pale patch and waited. And she began the fashioning of him.

Henry Holtz told me once, the wolf goes first and next the bear and then moose and last the deer. Only coyotes stay around when man comes. That is a real unhappy thought for me.

On the oil company-handout maps there is a little blue ring, perching like a period at the eastern end of Muskrat Lake. It is labelled Sandy Stretch Beach, and the ring indicates a year-round population of less than a hundred souls. This information is misleading. In winter the population is reduced to the veteran and his wife, who have the store, and in summer it can rise to upwards of a thousand. The name also is false. There is no local sand. Such as there is has been brought from a pit on the reserve and it costs ten dollars a load, plus the trucking. The money from this goes into the Big Fish funds. Before each picnic the Lions bring in several loads and a cat is used to spread the sand so that children can play in it; but if they get to scraping too deep, then they'll need the lake to clean off in, before they'll be allowed back in the car.

The people of the area call the resort The Beach, and it is sufficient identification, because to date the property syndicates have neglected this lake in favour of development zones nearer to the city, and there is no other beach on the lake. The resort is dominated by the Lion's Park, a cleared stretch of grass. Cottages straggle along the water-front for about a mile on each side of the park, a Lions' project equipped with swings and teeter totters, and a square of board tables with seats.

Here the Lions hold their picnics, three in every year, a chicken roast in June, hot-dog barbecue in July, and corn roast in the fall. The get-togethers are pretty set in their ways, eating and meeting in the afternoons; races for the children and horseshoe tossing for the older men; bingo and baseball for the remainder, the latter on the top of the hill above the beach, and it is up there that most of the empty bottles will be found on the morrow. Later in the evening when the children have been taken home to bed or the television, their parents drive in to Redville to finish the night at the hotel, while the teenagers whoop it up at the picnic dance in the Community Centre.

The track side of the cottages is testimony that a man can be a

60

pioneer at week-ends without losing his week-day community spirit. Guarding the entrance to one stand whitened wagon wheels, beneath a board which reads 'Roll Inn Pardner'. Whynot Cummin had a 'His' sign over the house and a 'Hers' over the outside toilets, birds and squirrels spread their droppings impartially over both. The weed on the lake frontages grows more quickly the oftener it's cut so that the lot-edges are like boxes of giant watercress, and over these clouds of mosquitoes hang, undeterred by transistors, waiting their transfusion of rich city plasma.

All through summer the cottager teeters on his masochistic see-saw, between the hot hell of the city and this lakeside purgatory. To the locals, these poor souls are a queer bunch of cattle. Everybody knows that they are secret drinkers, their lakeside places are dens of vice, love-nests, booze-joints. The hot, worried-looking woman, dashing into the Beach store to replace forgotten bread, is a floozie on the make.

'That one's a real fire-ball!'

'Did you see those shorts? Man! She could have painted her ass and been more decent.'

But the picnics are for the locals and not these transients. On this, Corn Roast Saturday, the early morning walk to the pump became a quick weather-forecaster for intending picnickers. Signs were good; Old Sun going off again, like a weasel searching out and cutting down to nothing the shady places; dogs lethargic at the breakfast scraps; chickens bad-tempered and pecking; flies noisy around the head. This was going to be another humdinger, a real hot, straw-hat humdinger of a day. A score of farmers spread over many miles would echo phrases on their early walk.

'Never knowed a Lions' picnic to get rained off.'

'Never knowed that yet.'

Upcreek was having a quieter-than-usual Saturday morning. Most folks had stayed home to get rid of the chores, and apart from the occasional youngster sent down to collect the mail, there was little movement on the street. Helmut Golding stood at the store window and watched fat flies, trapped by the screen, hurl themselves in frenzied spirals through the dust-specked sun rays. His thoughts were dark and broody and full of Julie. She had been aloof ever since she began her job. She had avoided him as much as she was able, keeping close to Sarah when he was around.

And yet he suspected that it was not for protection that she was doing this. She had looked at him and the looks had been such that he felt quick urges. There were times when he thought she was playing him, as a fish might tempt the fisherman, gleaming from the safety of uncastable waters. He must wait. She might find the waters deep yet. He must wait to see what she was about. Sarah seemed to have taken well to the girl and Julie spent all her time in the house, only coming to the store when groceries were needed, or to bring drinks to him. She did not speak even then. She walked around the shelves looking for what she wanted, and then went back, her slacks pulling tight against her all the way up the stairs. He couldn't get the thought of her out of his mind, her dark eyes and the red mouth, her pale bronze skin—she made him think of silk and smooth nylon. His heart quivered when she was near or when he scented her.

He watched the trapped flies soar in their frantic searchings, knew they were being slowly cooked and dehydrated beneath the glass. He shook the screen with his fingers to frighten them, and he wished for a spider.

Sarah was working at the bureau. She was catching up on business correspondence. Marjorie had gone to the reserve to see the English girl and Julie was dusting over the bedrooms. Now and again she called out to Julie and they made a little conversation. Sarah liked this. She was feeling the benefit of the help, the girl was clean and well-mannered and didn't need telling what to do. She was deferential and had already asked Sarah's advice on little matters, on cooking and such. Julie would do very nicely, she thought. Yes, she would train Julie up real good.

The Indian girl moved away from the mirror in Marjorie's room and put the dress back into the closet. She liked the dress; it had a large floral design on a white ground and she knew she would look good in it. It would be right for the picnic. But she also knew that it would be too risky. Marjorie would be there, she would be bound to see and recognize it. Maybe some other time, she thought, and closed the closet door, and began to search through the drawers.

'Jeez! Black undies! That Marjorie! Bet her old lady doesn't ever see her in these!'

Sarah called to her. 'Is it time for coffee, Julie?'

'Okay, Mrs Goldin'. I nearly finished in here. Be right out.' She took a nylon slip from the drawer and tucked it under a corner of the bed near to the door, where she could easily pick it up later in the day. Then she made up her mouth with one of the sticks on the dressing table and went out, carrying dustpan and brush.

'I got the bedrooms done, Mrs Goldin'.'

'Right, Julie. Would you take Mr Golding his drink, four lumps mind, then come and sit down awhiles.'

Julie carried the big mug through the connecting door into the store and walked carefully down the stairs. Only the storekeeper was in and he came quickly when he saw her.

'I brought your coffee, old man.'

'Gee Julie! I wish you didn't call me that. I ain't that old, I ain't an old man.'

'What you want me to say then?'

'You call me Helmut, like everybody else does, uh?'

'I don't think she's gonna like that.'

'She don't care, Julie. Don't worry none about her.'

'I'm not worryin' either. I got nothin' to worry for.'

She turned her back on him. He watched the jeans tighten from side to side over her rump as she climbed the stairs; he saw the line made by some underneath garment. He stretched his fingers to stroke her but he had hesitated too long and she was beyond his reach. When she arrived at the top she stopped for a moment, then turned to look down at him. For a few seconds they stared at each other and then she said with a smile, 'Maybe I'd better call you Daddy. How's that then?'

'Sure Julie, sure, sure!'

She opened the door and went through into the house. He took the coffee over to a box and sat on this but his hands were trembling and the hot liquid spilled out on to his lap. He looked down at it and saw what she had done to him.

In his garage next to the store Little Moise was replacing a muffler when he heard footsteps and saw the neat, slim ankles come alongside the car. He recognized them, he had looked often at them. He looked at them now, at the miracle of nylon shine over curved bone, the polished shoe. Then the shoes began to walk along the car towards the back of the garage.

'I'm right with you!' he called and rolled out on the trolley. 'Hi Joan! What can I do for you?'

'I'd like to ask a little favour, Moise.'

'Sure! Is it a rush job?'

'Oh, it's not the car.' She hesitated for a moment. 'You'll probably think I'm crazy when I ask you. I want to get hold of a bottle, something to drink. I can't get away from home and I thought, if maybe you might be going by a beer parlour . . . it's all right if you can't do it, Moise. I was only thinking, that's all. I hope you don't mind me asking you, I sure couldn't think of anybody else.'

'I don't mind, Joan, not a bit. Fact I'd be glad to.'

'I'm not putting you out, am I?'

'Not at all! I had it in mind to go up anyways. What was it, anythin' special you thinkin' of?'

'No, a few bottles of beer would be right.'

'Havin' a party, then?'

'Not a party. A few drinks at the dance, that's all. But you know how it is at our house—beer's a dirty word, my dad's death on it.'

'He sure is. Say Joan, I figure maybe twenty minutes I'll be through here. Then I gotta deliver this heap and that's it. I'll go right off then and see what I can get for you. Are you gonna come around later and collect?'

She dashed that hope. 'I doubt I'll be able to. I've got to take them over to the Beach. No, I don't think I can make it back here. Can you leave it some place near? Somewhere I could pick it up?'

Intrigue stimulated him. He thought of the area and a picture sprang to his mind. 'Say, you know Old Powers's place? He has the first quarter after the Beach, towards Redville. Why don't I leave it in his mailbox? He's not gonna be lookin' in that before Monday. I'll stick it at the back of his box, cover it up with a *Herald*. How would that be then?'

'Great! Yeah, that would be okay, Moise. I could slip away, pick it up there. Nobody would see that. Would you do that for me, Moise?'

'Sure, Joan, that wouldn't be nothin'. Anytime you want somethin', anythin' at all, you gotta ask. That's what you gotta do, anythin', anytime.'

'You're swell, Moise. Say, what will I owe you?'

'Forget it! This is on the house.'

'Well, thanks again—I really do appreciate it. I'll have to go now, the folks are waiting.' She smiled at him and went out, standing for a moment so that the sun shone on her fair head. Then she turned and lifted a hand to him before going away.

'Jesus Christ, that's a shame!' he said. 'A swell kid like that having him for an old man. He makes like he's a goddam Moses leading all the Upcreek folk to the Promised Land. All 'cept me 'n' Ivor. I'll get her a bottle sure enough, the best bottle in that liquor store. Maybe later, if Rosie stays home I'll help her to drink it. But she'll know when she gets that bottle. She'll know then what I think of her. She'll know it right enough.'

Ruth ate an early, leisurely meal with Marjorie and afterwards they sat on the porch until it was time for the drive to the Beach. Several children came to play close by; they had nailed can lids to long sticks and were racing with these along the car ruts. She watched, marvelling at the speed and surefootedness of the little brown feet. The laughter coaxed smiles from her. It was hot, but so peaceful.

After the children wearied of their games and went away she closed her eyes; lulled into a lazy languor she could have slept the afternoon away. Thoughts drifted, became the dreams that she had forbidden herself in the sun, of a man of darkness. Though she had accepted him into her secret life it had been conditional; he was not to intrude beyond that, he was to be of the darkness and in the darkness. Now here came the weakening. Already she was breaking the conditions she had set, she was allowing him life here, in the sun, in the light of day.

Or was she? Was it not rather his bush, this home of his all around her, that forced its attentions on her? His environment was a part of all her days; at any moment a scent, or a slow movement of dark limb could bring him to mind, and once summoned, he would not easily be dispelled. This was the danger that she should have foreseen (perhaps she had foreseen, and ignored it; she had been so hungry that night) that once fashioned as a dream man, he could claim a bigger share than she was prepared to give. Scant yards across the baked mud was his bush, its first fringes were a speckling of colour, the hiding dots of a Seurat. Within a stone's throw a hundred rabbits hopped; last week, so they said, a bull moose strode out of those fringes and stood at third base on the ball diamond. He was there for a full five minutes and there was not a gun to be found, they were all miles away hunting for moose. The beast must have had a good look around during those minutes. He must have seen the school and its swings, and the ferry, of course—he had to see that. Perhaps it was on the move while he watched, that would have given him a thrill; some prehistoric remnant in his marrow would surely have quivered at the sight of that many-humped monster crawling through the water.

The little boys claimed to have chased the monarch back into his forest but she preferred to see him stalking regally, a crown of buzzing flies at his head and between his legs the dangling pouch of the future of his kind. The boys and the old men would be following behind, breathing the stench of his snorted breath and telling each other, 'Moose!' 'Moose!'

He could be there now, beyond that concealing cloud of colour, in its inner darkness, watching. The moose or the man.

Here I am, she thought, convincing myself how I can keep him away yet this very act brings him. I can almost feel his hand.

And if you are there, John Blood, and I come, what will happen

65

to me? Will you find me smooth as Julie—you would find me pink, not brown like she is. I would turn blue at your squeezing, not black. I would bruise easily from your strong fingers, I have bruised before and he was not as strong as you. He was not strong at all, John. Oh, you should have seen him run! Could you be gentle in there, or would its wildness be in you also, would you become cruel? What does your bush do to you? What would it do to me, what would it do to Ruth Lancaster?

A sudden bump interrupted her fantasy and she knew that Marjorie had thrown the book to the floor. A moment later she heard the girl's chair scrape the boards and then the sound of her feet on the steps. She opened her eyes. Marjorie had gone to the swings, she was sitting on one, her feet dragging as she swayed. Her face was towards Flanagan's house.

Poor Marjorie, she thought. You have your dreams too, and you have still to learn from them. You came so early hoping to see him; you sit on his doorstep hoping that he will see you, in pain with loving and not even noticed. He is probably sleeping, he does not even know that you are here. You aren't the only dreamer, Marjorie. I was at it too. You and I and all of us, making dreams, making fools of ourselves in our dreams. We are betrayed by them, they make us weak, but what are we without dreams? We must have something to build, we are the creators, we fashion with our bodies and our minds. And once a man knows he is in our dream, what then? In our minds or our bodies it's the same, we have given him a licence to hurt. Man can't build, he can only destroy. And if he knows you have a dream about him, he will destroy that quickest. Don't show him, Marjorie! Whatever you do, don't let him see it. No man will ever see my dreams again.

She called out, 'Isn't it time for us to go, Marjorie?'

The road to the Beach had already been well used so that clouds of dust hung, a long, smoke-like strata between the trees. They added their dust to this, passed a wagon laden with Indians, and the children on it called out and waved to them. The unshod horses chased after the car, enjoying the luxury of a long run after weeks of timber-hauling. But they fell farther and farther behind, and after a couple of bends were lost to sight. Marjorie said, 'John Fall and his family.'

'That was a lot of children for one family.'

'They aren't all John's. He only has two. The rest are his brother's, George Falltime.'

'Which is it, Fall or Falltime?'

'Both. John's dropped the end, that's all. His wife is a breed.

'I don't like that word. It makes my skin creep.'

'Sorry, Ruth. I didn't think it up. It's how it is, it's what they call themselves. It's the Indians who call us white, we don't, do we?' As she spoke another car came alongside. It was going very fast, its horn sounding all the way. Marjorie pulled over so that it could pass, and gravel and dirt pinged from the windshield as it did so. 'Those guys are sure in a hurry,' she said, 'it looked like the Miller bunch.'

'Are they from Upcreek?'

'They farm over that way. They're a crazy bunch, never out of trouble those boys. I wouldn't like to be in a car with them. That one place I sure wouldn't like to be.'

'I should think not. They're insane, driving like that.'

'I wasn't talking about the driving.'

They reached the park, paid their way in and walked across to the picnic grounds. Ruth found herself being welcomed to the district and shaking a succession of hands. She met the doctor who was wearing a baseball cap; the Redville Police Force and his wife, and Louis the Traveller, 'that's what all the boys call me on account of I've been every place. Sure! You ask me: London, England, I've been there; Paris, France, same thing too. Every place I been, that's why they call me that, that's why they call it me.' She met farmers by the herd, wheat, hog, chicken and mixed, and one old man with tired eyes and a quiet voice who ran sheep.

'Scarce they are, scarcer than charity in this part of the world. These folks don't know the sweetness of a lamb roast; all they want to do is gorge up on steak. That's why they get the ulcers. Come over some time, see my dogs. Pull a coyote down faster than you can think, those dogs can.'

They wandered among the stalls, threw darts at balloons, guessed the weight of a piglet, drank Coke and tossed horseshoes. The bank manager wanted to sell them roasted corn. He stood behind his table, an ice cone in one hand, cigar in the other. 'Aw, come on girls!'

'No, thank you kindly, Mr LaFrance. We've got figures to keep,' Marjorie laughed.

'Well, be sure to come and see me at the bank, Miss Lancaster. Be glad to have you visit us.'

'She'll be in come cheque day.'

They saw Julie and another Indian girl sitting with some white boys in the back of a car. They were clapping hands to the beat of a transistor. There were more Indians; Ruth met a cluster of children waiting at the ice cream stand. Their parents stood a little away. The father was a dark and heavy contrast to his small,

67

paler-faced wife. He grinned when Marjorie greeted him, but he did not speak and neither he nor his wife came forward.

'Hi John! Anna! Hi kids, having fun?'

'Sure teacher! Hi!'

'John who?' Ruth asked, when they had moved on.

'John Fall. We saw them on the way in, don't you remember? That's his wife. The kids are theirs and George's. George is——'

'His brother. I remember that.' She felt hot and tired and a little overcome by the noise and the crowds. 'I'm tired, Marjorie. Can we sit down somewhere? Not here, let's find a quieter place.'

'Me too. I'm pooped!'

They found a patch of grass beneath a tree on the edge of the lake. Here they sat and listened to the many noises around them. Through extension speakers in the trees came the unending hymn of the bingo numbers, punctuated by announcements which were greeted with partisan cheers. 'Hold it folks! I've got a score in from up the hill. Bandits in front, seven gives two. And the number now is——' Marjorie said, 'He's got the whole world in his number-picking hand.' And then, 'Hey! Did I say that?'

'You did. I heard you.'

'Man!'

A dragon-fly zigged and hovered—a blue streak against the water. A young girl in the lake screamed as a youth threw a handful of sludge at her. A sudden breeze sent a million leaves into a dance, a balloon popped, a horseshoe clinked.

The Millers had parked near first base. The five boys were sitting on the front of the car and dividing their attention between an unfortunate baseman and any girl who dared to pass in front of them. They had a bottle of beer each but were in no hurry to finish these, as the remainder of the crate was hidden in a ditch outside the Beach. They were noisy, but Peter McKenzie was much the worst. His companions, the wild drive, the beer and the freedom from domestic restrictions all helped to excite him. His chief victim was the fielder, whose performance did not improve under Pete's stream of invective.

'Christ man! Get your goddam hands out of your pocket!'

'Catch it with your ass!'

Henry Ramsey said, 'Hey Pete, quiet it down. You'll get us guys run off the park if the Patrol hears that kind of talk.'

'Patrol shit! Who's scared of the goddam Patrol? You don't like it, you shove off. We don't have to have you.'

'That's right too,' a Miller said. 'Don't stick around Henry if you've got the shits. Like Pete says, we don't have to have you.'

'Maybe I'll do that. You guys are lookin' for trouble.'

'Pack your can, boy! Get the hell out of this car!'

'Take off!'

'Hey, your Momma's missin' you, too. Go home to Momma!'

'I will so. I'll get, and I'll take the rest of my beer. Sure, that's what you guys are drinking right now, my beer. Well, you don't get any more. My old man gets the rest of that box. You guys have had it off me. To hell with you!' The Millers put back their heads and filled their thick throats with laughter. Tommy K. and Pete joined in.

'Ain't he a tempered son-of-a——!'

'He's chicken, that one!'

Michael Miller flicked life into the engine and turned the car in a tight arc that faced them away from the diamond. He said, 'Let's go for that beer.' They cut over the side of the hill avoiding the bottleneck of the track. They passed the Ramsey boy, and Miller pressed the horn and the others howled through the open windows. Young Ramsey stood, open-mouthed and startled; then, realizing where they were going, he began to run. They roared with laughter again and tears of hysteria ran down Pete McKenzie's face. 'Jeez you guys, I got hiccups!'

7

Right now I walk the blocks and there's cars all around and lots of noise but inside me there's a big shout for bannock and for hearing the singing and the dogs.

The Fall family took a long time to get home from the Beach. They kept to the ditch, it was cooler and wide enough for the cart, though they had to go up on to the road whenever they came to a culvert. It was quieter down there, they didn't have to keep moving over for cars and there was less chance of the horses being cut by flying stones. But it was dustier, too. They sat the wagon like grey ghosts of evening when they rode into George Falltime's yard.

The Falltime kids scampered away but Anna restrained her boys. 'You guys sit! You don't go no place.' The two brothers sat at the woodpile and talked, and after a while came over to the cart where George spoke to her.

'Hullo there, Anna.'

'Hullo, George.'

'Was it good then, that picnic?'

'It was not bad.'

John said, 'George, he's figurin' on buyin' that old Ford of Benny's.'

'Is that right!'

'Uhuh. When I get that car, Anna, you gonna look at it for me uh?'

'Sure, George!'

When they were on the road again she asked John about George's deal. 'How much is Benny askin'?'

'That son-of-a-gun! He's askin' three-fifty! George figures on givin' him three hundred. He's puttin' his Chev up for two hundred of that.'

'Where does George get that other hundred, then?'

'They got a contract for root pickin'. They're goin' next week, the whole bunch. Maybe we should go along too, help those guys.'

'Where at?'

'White acres. Over west from there. Fifteen bucks an acre.' The two boys were silent listeners behind them. Root picking meant a trip out of the reserve; it meant sleeping in a tent a long way off and working in the fields—pulling out the bush roots that the cat had left behind in the black earth, and stacking them for burning —maybe even setting the fires. Best of all it meant they would be away from school for two or three weeks, and when they got back there'd be lots of money, and new clothes and store food. They waited, and when John asked they screamed, 'Yes! Yes!'

'You kids sit quiet!' Anna called out.

It was coming dark by this time. The trees were high shadows but there were shadows even higher. John shook the traces and the team trotted on.

'We're gonna get us some rain!' he said.

The Miller boys and their two companions were on a country road east of Redville. The crate of beer had long since been finished and also six bottles that they had got at a breed's house in Redville. They were cruising along, waiting for oncoming traffic. When they saw the lights from an approaching car, the older Miller, who was driving, moved into the centre of the road and picked up speed. Three times he had done this and each time the other cars had taken to the ditch with screaming, smelling tyres.

'Chicken bastard!' 'Chicken bastard!' they shouted through the open windows.

'Where's that stuff of yours, Pete?'

'You know Old Powers, that old bastard by the Beach? Well, it should be in his mail box.'

'What you mean it should be? Ain't nothin' there kid, we're gonna twist that thing right off you.'

'Aw shit, Mickey! It'll be there for Christ sake! If it's not there's somebody I know is sure in for stretchin'.'

'Well, let's go see. Christ! I'm dry as a whelping sow!'

The car sped onwards, screamed through Redville and out on its far side. They were on the Beach road. In the twilight its blurred, unbroken bush flashed past. They fell silent, each in his own alcoholic dream. At last they came to the gravelled road that paralleled Powers' land. The mail box perched on its pole, white in the gloom. Pete got out of the car and went over to it. He read the name on the side of the box and shouted, 'This is it!'

'Then open the goddam thing,' Miller answered. 'Open it up and let's see what the mail man brought.'

They saw Pete lift the flap and reach in and throw a crumpled newspaper into the ditch. Then he gave a shout and ran back to the car. 'Now you guys, whose prick gets twisted off now?'

'What you got then, Pete? Holy Christ! It's goddam Scotch!'

71

'Who laid this on for you, Pete?'

'Does it matter? We got it, haven't we? Let's get at it. Who's first?'

'You start her, Pete. That's fair, ain't it boys?'

'Sure! Just so he don't drink all of it. Jesus! Scotch!' Pete lifted the bottle and drank. It was the first whisky he had taken and the strong liquor had an immediate effect on him. He had tried to swallow too much and his system refused, forced it back through his nasal passages. He sneezed and coughed, and his eyes ran. 'Hell! I'm burnin'!'

'Give me a bit of that old burn, boy.'

'Put me on fire, you mail man!'

They passed the bottle round, and round again, and then Tommy K. asked about going back to the dance. Pete said, 'Sure we'll go back, but first we should have us some fun. Listen to me, you guys.'

'The way you holler, we goddam got to.'

'Aw shit, Tommy! Listen, why don't we dig around on the Big Fish, get us some women. Jesus! Some of those kids, they're really stacked. Tits bigger than a cow's some of them got.'

Michael Miller said, 'Man, that's true! One time I had one——'

But Pete interrupted. 'That Julie! Saw her at the store today. Wow!'

As if in agreement a sudden thunderclap rolled across the sky, its echo rumbling over the trees. A spatter of rain streaked the windshield and Miller switched on the wipers.

'Don't that just beat everything! It's got to goddam rain.'

'Them girls gonna get wet asses!'

They thought that was really funny, they laughed a lot at that. All the way in to the reserve they laughed.

Flanagan did not arrive at the dance. Marjorie mooned and Ruth found herself taken over by one of the town's heroes. She listened to him for an hour, politely and with a little interest for the first few minutes, and after that with less and less patience. He was an athlete, he had won all kinds of letters, he was just twenty, was tall and had clipped red hair and speckled skin to match. He talked incessantly and his subjects were as constant; baseball, ice hockey and baseball. When they danced he charged like a footballer at third down and was recognized and given way over the floor. He filled each interval with diamond and bat and muscle, and it got so bad that she could have screamed. He prattled on during supper and she knew enough. She finished a chicken leg, put its pared bones on to a plate and wiped her fingers with a paper napkin. He was still talking, 'If you want to get the stomach muscles real good then you got to do the press-up and you got to make it every day. Take me. I do twenty every morning. Have done since I was fifteen. Look at that now.' He prodded his stomach with two stiff fingers. There was no give. 'That's with doing press-ups,' he told her. She said,

'I should try pressing down for a change. You are old enough now.'

She stayed long enough to see the muscles gather between the eyebrows, then left him and sought Marjorie.

'I've had enough. I don't know about you, but I'm ready to go. I can't go on being Auntie any longer.'

'Auntie?'

'Him!'

'Oh, Red! He's a very good athlete. Did he——?'

'He told me. He's been telling me since eight o'clock. If you want to stay I'll go outside for a while.'

'I was waiting for Matt. It doesn't seem like he's coming.'

'He's not. Not now.'

'We'd as well go then.'

When they reached the street the first thing they saw was the white Pontiac. It was in front of the Western. Marjorie said, 'That's where he is. That's why he didn't come.'

'Of course. You're really dying for him, aren't you?'

'Me! Dying for Matt! Whatever gave you that idea?'

'All right then: you aren't. But I think you are, and you can't die out here. Come on!'

'Where?'

'In there. Where he is.'

'Oh, we can't! We can't do that.'

'I can.'

She walked towards the hotel and Marjorie trailed behind her. They had just reached the door when it opened and a man came out. Marjorie called, 'Hi, Bill!' and the man stopped and turned to them. 'Hi, Marjorie!' he said.

'Is Matt in there?'

'He sure is. He's been there a long time too. I guess he should be goin' home soon.'

'He's had too much?'

'He's had enough, that's for sure.'

'Oh Bill, this is Ruth, Ruth Lancaster. She is with us at the Big Fish.'

'I know that, Matt told me.'

Ruth and the farmer shook hands. He had a strong grip, her own long fingers were quite lost in his fist, and he took off his cap and held it in his other hand. 'Were you guys going in there?' he asked.

'We were thinking of doing. Would you take us in, Bill?'

'Be glad to. I was goin' home myself but I don't mind another few minutes.' He led them into the Western, and the thunder roll that the Millers were hearing rode over the town. But it was lost in the noise that greeted them as they entered the beer parlour. The room was long and low and dimly lit; it was full of smoke and tables, and men and their talk. Bruchk pushed his way between the tables and they followed, Marjorie first. Conversation ceased at each table as they passed, and redoubled after they moved on. They were a spectacle and Ruth knew it. Men sat back, shifted chairs, got to their feet, or just leaned forward and stared. She had to squeeze herself within inches of some of the eyes, and she knew what they were up to, though she kept her own to the front, pretending indifference. But you can't not know, when a dozen pairs of eyes are unclothing you. 'The wish is father to the thought,' she told herself, and then, 'the bitch is busy in me tonight. But how can a bitch be a father? That would be virgin birth in reverse. Or would it?' Such thoughts carried her past the last group and she saw that Bruchk had brought them to a small alcove. It was plushier and better furnished and it held vacant tables. They sat. Bruchk put his cap under his chair and coughed. He had a slender face, its cheeks and the nose were long, the hair was fair, but withdrawing. He coughed again and said, 'I guess I'm a stranger up here myself. I don't often come here. You have to be with a lady to sit here.'

She said, 'Thank you,' and when she saw that he had not understood, added, 'for recognizing us.' She laughed and his face reddened, she saw the flush even through the wind-burned skin of his throat. My God, she thought, he is embarrassed, at that! He shouldn't be in here with these people. He doesn't belong. He couldn't rape a balloon.

Then Marjorie said, 'Guess which little gentleman is coming here right now. Bill, he has been drinking!'

'Yes, he's been in a long time. I guess he's had a lot to drink, too.'

'Judas Priest!' Flanagan said, when he reached them. 'What in heck are you guys doin' here? What you doin' with this old man? Why aren't you in that dance then? What you doin' in here?'

'We got hot, Matt. It was awful hot in there so we came out,

74

and we saw Bill here, and he said would we like to come in, and so we did.'

'That's right, Matt. I asked them in.'

'Good old Bruchk boy, old cotton picker.'

'Sit down, Matt.'

'Sure! Too goddam right, I'll sit. Gonna pack my can right here. I'm gettin' you guys a drink too. What're you havin' then, Marjorie?'

'Can I have a tomato juice?'

'Have what you goddam want, kid. And what about you, you havin' the same?'

Ruth said, 'I don't like tomato juice.'

'Then it's gotta be beer.'

'Thank you.'

She found the beer very cold and she shivered as its chill hit her stomach. Flanagan laughed. 'Get that down you, English, you're gonna be one hundred per cent.' She ignored him. She turned to the other man:

'I haven't heard your name before. How do you spell it?' He spelled it for her and added, 'It's a Uke name.'

'What is that?'

'Ukranian. My folks came from over there.'

Flanagan said, 'It means his folks came out here with bare feet and hungry bellies. That's what he means.'

'Matt!'

'Christ! It's so! Your folks too, Marjorie. And mine. This country was built on hungry bellies. What's to be ashamed of? My old man, his dad came out of Ireland. One jump ahead of the cops he was. You know what—those were goddam English cops, too.'

Bruchk said, 'Matt, we're going to have to leave if you go on like that.'

'You don't have to do nothin', Bill. You don't have to, 'cause me, I'm goin' myself. You guys stay right here.' He got up and wandered back to his smoke-gloomed fraternity and Louis the Traveller slid into the vacated seat. 'I'm gettin' you guys a drink,' he informed them, 'and then I'm tellin' you a little story I heard at the Beach.' He cocked his head at Ruth and asked, 'You 'member me?'

'I remember. You're Louis the Traveller. You've been everywhere.'

'Hey, that's right. You 'member good.'

They never did hear his story. Louis was only the first to cross the unmarked line. Tyler almost tied with him and the party grew. Ruth liked it. She enjoyed an hour of it and it was the best hour she had spent since she arrived in the district. She knew that she was the draw—a new woman in a closed community. There was flattery in this and it was pleasant. She saw the contrast between her long bare arms and their knobbly bones, between her pale skin and their tanned and burned faces and necks. Her femininity was elicited, causing her to emphasize this. It was a long time since she had felt herself react so—and it was reaction. She had no desire to be one of the boys. They plied her with drink some of which she took, some she pushed away; they inveigled her, told stories with an eye to her response, finally loosening her tongue. She knew they had managed this when she heard her own laughter at the little grey man's remarks. Then a big farmer, a huge-framed man, slapped his thighs and challenged.

'Hey, Honey! Bet you daren't come sit here!' She laughed and looked at the others, and saw the flush rising again on Bruchk's face.

'What about that, Honey? Are you comin' for a ride?'

'Big Tom, he'll give you a good ride,' the little grey man told her, 'best ride in all this town he'll give you.'

'No, thank you. Not tonight.'

'Aw! Come on, Lady! Be a sport!'

She dithered. There was a great urge to do just as he invited, to sit down on his knee and see what happened then. The tiniest of pushes would have sent her to him, but he stretched out to take her arm, and Flanagan, who had returned a few minutes earlier, reached forward and knocked the man's hands away. 'You keep your goddam hands to yourself!' he said.

'Well, for Chrissake! She wants to come and sit, she can. She don't want to, she don't have to. You mind your own self, you little bastard, or I'm gonna put you out there on the sidewalk.'

Ruth said, 'For goodness sake!' but Flanagan was already swinging. He missed. The big farmer did not, and Flanagan, table, glasses and beer, all flew, all fell. There was a scattering to avoid the beer. Marjorie began to weep. Bruchk cautioned, 'Hold it, Tom!' but the big man shook his head.

'Did you see that little bastard? Took a punch at me, he did. I ought to break his goddam neck, that's what I ought to do.'

Ruth decided, 'I think you've done enough. You'd better help us to get him outside.'

'What, me!'

'We have to take him home. I can't carry him by myself.'

'Give me a hand, Tom,' Bruchk said. The farmer shook his

head again. 'Little son-of-a-gun!' He took Flanagan under the armpits and Bruchk took the feet.

It was raining hard and the porch gave scant protection. They propped Flanagan against the wall and his head lolled forward on to his chest. Bruchk said, 'You hold him, Tom, I'll get my truck and run him home.'

'Shouldn't we take him, Bill?'

'I think I'd better, Marjorie. I'll handle him okay. The roads are going to be bad slippery after this rain. I'll go in front. If you get into any trouble give me a flash. The roads will surely be bad. They're going to get real greasy.'

The two girls ran through the rain to their car. When they were in it Marjorie began to shake. Ruth asked 'Are you all right? Are you sure you can drive?'

'I will be in a minute. I'll be okay. It was so quick, what happened in there. It put me out, I guess. I'm okay now. What did he act that way for?'

'I wasn't surprised, I expected something like that.'

'Why?'

'Well, you could see, couldn't you? He's had too much, poor man.'

'Why do you say that? Why did you call him that?'

'I don't know. I'm sorry for him, I suppose.'

'For Matt? Sorry?'

'Yes. He's a sad man.'

'What is sad about Matt?'

'I don't know. It's a feeling he gives me.'

But there had been a moment when she had seen Flanagan as an ended thing. When she had seen that what she had taken for fire was despair. It was a quick illumination, gone almost as soon as it appeared but it gave birth to her words. There was a silence between them while Marjorie steered the car out to the road and took up a position in the rear of Bruchk's truck. When they were settled in convoy she said.

'He lives on crackers and cheese and beer and I think he has an ulcer, and his wife walked out on him, and he worries himself sick about every kid in the school, though he pretends he does not. That's what's wrong with Matt Flanagan. I should try to change all that!'

The road was bad. Its top surface was an inch of treachery and Marjorie had a hard time controlling the car. It frequently went into a crab-like slither and she had to spin the wheel madly to correct this. Mud splashed high on the windshield and was turned into a brown smear by the wipers before the rain washed it away.

These seconds of blindness turned the drive into a frightening ordeal. They could see the tail lights of the truck veer and jump and the spouts of water shoot up from its wheels. Ruth said, 'What a night! You wouldn't have thought it could end like this. Be careful! He's stopped.'

Bruchk's lights had discovered a shadow on the road. He saw that it was a man running, staggering. He stopped the truck and the man came to it and leaned over the front wing. Bruchk heard him moaning, 'Oh Christ! Oh Christ!' Bruchk recognized him, he was one of the boys who lived in Upcreek. He got out of the truck and pulled the boy up.

'What is it, son?' he asked. 'What're you doin' out here in this weather?'

'Oh, Jesus! They're in the ditch, Mister. They're in the ditch.'

'Who's in the ditch? Tell me, who's in the ditch?' He grabbed the boy and shook him and asked once more,

'Who is in the ditch?'

'Millers. And Pete. We rolled, they're in the ditch.'

'How far? How far are they?'

'Up there. I been running. I got throwed, then it rolled. Nobody was talkin' I just run.'

'Did you switch off? Did you turn the engine off?'

The boy looked at him. 'I don't know. I can't remember. I was runnin', that's all I remember.'

Bruchk seized him and ran him back to the car. Marjorie said, 'What is it, Bill?' He opened the door and pushed the boy in.

'A bunch of kids rolled over, up the road. I'm going on fast as I can. You follow me but keep out of the ditch.'

'Right!'

He slammed the door and as he began to run through the sheeting rain Marjorie shouted, 'Who are they, Bill? Who are those boys?'

'Millers.'

'That wild bunch!' she said.

'I just kept runnin', Marjorie. I kept runnin' to get help some place. I wasn't running to get away. Honest, I wasn't. I think they're all going to be dead.'

Ruth turned and said, 'Stop talking like that. They'll be all right, I'm sure they will.'

'No! Nobody was talkin'. Nobody at all. It kept goin' over and over, and fast—I could hear it.'

'Keep quiet!' she told him and this time her words were an order and he became silent.

They soon saw the truck. It had been pulled to the side of the road and as they slowed to approach it, Bruchk waved them past and came after them. 'I found it. I think you'd better go on, find a telephone. Get some help down here. I'm going back, see what I can do. It's a mess. We'll need a tractor and ropes. Hurry it up, eh Marjorie?'

After they left he went into the ditch; into the dark, wet jungle of weeds and bracken and branches, and steel and tin. The roof of the car had crumpled in, its frame was buckled, a door hung loose. Steam spat as water dripped from leaf to bared block, its sizzling was loud against the quiet falling rain. Three boys lay and were silent in this jagged, shadowy mess.

'Hey, in there!' he shouted. Then he got down on his knees and crawled under the triangle of door and ditch side. 'Hey, you fellas!' he called again and waited, but there was no answer. Nor had he expected any from within this mechanical anarchy. He groped in the darkness, his seeking hand found and slithered along a wet cushion, and he stretched it, reaching until steel dug into his shoulder, but he felt nothing. He brought his hand back slowly and his trailing fingers touched cloth and a button. He followed the cloth and found a hand. It was cold. He said, 'Oh Christ!' and let it fall. He was suddenly very much afraid, and he crawled backwards out of the wreck and got to his feet. As he did he heard a shout, and looked up. He saw Flanagan's silhouette at the top of the ditch.

'What the hell's goin' on down there?'

'There's a bunch of kids in this.'

'Judas Priest!'

Flanagan slid down to him. He wore no cap, it was probably back in Redville. His hair was plastered against his face, the shoulders of his shirt were darkening.

'What's that about kids?'

'There's two or three, I'm not sure. There's nothing moving. I felt one, he didn't feel so good. You can't get in, I've tried to. We'll have to wait till we get some light down here.'

'I'll take a look anyways, Bill.'

Bruchk heard him scrabbling beneath the wreckage, but he soon returned. He wiped his hand across his face, then held back his head. 'Thank Christ for this!' he said. 'My God, I could use a bucket of water. I don't know if I'm goin' to be sick, or just bust my head open.' He used his hand repeatedly, rubbing the rain into the back of his neck and slapping his face. 'Judas Priest, Bill! What a goddam, stinking sod of a night. Say, did you look around? A guy could drown in that.'

'By God, I didn't!'

They scrambled into the water and moved along it, feeling with hands and feet. Brushk said, 'I sent the girls to get a bit of help.'

'I guess I was pretty goddam stinkin'.'

'You was too.'

'I should fall down in this and drown myself. Who's in that goddam heap?'

'Peter McKenzie. The Miller boys.'

'The stupid bastards! Hell! They're but kids.'

They followed the deep gouges that told of the last frantic seconds of the car's journey, and Bruchk saw a darker patch on the far side of the ditch. 'Matt!' he said, and pointed. They scrambled to it, but Flanagan was quicker. He was already kneeling, putting his arm under the spread-eagled boy when Bruchk reached him.

'Go easy, Matt. Maybe he shouldn't be moved.'

'Nobody can help this kid. Not now they can't. Look at him. He's emptied all his blood out.'

'That's young Pete.'

'I'm not leavin' him here this way. Help me get him up top.'

They struggled out of the ditch. It was not easy and they picked up a lot of slime before they reached the road. Then they carried their burden to the truck and put it in the back on the wet floor. Flanagan said, 'Sorry, Bill, I'm gonna have to throw.' He went away and Bruchk heard him retching. When he returned they stood, silent in the rain, waiting.

The girls came back. Flanagan gave his news, his words were few and muttered. They listened to him and to Bruchk and saw the men's dejection and became forlorn themselves. Marjorie wept quietly, huddled behind the wheel. Ruth listened to her and to the beating above her head. The boy was only a name, and that since only a few moments. There was no face to remember, no arms or legs, or laugh. She could not pretend for a name in a night. But there were two men, shut away now by the rain across the windows. She remembered their dejection, she remembered Flanagan's misery. He is a sad man, she thought. I was right about that. He hurts for things. It must be terrible to be like that, especially nowadays, to feel the knife, to feel the bite. I am stronger than he is. Right now I am stronger. In ordinary things, in living, I can do that, I am strong at that. It is only between the legs I get weak, when I am attacked there. And here's a rain to cool even that. To hell with pain and sick-making things, she told herself, and she slipped off her shoes, opened the door and got out of the car. The mud was cold around her ankles, the rain quick on bare shoulders and arms. She stepped carefully across to where the two men stood.

'It's raining hard, Miss,' Bruchk told her.

'Yes, Bill,' she answered and the deluge embraced them.

After a time she said, 'We left the boy at a farm. The people were very good. The farmer is getting his tractor out and his wife is phoning to all the people around here. There should be help soon.'

Flanagan replied, 'Thanks.'

'How are you feeling now?'

'I'm okay. Better than I should be, that's for sure.' She put her fingers to his arm and said, 'Never mind about that, Matt,' and at that moment Bruchk placed his coat about her shoulders.

And then moving beams of light broke into the darkness and the quiet of the night was no more. She returned to the car. Her clothes were saturated and she sat and leaned in wetness, but it did not matter. She watched the dark shadows criss-crossing the headlights and heard the tractor sliding about as it tugged or dragged, and returned time and again to the lip of the ditch. She heard some of the shouts:

'Give us more light!'

'Ain't it wet down here!'

'Take it slow now, slow!'

There was so much shouting. They are like little boys who whistle louder in the dark, she thought. They are afraid of what is to come. Someone will have to do the touching. Then the tractors cut out and the shadows converged and disappeared. Silence descended over the ditch and she felt Marjorie's hand seek her own. At last, a man came towards them and they saw that it was Flanagan. She rolled down the window and he bent to them.

'They're both dead. We're gonna be a long time here. You two should go home, get some sleep. Marjorie, you stay the night at school, don't try drivin' back to Upcreek.'

'I'll see she stays.'

'Give her a drink. There's a bottle of rum in my bedroom, bottom drawer, right side. See she gets a shot of that, will you? You too, you have a shot.'

'Right. I'll do that.'

'Well, you'd better go then.'

'Matt!'

'Yes?'

'Say goodnight to Bill for us, please.'

'Sure. So long now.'

.   .   .   .   .

There were a few moments, before the nothingness of sleep, during which she could think and remember. She had bedded Marjorie, and then taken a bath and a lot of Flanagan's rum, sipping this while still in the heated water. On her return to the bedroom, she had gone to the mirror to look at herself. It was then, while looking at her body, that her mind, leaping the horror of the crash, returned to Redville and her hour with its men.

Poor Bruchk, he was so dreadfully shy. I wonder if it hurts him when he goes red like that, I wonder where it starts. I don't remember him saying anything. No, I don't remember a word he said. But the big man, there's a one! I should have taken him up. I should have parked right there on him. That would have shaken him, I bet he would have lifted me up with it. His hand would have covered half my ribs. 'And you too,' she told the stiffening nipples. 'You're greedy. Ted treated you too well. He spoiled you. He had a thing about you.'

She took these memories of her late lover to bed and thought of him for the first time without shame at the way he had cast her off. He had been so afraid—the great seducer who scuttled at the mention of divorce. But was he the seducer. Ah yes, she thought, he was the undresser, he was the love-maker, the teacher. But I had been waiting so long there would have been someone, there had to be. I must have guessed what he could do for me. And after he had done it, after he had discovered the void in me, or let me discover it, I could have devoured him. That is how hungry I was. I had been empty for someone. Ted wasn't my seducer, not really. And the next time—why do I always think about the next time? There's too much confusion in it all, the mind and the womb don't get on at all, not in me. It won't be like that for Julie. Her body will tell her all she needs to know. And John Blood too. No reasoning for that dark wretch. Drive home the hand! Drive in the man! Force and blackness. And love? For them? The shared smell of the bush. The shared explosion in the darkness, the overcome mind. That will be their reward for obeying themselves.

Just before she slept she realized that the rain no longer beat against the window. It has all gone, she thought. The sky has drained itself. It is as empty as I am, a great empty womb. Tomorrow the sun will enter it, and fill it with power.

Tomorrow! Those boys! How sad to be like them, not to have tomorrow.

8

Everybody is talking about the kids in the crash. Do I know these guys?
I should tell them about when I was with the Millers that time they were
gopher hunting. Those guys had some beers. They were sitting drinking
beer. When a gopher puts his head they shot it off. They sure laughed then.
They shot lots that day and drank a lot too. That hill was all mixed, dead
gophers, dead bottles.

A few days after the crash Flanagan had a visit from John Fall.
The two men sat on the earthing frame at the foot of Flanagan's
house. The Indian had not shaved for several days and showed a
dark stubble. He was wearing drills and his thick hair was
topped by a red cap, set far enough forward to keep the sun
from his eyes. They smoked through half a cigarette before John
began the trail of words that would lead to the real reason for his
visit.

'Jeez, Matt, you look in awful bad shape. That must be some
dilly you laid on there.'

'It's been worse. It's coolin' off, I guess. It was a dilly, too. Some
day I'm gonna say finish and then that's it for me.'

'That's what all us guys say, uh?'

'I'll mean it when I say it. How long since you were on a beer
drink, John?'

'Oh, say maybe three, four weeks. Maybe longer than that.'

'When you go, you'll find a bottle in the barrel out back.'

'Thanks. Say, Matt, them kids of mine. I don't think those guys
gonna be in school any, next week. Is that okay?'

'No, it isn't. You know that without askin'. Where are you
takin' them?'

'Off aways. We got a root pickin' contract.'

'This time of year?'

'It's late, I guess. Some guy missed his figurin'. Maybe he
couldn't get help before this.'

'Who will be in your party?'

'George's bunch, me and the missus.'

'That's not gonna leave any kids in school if we take out yours
and George's.'

'I got another in the basket.'

'Judas Priest! What do you guys eat?'

'It's these womens, Matt. Always won't leave us guys alone, always chasin' after us. Worsen' rabbits.'

'Wait till I see Anna. I'm gonna tell her, her old man says she's a rabbit.'

'Jeez, Matt! Don't ever do that, she'll kill me for sure.'

'About the kids: you tell those guys, they've got to work like hell when they get back. They gotta make up this time. When do you figure on goin'?'

'In the mornin' some time.'

'Well, remember what I said, John. You tell those kids what I said.'

Ruth was in the living-room of the other house. She was working on a series of sketches of birds and mammals that she intended using as teaching aids. Their words carried through to her, first as a mumble, then as recognizable voices. She went to the window and watched the two men. After a few minutes she returned to her work but found that she could not concentrate. She went back to the window, watched again and then walked to her bedroom where she checked her appearance. She unzipped her slacks, tucked in her blouse, re-zipped and smoothed down her hips. When she was satisfied she went out of the front door and on to the porch. Flanagan saw her come down the steps and paused while he appraised her. He thought that she looked much better now than she had when she first arrived. Slacks are good on those long legs, and boots too, he mused. He watched her pick a careful way through the mud and remembered her calm ease of that bad night. 'I guessed her wrong,' he told himself. 'I was too quick that time. I think she's gonna be okay. I could be damned glad she's come.' As she approached he called, 'Hi! Are you takin' a walk?'

'Not really. I came out to get some sun.'

'Did you meet John here?'

'I don't think so. Did I?'

'Well, this is John Fall. I guess your kids will have told you about Miss Lancaster.'

'That's for sure,' the Indian said. He got to his feet and offered his hand. He made a solemn business of the handshake. She had noticed this custom among the Indians, the taking of hands in silence, making a true greeting of it. And now that he was standing she thought that she had met him before. She asked him about it. 'Weren't you at the picnic? I think you were with some children.'

'We were there sure. The whole bunch.'

'Yes, I remember seeing you.'

Flanagan suggested, 'If you're not in a hurry, why don't you sit down and listen to John here. He'll tell you all about his kids, won't you, John?'

The Indian grinned at her and she smiled. She said, 'Thank you!' and seated herself next to Flanagan, folding her arms over her knees so she could lean forward and see the Indian.

The men had been discussing trapping and they resumed their conversation. She listened without great interest at first but this soon changed. With one sentence the Indian claimed her attention and he never lost it.

'What furs do you get up there, John?'

'Oh, them squirrels, and mink, you know. And weasels too, and lynx. That's mostly all.'

'What snares do you use?'

'For the squirrels? Oh, we use that rabbit wire. Same stuff. We make a little noose, we put it on a leanin' post. We try to put it where the she has run. Then we get them fellas when they come after her.'

'Skinnin' them's a chore I guess, John.'

'It's not bad. We can do a hundred in one night, you know, skinnin' and stretchin'.'

Ruth looked at his hands. They were thick and blunt-fingered. She tried to imagine these fingers at their work, tearing fur from flesh. They looked strong, the knuckles were big and she saw a covering of fine black hairs on his arms. This surprised her as she had always understood that Indians lacked body hair.

Flanagan was asking about lynx.

'He's kinda hard stuff. You make a fence for him, just little dead sticks, any little bits of sticks. Then you set your trap in there so he can't get. He's pretty sneaky stuff to get in there. You've got to put your bait in. If you don't put it where he step over, then you don't get him. That's a hard thing to kill.' He halted, reflecting, and there was a pause until he continued, 'For them things we use mostly liver and stuff, you know, all rotted out an' smellin' awful hard. Any kinds of liver. We put it in a can and we rot it out so it smells awful. We put it where the lynx go by with the wind side about hundred yards. You have to know how to set your trap.'

She spoke for the first time, 'Don't they suspect anything when they see the row of sticks?'

'Oh no! They go right in there.'

There was another pause. She wanted him to go on talking. He was a slow speaker and he broke up his sentences with these pauses and with chuckles at the cunning of the things that he slaughtered. But these breaks seemed natural to such a subject. So did his voice, deep and strong, showing to her the life on the other side of that fringe. She had seen its insects, and heard its frogs and birds, but of its larger animals she knew nothing. Here was a man who knew them as she knew books, who could read them or their actions with a matching ease. He would foretell an ending with accuracy, would see their traces where she would see nothing. He would smell them, he would hear their breathing. He would catch them by reading their urges.

Put it where the she has run. Catch the he's while they are panting with lust and choke lust and life from them with wire. There was excitement in the thought and its connotations, the power of the she. She found herself breathing deeply, wondered for a second if they had noticed it. But Flanagan was lighting a cigarette. She said, 'Tell me something about wolves.'

'Wolves? What you want to know 'bout them fellas?'

'Well, are they dangerous? Why do they howl at nights?'

'I'll tell you, the only things he howls for, he smells somethin'. Maybe a trap or somethin' in the bush. If he smells that he howls right away. Bad weather too, like coyotee, same thing with coyotee.'

'How's about moose, John? That's what keeps you fat.' But he is not far, she thought, leaning forward fractionally so that she could see him. Her eyes dropped to his waist. The tan shirt was tight across his stomach, it was open and she could see his skin. Below this, his pants were taut over the thighs. He was not fat but neither was he thin. Flesh would be firm over his bones, there would be muscles across his shoulders and around his legs.

'I've killed some big moose, weight ninety-five or a hundred hindquarter, more even. Some go to five hundred dressed. That's a big moose. Fall time, that's the best, that's when they're good.'

'But you're hungriest in winter.'

'That's for sure. You're hungry, that's when you got to have some. Yeah! You know, first thing when I kill a moose in the bush, and I killed lots of them, I make a fire and I cook a steak. Right there!'

'Just like that.'

'Point up a stick and tie your steak on that, by the fire. That's the first thing I do. It's wild meat, you know. When I'm going on the trap lines, the nearer I go, I get that much more hungry. Far as that goes, deer is a little better than moose for myself. But he can smell real good, that guy.'

'Is that right?'

86

'You've got to know how to hunt. When you see a track, you know. They go this way and that and you know they're gonna set. They lay down in that spruce, they sure can see in that spruce. When you move your legs that's what they see, they take off. It's the legs those guys watch for. When a moose is feeding here like, then they go right round and . . . sit here!'

His knife blade, which had been scratching paths and circles in the dust, stabbed suddenly and remained in the dirt. Her eyes followed his hand from knife to its resting place on his thigh. He went on without urging now and she knew that this was no longer story to him, he was seeing, he was living his words. 'You have to know which way to circle them. You look round, see how the timber is, which way he's gonna go, where he's gonna set. If you know the bush, you know for sure.' He was silent for a moment, his face still, the hand on the thigh, palm upwards and open. Then he closed and turned it. 'Come to that, killin' is easy. It's packin' that's hard. Nobody takes horses in there now, you've got to bring him out on your back. Jeez, that gets hot! When that snow's deep, it's what gets you for sure. You don't go far to have a rest.'

'And the next steak,' Flanagan added. While they laughed she looked again at John Fall. She tried to see him staggering through bush and snow, with a huge, bloodied quarter on his shoulders. She looked once more at the man's hands, imagined them deep inside a carcass, pulling and ripping, with blood on the wrists and in those black hairs. Breathing deeply but quietly, through widened nostrils, she could smell the burned wood and animal scents of the forest. The smell of her nights, of the bush and its people. Then the Indian got to his feet and rubbed his mouth with the back of his hand.

'Maybe I should be goin'. I've got things to fix for mornin'. I want to see George too.'

'Okay, John. Call in round back, and have a good trip!'

After he had gone, she stayed for a while with Flanagan.

'I guess you found that interestin'.'

'I certainly did. I've never heard anything like it. Why, I could almost smell the animals. I could have listened to him all day.'

'I figured so. He sure knows his bush. Say, my throat's slit. Time I gave it a drink.' He got up and walked to the door. He stopped there and turned and said, 'You fancy a beer?'

'Yes, please.' She got to her feet and brushed the earth from her seat. The bottles were wet when he brought them and he had to towel them before flipping their caps.

'Do you want it out of a cup or straight?'

'Straight?'

'Out of the neck.'

'How do you have yours?'

'Straight.'

'Then don't bother about a cup for me.'

The beer was bitter at the first taste. She gave a little shiver, laughed and said, 'I'll soon be a hundred per cent.' Then she walked to the table and eased herself on to it. Flanagan said, 'I have to tell you somethin'. I first met you I figured you for a real——'

'Go on.'

'Skip it! You're not anyways, you're okay. And you sure got a kick out of old John and his bush jaw.'

She nodded. 'He was very interesting, he really was. I would like to listen to him again some time.'

'Yeah, he's an okay guy, John. I'll talk with him, see if I can fix it for a trip in the bush this winter. You might see some of this stuff he was talking about. How would you like to see a couple of white tails?'

'White tails?'

'Deer.'

'I'd love to. Do you think he would take us? Could you persuade him to?'

'Sure. It won't be any trouble persuading old John to go up there, 'specially if he gets a ride in.'

'You keep calling him old. He isn't so old.'

'I'm older. But he'll die quicker.'

'Oh!'

'Well there's more chance, put it that way. How's a guy to get knocked off, teaching kids?'

'I like John. He seems different.'

'From the other guys around here—is that what you mean?'

'Yes. I could understand him.'

'Don't count on it.'

'Why not?'

'I've known John. I don't think I understand him.'

'You have been with them for a long time—if you don't understand them, who will?'

'Three years! Judas Priest, it's gonna take more than that. Can you tell what goes on inside a spruce, right deep inside? It's the same thing. We got a lot of experts. Guys come from over the east and nose around a little with their portable tape recorders. The Indians tell them what they want sayin' and pocket a little hooch money, then they go back and write a paper. Those universities must be filled up with papers like that; any guys want an easy tag to their names they can pick it up here. And what have they done, what have they taught us? What do they know 'bout what goes on in an Indian's mind? Nothin'! No more than we do. No more and no less because it's got to be nothin'!' He thought for a moment before continuing, 'I guess we got too many experts. An expert never cares. His subject becomes his baby, he totes it all over, like he was the proud daddy who made it. But he doesn't care. It's all brain, there's nothin' else. This Bureau is loaded with experts and I don't suppose there's one gives a goddam 'bout a single Indian kid. There was a time in this country when an agent lived with his Indians, he was a real father to them. He got down off his horse and used his shoulder when they wanted help. But that's out. Today, he's a city cowboy, comes out when he's got to, and then it's in the latest model and totin' a brief case. Can you see Sam Smythe dirtying his suit to help an Indian?'

'I don't know Sam Smythe.'

'You will. He's agent for the Big Fish. Comes for the meetings. Wouldn't bury his own mother without six permits.' There was a short silence. Then he said, 'I'll tell you somethin' about these people here on the Big Fish. They're survivors. They're what's left of scores of bands that lived in the west before the whites came. Out of all those bands, these are one that got through. They beat out the others, they beat the bush and the winters and they came through. They even survived when the whites took away their food and gave them hooch and pox. They were toughest when times were hardest, and they did it on a code of honour. You know what, a chief died, they left him in his tepee with all his stuff around. They didn't build no goddam pyramid over him. They didn't need to. No Indian would touch anything. A man had to be a man quick, and carry the weapons, his woman walked behind and carried the fire pot and the baby. It was done on the code. You know John Henry Burn Stick? And Baptiste Long Leg? Well those old guys they still have a bit of that left.'

'The others have lost it?'

'They've had it stolen. Now they don't want it back. They've found it easier livin' our way, cheatin', lyin', twistin'. We taught them. Boy, we taught them good, and they learned it good! We stole their land and we figured they'd die out nice and quiet, so we gave them a pension while they were dyin'. But like I said, these are survivors. They're adjusters too. They can take a bit of this and a bit of that, but they can't make it all the way. They've got somethin' inside that stops them, somethin' warm. Listen to them at a funeral, you can hear them bleedin'. They can't get rid of that, they can't get hard enough to go all the way across to us. And there's that other little thing. They sunburn easy. Folks round about a reserve don't bother too much, but you go to the city. You stand on Mountain Avenue with one—with old John, say—and you watch, when they go past you. Watch what their faces are like when they see him. It's not only in the west; those bastards in the east are the same, croaking their guts out about how many languages there should be on a box of corn flakes. Tell them they're right, tell them English should be scrapped, and then tell them it should be Cree instead and watch their faces. Christ! I'm sick in the guts at this country and don't think that's an easy thing to say to a Limey.'

She let him calm down a little before she asked, 'How is it going to end?'

'That's anybody's guess. Mine is they'll try and force them off the reserves. Then we'll have thousands of vagrants with us for the next fifty years.'

'Isn't education the answer? Aren't we teaching them? Can't they be trained? What about the boy who is in the city? If we can get more to be like him, to really benefit from education. There's hope then, surely?'

'You mean Francis Littleleaf. Say I'll make you a little bet about that. You want to take it?'

'When I know what it is I might.'

'I'll bet you an even buck that he doesn't go on. I'll bet you he doesn't ever spend one day in university. Will you take that?'

'Yes. And I hope I win it.'

'So do I. I'd pay it smilin'. But I won't have to.'

'You want him to do well.'

'I want it for all of them, not just him. I want them up off their fannies and kickin' hell out of each other. I want them to burn down their shacks and get the hell off the reserves and earn a goddam livin' for themselves. I want them to stand on their own two feet, anywhere in this country, in their country, with their heads up here. But they've got to be able to do that first! I get madder'n hell at the whole goddam mess. A race of people sittin' stinkin', while the government leeches away what last little bit of yesterday they've still got left. Allowances and relief! You can't pension a people and then ask them to respect themselves. Not when it's so easy to make hooch, you can't.'

His face was very pale. She thought she saw sweat at the corner of his mouth. He is one man who does care, she thought. I could

90

not feel about things as he does. I would not want to, it is dangerous. It is a weakness to care like that.

'I don't want them to be dyin' off in our ditches, like country bums.'

'And where does drink fit into this?'

'Hooch! It's the best equalizer these folks have. They drink it like you shut a door.'

'To keep things out.'

'So they don't have to face up to what they're gonna have to face.'

'And John Fall. Is there any of yesterday in him?'

'He's okay. He's a good mechanic. He can do a day's work. I like John.'

'But?'

'But what?'

'Has he a future?'

'John, he'll be okay till the poison gets to him. Then he's had it, he'll be as bad as any.'

'And the poison is drink?'

'Judas Priest, Ruth! I thought I'd been tellin' you. We're their poison. An old Indian told me once, he's dead now, that guy. He said, 'wherever you whites put your boots you leave poison in the earth. Nothin' good grows any more.' Think that out. Take a good look everyplace. Worst thing that happened to this world was when the white folks got itchy feet. By Christ, a lot of people have suffered for that! No! We are their poison. One way or another, givin' or takin' away, it doesn't matter which. Don't ever try to do anythin' for an Indian. All you'll be doin' is puttin' a rope round his neck. There never was an Indian yet got away with bein' helped by a white.'

'But you still try.'

'I still try. I'm crazy, I guess. I hope when John gets it, it isn't from me. And I talk too goddam much for one bottle of beer.'

She commented, 'Marjorie says it is living in the bush that affects them. She says there is evil in there and that it rubs off on them, that living close to the animal brings out the animal.'

'She could be right, too. Between us and the bush what chance do they have? What the hell! Forget it, they'll make out better'n we do. You havin' another beer?'

'No, thank you. I was doing some work. I'd better get back to it.'

'Your work's gonna have to wait. We have us a visitor.'

She looked through the screen and saw that a truck was approaching the house. It drew up in front and she recognized

Bruchk as he climbed down. It was the second time he had come visiting since the bad night.

Flanagan wouldn't let her go. He threw together a five-minute, out-of-the-can lunch. After it was eaten they sat around and talked a lot. She wondered afterwards why the farmer had bothered to come, he took so little part in the conversation. Then he and Flanagan drove away. Flanagan invited her along but she refused, she really did want to get on with her painting. But she watched them go then turning saw the white stump out on the ball diamond; she looked at it and remembered.

There was a mad moment when the post became a finger, reaching out of soil and beckoning to her. She found herself walking across the ground towards it. The sun was full of power, filling the world with light and heat, making her into a black ball at her own feet. She stopped and held up her face to its warmth, eyes shut and mouth smiling. Then she walked on—slowly. There was anticipation that could be so easily destroyed. Nothing else moved, everything human was hidden, all were tented, King Sun ruled. She came to the post and leaned herself against it as the Indian girl had. She was alone, but she could easily alter that. She could easily make herself feel the wanting hand on shoulder, on back, and down there. The shoulder was waiting for it, and the back, and down there, what was waiting most of all. It was always waiting. Ted Swift's soul, marching on. She tightened herself to receive the hand and suddenly everything inside her seemed to shiver. She clung to the post, tightened her legs around it and pressed herself hard on to it, until the shivering ceased. Even then she stayed. To an onlooker she would have appeared to be sleeping, pinned by sun to post, fixed by its whiteness.

At last she turned and faced the bush. She looked at the forest where moose strode in circles and squirrels hung in wire circles, where flowers opened at night above their decaying sisters, where every living thing ran or flew, or crawled in danger. She walked away from the post, passed by the swings and Flanagan's house and climbed the slope, where mud gave way to dark soil, to first stubble and first thorn. She passed all of these and entered the bush. It shut her off immediately, folded its arms around her; made of her a child searching forbidden places. Above her head leaves and branches nursed a fragmented sky, beneath her feet dark, leaf-moulded earth steamed gently. A rash of choke cherries bled upon their spikes; the spaces surrounding her were depths of sunlight and shadow—moss, scrub, and leaf. Each seized and held its tiny share of golden ray. She put out her fingers to touch the leaves, stroked the bark and its glow came green on to her palm— she walked with her cupped hand showing the green, holding the glow. I am quite alone, she thought; I am being led deeper and deeper into their bush; being led by sun spot and green shine and berry glow. How warm the sun is, even here. It is making day all around me, making life, pouring it through all these leaves into hungry stems; everything here is living and breathing and taking in sun. She gave way to fancy and addressed herself to the sun:

'Light up your bush for me. Show me the world of John Blood, of John Fall. There is no one else to see, only me.' She sauntered along, unaware that within yards, the long deserted shack of Fat Mary Littleleaf, whose son was poised at the entrance to a new life, rotted quietly. She followed Mary's trail and in time she came to the creek. When she first saw it she stopped to watch the racing rolling water and the rubbish that rode with it. She saw a branch twist with the tide, its leaves cowering; and she was watching this, waiting for it to catch against the bank, when a man's voice sounded close to her. She was startled for a moment, then the voice sounded again and she knew that she had not been seen. Curiosity drove her forward, and through the screening leaves she saw an Indian.

He stood below her, on a small ledge that overhung the creek, and he was naked. The water beneath him was dark and caught no sun. It was still and silent, a pool in the looping arm of the creek, an overflow from the swollen stream. The bush was dense down there, almost hiding the shack from which the man had come. It was a silent place, a private place. Another man came and stood by the first. He was naked also but he was smaller and thin. She had no eyes for him. She crouched in the concealing thicket and the sun lit up the strong, bronzed body of the first, showing him to her. She recognized John Fall. She watched as he rubbed his flanks, heard the slap of his hand against them. When he balanced at the edge of the bank she saw his dark loins and their awesome bundle. Then he dived, taking the sun with him in a steep curve to the water; and the pool split and jumped as it received them and covered him. He seemed to be hidden for so long that she was terrified he would not reappear. But a flash of his skin calmed her. She saw the sparkle of sweat on her wrists, and reaching, felt more on her brow.

When she looked again at the water both men were playing, splashing and criss-crossing the pool. John chased the other; she saw their bodies, so pale in that darkness, flip and turn and sink and vanish. She felt fear once more, but they emerged, gave up their playing and came to the side. They stood at the creek's edge, shaking the water from themselves like soaked dogs. Then they climbed the bank and walked beneath and past her. For a few seconds she owned all of him before he went, laughing, into the hut.

She left the creek and its path and walked deep into the bush. She found a stretch of moss and making sure that she was alone, she took off her shirt and her bra. She laid the shirt on the moss and stretched herself on it. Looking upwards through the latticed leaf work, she was awake to every movement, every twist of leaf, each tiny rustle, each passing insect, every flicker of light. She was motionless herself, relaxed, breathing easily, allowing her imagination to have its way: 'That was why I was tempted here. The bush has shown me one of its sons, a child of the forest, a man of the band, whose generations are conceived here, beneath these floating feathers. Their women are pressed on these mosses; their families are fed by its animals and hidden by it; and when they are ended, they are buried and become bones in its depths. Children of Adam we called them, Marjorie and I. I who am a daughter of Eve.'

A butterfly came near, a hovering dab of too-bright colour. It hung above a floral tube and she watched it, marvelling at its adult beauty. A few days ago you were sleeping, she mused. Now you are brighter than the flowers you feed on, you have stolen their glory. In another few days, an hour perhaps, you will be dead. But first you must seek a mate. I wonder what you are, male or female. You must be male. You have to be. This is a day for males to show themselves, to vaunt. The insect fluttered towards her. She kept perfectly still. She was wishing, willing it with all her silent strength. It came nearer, made two tentative swoops and then folded its wings and she could have sworn that it touched her. For one second only, on the smooth slope above the navel and then it was gone. But she was smiling, it had been a male, it had touched her.

Little Moise was not enjoying such a pleasant afternoon. Upcreek knew about the whisky. It bridled with anger. It flexed its moral muscles and cursed with rage. It grouped its citizens on corners and in store and station, and the little man, who knew now how he had been used, also realized his danger.

'Who would give kids that stuff? Who's gonna give whisky to a sixteen-year-old boy? A man gives whisky to kids—he ought to be shot!'

Through a whole day he had suffered on the rack of fear and

impotence, ever since the news from the autopsy had leaked that morning. He prowled the streets in search of hopeful titbits which might be to his advantage, but found none. Nor was there sympathy for his various suggestions: that maybe those boys were regulars at the drinking game; that they got the liquor at the dance; that perhaps they had got it in the city. He was too smart to press these points, he merely put them out as feelers and was quick to agree with their rejection. No one was stronger than he in condemnation for the source of the liquor.

The town had its teeth into a scandal and was shaking it with all the fury of righteousness. Little Moise also shook. He hoped that Joan McKenzie's fear was stronger than her conscience, and he knew by the Holy Ghost, that he would never again look at a woman other than his wife.

And a couple of miles farther south, Bruchk was back at work again on his farm, and pondering the wonder of Ruth Lancaster. That a woman such as she, cultured, beyond touch of farm dirt, a woman of that other world, should sit at his table, should drink beer with him, should stand beside him in the rain—all these thoughts were not credible. He had to keep remembering, to keep retelling each word that had passed between them. There had been so few. The more he tried the harder it became to remember her face. All he could think of was the wonder of her presence, when she had stood beside him, and how he had put his coat on her shoulders.

They sweep up the leaves when fall is over in the city. I'd leave them in the road. It's something to remember it by until the snow comes. I like to pick up a handful of leaves in the city.

The inquest was held in the depot waiting room. It was the biggest room in Upcreek, take out the store, and Golding had not offered this. It was also in the shade of the elevators which cut twenty degrees from the temperature. Long benches already lined three of its walls, and the sub-agent had filled the centre well with chairs from the County Women's League's stock. Unfortunately some little fingers had opened holes in the window screens, and a swarm of flies disputed possession of the room throughout the proceedings.

Most of the Upcreek citizens had gone to share in the judgement. They were sure that there would be naming of names and pointing of fingers, and when that happened there would be no hesitation about the first stone. That was why they grew impatient at all the talk about who did the finding, and the state of the car and all that. They were waiting for the surviving boy to be called, and it was when this happened that necks craned, and people at the back stood, and even the women shushed.

'Yes, they had been drinking. They'd been to the reserve but it was raining. They'd gone over there for a ride. Yes, they had some beer. What else? Oh, they had some whisky. No. He didn't know where it came from. No. He didn't get it. He just had a little sip, that's all. He didn't like it. Who? No, not the Millers. Yes. Young Pete McKenzie. He'd got it. He hid it in a mail box. No, they hadn't paid for it. Young Pete must have done that.'

It was then that Arthur McKenzie put his head down into his hands and his wife began to weep, and it was very soon after that Little Moise left his seat at the back of the room and pushed his way out.

And that was all the listeners got for their sacrificed morning. No names, no pointed fingers.

All those bodies had jumped the temperature back up. The flies were a pesky nuisance, there was sweat around shirt collars and the chairs were hard as hell on the rumps. Most of them were glad when it ended and they could get out of there. The verdict

96

was as expected—from misadventure, and with regrets to fine parents, plus a little homily on teenage drinking that brought on more tears from Helen McKenzie and a bout of clapping, until the coroner stopped this. There was a quick exodus and the room was left to its flies and the sub-agent's broom. The women went away quickly to their chores but the men lingered outside, passed cigarettes around and stood quietly, looking at the rails while they smoked.

Flanagan said, 'Where are you eatin', Bill?'

'Here I guess, at the café.'

There was disgust on Flanagan's face.

'Have to eat some place, Matt.'

'Call that eatin'? Bet you wouldn't take one of your hogs in there.'

'Maybe not. My hogs are choosy, gettin' good grub the way they do.'

Marjorie offered, 'Why don't you come home with us, Bill?'

'Thanks anyways—I guess you Mom's gonna be busy enough with you folks. No, I'll eat down the street if it's all the same. Maybe some time else.'

'Suit yourself, Bill. You're welcome, come or not.' She began to walk along the platform and Flanagan followed. Ruth said, 'Goodbye then, Bill.' He took off his cap as she left him, and he cursed himself, he was that annoyed. He could not understand why he had said no to Marjorie. The words had jumped out of his mouth it seemed to him now.

He did not eat in Upcreek after all. A group of the men were making up a party to go to Redville and he was asked along. They ate at the hotel snack bar and went from there to the beer parlour. Tom O'Malley, the big farmer was in the group, so was Louis. It was a noisy gathering, they drank a lot and laughed a lot. It was a long time since Bruchk had passed such an afternoon. Listening to these men and seeing their careless companionship, he thought that he did not do enough of this, that he should get around more. 'Does a man good,' he told himself, 'helps a man unwind a little.'

O'Malley said, 'Say Bill, that Flanagan, he's sure a son-of-a-gun. Passed the time of day with me this morning. Never said nothin' about me hittin' him that way. Jeez, I was sorry I done that.'

'Matt's okay, Tom. He gets worked up, I guess.'

'Who wouldn't on that job he's got.'

'That's a nice kid too, that other teacher. That English one.'

'She sure is.'

'Leave that girl be,' Louis said. 'Me, I'm gonna set myself up with that one. Tom, you keep your eyes right off that girl, or I'm tellin' your missus.'

'Fritz!'

They drank more beer and then the bar phone rang. Fritz answered it and came back to them. 'It was Suzanne again. She wants somebody to take some beer to her place.'

'What did you tell her?'

'Said there wasn't nobody in the bar.'

'Which she'll know is a goddam lie anyways. All she's gotta do is look out of the window. She's gonna see the trucks out front. When is he back?'

'Week-end. She'll never last till then. She'll be in. She'll be in tonight.'

'How's a woman get like that?'

'Same as a man. There's guys come in here as bad as she is.'

'I blame her husband. He knows he's goddam torturing her, leavin' her dry in the house three weeks together.'

'It's his job, Fritz. She knowed that when she married him. She knowed he was a driller.'

'All the same it's hard. I seen her like this, she gets sores all over her hands. Christ! You should see her scratchin' those sores. Makes me goddam sick!'

'That's how she'll be right now.'

'Any of you guys soft enough to take a crate over there?'

'No sir! That bastard would shoot a man who went into his house while he was away, especially takin' beer.'

'She'd lie right there on the floor for a can of this stuff.'

'Who's gonna lie on the floor?' Tyler had joined them. He did not wait for an answer.

'Did you guys hear that one about Hereafter Jones?'

'No, I never did.' Big Tom shook his head, so did the others.

'Well, this Jones, he got himself hooked up with this Salvation girl. One night she has him in the back seat of his car. She's workin' like hell, doin' her damnest to save his soul. But Jonesie, he's all steamed up, 'cause she's such a temptation. Then she says to him, "Willie, do you believe in the Hereafter?"

'Jones says, "Sure I believe in the Hereafter, and I knows what I'm in here after. An' if I don't get what I'm in here after, then you're gonna be in here a long time after I'm gone.'

'Hey, that's good!"

'That's one for the missus!'

Bruchk began to feel restless. If this was going to develop into a Tyler session, he would buy the next round and then pull out. His memories of his wife were strong, she was his only knowledge of sex, and what they had shared was too good to be dirtied in a beer parlour. He listened with a part of his mind to the conversation while his thoughts drifted from past to present. He found himself thinking of another woman. He tried to recall his wife and he found this was not easy, Ruth Lancaster kept intruding. He tried again, but the tall, dark figure came again to force away his wife, and there was no difficulty now in remembering the face. He could see the table at which she had sat with him, the chair she had used. He could turn his eyes from it and still see her; the tall girl who had stood in the rain, her wet dress clinging to her. She was so different from these people, from Big Tom and Louis, from Tyler, from the wives of these men. He thought of Suzanne sitting in an empty house and itching for the drink that her husband forbade. How clean and different was the English girl!

What does she think of us, he wondered, what does she really think beneath that quietness. What does she think of us. What does she think of me. I wish to God that I could talk, I wish the words would come, the ones that I need. I wish I could use words like Tyler here, or like Louis.

He bought a round, left himself out and went as soon as he could. He stood on the sidewalk near his truck. The shadows from the buildings opposite reached across to him though it was still early afternoon. A leaf flicked by, rested at his feet and then moved on. They spoke of many things to him, the leaf and the shadows; of wood to be sawn and shingles to be checked; of oil that had to be ordered and walls to be stuffed; of cattle that had to be moved up and machines stored. In the convent garden, below the steeple-centre of this French town he saw the paired nuns walking, six pairs walking and praying. They would be praying for other people, not themselves; praying for Redville and its sad ones, perhaps even for Suzanne. He climbed into his truck and drove out of the town.

After the inquest came the funerals. Pete McKenzie was buried over in the city, where his mother had lived. A lot of the country women from Upcreek went, Helen being the President for the year. Sarah Golding was in the fifth car which Little Moise drove. He had spent a whole morning cleaning and shining it. After the convoy had lined up on the street and driven off there was an unusual quiet in the town. It was especially quiet in the store and Golding decided he would lose no custom if he went to collect his mail. Sarah usually did this—the storekeeper and the little Welshman were like cat and dog in the same box, and that office was no bigger than a box. This morning she had not the time, so he must go himself. The postman pushed an armful of newspapers and letters towards him and went away. Golding returned to the store, took the mail behind the counter and began to go through the letters. Some time later he heard a bang from the door leading into the house. He looked up and saw Julie at the head of the stairs. She held a cup, and while he watched she came down the stairs and brought the cup to the counter. 'Here's your coffee, old man.'

'Julie, I told you about that, didn't I? Don't want you callin' me that. It ain't a nice thing to call somebody.'

'Aren't you an old man then?'

'No! I'm sure not. Anyways, I'm the strongest guy in this town, you bet.'

She laughed at him. 'Who says so?'

'I say so. See, I show you.' He came round to the front of the counter and leaned to wrap his arms round a swollen sack. He straightened his back and she saw the sack lift clear of the floor. He bent a knee and used this to support the sack and then a quick heave brought it up on to his shoulder.

'How's that then?'

'I seen other guys do it.'

He dropped the sack with a thump at her feet. 'You try it, Julie. I give you five bucks if you can lift that off the floor even.'

She looked at him for a moment, using her tongue against her upper lip while he waited. Then she gripped the corners of the sack and tried to lift it. 'Shit!' she cried, and stopped trying. 'That's a heavy cow in there!'

'I told you. Me, I lift all these sacks, all these boxes—every goddam thing. Nobody in town could do what I do nobody on the Big Fish neither.'

'Your coffee's gonna get all cold.'

'You gonna stop callin' me Old Man?'

She licked her lips again, and then she smiled, 'Okay, Daddy.'

'You gonna stay down here awhiles?'

'Me, I want my coffee.'

'You have that. I don't want.'

'Okay!' She brushed past him and stood at the counter, her back to him. She picked up the cup and began to drink from it, nursing it in her hands. She listened to the storekeeper who was moving about behind her. She heard the lock of the door spring to, and then the lowering of its blinds. Then she heard him returning until he was close behind her, and she was smiling when the hands made their first touch, one to each of her hips. When she did not move they became stronger, the touch became a grip. She continued to drink without hurrying and then placed the cup on the counter. Then she turned within his hands. 'Me, I'm too heavy for you, I bet. You can't lift me like that sack.'

'Jeez, Julie!' He slipped an arm behind her legs and the other across her back and swung her with ease from the floor. She placed an arm around his neck and with her other hand she patted her hair into place. He saw the pink tongue again, wet and touching, leaving a shine on the upper lip. 'You got some beer up there in that refrigerator, haven't you, Daddy?'

It was almost noon when Julie got up from the bed. She pulled on her slacks and went barefoot to the store. She opened the cash drawer and took out a ten dollar bill which she put into her shirt pocket. Then she went back upstairs. Golding was still lying on his back, as he had fallen from her. 'Ain't so strong now, Daddy. Guess you couldn't lift no sacks right now.'

'Come here! Come back here, Julie. Please, Julie, come back.'

'Again! You want another! Nossir, you had it enough for one time. When I'm ready next I'll tell you.'

'Please, Julie.'

She sat on the bed while she slipped on her shoes. He reached for her but she pushed away his hand. She laughed again and said. 'Jesus, you sure are a daddy to me. Thanks for the money.'

'What money? I didn't give you.'

'I took it anyways. Be good, Daddy.'

She went out of the bedroom and down the stairs. She raised the blinds, left the store and walked across to the Post Office. The Welshman was in, she told him, 'Want a money order for five dollars.'

'Who do I make it for?'

'Make it for Francis, Francis Littleleaf. And I want an envelope too, with a stamp.'

She took the envelope, put the money order into it, and pressed down the self seal. Then she wrote the address and dropped the envelope into the collection slot. After that she went out to the front and stood in the street. She could hear some boys at the ball pitch but she couldn't see anybody. She looked across at the store but there was no sign of life there. She laughed, 'I done enough work over there for today.' Then she turned and began to saunter away towards the turn-off to the Big Fish.

The road was deserted and she walked undisturbed in the heat of the afternoon. Her only companions were the flies above her head and the darting hornets. 'That was a strong one for an old man,' she told herself. 'Goin' twice like that. He'd have gone again too, the old goat. Bet he gives that old lady hell.' A little farther on she said, 'That Francis, he's gonna have a real surprise. That Francis boy!'

Thinking about Francis Littleleaf brought excitement that she had not felt with the storekeeper. The fun there had been in getting the old man so hot. This excitement was different, it was the big thing, her own inside thing. Suddenly she needed to get back to the reserve, she had to get to Martin Crow. He was the only one who could help her when she began to feel this way. It was a good thing that he was crazy; not bad like Pete, his father, but stupid crazy. He did what he was told and he didn't ask anything.

She found Martin at the creek, he was fishing but he had caught nothing. 'Put that away!' she told him, and he hid the rod in deep grass. 'Come with me and hurry up!' She was impatient, afraid the excitement might escape from her before she had answered it. They hurried through the bush, Julie leading and the big Indian boy trotting behind. When they came to the shack she took him by the arm and led him inside. There were scurryings at their feet and on the roof timbers but she ignored them.

'We're gonna play our game again, Martin. You're gonna be Francis for me. Right! Now get hold of me, here, like that. Give me your hand. Here! Now squeeze me. Not that hard, I told you already. That's right! Oh that's right.' After a while she began to moan, 'Oh Francis boy! Oh Francis!'

Francis Littleleaf had never touched her. He was one of the very few men who had not tried to. That was a big day when she met a man who could keep his hands off her. She had known ever since she was twelve years old that she caused something to happen to men, even by going up close to them. The old ones were the worst, it was as if they were trying to take her young life out into their fingers, into their own bodies.

Her own uncle was the very first. She was baby-sitting for him and Zella while they were at the card game. He came back, he said he'd forgotten something. He stayed talking and laughing with her, and then he got hold of her and took off her jeans and put her on the floor. She was too scared to tell anybody about it, and it happened again; it kept happening until her mother caught them one day in a car, at back of the house. She chased off her brother and told him she'd shoot him if he came again. Then she took a stick to Julie and whipped her until there were lines all over her legs. But Julie knew that it was for who she'd done it with that she got licked, not for doing it. When her uncle didn't come around any more she got hurts for him. They were awful hurts, they made her cry she hurt that much. Then one afternoon when she was like that, she met Martin Crow and had her idea. 'Come with me, Martin!' she told him. He was a year older than she and a lot taller, but he could not think for himself. His father was Pete Crow, the screw head. Martin was stupid, too, but he was a good boy, he did what anybody said. That first time she had taken him into the bush to the old place where he had once lived. Someone had boarded up the shack doorway and windows. 'Kick it in, Martin!' she told him, and he obeyed, kicking and kicking until the boards were broken and there was entrance.

'Good, Julie?' he asked.

'You fixed it good. Come in, Martin.'

He hung back. It was gloomy inside the shack and he was a little afraid. She laughed at him and taking his hand, pulled him into the darkness.

'Julie,' he said.

'Shad up, Martin.' She was taking off her sweater, she rolled it and stuck it into a crack in the wall. 'Come here, Martin! Don't be scared, it's only me, Julie.'

'Julie.'

'That's right. Give me your hand. Put it here. Now open your mouth. Open it, Martin!'

There had been many trips to the shack. After she had gone to the city there might be months between the visits, then she would reappear as she had today, and call him and he would go with her. But it was after she had been in the city for some months that the meetings changed, became the game in which he played the part of Francis Littleleaf.

She had a succession of boy-friends in the city, white boys they were, and white men, and old white men. She took all they offered, presents, liquor, or just taxi rides to the reserve. In return she allowed them to get excited over her. If they wanted it they could have it. But she didn't think she really gave them anything; she could have slept through their frantic struggles, she often laughed inside at the way they worked so hard. It was only when she wanted herself that they got a real ride. Except for those times she didn't think that she gave anything.

She had her own dreams of love, and their subject was far removed from these men. Some day, when he had given up this idea of going through college; when he stopped trying to be a white himself; when he returned to the reserve she would marry Francis Littleleaf. She was sure of this, and she could wait. But he had not to be like the others. She did not want him to touch her, not like they did, she did not want his hands like that. He was going to be for ever and ever, and she was going to be for ever and ever for him.

All she had wanted in the city was to walk with him under the lights and listen to him. He did not know about how she felt, he would be the last to know. There was time, and there was no other girl, she knew that. If any other girl tried that she would bite her to death.

It was funny how it happened, how she had fallen for a quiet boy like Francis, walking the blocks, round the stores, listening to his voice, listening to his poems.

'Write one about girls, Francis.'

'I already did.'

'Tell it me then. You scared?'

'Do you remember that old bush man, Julie? When we were kids did you play that too?'

'Sure. You get the one wish.'

'What did you wish then?'

'I wished for me a new dress with a sky full of buttons.'

'I wished for me that school quit for ever.'

'I wished my momma didn't shout no more.'

'Maybe that old bush man he's still out there. Could be he isn't an old man, just a big old moose. Maybe his ears are full of ice, he don't seem to hear too good. Maybe he's listening right now. Old bush man! I wish for me to get grade twelve.'

'Francis, there's no bush man. No Santa, either. I know that.'

Nobody could take anything away from her, no matter how hard they jigged. Not when she was saving it for him. When she got him, then she would give. He would think the sun fell right down on him. 'I'm gonna make the sun come right down on you, Francis,' she promised aloud. Thinking of him like that, while Martin was playing him made her too happy. She began to cry. 'Kiss me here, Francis,' she said, and taking Martin's head between her hands she put it to her breast.

One night, late in October, Marjorie drove Ruth to the city so that she could choose a winter wardrobe. They had a spree in the stores, bought lined jeans and parkas and several sets of leotards. Later in the evening, when they walked out of a cinema foyer and the first frost met them on the street, Ruth wished that she had changed in the store. People began to say that it had been a long summer and this was a sure sign that fall was coming to an end. The first snow fell, and was followed in unusual and indecent haste by the second—so soon after, that the earth hardly showed itself between each, and people were cheated out of their lovely

Indian summer. There was a hasty repairing and shoring up of defences by people whose faces had been uplifted to the sun for so long that they had forgotten it was only on loan.

Little Moise, working long hours in his garage, replaced countless quarts of oil, and empty anti-freeze cans piled up at the rear of the shed, covering the lower bosoms of his gallery. Ivor Jones, and across the west a high percentage of his generation, made his semi-annual switch of underwear, Long John heavies for lights. Bruchk took the scraping blade from off the grader and replaced it with the huge, shining, snow-sweeping arm. Everything that needed doing on the farm had been done, he had noted the leaf and acted. Now he waited, and wondered how many hours he would spend on that high platform watching the shearing of the snow.

There was a mass evacuation from the Beach. Cottagers packed, cleared closets and pantries, put up shutters, locked doors and outside toilets and departed. The veteran from the store walked the deserted street on the morning after that last Sunday rush and saw squirrels already scuttering over the roofs and blown leaves in the porches, and he remembered once more that long-ago walk in the desert of Dunkirk. Helmut Golding replaced his screens with storm windows, blew the husked flies from the frames and spat upon a scuttling spider. Fritz had wooden porches built around the entrance to the Western, for its inhabitants must be as warm as the beer they drank was cold. Flanagan turned up the oil in school and took a reading of the fuel gauge. The people of the Big Fish made ready also. Tents were taken down, families moved back into houses leaving the tent poles to stand as skeletons in the pastures. Rags were stuffed into broken windows, hides taken down from tree crotches and spread across floors, tins were filled with coal oil and earth was scraped together and piled against lower logs. Men who would soon be patrolling their lonely traplines, hauled dead timbers from the bush for the women and boys to split into kindling. John Fall, deciding that it was going to be a long and cold winter, figured he might as well spend it in taxi-ing and to hell with the trapping. He sold his team to Pete Lefthand, and used this money and what was left from the root picking, plus a little loan from Band Funds, to buy a '55 Chevvy. He got it on a week's warranty from the 43rd Street Car Gardens. It used oil but its tyres were good.

Finally, in official acceptance of the inevitable, the sand boxes on the hill crests were filled, and the police shucked their tans and put on dark blues and fur tops.

Thus prepared, the people of the west ate their Thanksgiving

105

turkeys and awaited the onslaught of their implacable, inexorable, uncompromising enemy.

The inhabitants of the forest made their preparations also. Some tunnelled deep below the frost line, and dragged straw stubble, mosses and leaves into their burrows and wove these into webs of insulation. Frogs bored into mud; toads sought holes beneath rocks or in trees; muskrats built houses even higher, using their tiny, banana teeth on water weeds and reeds, until the tips of the roofs peeped above the water, ensuring ice-free entry or exit.

Rabbits grew as white as old men overnight; and weasels also switched suits to balance the odds. Squirrels worried and chattered inside their hiding places, unwitting of future waiting poles—they left untold piles of little cones to lie forgotten beneath snow and give birth to a new forest in a new spring. Bears, padded with winter fat, rolled like furred pigs in their dens and gave the first snores of the long sleep. Those animals that would brave the elements, moose and deer and elk, grew thicker coats, sweated oil into these, and began to move out of the hills. With them came their living shadows, the hunters, cold-eyed and silent padders. Birds also made ready. Ducks gathered in families, in groups, in flocks, until the surfaces of the fast-shrinking lakes were so crowded that relays must always be in flight. Then came a final, sky-darkening wheel of wings, and after that the sky was silent except for occasional yelping of geese—those transients of the north, late, in a hurry, and soon gone.

Now the great exterminators showed mercy as the Whooping Cranes came through. Their flight path was beamed on the radio and shared the same page as Li'l Abner. A count was made, and great was the joy when this showed an increase of three over the previous years. Folks knew those cranes had sure enough been whooping it up in the north that summer.

It had been a long summer and a short fall. Frost arrived now with each failing of the light, and in the skies stars became brighter and the Northern Lights danced their stately minuets through the dark ballrooms of night.

WINTER

1

It's going to get cold for those little kids on the Big Fish. The mommas and poppas going to get closer together at nights and that means more little cousins for me.

The true snows of winter stole into the streets like members of a coup, secrets in night's dark, unseen, unheard-flakes that took possession silently so that the early riser was presented with a *fait accompli* of several inches in depth. However, the sky was clear and bluer above the white spread, the descent had been gentle, its weight was picturesque, and countless flakes had stroked the air into a crispness that was energizing.

On mornings like this, well-wrapped, with tingling face turned to bright sky, a man was glad to be out of doors. It made him feel good, a little younger than yesterday, a tough son-of-a-gun with that shovel in his hand. He was glad to meet the other men and swop jokes about mosquitoes, and kick snow pads from his boots while he talked. They attacked the enemy, opened roads, out-flanked and reduced white citadels, drove into his very guts—pushing him back until there was freedom for the young faces at the window and access to each door. After that he could go inside and let the whisky or rum or plain hot coffee build a warmth inside to match the burning cheeks and ears, and then, by God, let the wife look out or her backside would get nipped and not by the cold. That's how it happened one morning, a gentle introduction almost like the homecoming of an old friend. But before there could be too much celebrating, from out of the north came the winds, Gothic horsemen of winter, and everything quailed before them. Exhilaration departed, humanity became housebound and the creatures of the wild, hunters and hunted alike, cowered in the depths of the forest.

Ruth saw the storm at first as an early afternoon greying of the sky, a mist growing thicker in the lakeside bush. It caused her to put on the classroom lights and this sudden brightness acted as a unifying force; work almost ceased, all heads turned towards the windows. And then the first flecks appeared, dancing dots, rising and falling and circling, and some, touching the panes, became spots of twinkling moisture. She went to the window and her children came quietly around, together they watched the greyness of the bush gather strength. Suddenly, with a great rolling heave it was up above the trees and taking possession of the sky. It was a monstrous emergence. Within seconds the intervening ball park became a whirling mass of snow flakes. The windows were turned into dark patches, their sashes rattled beneath the onslaught. Ruth got the children back into their seats but they were unable to work. Nor could she. There was a constant roaring from outside, the windows shook at each fresh gust of wind and Flanagan entered the room. He said, 'The sooner we get this bunch away the better. It's making up into a real storm. Could be a day or two before it clears.'

'Is it safe to let them go out in it?'

'They'll be okay. Most of them will stop around here anyways, they've got all kinds of aunties and uncles. They'll be all right.'

'Come on you little snow guys!' he called and they shouted and cheered and ran in search of their clothes.

They had sent off most of the children. Only the two Fall boys and three of their neighbours remained. Paulie told her, 'My dad, he's over at the Old People's. He's gonna take us home.'

'Will he know that school is finished?'

The boy nodded. He pointed with a jerk of his chin in the direction of the departed children. 'Those guys will go over to the card game. He'll ask them. Then he'll come for us.'

'Which card game?'

'Old Lady Potts, he's got a card game.'

'*She's* got a card game.'

'Yes, teacher. She's got a card game. She's blind, that old lady. One day she's chasin' her cat on the prairie, she run all over. When she catch him, that's a gopher she's been chasin'.'

'Teacher, what do those bees make?'

'Honey.'

'Teacher called me Honey!'

'You be ready when that car comes or you'll get honey where you don't want it.'

'That's him, teacher. My dad's come!'

She had not heard the horn but she had learned already how sharp the senses of these children were. She said. 'I'll see you to the car,' and she put on her parka and overshoes. As she opened the door and led them out, the howling wind flew at them claiming and buffering. She felt a momentary panic at the sudden isolation. She seized the children and held tightly to them while she shouted for their father. But her voice was a tiny thing in this wilderness. It was stolen from her and tossed away with the flakes. She was about to fight her way back with the children when she heard him answer. The walls of snow seemed to open and John Fall came through to them. She saw his bulk, huge, in its swathing coat, strong in great boots—hunched against the storm but unshaken. She staggered to him and his arms came about them all, steadying and holding. She looked into his face, its black growth was flecked with snow and mingled with the animal hair of his headgear. She saw the strong nose and lips and the flash of his teeth, and knew that he was grinning.

'There gonna be school, mornin'?'

She shook her head and he said, 'Snow holiday!'

Ruth nodded and laughed with him, and he took them to the car, keeping the worst of the wind from them. She sheltered in its shadow while the children scrambled into the vehicle and her thoughts were as wild as any of the winds that sought her.

There had been such strength in his arm. She gave not a damn for storm or fury, she wanted his arm around her again. She wanted those children away and his arm for her only, around her, holding her, and she wanted that quickly. Then the car door banged and he came to her. 'We'll be goin' then, Miss.'

'Help me back inside.'

'Sure.'

He set off in front, lifting his boots to smash down the snow, and she took hold of his coat. She could smell him, even in that stealing storm she could smell on him the scent of the bush. She stumbled to her knees and he turned and lifted her and they returned to the school with his arm around her as she had wished and she leaned against him. All the leaping emotions fused, filling her with joy and unconcern. She closed her eyes and put her face to his shoulder and let him lead. He could have led her anywhere, he could have gone on, past the school, down the dark tunnels of the storm, into his bush. But he didn't. At the school his arm fell away, and he pulled open the door and kept it open with one of his boots. She staggered past him and the door banged behind her.

Later that night she took off her clothes and walked naked around her house, matching her inner wildness against the outer fury. When she dreamed in her bed it was not of John Blood, but the other John. It was as if she stood again in her hiding place above the creek and could see herself in the water below. She saw her white body twist and float like a waiting lily and then the bronze flash as John Fall dived to join her. She saw herself spring away and he in swift pursuit of her. And then she watched them plunge together into the depths. There was nothing more to her dream, nothing beyond that black water. But somewhere in its depths she knew that the bronze fish would catch the white and then the biting would begin.

For days the winds blew—out of November and into December, until at last one day the world went quiet again. People ventured out, timidly at first: the length of the porch or down to the gate. Then, like exposed ants in an upturned nest, they scurried in all directions—repairing and cleaning up the damage; pushing out and meeting each other on paths and sidewalks and roads, and agreeing that it had been a real son-of-a-bitch of a wind.

Bill Bruchk stood high on his shaking platform throughout the long, cold day, bringing relief to farms and homesteads with his shining blade. He climbed down and drank innumerable cups of coffee and swopped news—the lines had gone down of course, on the first night—and then remounted to turn the plough towards another blockage, another besieged family. He worked on into the night under the flashing blue light, knowing that Christine was safe in the village, and that his livestock were being cared for.

A man got plenty of time to think, up there on the snow plough and the snow itself seemed to lull him, and bring things back to his mind. There was something new to think about this winter. A new face to add to the collection of memories that kept him company during his vigils. He had the thought of Ruth Lancaster, her face sometimes quiet and remote and with the hair wet around the cheeks, and then smiling and laughing as he had seen her in the hotel. He wondered how she was coping with her first northern winter, and he admitted to himself that his non-stop labouring had another reason than the bringing of relief to the township. He knew the road to the reserve, knew how badly it drifted up, and he was impatient to be free to cut a way through to the school. He did not like to think of her being stuck in there. She was not used to that, she would not like it.

First of all, though, the township's roads and then the extras. He drove on into the night, and only stopped for sleep in the early morning, when exhaustion stiffened his frame, when he could no longer open his fingers and he was in danger of falling off the plough. He slept at Peterson's, on a couch in front of the stove, and when he awoke he was red-eyed and still weary.

He breakfasted on ham and eggs and scalding coffee in a thick mug. How many cups of coffee since this time yesterday, he wondered, a dozen, a score, a hundred? Always cups of coffee in the West, a man's stomach must be brown-lined—caffein-coated stomach, nicotined lungs, he thought. God help our poor insides! His overboots had stiffened in front of the stove and he worked on those for a few minutes, pulling at the tops to soften them before he dragged the boots on. Carl Peterson said, 'Take this along with you, Bill, you'll be needing a nip before long,' and he pressed a small bottle of rum into Bruchk's hand.

'Well thanks, Carl. I sure could've used this last night.'

'Thanks for getting through to us so quick anyways,' said Carl, as they went out together to the yellow monster in the yard.

It was a fine morning; the sky was so clear a blue that Bill felt that a shout might shatter it, and it would fall to pieces around him. But it held firm, even when the snow-plough roared.

Bill Bruchk, Uke-boy, whose father, failing to scrape enough from his native soil to feed his children, had been persuaded away from it and put to building a railroad. For his labours the man had been given a patch of bush and swamp but he had died because there was not enough work left in his muscles to beat it. His son had grown up fighting the bush. He was a dogged man, and this was the Uke in him; and a little stupid about this, his own land, which could have been the peasant in him. He fought the bush where it hurt—at the roots—and he kept his eyes there and not on the impossible mass ahead and around. Spring followed spring and each had its quota of clearance. A house took the place of a hut and a woman came to share it with him. They walked together through the steaming soil in summer and they smiled at each other and he knew that she shared the beauty of the rising green lances though she did not speak of it. Then she died, birthing their own crop, and he had supposed there would not be another such sharing.

'She will be lonely in there,' he told himself. 'She is not one of us. She won't like it, being stuck in there.'

Bill Bruchk, farmer. Earning winter money, keeping open the roads, and better doing that than sitting. Moving this big machine along the roads, one side then the other. Piling the pebbles, slicing the crusted mud, shifting the snow like just now. Cutting through to people, to the reserve, to Matt and the Indians. To Ruth Lancaster. A Uke-boy can have a dream.

2

Poor moose. He's got to eat. Everybody is waiting for him to come down for his food. Come on down, old man don't keep them waiting.

> *The women wait, the children wait,*
> *The scraping stone in the hand.*
> *They'll cut your hair,*
> *Old Moose.*
> *Food and clothing of our Band,*
> *Come down to us.*

Early in winter the wind ripples had ceased to flutter the water at the Neck and its surface solidified. The first ice was a fragile covering easily broken by sticks or rocks tossed by impatient Indian boys. As the temperature fell, each day added new laminae to the thickening crust. The ice was soon a foot deep, trapped reeds were crushed to death, spring nests of the wild duck veined the glassy slabs. Snow fell, turning the lake into a vast white valley, and beneath this covering more layers were added and still more, until the thickness of ice was in feet, not inches. Only in the muskrat houses and at the axed water-holes was there free water. The dark hours were the deepest freezers and these were many, for days were dieting now, their narrow waistlines measured but a few hours.

The view from the schoolhouse became a monotony of blacks and whites, startling under the sun but more often greyed over and blurring into far distances. Silence descended with the snow, an unbreakable silence respected even by the dogs. The world became a still place disturbed only occasionally by tiny, isolated figures which straggled across the white wilderness, black and bent over and locked within their parkas. But for most of the time there was nothing to break the pattern, nothing to catch the eye and lure it from the sombre frieze. Ruth found herself confined too much and alone too often. Her mind itched to make some kind of break-out. It was with a sort of desperation that one Saturday she went on to the lake. She could no longer have stayed in the house. Several cars were parked, far apart, on its surface. Near to those blocks of colour were smaller dots—their owners, squatting over holes in the ice, crouching in the cold above their fishing lines.

She stopped by a fire that one party had lit and chatted with a woman, until she realized that the woman's husband was eyeing her. As she went from them she heard the raised voice of the woman, and felt anger at them both. You argue over me as if I were an animal, she thought. You would make a Julie out of me.

Thinking of Julie reminded Ruth of the last time that she had seen her. She had been in the store and Golding had been checking her things. Then he had moved, quietly so that she had not noticed, she would have missed the whole thing if Julie had not been wearing a white blouse. But she caught the flash of white in the mirror at the back of the counter and she looked up to see Julie's reflection. The girl was at the far end of a bay and while Ruth watched, the storekeeper came into view. The two faced each other, the length of the bay apart. For a moment they stood like this and then Julie used her hands to make a quick sign. The man's back stiffened and Ruth guessed that the sign had significance for him. Then the girl disappeared and Golding came back as unobtrusively as he had gone. He finished her order and she carried it to the door. The happening was over in seconds but she knew without doubt that there was a sharing between those two, that it was a sexual sharing.

After that the pictures began, the mental pictures that could be varied without limit, that could begin in disgust and end in fascination. The gross giant and the girl, the brown cat wrapping herself around him, using her body as the final sign.

A cold wind blew across the lake. It lifted grains of snow and threw them against her and she dithered and thought of returning. But no one was beyond her now, each step she took carried her into empty space. She went on, and as she walked she wondered about Julie and what she did and how she did it, and what she said, until she reached a point where she became Julie and said those things herself. But not to the storekeeper.

She reached a wall that had been formed by the upturning of expanding ice. Snow had drifted against this, turning it into a series of humps that zig-zagged from shore across to far shore. She climbed this hump and turned to face in the direction from which she had come. The black fringe of the bush sprang like a beard from the far edge of the lake, its needles and spikes scratching at the sky. The fishermen were tiny specks that shivered as the wind brought tears to her eyes. She felt a great loneliness. The cold, the vastness of space and silence affected her, and she had a compulsion to move quickly, to return to those specks before she herself was frozen into a thorn on this hump. 'There is nothing here,' she told herself, 'but ice and bush and cruel winds and pressing cold.

How it presses, this cold! It squeezes like a lover but there is no love in it.'

She climbed down and began to retrace her steps. As she drew nearer to the couple she told herself again, 'They would make a Julie of me, those two. The man with his greedy eyes and the woman with her fear of me. They must have seen something in me, that I was a possibility and a danger. She was afraid of me and I had done nothing. I only stood. How wives must fear that other woman, she has only to walk, she had only to be and there is fear for them.'

She avoided the fisherman and she spared his wife. She began a new set of snow prints that would take her back to the thin wisps of smoke above the spruce, to the green roof, the brown-faced children, and to man. And man now meant John Fall.

If I wanted you, she thought, like that, how hard would it be to get you? Not hard! You have told me yourself how to do it. Your own words would sell you out. You would be the hunter, you would think that. You would come sniffing and I would spread a good scent for your thick nose. And if you were caught, John, caught in your own trap, I wonder how you would squeal. I wonder if you would squeal at all. Or would you be a happy prisoner?

The wind forced tears to her eyes and froze them to her cheeks. It pressed against her, below the padded coat her thighs were numb.

I hurt like hell, she told herself. I'm one great pain for that man.

The man for whom she hurt was talking to Flanagan. They had met outside the post office.

'Jeez, Matt, I'm loaded. I just got me a check for all that taxiing I done to the hospital.'

'Rich guy, uh?'

'Sure! Hundred-twenty dollars rich.'

'Keep it in your cap, John.'

'Keep it in my cap, for sure.'

'How's about that trip you're gonna take with us? Did you forget that?'

'No, I didn't forget. Any time you want. Jeez, I'd sure like to go up there too. I'm kinda missin' that stuff since I did this taxi. My belly's ready right now for a bit of that wild stuff. It should be good about now, those snows all settled. Old moose should be walking about I guess.'

'Well, we're ready when you are.'

'The mornin'. That would be too soon?'

'No. That would be okay. I'll tell them.'

'We go in my car, Matt?'

'Have you got a heater in there?'

'I have, but it don't work.'

'We go in mine. I don't want to get my rear end all frozen up.'

'You wanna go north or west?'

'I'll leave it to you. You find some good thick bush and something on four feet.'

'Well for me, I'd figure north is the best, over by the Fort. Who is gonna be coming along?'

'Marjorie, and Ruth Lancaster. Nobody else.'

'They'd better don't go shoot us none.'

'They won't be shootin'. They're comin' for the ride.'

'Jeez, Matt, the old lady—she can shoot the ass off a squirrel that one.'

'Is that right!'

'She sure can. Gets herself more squirrels with that little gun she got, beats me all to hell.'

They paused for a moment. Matt knew what the other man was waiting for. He did not offer. Then the Indian said, 'That's all fixed then for the mornin'?'

'What time do I pick you up?'

'That don't mind me none, Matt. We wanna be up there and catch those guys takin' their first walk. That's just with the light, they walk around. You come by when you're ready, it don't mind me none, the time.'

They parted and Flanagan went inside to see Ivor. He was worrying. He wished now that he had made the offer. I'm as big a bastard as any of them. I make like I'm his brother but I don't want to see his wife sitting in the back with the girls. He knows, he won't ask again. What in Christ's name makes me like that? I want to stand up and shout murder against it. And if I did, what words would come out? 'John Fall's as good as I am, but his wife should run around on four feet.' Judas Priest! What a world!

They got their early start. When they stopped at John's house he was at the doorway waiting for them. Ruth peered through the car window. She saw the Fall cabin for the first time, a squat, angular darkness, fronted by a trampled white square and surrounded by mounds of the same whiteness. Huge shadows flitted across the square, she saw that these were being caused by the bobbing and ducking of children's heads in the lamplit windows. She waved, but Marjorie said,

'They can't see us.'

'I suppose not. They should be asleep. How crowded they must be in that tiny place.'

'That's nothing on Old Lady Shortleg. Holy Smokes! She has three bunches all livin' at her place, and it's no bigger.'

'Shh! They're coming.'

The two men got into the car. The Indian turned and said, 'You guys up kinda early.'

'We didn't sleep yet,' Marjorie told him.

'We got a long ways. Maybe you'll be sleepin' before that.'

'Right now, John,' Marjorie told him and they all laughed, but she curled herself up in a corner and wedged her jeaned buttocks against Ruth. She was sleeping before the car left the reserve. Ruth was glad about that. Flanagan was intent on his driving and she felt herself alone with the other man. She leaned forward and breathing slowly through her nostrils she took in the familiar smell of burnt spruce that he gave off. She stayed like this for some time, deliberately, savouring the pungency. It was almost as if she were testing him, tasting him. Here was the first contrived intimacy. She did it without deceit of herself and she learned that she could accept him and his odours. Only then did she speak, softly, and using his name for the first time. 'Were the children awake, John?'

'Those little guys! They sure won't sleep, they know I'm going off some place. Old lady, she'll chase them around I guess.'

He spoke of his children. She recognized his pride in them and in the low-spoken stories of their doings. The air in the car became hot and thick with smoke. Their conversation slowed and finally died. She slipped off her parka and folded it into the corner and lay against it. Marjorie's rump followed her but she pushed it away. She could see the shape of the two heads over the seat. There was contentment in that and happiness in the coming day. She reached out her hand and put it against the seat in front of her. Her fingers stroked the seat and then she slept.

When she woke the moon had left its cloudy refuge and was flooding the world with light. The car was climbing, they reached and crossed the crest of a hill and she saw, far below, a frozen snake, coiled and still. This was the river that Flanagan had said they would cross. She watched it approach, saw trestles loom overhead, and then they were crossing the bridge. When they emerged on the far bank she saw buildings once again.

'The Fort,' Flanagan announced.

They all came to life, even Marjorie. 'Have I slept? Where in Pete's name are we?'

'The Fort,' Flanagan repeated.

They drove along and out of the one street, past the shacks and the bakery, past the poolroom and the hotel and the railed-off pyramid of river stones—memorial to days when boat brigades came singing on the spring tides. They followed the road of a newer century, the graded, gravelled tunnel cut as straight as a ploughed turn through the forest.

John Fall asked Ruth, 'Do you have moose in the old country?'

'We don't have moose. We have some very big rabbits.'

'Sure good eatin' too, them rabbits.'

They laughed, but he had taken her words seriously and this gave her thought. That would be something. Rabbit hunting with John Fall, Indian. Creeping through the lettuce and into the blackcurrants. Catching the bunnies in the orchard and roasting them over a fire on the lawn. Taking burned flesh from him. Eating with him, his woman at his fire. That would be something! That would give the *Telegraph* a story! Then John said, 'One mile, we leave the road.'

'Which way?'

'West. There's an old place. We turn off there.'

Flanagan slowed as a shack appeared ahead.

'This is it, Matt.'

They pulled off the highway on to a trail that led beyond the shack. 'Maybe I'll go in there. Say hello to those guys.'

'Sure, John. And we'll have a stretch while you're in there.'

They got out of the car and walked around. Ruth brought out her camera and opened the shutters. She moved about and took several snaps, hoping to get one that showed the streaky dawn light in the cabin. Then John came out with another Indian and they spoke with Flanagan. The three men came to the car and Ruth saw that the newcomer was carrying a rifle.

'This is Dan Bigbear. He knows the bush good. He's comin' with us.'

The trail they followed from the shack was narrow and over-hung with snow. The bottom of the car dragged and Flanagan drove very slowly.

John Fall said, 'Better put down the windows, case some old guy come out the bush and we want to get in a shot at him.'

'They come down the road when they walkin'' Bigbear told them. 'That snow crust, it icy, hard on those knees. Makes them sore. They sooner walk down the road, they don't get sore that way. You gotta be ready.'

So they drove through the forest with windows down, and it got very cold in the car. The light grew stronger, the shadows of the bush, pseudopodia of the night, withdrew. Dawn was suddenly with them.

Several times the men got out of the car to inspect tracks. Each time they returned with the same report: 'Old stuff.' At one such stop Ruth got out also. She followed them, and when Fall bent and then said, 'No good,' she asked him, 'How can you tell?'

He looked up at her. 'You got to feel in here.' She went to him and bent over the tracks. They were deep holes without shape. 'Feel down in there,' Fall told her. 'That little heap. Can you feel that? That's off the hoof. When it's all froze, then it's old stuff, maybe days even. When that's kinda soft, you know, when it ain't froze—then it's new. That means he's pretty close, that guy.'

'I see. There's logic in it.'

'What's that?'

'Seeing something that's happened, and asking why, and finding a reason for it.'

'Oh sure, there's plenty of that.'

'There's more too,' Flanagan said. 'He used logic, sure, but he can toss it right out of the window and just sniff things out. Right, John?'

'I guess. You just know. That's how you learn to hunt.'

'So if you're gonna learn, Ruth, you got to watch John here. See how he figures things out. Then you got to watch him sniff as well. That's the only way you'll learn to hunt.'

'I'll do that.'

All the tracks they found were no good, their little humps frozen. They saw nothing in the surrounding bush, no old moose walked the trails they crossed, nor deer, nor elk. The rifles were lowered and the cameras also. At last, at the end of one track they found a deserted lumber camp. There were upwards of a dozen shacks, little boarded boxes that were falling to pieces under the weight of snow and wind. Their tar paper flapped, scrub crowded in on them, it was a ghost camp, and the greatest ghost was the snowed-over mountain of sawdust that towered above them.

They sat on a rail, where they ate sandwiches and drank coffee. The men lit cigarettes and then John Fall walked away from them and disappeared behind the shacks. Ruth listened to Marjorie's chatter and Flanagan's answers but her mind was not following what was being said. She knew why the Indian had gone and she knew what he was doing right then. She was thinking how easy it would be to contrive another moment of intimacy under cover of these buildings. She got up from the rail and walked into the road. Here she turned and snapped a shot of the others. Then she walked between the shacks, pausing to take further snaps. She did not hurry at all. At the last hut she turned and went out of sight of the other three. The snow here was knee-deep. She stepped through it to the end of the hut and came to the back of the shacks. She paused on the corner but the bush had grown so close to the walls she could see nothing of the man she sought. She pushed through, holding up an arm to protect her face from the whipping branches. Then she found him. He was bending, looking at something. He had not seen her and for a second time she watched in secret. This time she studied him carefully, seeing his big frame, the hands spread on his hips. She guessed the power there would be in those hips, and looking at his jeans and the boots, remembered the muscled legs. She moved and he heard her and looked up.

'Jeez, Ruth! You want to see somethin' real cute? You can get yourself a real good picture here.'

'What is it, John?'

'Take a peek.'

She came to where he stood and crouched with him. The smell of him was strong in her lungs, his shoulder was almost touching hers.

'See them little guys. Ain't they cute?'

'They really hot in there, those guys.'

'Real cute, uh?'

He straightened and she was left crouching, looking at the pushed-away snow and the white rib cage of a long-dead coyote. It was packed with bluish-grey hairs, and now Fall bent again and stirred the mass and there was quick movement. She saw the mice for a second before they burrowed away.

'I see'd the tracks, figured they was under here some place. Them's moose, them hairs. See how the little guys get help from the big guys, uh?'

She answered, 'Yes, John.' Then she levelled her camera and photographed the nest. She reached out her mittened hands to bring back the snow. Then she got to her feet and he turned to lead her back.

'Wait a minute, John.'

'Uh?'

'Stand here, will you. I'd like to get one of you next to it.'

'Sure.'

'Can you bend over, like this.' She touched him with her mittens, moving him into the position she wanted.

'I got to laugh, uh?'

'Yes, please. That's right. Keep still, John!'

He got up and dusted the snow from his knee and they went back to the others. Such was her first moment of real privacy with him and it gave to her a new idea. As I smell him, she told herself, so he must smell me.

And thus began the hunt within the hunt.

Dan Bigbear was working out plans.

'We're not going to catch anything out walking. Not now. They're all goin' to be gut full and settin' in a yard, some place. We got to wait till they goes again, or we got to get in some place, see can we find up with them.'

Marjorie said, 'I think we're the only live things around here,' but Fall corrected her.

'Oh no! They here all right. You gotta find, that's all. Like Dan says, they're settin'. Maybe soon we'll go in and chase those guys round a little.'

'Why not right now?' Flanagan asked.

'Not right now. That snow's all iced over. Best when the sun gets on it. It gets soft then. We don't make so much noise.'

'What do we do till then?'

'Cowley's place?' Bigbear asked. Fall nodded, 'Sure. That's a good place, Matt. We can rest up there. Light a fire.'

As they were approaching the Cowley homestead they saw tracks on both sides of the trail. Flanagan stopped the car. The men got out and went down into the ditch to examine. Then Flanagan called Ruth out of the car.

'Well, here's your chance,' he told her. 'What do you make of those?' She squatted and reached into a hole. There was a difference, the snow inside was soft and separate.

'They're fresh,' she cried.

'That's right,' Fall agreed, 'And which way did those guys go?' She studied the tracks, tried to see some reason for an answer, failed and guessed. Fall and Bigbear both laughed.

'It's the other way,' Fall told her, 'but you doin' okay. You nearly had that right, too.'

'Are we going after them?'

'We go in now, they hear us for sure. Ain't got big ears for nothin', they ain't. They'll set. Later we go get them.'

The owner of the cabin was absent, but this made no difference. Dan unwired the door and Fall and Flanagan followed him into the house. Ruth looked around the veranda. There was an old board seat, into one of whose slats an axe had been deeply driven. Under the bench was a scattering of split logs, and over it hung a storm lantern. A torn coat dangled on a nail and some dirty clothes were in a bath by the door. She focused her camera and took the scene. Two whisky-jacks hopped around among the pile of tins and scattered garbage, searching for scraps. She photographed them also, marvelling at their impudence as they strutted about, darting their beaks between boards and fleeing with discovered seed or dung titbit. Then she went into the house. The stove was the most important thing in the room, a fat queen sitting amongst the rubbish of her court, the wood chips, the cans, the trousers and socks. Four-square to the floor, it thrust its pipe upwards, through a maze of cobwebs into the roof.

Fall had the stove door open and was building a fire. Marjorie prowled around, poking and searching. She looked up when Ruth entered and signalled to her. She was staring at a calendar. 'Look at that picture! The dirty old man!' Flanagan's voice said from behind them, 'Poor old guy's gotta have something to keep him warm at nights.'

'Matt!'

'You know what they say, go peekin' you'll get your nose pecked off.'

'We're not peekin', are we Ruth?'

'Yes, of course we are. Who lives in this hovel, Matt?'

'Ask John. Hey, John, who is this Cowley?'

'He's just a guy lives over here. He's got his trap lines out here. He's got this place and there's a cabin west. There's creeks between. That's his trap line. Two, three days he stays here, then he goes along, picks up those traps and does his pelts up, in the cabin. Then he comes back.'

'It's okay for us to use this place?'

'Sure. All us guys stop by.'

'How long has he been here?'

'All the time. Before him his folks had this place. They cleared out around. They had crops, I guess.'

'What happened to them?'

'They been dead long times. He buried them out there some place. He don't farm none himself. He just traps, that's all.'

Ruth asked, 'Is he married?'

'No. I didn't never see no woman around.'

She went back to the veranda. Dan Bigbear passed her, carrying a bucket packed with snow. 'We'll have coffee right now,' he promised.

She looked across the snow-covered pasture. Here, long ago, an Englishman and his wife had toiled together on sunny afternoons, on frosted mornings, below red skies, in downpours. They had cleared land, sown crops, built a home and watched their wheat grow golden heads. Their own seed had grown also but he had not shared their dreams. The land had claimed him, the creeks and their animals, the watching bush. She saw this as its revenge on the parents. She wondered where they were buried and hoped that there was some mark, some rock or tree, to speak for their years in this lonely place. She turned her eyes to the bush and remembered the animals that hid there, sleeping perhaps, safe and not knowing. Soon they might be dead, one or all, they would walk no more along the trails nursing their tender knees. They would take their part in the gavotte beneath the branches; sought and seeker; panter, luster—in measured movement towards the final bow.

Somebody called her name and she went back inside to find hot coffee, Dan Bigbear's fulfilled promise. After they had rested, Marjorie went out with Flanagan to learn how to use his rifle. Ruth stayed. She was sitting on the bed. The two Indians were playing cards. She watched them and listened to their remarks. They spoke about Cowley and his pelts. 'He gets them real good,' Fall told her.

'All this talk about pelts. I have not seen one yet.'

'You ain't? Jesus!'

Bigbear said, 'Maybe in the barn, some skins uh, John?'

'Could be. He keeps them there.'

'I'd like to see some, John. Will you show me, please?'

'Sure.'

She followed him, hoping that Bigbear would stay in the house. Fall took her down a trodden path to the barn. She was close behind and could see the black hair, thick on his neck, the big shoulders and the strong unmittened fingers. She thought, I could reach out and take his hand; it would be that easy. He would jump out of his skin if I did.

They entered the barn. The half darkness closed them in and she waited, not sure what she wanted, or what she would do. Then she said, 'Close the door, John', but he spoke at the same time and her words were lost.

'Jeez! This guy got some beaver!' He took down some skins from the wall and turned and held one up for her. It was a shining circle of thick, dark fur. The Indian stroked his fingers through it and she saw the hairs spring back. 'Ain't that sure good!'

'It is. It is beautiful.'

'That's gonna make some good coat, uh?'

The hand still stroked. She watched it, not the fur. Her eyes followed its movements up and down. 'Skin like this worth twenty bucks. Can't figure why this guy keeps them around his place.'

124

And up went the hand and down it came, and the hairs sprang beneath his fingers. The slow voice of Dan Bigbear said, 'He keeps them, John. I seen these before.' She had not heard him come into the hut and she stepped back. Then she took off her toque and shook her hair loose, patted it and replaced the toque. She said, 'They are lovely pelts. I wish I had that one. I would like to buy it. Do you think he would sell it to me?' Bigbear said, 'I don't know. I guess he would but I don't think we see him today.'

They went out of the barn. They were quite close to the house when Fall said, 'Ruth!' She turned. 'Yes, John?'

'You really want a pelt like that, I get you one. I get lots better than that in the spring.'

'That would be nice, John. I would like that. You won't forget?'

'I won't forget.'

In the early afternoon they drove back to the tracks. John Fall and the two girls followed these into the bush while Flanagan and Bigbear skirted wide to the west. Fall led the way, gun pointed to the ground, Ruth was next, then Marjorie. The snow was very deep, its crust still crunchy and the Indian stepped carefully, using the tracks themselves as much as he could. Ruth used his but had to stretch her legs to do so. She could hear Marjorie struggling behind and guessed that her shorter legs were proving a handicap. Her own thighs began to feel the strain of constantly lifting the boots out of the holes. The sun was strong now, pockets of sweat began to collect and run, but she did not complain, neither did she slow her pace. They went for some distance and then Fall stopped. He pointed, and she approached and saw animal droppings. He bent to pick one up and crumbled it within his hand. He wiped the hand, first on the snow and then across the seat of his jeans. 'Fresh! It ain't iced over yet.'

'Where are they?'

He used his chin, as she had seen the children do so often to indicate direction. 'They was settin' here,' he pointed, and she saw the shine of ice on packed snow. 'Them guys heard us. They out walkin' now. Maybe they'll set again. Maybe not, if we throwed a scare into them.'

She looked around. The bush here was such a tangled mesh that an animal could be, perhaps was, twenty feet away and concealed. It was a good stage, a proper setting for the gavotte she had imagined. Here was the thorn heart of an earlier imagination. This was a cruel place.

She realized that Marjorie was no longer with them. She was

glad of this and hoped that the girl had given up and returned to the car. She watched the man as he moved forward, and did as he did, a few paces and stop and listen. Was he sniffing? Sniff, Flanagan had told her. She tried, and smelled Fall. She stepped as he did, crouched when he crouched. She saw him bend and knew for certain that he was testing the air, hoping it would betray his quarry. He moved the gun, raised its barrel and his hands worked at its breech. She levelled her camera, found him in its sights and was about to trigger it when she realized the damage she might do. She lowered it and as she did this, though no sound had been made, though nothing had disturbed the stillness, Fall raised an arm and pointed, and she knew he had found his quarry. Then he was running, so suddenly that she was left behind. As she set after him her boots slipped and she sprawled in the snow. She lay and heard crashing sounds close by and Fall's voice shouting. There was a shot, and almost as an echo, a second. She scrambled to her feet and pushed through the scratching strands.

'John!' she shouted. 'John! Where are you?' He didn't answer, but she heard other voices and shouted, 'Over here, Matt! Over here! We've found them. John! Where *are* you?'

She was angry. She was afraid that others would find him before she did, and she swore at him. Then she saw him and her anger fled. He was kneeling in the snow, against a dark mound. As she ran towards him the mound moved. She stopped and saw a great head lift up behind Fall, turn towards the man and drop again. It was as if the animal were helping at its own death; as if it had held its neck to the tearing, slicing knife in the Indian's hand.

She was filled with horror and turned away. But she had to look again. She could not resist. A flush of blood spouted into the air and bubbled on the snow. She quivered under the brutality and her stomach retched as frantic hooves kicked scarlet slush at her. She watched the man, watched his hands in their unceasing slashing, turning movements. She saw the shoulders strain beneath the coat and heard his gasps. She saw strong back and buttocks and she knew the hunter, the conqueror. She lifted her camera and photographed him, snap after snap, intent face, bloodied hands, knife, knees and back. She came so close to him that his hands almost filled the viewer. When she had him, all of him, trapped in her little box she rose. The voices that she had been ignoring sounded very close. 'We are here!' she shouted, and John Fall heard and looked up at her.

'Jesus, Ruth! This's good meat. And this is a cow, see the tit?' and he reached under and pulled at the belly and between his fingers she saw the dug.

3

Julie, your beads are shining in the store. Come and see your shining, shiny beads.

Helmut Golding had a problem. It was not Julie—rather did she seem as a miracle to him, a wonderful thing that no man of his age should expect or hope to have. She had mastered him, she ruled him, she ruled him with her person, her casualness and her insolence. She had mastered Sarah also, but here she had used cunning. No daughter could have been more of a listener or heeder.

She was not a problem, but Ivor Jones was. A constant nagging ache, he had on this morning become a raging pain. It was Allowances Day, when Government cheques arrived for fertile mammas and these were many on the Big Fish. They came to Upcreek to collect their cheques, rewards for gay and careless nights, and usually the storekeeper was on hand to settle outstanding accounts. Herein sprang the enmity between himself and Jones, for the postman refused to allow his office to be turned into a collecting shop. Golding had to keep close watch, and come quickly from the store whenever an Indian cart trundled up to the post office. There was little dignity in standing on a street and accosting Indians but there was no alternative. They would slip away, like shadows at noon, and with them would go their cheques—and his money.

Golding had tried hard to be accommodating, he had gone further out of his way than he would with any other man in Upcreek. But Ivor Jones, who had served in neither, was still fighting both world wars. This morning had been typical, but the firing had been heavy and the storekeeper had been routed. He had tried being friendly too, the very remembering of that filled him with fury at himself.

'This is sure a nice winter we're havin'.'

'I said, this is sure a nice winter, Ivor.'

'I ain't been out.'

'Haw! You sure keepin' busy, uh?'

'Yup!'

'Is it all this Christmas mail then, Ivor? Is that keepin' you busy?'

127

'It's mindin' my own business keeps me busy and that's like nobody else on this street.'

'Now look, Ivor, there's no call for creatin' that way. You're busy. Me too, I'm busy. There's lots work this time of year for all of us, that's all I was sayin'.'

'You got your mail.'

'Thanks. Say, I guess I'll take Willie Henry Littleleaf's too. That guy, he's asked me to hold it for him.'

'You ain't Willie Henry Littleleaf. You don't get his mail.'

'Now look, Ivor. This guy, he's in to the store for forty-eight bucks. He's fixed it with me to collect this way. They do that other places, you know that. You just gonna be awkward with me. Jeez, I don't know why you act this way.'

'Other places! I don't give a goddam 'bout other places. This is my place. I don't do it. You want to run up accounts with Indians that's your business. If some of them puts it over you, good luck to them. You've skint 'em often enough your own self. You get nobody's mail off'n me.'

'I got a paper here. See, that's all signed up, there, see? Willie Henry wrote it. That makes it legal. You got to do what that paper says. You got to give me that mail, it's same as giving it to him.'

'You can use that paper on your ass. You get no more goddam mail from me.'

'Give me that letter, Ivor.'

'Nothin'.'

'I don't forget this. I show you about this.'

'Get out of my house you fat bugger of a German. Go on! Git! Before I come round there and give you the boot.'

Thus had begun a day of fuming and a resultant belly-ache that not even a double dose of the little white powder could shift. It had not helped when Willie Henry Littleleaf arrived in town, avoided the store, and then became as invisible as one of those noonday shadows, leaving his wife dumb as a rock and chequeless.

Such had been Golding's day, and not even Julie could bring joy into it. But if wars must be fought, then victory goes to he who wins the last battle. The storekeeper had taken all he could. He put in a call that he had thought of doing for some time.

'George? Helmut, yeah, Helmut Golding. Fine, George. Everybody, sure. And you? That's good. Tell you why I call you. I got a piece of land comin' up that's for rent this spring. You be interested in workin' a deal on that? Uhuh. Sure, I thought you would, that's why I called you. Say, why don't you come over, we can maybe fix this deal. Yeah, right now. I'll see you then, George.'

They were two eager beavers, those Telmans. George was aiming for a quick rich day and his wife, she was in a hurry too. She was wanting to be somebody. Folks said that she couldn't wait to push her nose in for polishing. She was making it quicker than George, because she was getting close to Helen McKenzie—closer than Arthur, the same folks were saying with a snicker. There was a shiny piano in the McKenzie house and Monica Telman was the only woman in the township who could play it.

'Doesn't she play beautiful, Arthur?'

'She does indeed.'

'I just love the way she plays that Chopin.'

She was that close to Helen McKenzie, whose husband was town mayor and could sign letters as such, and who had lost her son through drink. One thing only was holding back the Telmans and Golding had plenty of it—land.

George Telman came quickly and parked his pick-up in front of the store, himself in front of the counter. They smoked cigars and talked weather and then got on to the land deal. After that they smoked another cigar and Telman, who was shrewd as well as ambitious and knew that he wasn't going to get anything from the storekeeper without there being some call on his services, waited for this call. Golding, who was shrewder than Telman, knew that he was waiting and played this game for a little while. Then he said, 'Town is building up nice, George.'

'Sure is. New folks moving in, I see.'

'Uhuh. It's a good town we got for sure.'

'That's right. Who in hell wants to go over there to Redville when they can come here? It's a good town for a farmer to come into. Can get everything he needs here, a farmer can.'

'I been here long time, George. Know how long? More than thirty years.'

'That's a hell of a long time too.'

'It sure is. I've seen everybody come here. Man and boy, I've seen them all. I guess our town growed up around this here store.'

Telman agreed with him, ignoring as Helmut had, both the grain elevator and the depot. He knew that he was not going to be kept waiting much longer. The old man was pushing the town at him, it was something to do with the town, or somebody in it. Then Julie came down the stairs. Both men stopped talking to watch her. She walked past them and went along the store.

'Workin' for Sarah,' Golding said.

'Yeah, I heard that. Is she an okay worker?'

'Sarah likes her. That's all I'm bothered.'

'Sure. From the Big Fish, uh?'

'That's right.'

'What was that you was saying, Helmut? 'Bout livin' here and that?'

'I was goin' to say how one thing was spoiling livin' here. Can you think what that is?'

'One thing? Flies. Is that what you mean?'

'They got flies everyplace. I don't mean flies. I mean one guy, one fella that's turning' all this nice town into a rotten barrel—you know when you get the one apple.'

'Who is this guy, Helmut?'

'Christ, you know sure enough George, who he is.' Telman thought quickly, and remembered other conversations. He guessed. 'Could you be talkin' about him over there?'

'That's who I am talkin' about. That's one guy who is spoilin' this place from comin' real good. That Jones, George. He's gettin' all dirty with how he talks and you know, all the time he's on the bottle. Can't go in there without he's been drinkin' and folks got to go 'count of the mail. Like Sarah, she don't like to have to talk to him, but she got to, don't she?'

'She sure does. He's the same with everybody, that guy.'

'With your wife too, uh?'

'She don't ever go in there, Helmut. She asks me to get it. Monica wouldn't go in that place for nothin'.'

'And the other womens the same. Ain't that a goddam shame when good womens like them can't go into their own post office on account of being shamed like that.'

'He's got the contract, Helmut. I guess we got it to live with. No way I can think to change him. He's too fixed, Old Ivor. He's never gonna change, that I can see.'

'He don't have to change. He has to go, that's what.'

'Oh!'

'Don't you think it's right?'

'Sure. But how do you shift him? It's Federal, that is.'

'That's right. And don't those guys watch? Sure they do. They find out how Jones is, then he goes quick. Soon as they find it out.'

'I guess he would. But somebody's got to tell them. Somebody should write, is that what you were thinkin', Helmut? I mean, I suppose I could do that, couldn't I? I could send a letter if I knowed who I should write it to. Would you know that?'

'Sure you could, George. But it's gotta be somebody they'll listen to, good. No offence, George, but it calls for somebody pretty high, don't it? Say somebody like Arthur McKenzie.'

'Arthur?'

'Uhuh. Ain't he Mayor? That would be official if we could have Arthur do the complainin'.'

'Hadn't thought about Arthur.'

'Your missus, she's good friends with Arthur's wife.'

'That's right.'

'If Old Jones let into your wife and she brings it up with Helen McKenzie, then maybe she'd get Arthur to write to Ottawa.'

'If he gets cussin' her.'

'Well, now. I guess she knows how to do a bit of stirrin', George.'

'Christ! She sure does.'

'Better yet if Jones been on that bottle.'

'Arthur's real set against that. Since young Pete got killed he's talked nothin' 'cept drink. Say, Helmut, how many years did you set for that land?'

'Five years. Then first call if the crops have been good.'

'They'll be good. I'll get under there and push the goddam stuff out if I have to.'

'And Jones.'

'First thing in the mornin' she'll be down there waitin' for the mail. All she has to tell him is how he's got a dirty goddam shack and he'll blow. Then she's got to remember what he says. She remembers good, she does. Don't I know it!'

As the door closed after him, Julie came from behind the stall. Golding said, 'What are you gettin' then?'

'Things, Daddy.'

He felt his immediate springing at her choice of word and went around the counter.

'Julie.'

'What?'

'Come here, Julie.'

She laughed. Then she walked towards him, putting her collection, can by can, on the shelves she passed. He moved so that there would be cover from window and stairs and she followed and went right to him. Her bottom lip was lowered and he could see the tip of her tongue balanced on teeth. Its pink sparkle fascinated him, he was staring at it when she put her hand between his legs.

'Jeez! You sure are proud tonight, Daddy. That's no good with Old Lady upstairs. This is gonna have to wait. Maybe Wednesday, uh? Old Lady's doin' her Christmas shopping. Gonna be away all day. That's a long time for us to play, Daddy.'

'You got me right now, Julie. I can't wait till Wednesday.'

'You gotta. Old Lady's upstairs. She's gonna be shoutin' if I don't go back up there.'

'You tell her you got to be home early. Wait down the road. I'll meet you down there some place.'

'Right now?'

'Wait! This is good.'

'Somebody coming!'

She was away from him in a swift and smooth movement. Before he could return to his place at the back of the counter she was hidden. The door opened and Ruth Lancaster came in.

'I'm not too late, am I?'

'No. Go right ahead.'

'I'm sorry. I didn't realize what time it had got. We have been planning the Bingo for the Christmas party.'

'That's a Wednesday, uh?'

'Yes. Are you coming?'

'I guess not. I don't bother much these days. Gettin' old, I guess. But tell Matt he can put me down for a turkey like usual. He can pick it up when he's ready.'

'Thank you. I'll tell him that.'

'If it helps those little kids to have a good Christmas. I like for those kids to have a good Christmas. They don't get that much.'

She wondered if it were her imagination that made her sense an edginess about him. She felt that he was watching her closely, and when she turned suddenly and caught his stare full on her she knew that something was bothering him. He's fancying you, she told herself, he's putting you on his list. She moved along the grocery stands, taking her time, knowing that he was watching. Then she stopped. There was something disturbing, some alien thing. She puzzled for a moment and then realized that there was a fragrance here that did not belong with sugar or flour or lard. She turned again and Golding moved his head too late. She smiled to herself and wandered back in aimless fashion, so that she was between the bays and the stairway. Then she turned suddenly down the blind side and as she had expected, there was Julie.

'Why hello, Julie. I didn't hear you.'

'Hi!'

'How are you getting on?'

'Okay.' The girl would not look at her. Ruth tried to make her, she wanted to see the full face, she wanted the eyes.

'Can't you find what you want?'

'I can.'

'Are you coming to the Bingo?'

'Maybe. I don't know.'

And still the girl avoided her. Ruth remembered Flanagan's

pessimism and prophecy, and knowing what she did about these two, she looked now for signs of the promised poisoning. She saw none. Everything pointed to the opposite—to a feeding, a nourishing. Julie was a blooming rose in this house of stacked cans, the glow and vibrance of life, an Indian rose smelling and flowering in the surrounding sterility. She told her so. 'You are looking very well, Julie. You must like working here. It seems to suit you better than school.'

At last Julie looked straight at her. There was such depth in her eyes. There was anger too and her words came quickly. 'I didn't like school. I didn't want it no more. I had enough with those teachers. Askin' all the time.—they got to know everythin'. It's the same with all them teachers. They're rotten old. Me, I don't like no teacher.' She pushed past Ruth and went up the stairs. She stopped at the top and shouted down. 'Mr Golden, if there's anythin' else, you'd better say. Me, I'm goin' early tonight.'

'I got nothin' for you to do here. You can go as soon as you're ready.'

As Ruth walked across to the post office she thought of Julie's words. She knew that the Indian girl had turned the tables on her, and remembered how her feeling of triumph had turned to anger. I should have smacked her face, she thought. I should have smacked her in front of her fat old lover. But her anger fled when she got her mail and found that the slides of the hunting trip had arrived. She put them into her pocket and went to the garage where she hired the little Frenchman to taxi her back to the school.

He asked her about the school and then about the kids and then about herself. He smelled of tobacco and oil and his arm kept pushing hers though she knew that the road was not all that bumpy. He chewed like a rat at her private affairs, a nibble here, a nibble there, a quick sniff and a fresh start after each rebuff. He would have asked about the slides if she had tried to look at them, he might even have wanted to look also. That would have given him opportunity for stopping the car. But the little package in her pocket was a box of magic to be shared with no one.

I will see them in the basement, she decided. I will take the Aldis down there and draw the curtains. I can use the big screen. But first I will make a supper and I will borrow a bottle of Matt's beer. A party for one with an unwitting guest. John Fall, to be viewed, dispatched or changed by flick of finger. She tried to remember all the shots she had taken and then gave up as little Moise spoke again. They were coming out of the last bush and it was getting dark but he was quick to see the truck outside the school. 'You got a visitor then. That's Bruchk's pick-up, ain't it?'

'I don't know. If it is, he is visiting Mr Flanagan, not me.'

'He don't visit you then?'

'Nobody visits me, Mr Montpelier.'

He was not easily put out. 'Jeez, that's a shame. I guess some guy will soon, uh?'

She did not bother to answer. She had recognized the truck, but she could not see the Pontiac and she feared the worst—that Flanagan was away somewhere and she would have to do the entertaining of his farmer friend. She paid Little Moise and waited until he had gone before she spoke to Bruchk.

'Hello, Bill. Is Matt not home?'

'I guess not. I was goin' already but I might as well leave this with you. It's for the Bingo. Maybe you'll keep it for Matt.'

'Does he know you're giving this?'

'He'll be expecting it. He gets one every Christmas. It's heavy. I should carry it for you.'

'Thank you, Bill. I'll get my key.'

'You left the door open.'

'Did I? I should be more careful, I'll be losing things.' He followed her to the kitchen. The bird was huge. It sprawled on the table, its white flesh a pale mountain between them. She said, 'It's very big. How much does it weigh?'

'I can't be sure. Over twenty, I suppose.'

'Are you coming on Wednesday?'

'Oh yes.'

She slipped off her parka and dropped it on to a chair. Bruchk picked up his mittens, 'I should be goin',' he said. She felt a sudden shame at her eagerness to see him gone.

'I am going to make myself a cup of tea. Would you like to stay and have one yourself?'

'That would be nice.'

'Good! Sit down!'

'Tea drinking is one of my bad habits,' she told him. 'I could drink tea all day long. You do like it? I never thought to ask.'

'Oh sure!'

'There is coffee if you'd rather.'

'No. Tea would be fine.'

'Matt tells me it rots the stomach.'

'Does he say that?'

'What he drinks rots it quicker. Do you have sugar?'

'Yes, please.'

'Help yourself.'

She watched his cup, noted that his finger was too thick to

fit the handle and began to worry. If he squeezes too hard the handle will come off, she thought. For the rest of the conversation she watched the cup, knowing no peace until it was returned safely to the table.

'Do you like it here, Ruth?'

'I think so. Mind you, this winter seems so terribly long. Is it never going to finish?'

'It's only half-way. Less maybe, depends on the snows.'

'As far as I'm concerned, winter is one thing you can keep.'

'You'll like the spring, though. That's a good time.'

'I'll believe that when it comes.'

'It sure is. Everythin' starts up, you know. And there's the birds, too. You'll like it.'

'We'll see. Another cup?'

'No, thank you. That was real good, too.'

'I'm glad you enjoyed it.'

'Have you fixed on next year yet?'

'Next year?'

'You goin' to be here, I mean?'

'I hadn't given it a thought. I've no idea yet.'

'It's soon to be thinkin' about it.'

'Yes, it is.'

'Well, maybe I should go.'

'Come again, Bill. Anytime you are passing I'll put the kettle on for you.'

'Thanks. I'll do that. Say, maybe some time you'd like to come over to my place. You didn't visit us yet. We'd sure like to have you for supper.'

'That would be very nice.'

'Can I fix that? With Christine I mean? She's the boss, you know.'

'She's your daughter, isn't she?'

'Uhuh. She keeps sayin' why don't you come over.'

'Well, you haven't invited me before, have you?'

'No. She'll sure be glad.'

At last he was gone and the house door was locked. The lights were off. Flanagan would think that she was asleep and there would be no interruptions. She set herself up in the basement, projector, sandwiches, and glass of milk. The curtains were drawn, she shut off the light and flashed the first slide on to the bare wall. The whisky-jacks strutted for her on the steps of the trapper's shack. The snow seemed bluer than it should have been, the bush a little darker, but there was gloss on the feathered bodies. She tried the next and saw John Fall leaning over the mouse nest. His face was turned towards her, its black brows and strong jaw, the flash of white between thick lips emphasizing his brown skin. His body was bent from the hips. I put him like that, she thought. I moved him, I used my hands to place him, to bend him.

She left this slide for some time. The cooling element hummed, filling the basement with its noise. It was dark behind the projector. She ate a sandwich, drank a little milk and then changed to the next slide. She went through the collection, coming eventually to those of the kill. The last was a surprise, she had not realized that she had photographed him at that moment. The teeth grinned down at her, the beast's teat was between his fingers.

She collected the slides and carried the machine up to her bedroom. She undressed quickly, threw back the sheets and lay on her bed. Then she reached back over her head and switched on the projector. John Fall crouched over her. His shoulders were huge. He was very dark on that white canvas. Looking at his face she remembered his body and then the body of her lover that had lain, slender and white like a thin maggot, on her eiderdown. The only white things about this man were his teeth, and these were big too, and strong. Everything about him was strong. He seemed too heavy for the wall. She imagined that weight tearing itself from the wall and falling on to her. She stretched her arms and legs to receive him. She imagined so powerfully that she felt his weight and she shouted.

On that Wednesday afternoon, school finished early so that the children could reach their distant homes in time to release their parents for the night's big event. Ruth was clearing up in the kitchen when she heard someone go down the corridor to the bedrooms. She thought for a moment of calling Flanagan but was soon glad that she had not done so, for when she went to investigate she found Marjorie sitting on a bed.

'What are you doing back so soon?'

The girl burst into tears and threw herself down.

'Marjorie, what is it? What is the matter?' she asked, although she had already guessed. The girl proved her right. 'Ruth. It's awful. It's terrible.'

'What is, for God's sake?'

'I went home. I went round back. The store was locked. I thought they'd all gone . . . to the city. I went in, there was nobody around. I heard the radio. It was my radio.'

'Go on. You'd better tell it all.'

'Well, I went in there,' she halted again. Ruth waited and she continued. 'He was in my bed, Ruth. My dad was in my bed.'

'Well? What's so terrible about that?'

'He was with Julie!'

'Oh!'

'Yes. They were in my bed. Him and Julie!'

'The little bitch!'

'What am I going to do, Ruth? I can't go back, not after seeing that. I can't face him, not he and Mom together. What am I going to do?'

'Do you think your mother might know?'

'I don't think so. No, she wouldn't take that from him. She thinks Julie is an angel. She really does. Isn't that something! She thinks that about Julie, and all the time——'

'I think you'd better stay here. It won't last. It's his age I suppose. Stay here until it blows over. It probably will now that you've found out. You will have given him a bigger shock than he gave you.'

'I've got to go home for Christmas.'

'You don't. Come to the city with me. Anyway, you don't need to worry about that tonight. You stay here. I'll run a bath for you, then we'll have supper.'

As she left the bedroom Marjorie sat up and said, 'There's something else, Ruth.'

'Yes?'

'Julie. She had on my nightdress. She had been wearing my clothes. They were all over the floor.'

As for Julie, when the scared old man had run from her arms she took the letter from under her pillow and read it again. It was the first she had ever received from Francis Littleleaf. She had received it in that day's mail and already she knew its every word. That was like Francis to write her a letter about an old car he wanted, and not a word about himself except how bad he needed fifty dollars. 'Could you start me off with the first two of that fifty?' He'd put that in for a joke, but maybe the joke could go the other way. Maybe she could give that Francis a real surprise.

She didn't get up. She didn't have to. She knew Daddy Golding would be back soon enough for his Baby Julie.

4

*There is a Chevvy in Benny's Car Garden. It's beat up but I could use it if
I could find a hundred dollars. Benny will take fifty down. Where could I
get fifty?*

> *One time its flowers spun
> Bright in the sun, black petalled.
> Now busted, fall-rusted
> It grieves in that garden.*

From out of the well-starred western night the bingo players came,
big-booted, muffled to the eyes against the questing wind, in
cars and trucks, on sleighs and on foot. They filled the school
basement, crowding into it and divided there, the few men
retreating to a corner, the women and children taking the rest of
the room up to the caller's table. Ruth heard them arrive while
she was dressing. She listened to the car horns and the shouts,
wondering whether John Fall was among them. She took a long
time preparing herself and she knew when she went in to them
that she could not have looked better. There was pleasure in her
reception, in the acknowledging eyes turned towards her.

Bruchk watched her moving among the Indians. She looked so
clean and different against the motley, so sure of herself. He
thought that she was the most beautiful woman he had ever seen,
and that at this moment everybody must agree with him. He
could not keep his eyes from following her. She saw him and said,
'Hello, Bill.'

'Hi Ruth!'

'You've got to work,' Flanagan told her.

'What do you want me to do?'

'Same as Marj. Collect. Ten cents a card. And watch 'em.
'Specially the old ladies. They'd sooner lose on a stolen card than
win on a straight.'

'Ten cents?'

'Ten cents.'

'Here I go. Wish me luck.'

She left them. Flanagan turned and saw Bruchk watching her.
'Isn't she making out,' he said.

'She is for sure. Is she goin' to stay, Matt?'

'Till summer, sure. Next year, maybe. I don't know. She didn't say yet.'

'She told me she hadn't thought it over.'

'When was that?'

'Monday.'

'I guess she hasn't then.'

'She's too good for this place. It's not right for her to be here.'

'I guess. Won't do her no harm. Hasn't done her nothin' but good so far. Lookit her laughin' it up with those women. Still, I guess they're all sisters under that thick hide.'

Ruth felt good. She knew she was being watched, she didn't need telling that, the basement was full of watching eyes and she kept her head high for them and her body straight. She caught glances from sly-eyed, teenage girls and thought she saw envy in them. It pleased her to think so. She moved among the women and knew what a contrast she made, and finally she reached the men.

'You give me that turkey card, Teacher, 'cause I sure got a hungry.'

'Always you got a hungry, Tom.'

'Teacher, don't you listen to that guy.'

'I pay for these. That makes forty cents you owe me, Teacher.'

'I take one more card I think. Have you got a real premium card for me?'

They were all going to win. They all had something to say but there was much more in their eyes than in their words. Dark eyes. Secretive. Watching eyes. Hunter's eyes, she reminded herself, and the thought followed, they have turned this basement into their bush. They sit here watching, sniffing, aiming.

At what?

'At you,' she told herself, and believed it.

She came at last to John Fall. 'You've got to know how to hunt them,' he had once said to her. 'You have to know how to set your trap.' His words.

Now he said, 'If I don't win this one I hope it snows for ever.'

She said, 'You won't.'

'I'm sure gonna try.'

'You won't win, John.'

'After the finish,' he told her, 'I'm gonna help Matt clean up this place. Then we'll take in the hockey.'

'Oh! What about your family?'

'I'll take them first though. Then I'll come back down here. Do you watch the hockey then?'

'Yes,' she lied. She could hear her heart beating right through her ears.

Later, after the last prize had been won and the exodus began, she accompanied the farmer to his truck. They watched the Indian cars pull away and as the green Chevrolet passed by she waved to the blurred faces at its windows. Then she said, 'You can get yours out now, Bill. I'll go in if you don't mind. It's cold.'

'Sure. You go in, you'll get cold like that. Say, I forgot. Would Sunday be okay for you?'

'Sunday?'

'For supper. Christine said to ask you over for Sunday.'

'Yes, Bill. Sunday will be fine. Are you doing the cooking?'

'I do the chores. Christine, she's the cook when we have visitors. Shall I come for you?'

'There's no need. Marjorie will drive us over.'

'Marjorie? Oh yes. Well, I'll see you then.'

'I'm looking forward to it. Good night, Bill.'

'Good night, Ruth.'

She went back to the basement. Flanagan and Marjorie were sweeping the floor. Flanagan said 'Hey! Take yourself out of here. You'll get all messed up.'

'Me, I don't count,' Marjorie said.

'You too. Take the money and check it. Go across to my place and start the set. John and a couple of the boys are coming over to take in the Leafs' game.'

They went through the house and out to Flanagan's. Here they put on coffee and sat through the final part of the Hitchcock Hour. Then Flanagan came in accompanied by John Fall and two other Indians. There was a reshuffling of chairs and the divan was swung round to face the set. Flanagan brought in a box of beer and pulled the caps and passed the bottles out. 'Everybody okay?' he asked, and then he flicked out the light. The commentator's face loomed large on the screen and his voice drove away the last ad. The second period of the game begun, the stick-swinging athletes swooped and leaped in their hypnotizing circles and the men in the room and Marjorie also, surrendered. But not Ruth. She sat in the darkness at the end of the divan, farthest away from the screen, behind everyone—and next to John Fall. She became a spectator, not of the game but of its audience. She saw how totally involved they were, shifting and leaning in sympathy with the players. It was easy to watch them, she had only to lean backwards to watch John's face, it was intent and still, the features seemed bigger, its shadows darker in the false light.

Time passed. The nasal hysteria screamed on, smoke drifted in front of the screen and the room became hot. Once, he reached for his bottle and drank, then turned to grin at her for a second

140

before going back to the game. He shouldn't have done that. Until then the impatience that had started in her was bearable, but from that point it became dominant. Her fingers trembled. She flexed them, looked and saw how white they were—white sticks, waiting. She placed her hand on the seat between herself and the man. She counted in her mind, giving herself up to ten, and at that she moved the hand till the fingers touched the tan drills. She felt their texture and slid the fingers up until the palm rested along his thigh and she could feel the warmth coming from the hard flesh beneath. Then she squeezed. From first movement to last she had not breathed. Now she did so, and the throbbing in her body was fear as she waited.

He did not move immediately, but she watched his face and saw that the game had lost him. He moved his near arm and she knew it was to hide her hand and she thrilled to this. Then she felt his fingers creep over hers and she turned her hand upwards and placed it in his. She felt his strength as he squeezed, and she answered it as hard as she could.

The game and the beer ended together and there was no reason for the party's continuance. Flanagan said, 'I'm goin' to the city on Saturday mornin', see what I can round up with this money. You two fancy a ride in there?' They answered together. Marjorie said, 'Yes, please Matt. Sure I'd like to come.' But Ruth was aware of the listener in the outer darkness when she spoke: 'I'd rather not, Matt. I have letters to write. I'll stay home and get rid of them.'

'Nine o'clock then,' Flanagan told Marjorie. 'You be ready, or I go without you. I'll pick you up.'

'Didn't I tell you? I've moved in with Ruth so I'll be on the spot. I'm here for good now.'

'Well you be ready. It's gonna take us most of the day.'

'I'll see she doesn't keep you waiting, Matt.'

It was a promise that she kept. She was knocking on Marjorie's door early and had the girl dressed, fed and out of the house right on Flanagan's dead-line. She watched them go from the veranda. The morning was cold but the sun promised a clear day. She went back into the house, cleared away the breakfast things and made her bed. Then she dressed. She put on black slacks and a red sweater and tied up her hair with a red ribbon.

There was nothing now except the waiting. She was that sure. When he came they would have to start again. There would be nervousness as they rebuilt towards the peak of the previous night. But there would be pleasure in the nervousness and in the building. She did not want to think beyond that. Whatever happened would be a shared thing, it would be done and there would be an end to thinking and planning and dreaming. She was filled with impatience, for the sight of him and went into a classroom from which she could look at the lake.

Already there were black dots and coloured blocks out there and she marvelled at these people who would make a sixty-mile drive to sit by a hole in a frozen lake in the hope of catching fish that they could buy in any supermarket. She watched an Indian drive across the Neck and disappear into the bush. Some of Flanagan's boys were playing ice-hockey on a small square that they had cleared of snow. They were using sticks and branches but had all the grace of the professional skaters.

Then she saw the green Chevrolet. It was crossing the front of the school no more than a hundred yards away. She pushed herself against the window, knowing that his sharp hunter's eyes would be looking for a sign, and then, thinking that he might miss her because of the glass shine, she ran to the door. When she got outside the car had gone. She waited for a few moments and then she saw it appear again but now, conversely, she did not want him to see her. He should come seeking. It was for him to approach, to take up from where she had begun. So she went back to her bedroom and examined herself and made improvements in her make-up. As she went out of the room she looked at the bed and the thought that she had suppressed came to mind. She sat on the coverlet and waited and she was like this when she heard the school door open.

He was standing just inside. She looked down at him and said, 'Good morning, John.'

'Morning, Miss.'

'Do you want something?'

He shook his head. There was a slight smile on his face. He said, 'I was just passin'. I thought maybe I'd stop by. I guess Matt, he's not at home.'

'There's only me here, John. They've gone to the city, don't you remember?'

'Sure that's right. I forgot that.'

Now came the uncertainty. They watched each other, both waiting. She thought, he is more afraid than I am. He is afraid of me. She said, 'Would you like a cup of coffee?'

'Do you have plenty?'

'I think so.'

'Okay. Thanks.'

He followed her and she was glad of her trim hips and her raised hair. She took him to the kitchen where she poured coffee while he thumbed the comic section of her newspaper. When she gave him his cup he said, 'Gee thanks! I got me a real thirst this mornin'.'

She wondered if his thirst was for the same reason as her own, if he had swallowed as much as she in those few moments. She moved a chair so that she could sit at a corner of the table, near to him and for a moment or two they were silent, he reading and she watching. She watched his fingers turn the papers, they were so thick and strong those fingers. She looked at her own and remembered how these had proved their own kind of strength. She thought of Flanagan and Marjorie, far away down the road and she looked again at this man whom she had brought here. Her eyes travelled over him, from the hands, over the body to the face. She saw that he was not reading at all and she said, 'I was not drunk last night, John.'

It was so easy. He reached for her and she went into his arms. She knelt against his chest, her face turned upwards, offering and asking. She closed her eyes and when their mouths met, hers leaped beyond the expected lip kiss, opened to his tongue and her own was subdued by it.

It was so easy. He led her into the living-room to the divan. His arm was as strong as she remembered it. His hands shook as he fumbled at her and she helped him, white fingers leading brown, unbuttoning, exposing. It was so easy. She took him to her bed and she knew as she stood beside it, looking down on his head while he took off her shoes, that she had thought forward to all this. His hands were rough against her skin, her belt resisted him and she helped him again but he did not want this from her. She lay on the coverlet wearing the red sweater only. She waited for him to undress but when she saw him unzip the front of the drills she turned away her head. A moment later he came above her, blotting out the ceiling with his darkness and she could scarcely breathe. Then she felt him and her arms went around him. She slid her hand under the waistband of his slacks and pressed it against the moving back. She held him like Julie, the brown cat would hold her men. She held him, and received him, and his seeking tongue broke into her mouth.

It was so easy. And it was done. She slept for a little while. She was surprised when she awoke. This had never happened to her before, this sleeping afterwards. John Fall was warm beside her. His arm was across her hips. She listened to his deep breathing and knew that he was asleep. After a while she lifted herself on one elbow and looked down at him. His skin was rough, more so than she had thought and she knew that it would have marked her face. He had shaved but the dark growth was close beneath the skin and would soon emerge. You didn't have to follow the she, she told him silently, and bent to touch his cheek with her lips and then with the tip of her tongue. His head moved and the arm rose against her, taking possession again. She looked into his eyes and laughed.

'Was it good?' he asked.

She laughed again and fluttered her lips against his cheek.

'Was it good then, Ruth?'

'Yes.'

'All the time I wanted. Ever since I first see you.'

'Tell me that again.'

'It's right. All the time. I get that way every time I see you.'

'Now you've done it.'

'Oh Jeez! That was good.'

'Was it? Tell me how good.'

His hand began to stroke her. 'I got to again, Ruth. I sure got to again.'

She was surprised. Ted had never risen to this. She doubted that a man could, but John was insistent. He brought her down to him.

'Make sure it's safe, John.'

'I did. I brought them.'

'You meant this to happen.'

'Ever since I see'd you I wanted it.'

'Then take it again, John.'

This time he was not as quick. She felt herself begin to move with him. She found herself rising with him, rising and climbing so high, and then suddenly, falling into a great darkness but she felt like a star, falling and bursting with brightness.

A long time after he had gone, she went out and stood looking at the bush. I could have done the same to any one of them, she thought. I could have any man on this reserve. Then she remembered that final moment.

'Dear God, that was wonderful!' she said. Its memory was a warmth that flowed through her again and again.

5

I wonder who that guy is keeps sending money orders to me.

Ruth bought her car. It was a white Volkswagen, two years old and a one-owner. It was bought after a crazed, exhausting day, during which Flanagan proved himself a fanatic about cars and an expert on handling salesmen. How they got out of some sales rooms without a fight she would never know. Then she gave Flanagan an ultimatum and at the very next car lot he bought the white Beetle and she parted with sixteen hundred dollars.

During that week she took her tests and became mobile. During that week also, Marjorie scared her half to death. They were sitting in the early evening, each waiting for the other to make the first move to the kitchen when Marjorie said, 'Don't keep it a secret, Ruth. Who is it you're in love with?'

The shock almost stopped her breathing. She waited until she had recovered, wondering wildly how Marjorie could have found out, how she had betrayed herself. Then she asked,

'Who says I am in love?'

'You do. You've been saying it for an hour.'

'What are you talking about?'

'That song. You've been singing it all day.'

'I didn't realize that. Have I really?'

'Sing it again. It's nice, I like it.'

'Love is a teasing, is that the one?'

'That's it.'

> *Love is a teasing,*
> *Love is a pleasing,*
> *Love is a treasure*
> *When first it is new.*

'That's what I mean. Who is he, Ruth?'

She could have laughed aloud, so relieved was she. Instead she said, 'Ah! But you don't know the ending,' and she sang it.

> *But as it grows older*
> *Love it grows colder.*

'That's not true. It can't be or it's not true love.'

She thought about this conversation later. She knew that there was no love in her relationship with John Fall. He was a man in her life. He was man, and man without trouble. She did not need to think beyond his manhood and the wonder of it walking towards her and the special wonder that it gave her. He had visited her again, and again she had been stirred to wildness and had enjoyed a final, overwhelming surrender. There was no love in this, she gave to him and took from him and she wanted nothing more. But that, she did want. As often as she could possibly have him she wanted him.

Suddenly it was Christmas. Joy to the world time, jingle bells time, drinking and eating time.

In the front window of the I.G.A. a whole hog lay in festive dress, decked with pineapple rings and polished with syrup.

It was Christmas time, time for Merry Gentlemen and mistletoe, and Helmut Golding sold out his stock of cranberries and Julie moved into Marjorie's room because Sarah thought it might as well be used. Queues grew in the post offices, shortened at the cinemas, clamoured at the travel agencies and fought at the turkey counters. On the city sidewalks Salvation Army nymphs rang their bells outside the multiples while inside, tinsels spiralled in the heated air currents and plastic calendars were handed out with the grocery checks. At the prefabricated grottoes, Santa Clauses hypocrised in rota, nine o'clock to five, giving away five-cent painting books for free, and filling children with wonder at the gullibility of their parents.

It was office party time, when nubile typists drank freely of the boss's liquor and waited for the seasonal democracy to lead them to darkened car or way-out motel.

It was nightdress-for-the-wife time and at a city hen affair, six bun-eating matrons went into hysterics when they discovered that each of their husbands had bought for them slinky, black, nylon wisps, and laughed till the tears flowed at the eternal optimism of their menfolk.

It was *Silent Night* time. Outside the Catholic Church on Mountain Avenue, impervious to sub-zero temperature, a plastic virgin leaned over the hope of the world, while the ancient truth was told and retold, helped by a taped *Adeste*; and occasional passers-by crossed themselves or bent a knee just short of the frozen slush.

It was goodwill-to-men time. And more drunks than ever sat in the city cells. And more bank balances sagged. And more lives ended on the highways.

146

On the Big Fish, the Indians drove around to each other's homes bearing greetings. John Littleleaf, George Painted Rock and Peter Bird came out from Toteroad with a trunk full of pelts and the separated parts of an elk tied to car roof. Far to the west, the John James Barnsticks sat on their pelts at a pull-in, thumbing down trucks which slowed but never stopped. Francis Littleleaf, who had received eight money orders from his mysterious benefactor was rich enough to buy a seat on the Northstar and felt the joy come again as the bus swung north from Redville.

Mike Bird came out of the Fort on early release and went home to the wife, for the beating of whom he had been put away. Simon Bigbear came too, looking fat and healthy, from the T.B. hospital. But he was feeling very dry and thirsty and in love with the reserve. O goddam that place! That Hospital! He was never going back there no more.

And from farthest away, from the southern city came Henry Burns who had been Burnstick before he had married white. He brought his boy with him for his old grandfather to see, but not his wife—she couldn't make the trip, not this time, nor last, nor the next either.

Their tracks led like spokes to a hub, like veins to the heart, and the reserve which was the hub was the beating heart awaiting the return of its children. For this was Christmas, best and most sure of the gatherings of the Band.

It was Christmas, time of goodwill, and during the Big Fish party somebody stole Santa's team from the front of the schoolhouse. On the morning after the party, Flanagan and the two girls drove to the city where they had booked at the National. They had a superb meal and then did the town, going to bed too tight to undress. Ruth wakened in terror from a dream in which she was lying in the snow and a huge, black, faceless man was pulling at her and shouting over and over, 'It's a cow! See the tit!' It was a dreadful dream. She lay for a long time after it, and she thought a lot about death before she slept again.

It was peace on earth time and Marie LaPlante, wife of bully-boy George, went home on the eve to find her Christmas tree smashed, her decorations torn down and her husband asleep on the floor amid his vomit. And Louis the Traveller travelled on, but in the manner of his going won a place in beer-parlour history. He was walking from the beer parlour to his truck, pausing now and again to give a fancy little dance or sing a snatch of French. He saw a fat figure standing in the shadows but he gave little attention to it. He started the truck and was on the point of reversing when the cab door was pulled open and he heard a voice say,

147

'Get down from there, you goddam French bastard. You're too drunk to be driving.'

'What the hell!' he said and then saw that it was the town policeman, for whom he had no love at any season.

'Oh, that's you, Kelly. You fat old son. Why don't you go to hell, quick.'

'You get down out of there, you smart-alec French bastard. Here's one Christmas you're gonna spend in jail.'

Louis gave the policeman a quick heel of the hand and slammed the door. He set the truck into a backward curve. As he came out of it he turned to jeer at his discomfited enemy and saw that Kelly was lying on the road. He shut off the engine, climbed down and went back to him.

'Oh my foot! My goddam foot! You've runned over my goddam foot!'

'Jesus! Quit that squawking!'

Louis grabbed the whimpering policeman under the armpits and dragged him on to the sidewalk. He staggered along the side of the I.G.A. store and into the back square, where he left the man among the ash cans. He drove fast to his house. Here he collected his scattered belongings and hurled them into the truck, clothing, food, bottles of beer, wrenches, everything he could find. Satisfied that he had got it all, he took down the phone and asked for Mr Smethurst at his home. He told him, 'Me, I'm just coming down the street, I see this guy sneakin' in back of your store, figures maybe he gettin' in there; maybe you'd better get there damn fast. Sure, take the boy along. Take a stick, man. That's okay, Mr Smethurst. You're welcome, sure.'

Then he got into the truck and drove away from the house. As he slowed to turn on to the highway, his headlights picked out a figure, standing with upraised arm, over a suitcase. He stopped and rolled down the window and saw that it was Marie LaPlante.

'Hi, Marie!' he called.

'Any chance of catching a ride?' she asked.

'Me, I'm going a long ways, Marie.'

'Longer the better.'

'Newfoundland, all that far, maybe.'

'That'll do me fine, Louis.'

'O.K. Marie. You come on up here then.'

As they entered the highway the first flakes of snow drifted against the windscreen.

'Hey, ain't that somethin'?' Louis called. 'We're gonna get us a white Christmas!'

．　　．　　．　　．　　．

On the fifth day of Christmas, Agent Smythe drove out from the Bureau and held a conference with Flanagan. They were closeted for some time and when he departed, he left behind him a furious Flanagan.

'I could kick that goddam ass higher'n that!'

'What has he done this time?' Marjorie asked.

'It's what the fat bastard is tryin' to do.'

'Matt!'

'So! What else is he?'

Ruth said, 'What is it that he is trying to do?'

'Shut down this goddam school, that's all.'

'He isn't! Surely he can't do that.'

'He's got himself a new word. Christ knows where from, but he's been giving it to me all afternoon. He's had a visitor. Some guy from the east, and you know what that means. That great white beast over there huffed and it's puffed, and it's gonna blow this place right over.'

'What is the word, Matt?'

'Huh! Acculturation. Know what it means?'

'I can make a guess. Do you, Marjorie?'

'Me!'

'It means a joining-together of the cultures. Not a take-over. Christ, no! We don't do that kind of thing. This is a give-and-take deal. Say, we give them our kids and they take them. They're gonna chop off our two top grades and bus them into Redville. Starts next fall if they can talk the Redville trustees round. You want to hear what our kids are gonna get out of that? Community purpose! Eh! You know what—Smythe believes that crap. He does so!'

'But it isn't so bad, Matt, if only the top two grades go. There are such a lot of younger children to come, it might even help.'

'And what happens the year after? I'll tell you. They'll have the next two grades. Don't you see, it's not the school they're after, it's the reserve. There's too many bloody Indians. They're costing too much. Take away the schools first, get the kids off the reserves and show them the bright lights. Maybe they won't want to come back then. Smythe and his buddy want to take a walk down 85th street. They'll see a bit of their goddam acculturation. They'll be able to buy an hour of it for five bucks.'

'Matt! That isn't nice.'

'Won't they?'

'I don't know. Don't get so excited.'

'Ask Julie Redstone. She'll tell you. And what about Julie? How long did she last in a public school?'

'Francis Littleleaf is still there.'

'Sure! That one boy! That one boy and all the time every time, everything's got to hang on that poor kid's neck. Smythe did it today. "Look at Littleleaf" he said, just like you. Poor Littleleaf! God help him, if he fails, the whole goddam Bureau collapses.'

Ruth said, 'I think you're looking on the black side of things. Smythe could mean what he says, a joining of the cultures. That could be a good thing.'

'I told you before, Ruth, we're poison for them. We should keep a thousand miles away. They shouldn't have to breathe the same air we do. And Smythe, him mean somethin'! He's a civil servant. Those guys never mean anything. He's at the mercy of the great white beast. When it huffs, he shivers. When it beeps, he creeps. Smythe!'

'Poor man!'

'Sure! But you didn't sit there and listen to his crap. This guy tells him he's building a nation and the fat ass believes it. Then he tries to feed me that. Aw, to hell with it! I'm needin' a beer after that lot. Any of you fancy a ride?'

Ruth knew that Fall was away and there was no possibility of a visit from him. She said, 'Yes. I would.'

'Okay! I'll pick you up after supper, the both of you. We'll have a ride up to Smallhill.' Later that night he warned them. 'That stuff I told you this afternoon. Keep quiet about it. I shouldn't have said what I did. It's hush stuff till after it's been okayed by Redville. It wouldn't do for the Indians to find out what's going on, though by God, I'd like to tell them myself. Can you forget I said it?'

They were sure they could.

On the twelfth day of Christmas, Helmut Golding visited Julie, having previously seen Sarah safely out of the way to a meeting. It was the first time for several days and he was unable to keep control over himself. Julie, for once, was lethargic and unresponsive, and so he was left feeling dissatisfied and frustrated. The girl only livened up when it was over, and she sat at the dressing-table toying with her hair. She sang the despairing words of a teenage song, making the notes flat and nasal, and as Helmut listened to her the knowledge of his age grew on him, and he became sad and afraid, and struck out in self-defence.

'Shut up that singing!'

Julie turned her head towards him and laughed. She said, 'I'll come and beat you with this brush, Daddy,' then she began to sing again.

'I said for you to stop that,' he called. The girl got up and came and stood over him.

'What's wrong, Daddy? Did you not get it this time? '

'You want me back in there uh?' She reached for him and laughed as he twisted away. 'Isn't that a little pup now. Oh you had it sure, you can't have it no more, not tonight, anyways.'

'What for, you no good tonight? How come you didn't do nothin'?'

'You want me to do something now, Daddy?'

'Git out, you goddam little bitch!'

'This my room, Daddy. Do I got to get out my own room? Is that it? Don't call me no names anyways, I don't like that.'

'You can't do no better, you'd better quit out of this job.'

'I don't wanna quit.'

The storekeeper was sore. Julie had moved in on Sarah's invitation, not his. The situation had become altogether too complicated with her under the same roof, too dangerous for him. He sensed that exposure was only a matter of words, or a mistake away; the whole thing was becoming a tug-of-war between joy and fear. If she couldn't produce the joy, she was hardly worth the fear.

'Maybe you'd better go too. I think so.'

'You got some other girl coming up here?'

'I ain't, either. Could be I don't like for Marjorie leaving us like she did 'count of you. Ain't right for my own girl goin' like she did.'

'You she saw, old man. You take up with girls you gotta expect, that's all. Marjorie ain't no kid anyways. She knows you got a busy one, down there.'

'That a goddam lie!'

'Folk on the reserve call you "Old Goat".'

Now he was annoyed and shouted, 'You'd better git.'

'I don't mind me none, you can be Old Goat round me just like anythin'. I don't care anyways.'

She returned to the dressing table and the hair brush, and there was silence between them. Then she said, 'What you gonna tell the old lady when I pull out?'

'Uh?'

'The old lady; what you tell her why I quit? You gonna say you got enough of me, is that right? Old Lady likes me. She ain't bad anyways, maybe I'll stay with her. Maybe I'll tell her how you keep after me, don't give me no peace.'

'You don't tell her nothin'! Jeez, I only funnin' you, you don't need to get mad that way. You got nice place here, all you gotta do is a little work around, that's all. Lotsa girls'd like it here.'

'I know all I got to do, Daddy, don't I?' Then, without a change in her voice she said, 'Daddy, I want fifty bucks.'

'Fifty bucks! Off me? Nothin'! That's for sure!'

'I think you're gonna give it all right, maybe more even.'

'What for I give you fifty bucks? Already you took plenty, already!'

Julie stood and laughed at him; she stretched her arms over her head and then she said, 'I got a real surprise, Daddy. You gave me a kid, old man. That's right, he's sittin' right here,' and she put her finger to her navel and drew it downwards.

Golding stared at her, stared at the white line the finger had left on the skin. He looked so funny, open mouthed and peering without his spectacles, that Julie burst into laughter.

'Ain't that good news for you then? Ain't it worth fifty bucks for you havin' another little one in the basket? It shows you're still good for that.'

'You goddam lyin' . . . ain't my kid . . . two months is all . . . that can't be no kid of mine . . . you lyin' bitch.'

'It's sure yours, Daddy. Oh yes, four months you've been shacking me up. It's yours for sure.'

'You goddam bitch Indian!'

'Me, I'm just Julie.'

'You goddam Indian tramp!'

'Just Julie, that's all; I ain't changed none 'cept now there's two of me.'

'You bitch! You bitch! You Indian bitch!'

Suddenly she changed. The humour vanished from her voice. She bent over him, her hands out at her sides and she shouted down at him, 'You called me that. You I warmed up . . . you I made jump all 'round that bed. I got you hot, Daddy, when you was all past. Ain't that worth no fifty? Ain't it right? Man! You was all dyin'. You was an old bull, stinkin' of it. I got you good . . . all 'round that bed—you was horny for ever. Old man, you got a damn good fifty bucks goin' up my road. What for you don't wanna pay now, uh?'

'You dirty Indian!'

'I'm not dirty, old man. I'm Indian, sure. Maybe this kid he gonna be better, uh. He gonna be half white. All down one side he gonna be white—one white ball, one Indian ball, uh?'

'Get the hell outa this house.'

'Like this, I gotta go out?'

'Get dressed—get out. You Indian!'

'Just Julie, Daddy. Just Julie.'

Golding sat on the bed and watched her dress. She moved about as if he were not there, picking up her clothes, smoothing her stockings, fastening her buttons, and all the time, on her face, that secretive, tormenting smile remained. When she was ready, she walked out of the room and he followed, desperate to see her go. She lingered on, holding open the door to the outer veranda, and she turned back to him and said, still smiling, 'I'll talk with Sarah about the baby. I guess I'll find her over to Mrs McKenzie's.'

'Get out, you bitch!' he shouted, and rushed at her and pushed her with both hands. She staggered backward through the doorway, lost her footing on the uneven boards and fell against the rail. He heard it crack and saw it swing away from the post; he watched her fall back and disappear from sight and heard the thump of her body as it landed in the yard below.

'Oh, Jesus Christ!' he cried, and scrambled forward and peered over the edge.

Julie lay still on the hard, shining ice, her legs spread wide. She was not moving. He ran down the steps to her and tried to lift her, but she leaned away from him as she never should have done and he knew that she was hurt badly. Then he knew that she was past being hurt or cold, or anything else. She was dead. He said, 'Don't be that, Julie! You can have it. Don't be that!' He shook her but she sagged. How she sagged!

He was filled with terror and ran back into the house and shut the door. He went into the bedroom that she had only just left, and then he turned and ran to the bathroom. Here he knelt with his arms folded over the toilet seat and moaned, 'What in hell I'm gonna do now—oh Jesus! Why did that have to happen— what in hell I'm gonna do?'

Thirty minutes later Golding had overcome his panic and was driving his car towards the Big Fish. It was a cold night and dark, and the wind was whispering snow grains over the road and across the windscreen. He was thankful for the bitterness of the wind and the moon's absence—there would not be any night walkers to see his car and remember and remark on his visit. He drove carefully and slowly, avoiding skids that might ditch the car, until he came to the place he wanted, the trail leading off the road and over Devil's Creek. He left the car at the junction, and lifting Julie across his shoulders, he walked up the trail. The night was full of noises; every branch in the forest seemed to be groaning within its ice; the wind brought a muffled drum beat from a distant party; his own breath was noisy on the air, his feet slurped through the snow.

He was surrounded by betrayal and full of fear.

'Can you pick me up, old man?' he heard Julie ask, but the voice was in the past. The head banging gently against his back had surrendered speech for ever.

'God damn it!' he wheezed. 'God damn it all!'

The bridge was a platform of thin poles, roped together and pinned to an undercarriage of thicker cross-pieces. There were no guard rails, these had vanished on some boy's fire, long ago. The poles were free of snow but a thin layer of ice covered them and pushed spears between them to point down into the frozen creek. It was a deep drop, all of twenty feet. The storekeeper looked over and saw below him a cushion of snow and the iron arms of a bedstead rising out of this. He let Julie's body slide down into his arms and he held it for the last time while he looked into her face. Her eyes had rolled away and her teeth grinned against the lipstick. Golding shuddered, and opened his gloved hands he let her drop. From his pocket he took two bottles of beer and he broke off their tops against the edge of the bridge. One he emptied over the dark shape below and then threw far into the bush; the other he placed on the bridge, close to where he had dropped her. Then he walked back across the bridge.

When he reached the far side, he turned and leaned over again for a last look. Although it was so cold, sweat beads collected on his forehead and ran down into his eyes. He lifted a hand to brush these away and as he did so his spectacles flipped away and fell into the whiteness.

'Jesus!' he swore. 'What for that goddam happen? Now I can't see even!' He scrambled down the side of the bridge and went back to his car. Already the windscreen was iced up and he had to use a scraper to free the wipers. He thought that the wind sounded stronger, and several times on the drive back had to cut through little snow dunes that were humping across the road. 'Come morning she's all gonna be covered over,' he mumbled. 'Maybe they don't even find her till spring.'

It didn't work out that way. Julie's body was found before he had got back to the store. He wasn't off the reserve when John Blood, the breed, coming down from a shortstick session, saw a bottle of beer lying on the bridge, and John never walked past either bottle or cigarette pack without taking a closer look. 'Sweet spring!' he said. 'There's beer here,' and he drank it. Then he said, 'What 'n hell! That should of been froze. Why ain't that beer all froze up? Some guy's now dropped that bottle. Some guy 'round here havin' a party some place. Jeez, that queer!

Ain't nobody here anyways.' He wandered to the edge of the bridge and looked over and saw Julie.

'Holy Christ! She got herself all drunk! She gonna be hurt for sure.'

'Hey!' he called. 'Hey, get up, uh? You gonna get all cold down there.'

*

Except for Tom Redstone the gravediggers were young men. They had waited two days for the wind to drop, but the tempest grew instead of abating, and on the afternoon before the funeral they had to go out into it and start the digging. Joey Bird brought a load of dead wood from the Old Folk's Town and they lit a fire over the chosen spot, building it up high into a pyramid. They huddled as close to this as the flames would allow, and the wind knifed into their exposed sides and through the fire, carrying great clouds of smoke and sparks away into the grey maelstrom. When the fire had burned down to ash and branch ends, they scraped these away and attacked the softened earth. They scooped out a trough a few inches deep, and then hit frozen ground again. They lit another fire in the trough and again they piled on the branches and watched the flames leaping. This would be a long job; a lot of fire would burn before they could put Julie deep enough. Through the rest of this day and the coming night and into the morning, the burning and digging would continue, and then, if they had it deep enough, they could bring Julie and put her away. Meanwhile the women of the Big Fish would sing at the Redstone house, and the teams would stand around with their tails to the storm, packing down the snow while their freezing breath welded their shaggy manes.

The fire died and the men stepped down into the trough with their spades.

At the monthly meeting of the Upcreek Chapter of the Country Women's League, the good women sympathized with Sarah, surrounding her with concern and spreading a net to catch any tittle-tattle titbits she might care to drop.

'It shows, don't it,' Rose Montpelier said, 'What you folks did for her and the way she pays you back, like that. I mean, going off into the bush and carrying on that way!'

Sarah said, 'We sure was hard hit,' and they all nodded and waited. She continued, 'Gave her a nice home, figured on helping her all we could. Treated her just like Marjorie, we did, and lookit! Poor Helmut, he's real put out. Ain't got over it yet. Keeps tellin' me, "Fancy Julie bein' like that, like all the others." Keeps sayin' it, he does.'

'That'll be a frosty day in July when you find one that ain't,' said Mrs Barwise. 'Scratch an Indian and he'll bleed drink, so help me he will. I said it before, ain't I, Shirl?' Her daughter nodded. They did not press the matter any further, Sarah was too upset, and after all, Julie had only been one of the reserve girls.

But some of the boys remembered her as just a girl, and were sad beneath their scoffing words, and wished that she could really be again, to wander in and out of their world as she had, at one with them, like the snow, or fishing, or the forbidden booze.

'Jeez! That was a waste! Before I could get to her. Man! Hey, think of that pair, uh!'

'Yeah. Me too. She was next on my list. I figured on datin' her, next chance I got.'

'Already, you guys!' the reputation-seeker claimed. 'Lots times I had her. She wasn't no different. Dames are all the same.'

'Aw! Gaw on!'

Ruth learned about the accident from Flanagan. 'It happened in the bush some place. She was drinkin', fell in the creek. Broke her back.'

'Oh! What a dreadful thing, to die like that. And Julie of all people. She seemed to have so much of life in her.'

'Did you ever hear of a rabbit dyin' of old age?'

'They aren't rabbits.'

'Sometimes that's how it seems. There's never a winter without somethin' like this. Not many summers either.'

'There's too much violence in their lives. Violence breeds violence. All this killing, this hunting. There's too much of it. Marjorie's right about the bush. There will always be violence in their lives as long as they live in it.'

Flanagan pursed his lips.

'You don't agree?'

'There's violence and violence.'

'What do you mean by that?'

'An Indian kills a moose, it's quick. Comes up from inside him. It's a true thing.'

'It's violence.'

'So is making second-class citizens. Tell me a worse violence than that.'

'I don't make second-class citizens.'

'Uhuh! Keep it general. We all do. We all got our own breed

of violence, and somebody gets it when we unload. You don't have to have a shiner to get hurt. These people, they take more than they give. A hell of a lot more. They're everybody's rabbits.'

'I don't like to think that anybody suffers from anything that I do.'

'Nor me. But they do.'

She remembered his words the next time she was with Fall. They had established a pattern to their meetings. He knew that she was available whenever her class lights were on. She would wait in the class for the tap on the door and then she would go with him to the nurse's room. This was in the basement and she kept the key. It had a bed. There was no need to put the lights on. He was always urgent in his approaches, as if he could never be sure of her until it was all over. For her part, she tried to delay him but usually found herself swept along with his urgency. The tides they rode were very high. They needed a resting-time afterwards. It was then that they talked, never before. As on this night.

'How well did you know Julie?'

'Julie? Well, you know. She was one of the kids. Yeah, I knowed Julie. Not much though. I seen her around, 'specially since she quit school.'

'Are you sure that's all?'

'Me? I don't know her much. Like I told you.'

'Did you ever do this with her?'

'Jesus, Ruth! She was a kid that one. No, I never. Not with Julie. Anyways, why you askin' me that?'

'I know one man she was doing it with?'

'Matt?'

'Good God, no!'

'I figured maybe you and Matt.'

'Then you figured wrong.'

'Did he not ever try, then?'

'Not by a touch.'

'Can't figure that guy. Him in that house. Why he don't go after you.'

'People can live without it, John.'

'Not me. Not now I can't. Jesus, Ruth! Nobody's good like you. I never been like this. Holy Christ! I can't sleep nights, I got you that bad.'

It was when he said this that, she remembered Flanagan's remarks. 'What am I doing to this man?' she asked herself. 'Is this my form of violence? Is he becoming my rabbit?' Then she reminded herself that she was giving as well as taking. If man

157

needed woman before he could reach the heights it was a dependence thrust upon women. It was not a cruelty to accept this. She reached for him again and he was soon roused. She whispered, 'Show me again how you need me.'

The Indians poured out their grief in a two-day burst of lachrymose self-pity that bore witness to their kinship in the unhappy winter world around them. Then they expunged Julie from their minds and returned to the business of keeping alive themselves. Only Martin Crow of the closed-in mind remembered, and either waited for her return from the city or sat in vigil beneath the creek bridge waiting for nothing.

6

It is not good for Julie
To lie like an earthed-up gopher.
She should die into water
And touch the rocks
And shine in the sun.

They had got into the habit of sitting over coffee when school was ended for the day. These little sessions became inquests on the day's happenings, and it was at one of them that Flanagan mentioned a little of Band gossip. 'They say the Chief has got tired of being everybody's pot-shot guy. He's quittin'. He's gonna tell Smythe so, next meetin'.'

Marjorie asked, 'And just who is taking over?'

'Tom Henry Littleleaf seems to be the favourite son.'

'Him! He's dead from here.'

'The Littleleafs have the biggest count. He's their front man.'

'Guess where the relief cheques will go if Tom Henry gets it.'

'Guess who'll sign them.'

'Mrs Tom Henry.'

'Right! But not to worry, kid. It has to be somebody.'

'If it has to be a Littleleaf I'll settle for Francis.'

'That poor guy. Now he's got to come home and be chief. Why don't you let the kid grow up a little?'

They argued a lot about this. Ruth listened, she took no part in the conversation but an idea came to her mind. She fashioned it while she was listening and the more she considered, the brighter it became. She was surprised that it had not occurred to Flanagan. Who better for Chief than John Fall? Young, strong, a man who could think, he had everything that any other man on the Big Fish could claim.

She did not mention this at the time. She never spoke about John Fall except when one of the others brought him into the conversation. But when she was with him next, and she suggested it to him, he was startled. 'Me for Chief? Jeez, I don't know. I hadn't figured on that. It's kind of for an older guy, that job.'

'How old are you?'

'Twenty-seven. How old are you?'

'I don't see that you need to be any older than that. They are saying that Tom Henry Littleleaf will win it.'

'He's no good, that one.'

'And that his wife will run the Band.'

'That's for sure.'

'And you don't mind. You'd let it happen like that? I'm surprised, John. I was hoping that you would try for it.'

'Maybe next time.'

'This time.'

'Hey! You're tryin' to talk me into that.'

'Yes, I am.'

'I got other ideas.'

'Oh! And what are they?'

'I been thinkin' about quittin' the reserve.'

'Leaving the reserve? For good, do you mean?'

'Sure. I could get me a job any place, I guess. Like right now with the taxi. That's not good for all the time, only for some days. I'd sooner get me a straight job. Can't do that if I stay here. I've got to get in some other place. That's what I been thinkin' about. What do you say to that?'

'Me? It's not for me to say, is it! It hasn't anything to do with me.'

He did not answer but there was a heaviness in his silence, and she had a sudden flash of insight. My God! she thought, and returned immediately to her original suggestion.

'John. You've got to try at this Chief thing. You need it and the Band needs you. I'm sure you could do it. I am sure you'd be very good. Won't you try, John?'

'How long are you stayin' here, then?'

'I don't know. I haven't decided.'

'You're here till summer, I guess.'

'I have to stay till summer. I can't leave before that.'

'You gonna stay after that?'

'I don't know yet. It is quite possible.'

'And we'd keep on like this, uh? If you stopped on the reserve.'

'So long as nobody finds out, yes. Otherwise I'd have to go.'

'Maybe I could get that Chief, too. Lots of guys, I guess would go for me.'

'I'm certain they would. Make up your mind, John. Go for it. Will you?'

'You think I'd be good at that, uh?'

'You'd be very good. Probably the best they've ever had.'

'You know what, Ruth. I'm gonna think about it.' Later he said, 'You didn't say how old you was.'

'Twenty-four.' It was too dark down there for him to read the lie on her face.

She returned to the election theme again until finally he agreed to put his name forward. 'But we don't tell nobody,' he said. 'We don't let Tom Henry know nothin'. He thinks he's got this all sewed-up. He's gonna find things, too.'

'When will you do it?'

'I figured the meetin' would be best. The agent's goin' to be there an' I can tell him then. Say, Tom Henry, he's givin' a pow-wow for his girls the same night.'

'That's a good way of getting votes.'

'Are you goin' to vote for me?'

'If I were a member you'd get my vote.'

'I'm gonna make you a member right now.'

She pulled his shirt from his slacks and slid her arms around his back. His skin was very hot. She spread her fingers and ploughed them along him.

'That's nice.'

'It's nearer.'

On the afternoon before the meeting she had another idea. The children gave it to her, black heads bent to books, a little community, with herself at its head. She watched them and worried about them and then remembered another conversation with Flanagan and saw how she could help John Fall. After that she had to see him, and before the meeting. She hoped that he was somewhere near, and feeling that way and it happened that he was, and he did. But she wouldn't let him touch her until she had talked first. 'John. What would happen if they tried to take away the children from this school?'

'What for?'

'To send them somewhere else.'

'There ain't somewhere else for them kids to go.'

'There is. There is Redville.'

'That's a white school.'

'Yes. Suppose they sent the children there.'

'They couldn't. There's no room there.'

'There could be for some of them.'

'They won't do that. Jeez, they can't do that.'

'John, what would you parents do if they tried to move any of the children?'

'They got to teach our kids right here and no other place. No guy's gonna take our kids.'

'The people would be against it.'

'By Christ, they would!'

'Then listen! I think I can help you to win your election.'

She told him her plan and he went for it at once. He was like a child in his quick enthusiasm and she kindled this and had him thinking of himself as Chief. There was more to it than helping John Fall. She had not liked his talk about leaving the reserve, she wanted no more of it, no more of his dreams of living in white-land with a white woman.

'Oh, you sure figured it good,' he praised her and she smiled and squeezed him and smiled even more when he gasped.

There was one thing you could be sure of about an Indian. If there was an inside story, someone would let it out. The men especially loved to do this. There is an importance in having an audience, it is rooted in their history. It can also build a bridge towards a loan. George Falltime brought the news of the meeting to Flanagan, but he was not seeking money. His reward lay in the presentation of his brother's smartness.

'So Tom Henry says sure, he's ready to stand for Chief. He gets this guy to name him and they're set on the deal. Smythe asks if there's anybody else wants to go. Then John gets up. He don't tell me nothin' that guy. He's sure of a son-of-a-gun. 'I got something to ask Mr Smythe,' he says. And Smythe, he says, 'Yes, John?' Then John, he says, 'Is that right you gonna take a lot of our kids away from the reserve school and send them to Red-ville?' Jeez, you should have heard that bunch then!'

'He didn't!'

'He sure did, Matt. Never told me that, he didn't, but he'd figured it somehow. Did you know that, Matt, about those kids?'

'No, George. Say, what did Smythe do then?'

'Him. He looked kind of sick, you know. He don't say nothin', and John asks him again. Smythe he says, 'I don't know what you're talking about. Anyways it got nothin' to do with our business. It's not on the list. 'Then you're gonna have it put on, Mr Smythe,' John says. ''Cause I know that you're askin' over at Redville for them to take our kids. You're gonna do it next fall even.' Smythe says, 'Nothin's settled yet.' He'd done better not to say that. We all knowed then. He'd done better to say nothin' at all.'

'John laid it out.'

'He sure did. That's not the finish. He says, ''Well I've got to tell you then, I'm puttin' in for Chief, too. And I tell you right now, if I get that, then no kids go off this reserve. That's what I'm standin' for. It's to keep hold of our kids.'' By Christ, Matt. You ought to have heard them shout.'

162

'So now they'll have to ballot.'

'That's for sure. You know what, John, he could win that, too.'

'How did he find that out? Did he tell you, George?'

'Wouldn't tell me a goddam thing. But he's smart, uh? He's gonna make a good Chief.'

Shortly after this, Flanagan received another version. This time the caller was the Agent.

'Could you tell me how he got that knowledge, Matt?'

'I couldn't.'

'You got no idea?'

'I didn't tell him, if that's what you're askin'. He didn't get it from me. Anyways, you work behind their backs, you've got no kick if it gets out.'

'I'm not working behind anybody's back. I'm engaged in negotiation and it's for the good of everybody. This could blow the whole thing. It could put these kids back years.'

'If you'd asked them 'fore you went ahead.'

'We thought it better to do some groundwork first. John Fall can have spoiled everything we've done.'

'Like I said, I didn't tell him. He's learned it from your end, or from Redville. You'd better tell those trustees to keep their mouths shut.'

After the Agent had gone, Flanagan went up to the house.

Ruth said, 'Good for John!' but Flanagan shook his head.

'Why not, Matt? Don't you think he'd make a good Chief? He seems to know what he is doing and you think he's all right. You said he was one of the best of the younger ones. Why don't you like the idea of him as a Chief?'

'John Fall as John Fall, sure he's okay. But as Chief John—that's different. He's diggin' a hole for himself. If they make him Chief, in no time at all he'll be dishin' out relief to the Falltimes and the Birds and gettin' kickbacks from the stores around. He'll be in every goddam racket and he's smart enough to think up some new ones of his own. No! I don't like it! But he's his own man, I don't own him.'

She nodded and she did not allow the smile that was inside to show. There is a lot about John that you do not know, she thought. You have to be with him like I have to know a man. You only see what he wants to show, but I get all of him. I know him when he is strongest and when he is weakest, too. He lies on me like a whale from which the sea has drained. Even at that moment, in the sunlight and among others, this thought filled her with lust for him.

Meantime the Agent had driven off the reserve. He chose the

track that led to the Chief's house, and as he had hoped, caught up with the Chief along it.

'Chief,' he said, 'I want you to come over to the city some time next week. It's important. I want to talk to you. Can you make the trip?'

'How's about the taxi? Who pays that?'

'It's Band business. You get the fare. What day can you come? I'd like it to be Tuesday. Could you make it then?'

'Tuesday. Sure!'

'One thing, Chief. Don't get John Fall to do the taxi-ing. Get somebody else. Can you do that?'

'Sure. I get Little Moise from up there.'

'John's not going to know you've come.'

'He don't find out.'

That night she went with Flanagan and Marjorie to the pow-wow. It was clear and cold and ghost lights were moving in the sky. The path was slippery from the tramping of many feet and snow squeaked underfoot. As they neared the Council House, they saw a red flickering on the trees. Shadowy figures moved and Ruth heard a snort and the shaking of harness brasses. The trees thinned and the red glare came to meet them and it was warmth from a great wood fire that crackled and roared, and drove back the shadows of the bush. Several men and boys stood by the fire, holding up hands to keep the heat from their faces and turning, like chickens on a spit, to equalize the roasting. From the Council House came the muffled thumping of a drum; then a door opened and somebody shouted above the din, 'Teacher's coming! Teacher's coming!'

'Here goes!' Flanagan said, and he led the way into the room, into the furnace where the people were dancing.

There were no squeaking fiddles, there was no piano, there was not even a harmonica. There was only the drum in the centre of the room, held by one man and being beaten by two others. Could that great noise be coming from the skin-thin, skin-tight circle of hide? Greater noise even than the roar of its owner when he was in lusting life and all the bush was his and the cows were near. Great noise, bouncing in the air and pushing against the ears, pushing and crushing and forcing the pressure into the brain, spinning and destroying the thoughts, so that the shout, when it came, was from the belly and escaped like a belch, unbidden.

Boom! Boom! B'Boom!

The drum, the stirrer of the blood, the soul of the Band—the beating haven of forgetfulness—the demanding drum.

Two more men stood beside it and all five sang, their voices rising and falling together as they searched for the feeling, and finding it common, translated it, not into words but into sounds. 'Ayee–a Ayee–a Ayee–a–a–a.'

Radiating from this group like spokes from a hub, in shuffling, shouting lines, the dancers moved—young children, old men, boys and girls, round and round, making the floor into a turntable, taking up the chant and swelling it into a shout of gladness, and sorrow, and hope, and life.

Lift them heels, point toes, hands by sides, round, round, round. Ho! Stamp feet, Heh! Dust in a cloud, shake the lamp, sweat on the faces. White the teeth, shine in the eyes, Ho! Ho! Kick feet out youse guys, hit them loud little chickens Heh! Heh! Ayee–a Ayeea O O O Ayee–a. Shiver that floor, shake that breast whenever I die, I will just die, Heya! Heya!

Among the swirling, smoke-wreathed mass, Ruth recognized many children and she acknowledged their smiles and waves. She said to Marjorie, 'This is terrible! I can't stand the noise, it's impossible!' and then, before Marjorie had time to reply, John Fall came to ask them to join the dancers.

'John, no!' wailed Marjorie, 'I can't do that kind of dancing.'

'I couldn't, John. I couldn't possibly,' Ruth said, but he was insistent.

'It's easy—all you gotta do is just go round there,' and Flanagan helped him. 'Get in there, both of you! Go on! Have fun!'

They were dragged into the throng, the lines of grinning faces, the chanting, swaying figures, and she allowed John Fall to manœuvre her into the centre where the crowd was thickest and she was farthest from onlookers. There the arm encircled her, and the fingers slid down to settle on her flank and in their squeezing she felt all of his yearning. His fingers were so desperate to know her. He bent his head to her and she heard his voice say, low and for her ears only, 'You're gonna be the Chief's woman.'

She smiled back in answer and then, Flanagan's face coming into view, changed the smile into a grimace of displeasure, so that he grinned at her supposed predicament. Then they had moved on and the hand reached down again and John Fall said, 'We could go in the bush right now!' She didn't answer and he said urgently, 'Jeez, I'm big for you.'

'What did you say, John?' Marjorie asked, from the far side, and Ruth heard her own laugh rise above the wailing and the drum.

165

The teachers did not stay long at the pow-wow. They left before midnight. Ruth stood at the window of the unlighted bedroom and listened to the rhythmic, muffled thumping from the Council House. It wasn't so much a noise as a trembling on the night air. She knew John Fall wouldn't be visiting her but she was too disturbed to sleep. He had wanted to take her into the bush. He had wanted her as an Indian girl in the darkness, within sound of drum-beat and smell of fire. His blood was hot, the blood of his race, primitive and stirred. He would have been strong, a raging bull in the dark. He had wanted her in the bush, not in a bed. These thoughts excited her. She slid out of her nightdress, left it on the floor and searched in the darkness for a few braided beads that she had bought. She found these and draped them over herself, tied one like a girdle round her waist so that its ends dangled below her stomach. She took her lipstick and drew lines across herself.

Then she returned to the window and the cold air streamed through the holes in the storm sash and played over her. She stroked her side where John Fall's hand had rested, and she wondered if he was still over there, circling the room or if he had gone out into the night, taking what was big for her to some other girl.

She heard the beating stop, and when it did not take up again she thought, 'They have started to eat the soup.' She flipped the curtains across the window and got into bed still wearing the beading, still painted. And John Fall came in spirit to rage with her.

At the pow-wow the drumming had stopped when the first bottle sailed across the room. Joey Bird threw it, not at anyone in particular. It was in his hand, it was empty so he threw it. But the splintering fragments fell among the Littleleaf group and Tom Henry's wife began to howl, and Tom Henry got down on the floor and hid under a seat. The children fled to the door laughing and screaming and jostling and spilling out, to stop after a few yards and return to watch from the doorway.

More bottles were thrown, and now men rolled over the floor and one of them touching the stove, began to scream. Joey Bird swung his pitching arm again and sent another bottle, dipping and curving. It struck a Painted Rock in the ribs, and he made no sound but fell and lay still among the scrambling feet. Now Joey found another bottle but someone held his hair from behind, and he felt boots coming into him, and he put his hand into his pocket for his knife. And then the Old Chief who had crawled along the side wall, reached up and turned out the lamp and all was over; the drumming, the singing, the pow-wow, the fight, everything.

For John Fall the two weeks between meeting and election were busy ones, as full of activities as any two weeks that he had ever lived through. He toured the reserve ceaselessly, passing his nights at card games or camping folks, sleeping more often in other houses than his own, building alliances, stirring up old feuds, until, as election day drew near, he had enough promises to ensure victory. Several times he awakened out of a stupor, not knowing where he was or what he had been doing, only that his body ached and his head protested. Once during that time he saw Ruth and then it was from the doorway of a shack and she was far away, a coloured spot out on the lake. Though he longed for her, he remembered how she had ordered him to stay away from her until after the election. So he did this, seeking solace in company and drink, and the men of the Band saw a correctness in his method of canvassing because he was going for Chief and everything has to be bought a little.

'That John Fall, he's a damn good guy.'

'He's gonna make a good Chief.'

On the day itself he ran his car endlessly, bringing his supporters from the Old Folk's Town, or from their scattered, away-from-the-others houses; and only when he was satisfied that they were there in strength did he himself go into the Council House.

Ruth, watching at her classroom window, saw the cars gathering and the people coming from the woods for the meeting. She was on edge throughout the afternoon. Time and again she went to the window to watch for signs of the break-up of the meeting, for the first voters to drift away.

She had missed him. She had regretted her chosen abstinence almost as soon as it had begun. Only then did she realize how much pleasure she got from his visits. Just to hold him and feel him fill with urgency for her had become a secret joy. To hold the rising man. She had missed him, and now that their reunion was only hours away she began to anticipate its passion.

On this morning she had managed to speak to him. 'Win or lose, John,' she had told him, 'come tonight.'

'You bet!'

'Yes. You bet.'

But she waited in vain that night. She watched by the window until she was cold and then she went to her room and took off what should have been a celebration garb, unbutton-me blouse and slim skirt; threw them in a corner and struck herself in rage.

167

She lay on her bed and wept as she thought of what had happened. She heard only the few words of Flanagan's: 'Election? There wasn't one. No! There wasn't. Smythe told the meetin' that the Old Chief had somethin' to say. He got up and told them he'd changed his mind. If the Band wanted him then he'd carry on some more. Then all the guys who'd been gripin' 'bout him changed their song. Reckoned it would be a good thing, his stayin' in the job. One after another they got in line. Only John and a couple of others held out. Smythe called a vote against havin' an election and that was it.'

'Didn't anybody vote against it?'

'Five. John, George and their wives.'

'Who was the other?'

'Joey Bird. John got himself out on a limb. Somebody went to work with an axe. They're gonna watch him damn careful from now on.'

'Who used the axe?'

'Sam Smythe. John went dead the minute he brought up that school deal. He should have kept his big mouth shut. He'd maybe be Chief right now, if he hadn't shot off about it.'

She slapped herself again, wanting to be hurt as much physically as she was inwardly. She was left to weep alone, for John Fall was drinking. And Anna Fall too, and George Falltime, and also Joey Bird and Tom Henry Littleleaf, who was with them. That night, in the shacks along Tophills the Old Chief wrote out new relief slips for the members of his family and there was singing and shortsticks.

7

I wonder what Old Bush Man is bringing me; glad thing or sad thing?

Slowly, as if it had always been, would always be, winter loitered. Weighted, snow-bowed, sky-bound, dreadfully oppressive and monotonous, short of day and long of night it crept out of January and still no birds sang, no green life sprang. Through long hours in the classroom, together in the intimacy of warmth and light and words, Ruth and the children came to know each other. She learned to accept the bonds they placed upon her, to shrink no more from their touching fingers, to shudder no more at their dirt or smells. She watched the pink tongues lick dust from lip corners, and fingers pushing into noses, without reprimanding. She listened to their stories.

'Me, I skate good.'

'Nossir! He don't skate good, that guy.'

'Me, I was in hospital with those Eskimoes. Gee, Teacher, those guys sure stink!'

'Claude, she's not coming to school. She's got bottle sickness.'

'Them birds, they call them Chuckeek. That's his name 'cause that's what he sayin'. Chuckeek!'

'Good soup them birds, Teacher.'

'My daddy, he's comin' home.'

'Teacher! Make your fingers sing,' they pleaded wanting her to play the piano so that they could dance.

Winter was heaps of overshoes at the outer door, and from these, a trail of wet that dwindled as it reached the higher-polished regions. It was thick, grey socks, floor-polishing socks good for sliding along floor boards and building up static that could be sparked on an unsuspecting ear at the end of the slide—girls' ears, of course—they scream louder than boys.

Winter was dry bread sandwiches in lard buckets, eaten on the stand or on the wander. It was two men staggering out of the bush, drunk and dancing, arms around each other's necks, and a delighted, prideful face: 'That's my daddy, Teacher. He's crazy guy!'

It was posters on the wall.

Flies make you sick
Mosquitoes Kill!
Drink Milk!

And winter was nights when she dreamed of what she would say to John Fall if only she had him in her bed, and days when she was disgusted at herself and what she had done with him, and allowed him to do. She had not seen him since the election fiasco, but she had heard through Flanagan that he had been in a drinking session that had begun on that night. Her moods varied, they could change on a drift of smoke from some unseen hut and she would become full of need. It was in this state that she left the house one day and walked, not to the lake as she had been doing of late, but along a new path that led into the trees behind the school. Old berries sparkled, tall grasses bore clusters of empty cases, the contents of which had long since been shaken free and eaten by the snow birds. Dead growth lay, reddish against the snow like hairs on a man's arm. There were yellow patches of snow beneath bare wands, where dogs had stopped to cock a leg. The matted mesh straggled like wire across a snow-man's land. It was a frozen, unwelcoming place. 'We're going to have us an early spring,' they had been saying for weeks now. But still the endless snow stretched. She made her way through it, seeking a way also through the forest of her thoughts, the sharp, black branches of anxiety and uncertainty and desire.

For some time she had been hearing a noise, a rising and falling, whining sound. She walked towards it and heard other noises, banging and shouting voices. She came to a clearing where she saw a white mountain, a smooth, snowed-over hill squatting in the centre of the clearing. As she passed and walked around it she saw that it was frosted sawdust and there was a mill behind it. Several men were working on and around this. Logs were being rolled from a pile. She watched the men pull one on to a steel platform where they drove hooks into it. Then the platform moved and as the log slid past the blade, she watched the bark peel back and saw white flesh emerge, naked and shining. Three times more the platform moved and then, the log squared and bereft of its covering, was hooked again and pulled to a new pile of similar lengths of wood. She saw, with a great inner excitement, that one of the men doing this task was John Fall. He was wearing a short, leather coat. She had not seen him in this before. The ear-flaps of his cap were turned down to protect him from the frost. His face was dark and she knew it carried several days' growth. She saw these things and she saw his thick body, and watching him move she knew that things were not over between them. Nor would they be, so long as his movements could affect her like this.

She walked nearer and knew that she had been seen because the shouting and singing ceased. She walked slowly to the mill and answered the greetings that the men gave her, all except John Fall. She stood and watched and waited and at last he looked at her. Then she spoke, 'Hello, John.'

'Hi!' He bent his head back to his work.

'Why won't you look at me? What are you afraid of?'

He did not answer. She allowed a moment to pass and then she said, 'Look at me, John!'

When he did, she said, 'I want you tonight.' She freed her hand from her mitt and lightly brushed sawdust from her bust. She saw his eyes following her action. That is my violence, she thought and turned from him and walked back to the frozen hill, around it and into the bush. But when she got out of their sight she began to run. She came to the school and went into the house. She could smell cooking and heard Marjorie singing in the kitchen.

He came, and they lay again in the dark room, on the narrow bed—he had been so eager, once she had started him. When that part was over and it was the time for talking; he talked and she listened.

'I'm givin' up on the taxi. I'm quittin' that. It didn't make me nothin'. It was too heavy on oil. Way I figure now is to get me a truck. I got a licence for truck drivin', all kinds of trucks I drove. When I get me a truck then I get in the money for sure.'

'Money, money, money.'

'You don't want to know what I want that money for then?'

'Why do you want the money, John?'

'I told you before. I'm quittin' this reserve. When you leave, then I'm goin' along. I got to have money for that.'

O my God! she thought. He still has that idea. He is still dreaming. Poor, dreaming John.

'I can get me a job any place. I can run the truck, maybe get me another one. We'll do good, you and me.'

'John! You are married. You have a family.'

'I'm gonna make me a family with you.'

'We can't do that.'

'You wait then. You'll see. I'll take you, this reserve is no good no more for me. I got to get off. And I got to be with you. That Anna, she's not gonna quit, you know. She's gonna stay right here with her folks and them kids gonna be all right.'

'Can't we make do with what we have got now?'

'I wish my kid was in here right now.'

'It is time you were going, John.'
'I quit out on the drinkin'. To hell with that!'
'I've got to go. Marjorie will be wondering where I am.'
'You gonna think 'bout it then?'
'Yes. I'll think about it.'
It was too dark for him to see her face.

'We're gonna have us an early spring,' they had said in February and they said it again in the first few weeks of March. They were saying it still, the prairie prophets, when the last days of March came round and passed the year on to April. 'We're gonna have us an early spring.'

Then came a morning when there was a scuttering on the stairs and a crowd of children, still wearing wet and dirty overshoes burst in on Ruth.

'See, Teacher! See!' In a small, protective hand she saw green shoots and on the faces, bright looks of hope.

SPRING

1

Hey, it's spring, Mr Littleleaf. You don't hear frogs in the city, you don't know it's spring. If I had a dollar for every frog on the Big Fish, I'd be Rockefeller.

Legs grow long in spring.
Toes twitch for mud.
Lost a winter yesterday,
Feel real good.

Springtime—time of the great release, the rising of the spirit and remembrance of the other way of life. Now a person can laugh at winter as a boy shouts at the darkness behind him; a person can take off the misery of winter along with his padding and his Long Johns, a person can put it completely out of his mind.

'It's a surprising thing—when the water is running and the catkins are out, a body forgets all about winter, 'cause he knows for sure how good this summer's gonna be.'

Spring came to the Big Fish not gently or slowly, but with a suddenness that increased the feeling of liberation. Already its armies were making inroads everywhere, even while winter still held outward sway. It came on an April morning, a morning which rose with expectancy, as if the bush had received the message from the night winds and was waiting. The breeze that arrived with dawn, crossed the snow surface and crept into the black mesh was a stranger. There was no cruelty in his breath, but he carried the sweetness from the south, a touch of warmth, a stroking of the sun.

Within days the snow began to look dirty, as true earth peeped through a million weak spots. Tree bark glowed with rising sap and although buds, in no great hurry to emerge, still held tight their sticky caps, there was a greening of the branches. With much cracking and rending, Muskrat Lake broke out of its icy strait-jacket, splitting this way and that, and from the bush came the first trickling, the first rivulets. Even though snow still surfaced the earth, beneath it the water ran, dropping always and joining, and joining and dropping again, until at last it reached the lake. Soon it poured in great torrents into the liberated lake, jostling the ice blocks and bearing the rubbish of the land, the dead leaves and insects and animals; and from the depths rose the snapping, hungry jackfish.

At the creek mouths, the Indian boys stood knee-deep and more in water with wire loops in their hands, fine wire to slip over the head of a fish and tighten behind its gills—fish for supper, fish for smoking, fish guts on the creek sides for the birds to turn over and fight for.

The prophets said, 'We need a good rain to get the frost out of the ground quickly,' but the frost was not waiting upon rain. The ice bond melted, inch by inch, and the soil particles crumbled into a new form, a slithering, clinging, unshakeable viscidity—gumbo. Along the roadsides, trees and fences carried notices reducing truck weights to half a load, and finally banning traffic altogether, even school buses, and children, white and brown alike, cheered.

The snow gave way slowly around the school. In one place where the children had churned up mud, Ruth watched a few small birds dig for seeds, their bobbing heads shining in the sun. Other birds hopped down into horse tracks to sieve the slush for the emerging animal droppings of last fall. She walked slowly, splashing her feet in the snow to help the break-up and in this way she wandered to the lake. A few spots fell on her face, the first rain in almost six months. She held back her head and let the rain strike her, until the downpour ran from her cheeks into her hair and her ears. She let it wash and wash over her. She had not realized how much she had missed it.

For days it rained, an uninterrupted downpour, and then there shone the clearest of lights, and the greens were so bright, so strong, so emerald as to gladden the hearts of the Kelly's. Among the trees came the first flutterings, but already the pussy willows hung heavily over the sloughs and the yellow dust was clouding, searching for the waiting pistils. Before long the velvet growth of early crops, bright gold patches of rape, would catch the eye. Roads would be whiskery-grey with cotton seeds. 'What with moskiters and fuzz a person don't want to stand around after church,' Mrs Barwise would say, and again this year her audience would nod agreement.

For almost a week no mail was delivered in the country districts, and children came walking, leg-weary, late and mud-laden, to school. Indian boys and girls hung cans from trees to collect the syrup drops. Above them the thieving squirrels were playing a similar game, nibbling away at the hard, sweet knobs. Across the land, plough blades curled away the soil and gulls followed in the wake, their sharp eyes missing no wriggle of pink flesh.

176

Suddenly the winds blew, warm winds, drying winds: and the water levels began to fall. Some of the smaller pools vanished completely, so that the nesting or pairing ducks were crowded together, until they filled every patch of water to the outskirts of the town. In these pools the young ducks up-ended as impudently as can-can girls, showing frillier and more downy bottoms. The winds dried the roads too. The pot holes and ruts were deep, the ridges high. A ride was a bumpy ordeal but Bruchk was oiling his great leveller, soon the roads would be bearable again. In the ditches, human debris shone every few yards—Carlings, Bohemian, Big Horn and the like, waiting to be rescued and returned to duty. The boy scouts of Redville put on their uniforms and went out along the highways and byways collecting the bottles, and their funds mounted sack by sack, cent by cent, but the little boys from the breed household behind the elevators found that their bottles weren't wanted, their help neither.

And all day long in the reserve playground, the swings squeaked under the weight of the little babies and their mothers. During recess the shadows slid up and down as the seats criss-crossed and the children screamed at the tingling in their stomachs.

'Teacher, today I seen them Spring Chickens dancing.'

'Me, I seen a gopher, right in the road he was diggin'.'

'You never!'

'I did too!'

Spring brought more than green grass to Ivor Jones. It was night time and he had began his supper when he heard tapping on his door. He went to answer it with meat tangled in his teeth and his fingers were at work on this when he greeted his visitor. 'Yeah? What you want?'

'Am I speaking to Mr——?'

'Jones. What is it?'

'May I come in, please?'

'Can't it be said right here?'

'It would be better if it could be more private.'

'Don't see how this ain't private, and I don't buy things, Mister. Come in then. Shut the door, I'm eatin'. Don't want no flies in here.'

'I'm sorry to disturb you. I should tell you before we go any further that I am an inspector of the postal services.'

'Is that right?'

'Yes. I should also tell you that I'm here because of complaints about the way in which the mail has been handled in Upcreek. We understand that your attitude towards the public has been, let us say, unco-operative. There are also complaints, and I say this without prejudice of course, complaints about you drinking during hours of business. There is a specific complaint here.' He paused. Ivor used a piece of bread to wipe and re-wipe his plate. The bread went into his mouth and was followed by a mug full of coffee and that by a bout of coughing and spluttering.

'Now, what was it you was saying, Mister?'

'You heard what I said, and I must add that your attitude confirms our suspicions. I would like you to be thinking over your answer to the complaints I have mentioned. Meanwhile there is another matter which I have seen for myself. As I came here I saw a man going away and he was taking mail. By my watch, about two hours after you should have been finished. You know the rules about timing, I suppose.'

'That was Matt Flanagan, Mister. He's my friend. He can pick up his mail any goddam time he wants.'

'In this position you don't have any friends. Everybody is treated the same way and has the same privileges. I'm going to have to put this in my report. Now, is there anything you would like to say about all this? I'm prepared to listen.'

'There sure is, man,' Ivor said, and got to his feet. 'Get the hell out of my house!'

'Now look here, Mr——'

'Mr Shit! Get the hell gone before I hit you with a goddam axe. You shined-up coyote. Git!'

'This will go into——'

'Git out, you bastard!' Ivor turned to the table and snatched at the plate. He hurled it after the departing investigator, and then turned and kicked over the chair. 'I should of smelled him at the door. Oh, those sons of bitches! Those goddam government bastards!'

For some time he fumed, then he went to the office and found pen and paper and began a letter:

Dear Lester,
    One of your snoopies was crawling around here today and last I seen of him he was running with his tail between his legs which he won't likely stop till he gets to Ottawa. And so I'm telling you to save you writing to me that I quit and you can have my job and you can stick it right up your ass.
                    With best wishes from,
                    Ivor Jones.

After re-reading this he crossed out the last four words and wrote over them, 'you know where.'

178

'Goddam,' he said, 'he's Prime Minister. I've got to let him have his bit of dignity.' Then he prepared a notice:

I QUIT.
THIS IS NOT A POST OFFICE
NO MORE.
GO TO HELL! THANK YOU!

He took this out and pinned it to the front of the house. Suddenly he felt very good. He turned towards the dark-faced store across the street and shook his fist. 'I don't know how you done it, you German bugger, but you're behind this, sure enough. But by Christ! I'm gonna camp you, you old goat. I'm going to visit up with you every day, man. You're gonna get sick of me comin' in that door, so help me! I'm startin' to enjoy what bit of life I got left. This town's sure gonna give me laughs to even out, that's for sure.'

Night-flying geese honked overhead as they sensed near-by water and Ivor, hearing them, took their calling for approval of his words and shouted up to them, 'You're goddam right.' Then he went back into the house and stood six bottles in line on the table. He began his usual search for the bottle opener.

John Fall did not keep his promise to Ruth that he would not drink. If there had to be blame for this then it was hers. Twice he had visited the school but did not see her. The nights were becoming lighter and people were about, and she was not prepared to take risks like he was. He saw her with Flanagan, and once he saw Bruchk, the farmer go from her house and apprehension began and increased when he could not be with her. When they did finally meet he hurled himself like a great moth against her glow and he was bruised. She took him quickly and sent him away, but she did not tell him it was in fear of being discovered with him, and despair attacked him. He was sure that she was cooling towards him and that at any time she might end their affair as suddenly as she had begun it.

She could do that by walking away, by quitting the reserve. She could do it and be gone and he would not know. He knew that no matter how her body had enjoyed its submissions it had returned after each to its fuller life and that he had neither part nor place in that life. It was only in drink that he could forget this. It was in drink that he could pretend her as his full woman. Drunk, he could forget how Flanagan and Bruchk were able to walk in and out of her house.

He began to hate Flanagan.

And he began to think about one way in which he could take her. It was not enough to put himself inside her, he must leave himself inside her after he had gone away. She must be got with his child. This idea, sprung from his despair, became as beautiful a dream as he could fashion. He imagined her as great-bellied and heavy-breasted and these thoughts gave him such ecstasy that he had to nurse them alone in the bush.

But Ruth was too careful. Even in her wildest moments she was too careful to be caught that way. He realized that it would never be managed in the house, in her place. He must get her into the bush. He must get her drunk and in the bush.

When he was drunk himself it was easier to believe in such a happening.

One night, when the girls were getting ready for a ride into Smallhill with Flanagan, he stole into the school and waited. He caught Ruth when she was going down to the basement. She would have sent him away, but his sudden appearance from the darkness below the stairs surprised her. Before she could exert any authority he had seized her. He encircled her waist with one arm and used the other hand to grip her buttocks. To quieten him he allowed herself to be led into the well at the foot of the stairs. Here they stayed for a few moments, and even though she was afraid, she felt the responses begin as he touched her.

'Jeez!' he whispered, his face close against hers, and she smelt the alcohol on his breath.

'You have been drinking,' she said, and tried to push him away. He was too strong. His hand gripped her and tore at her and she began to fight. 'Get off!' she hissed. 'Get off me!' He dragged open her dress and began to hurt her. Then suddenly he released his hold, and ran in a low crouch up the stairs. There was a faint flash of glass and she heard a squeaking hinge, and knew that he had gone into her classroom. Then the outer door opened and she heard Flanagan say, 'Who's that?'

'It's me, Matt. I was going out for some fresh air.'

'You haven't time. We're going right now. Aren't you ready?'

'I will be in a minute,' she answered. She was amazed that her voice could be so calm when her mind was so agitated, her fingers working so feverishly. 'I'll change my dress. We'll be out in a minute.'

'Hurry it up, then. I've been dry for hours.'

John Fall heard them speaking. As he listened to her voice he grinned. 'Jeez, I fooled you this time, Matt, that's for sure,' he murmured. He waited in the room until he heard the girls go past and the outside door bang, and then a car engine disturbed the silence and a beam of light passing across the classroom wall showed the flag and the framed picture of the Queen. He heard the car quicken as it reached the trail and the engine falter momentarily at the gear-changing, and then he was alone. 'I sure fooled you that time, Matt. Jeez, that Ruth! She was sure as hell hot and wantin'. She was only foolin' that fight. She was wantin' sure enough. Why she got to go out tonight! I'm that wantin' for her too. Aw hell!'

He went out of the school and crossing to Matt's house he tried the door. It was not locked so he went inside. He did not need a light, he knew what he wanted and he found it in the kitchen closet. He took out four bottles of beer and put one in each pocket and the other two inside his coat. 'I don't get her, I get this anyways. Jeez, I got to have somethin'.' Then he left the house.

Before he had gone very far he met John Blood and Joey Bird. He said, 'Hi fellas!' and they answered 'Hi!' and then they stood around and smoked.

'You fellas like a beer, uh?'

'Jesus, don't I, man! This old mouth, dry worse'n a summer day.'

'Sure John—did you ever know. Bottle of beer right this minute, that's what I gotta have.'

'Look at what I got then.'

They knocked the caps off against a tree, except John Blood who got impatient and knocked off the neck. 'You don't get no two cents on that bastard, John.'

'I didn't pay no two cents on any of these, anyways.' When they had finished the beer and tossed the bottles into the darkness, John Fall said, 'Jeez, I could sure go for a beer drink right now. for me it's one of them nights. It's like that for me. You guys ain't got no drink, uh?'

'I had wine, you sure could get it—if I had any,' Joey Bird said; and John Blood told him, 'Old man Greenery, he always keeps some by his place. Trades him off, he does, that old man.'

'What for does he trade these days?'

'Guns—then he sells those guns back. Or maybe for money. You got any money?'

'I ain't got no money, not right now.'

'Then what else you got? What else you trade in with him?'

'I got me that old thirty-thirty. It don't fire none anyways.

Maybe I get that old guy to trade on that. He won't go try that gun, he won't do that, uh?'

'Sweet spring, no! He won't do no tryin'. Hey, you bring that gun, John. Maybe me, I'll get me a pair of boots. Maybe they'll be okay for a couple of bottles.'

'I got dollar fifty,' said John Blood. 'I'll throw him in for three beers. That's what he says—fifty cents a bottle.'

'He's old bastard, askin' fifty cents for a ten cent bottle.'

'He asks that 'cause he's got the beer and we ain't. That's why he asks that much.'

'I'd like for to shoot him up the ass.'

'Not with that gun you couldn't. Ho! Ho!'

'Ho! Ho!'

'That old bastard!'

'He's sure a bastard!'

'Hey, let's go get that beer, uh!'

They approached the farm quietly and John Blood went in to do the talking, because he had once done some stooking for the old man. The other two waited in the shadows by the barn where the breed soon joined them.

'Okay, you guys,' he said. 'Give me the things—I've got to take them in—leave them over by the door. In thirty minutes I go back. He likes them, the beer is outside for us.'

'What is thirty minutes?' John Fall said after the breed had gone again.

'Damn long son-of-a-gun time,' Joey Bird answered.

'That's for sure! I get me more thirsty every day of that thirty minutes!'

Then they became silent. John crouched down against the barn wall. He could smell the cattle in there; the strong smell of urine came to him through the open knot holes from which the insulation had blown. He crouched and thought of the beer and of the girl and he thought: I could get her a kid. I could sure give her a kid. I get her in the bush, get her drunk, I could stuff a kid right in there. Then she's really my woman, she'd shack up then, for sure. Next time may be I put one there. I show that goddam woman. She don't say 'No John,' no more then. Jeez, I get her in the bush, I make her shout! Sure I make her shout that time! She's got to go. She's got to go!

They drank the beer at John's place and the fire was high and everybody was singing, even the children. And, man, was it hot—yessir, it sure was! Anna drank too, and then George Falltime came in with a whole jug; he swore it was store wine.

182

'What the hell! That wood alcohol all yeasted up!'
'You goddam liar! This hundert per cent. Sure is.'
'That horse piss I drink it just the same!'

It was a good party, though Joey and John Blood got to fighting and John Blood cut Joey's hand and his blood got all over the place. After the visitors had gone and the children were asleep in the corners, John Fall took hold of his wife, but she was pregnant and she pushed him away and told him, 'Nossir. You gotta wait. Not any more. Not this time.'

'Jesus!' he shouted at her. 'What I care! I know a white belly! I know it just like that,' and he pointed to her distended stomach. 'Just like that I know it. Sure! Any goddam time I want!'

And Anna laughed and laughed, and slowly, inevitably, silence descended on the cabin.

When Flanagan had seated the girls in the beer parlour he went to the phone, cranked it and took down the ear piece.

'Get me Bruchk's place,' he said and the girl answered, 'Sure.'

'Hi, Bill!' he said. 'This is Matt. We're here. Yeah, she's here too. You asked me to call you, I did it. It's your funeral, boy.'

He went back to the table and within half an hour the outer door opened and Bruchk walked in. He came to them and said, 'Well, hi! Can I join you?'

Ruth looked up and smiled at him. Flanagan asked, 'What are you doin' here? Sure, get yourself a chair.'

They had a pleasant evening but throughout it Ruth's thoughts kept returning to John Fall and the way in which he had behaved. She knew that drink had played its part. It and her refusal had inflamed him and lifted him over the danger line. For he was a danger. She saw that for the first time, and realized that he could hurt her in more ways than one. At any moment when he was drinking—right now, even, while she sat with her friends, he could be speaking to others about her. Once the boasting began there would be no reticence. He would expose her, the private woman, her actions—tell of her behaviour, repeat her words. This could happen at any time when he was feeling thwarted by her, or at any time when he was drinking. Perhaps right now. She became very afraid.

She worried about it while the others talked. She turned over in her mind all the possibilities in the situation. If he had not already done this, two things might keep him silent. His continued use of her and his hope of a future with her. Once he had lost those he had everything to gain, as an Indian and as a man, by breaking their secret. Before they left the beer parlour she had decided what she would do. She had planned to spend Easter in the city with Marjorie. She would use the occasion to book a flight home and would leave directly school ended. Meanwhile she would continue the affair, but in such safety as she could. And she would tell him nothing; she would let him nurse his dreams.

As they walked from the beer parlour she noticed that Flanagan and Marjorie had gone on ahead, leaving her with Bruchk. She was wondering about them when he spoke. 'Did you enjoy that, Ruth?'

'Yes, thank you. Did you?'

'Oh, I sure did. But you had me worried in there. You were kind of quiet. I thought maybe you wanted to go.'

'Was I quiet? I didn't mean to be. Matt doesn't give anybody else much of a chance when he gets going, does he?'

'And Marjorie too. She sure likes to jaw.'

'Do you come here often?'

'No. Not often. Sometimes I get things to do in Smallhill. I look in then, 'case I see somebody I know.'

'We come quite a lot now, two or three times a week. Perhaps you'll catch us in here again.'

'I hope so, it was real nice.'

They did not say any more, but as they approached the white car his hand sought hers. She took it and they walked the rest of the way like this, only parting when she saw the others. She had much to think about on the drive back home and Bruchk was an added complication. But this was not unexpected and neither was it so urgent as her other preoccupation.

The city was still in love with spring. Legs were on display everywhere. Gone the slacks and the boots, and in their place were the sleek, shining, shaven limbs in the clicking, high-lifting heels; and the clerks, the salesmen and the city walkers lingered between blocks, admiring wishing and regretting.

The acres of glass frontage were wild with the intoxication of spring. Gay outfits swaggered and boasted, sometimes in ranks that marched boldly down to the awe-stricken wanting eyes on the other side of the glass; sometimes in eye-catching loneliness, but always in the pre-determined pinks of this spring. Always with the one leg thrust forward, the coat swinging open, the head held back to catch a ceilinged sun, though the faces turned to the neon strips were already black-lacquered and shining.

The two girls added theirs to the worshipping eyes at the altars of the window-dressers. For two days they shopped, falling often

184

to temptation because they were lovely days, the city was so bright, its populace so happy. It was selling time for sure, almost as good as Christmas.

Then Marjorie departed for her cousin's home in Redville. Ruth waited until the Northstar pulled out of its underground park and then went to the travel agency. With the reservation in her pocket she felt more secure than she had since the night when John had fought with her. In a few weeks she would leave him and the reserve for ever. Meantime she could use Flanagan and Marjorie as protection, to ward him off. But the brightness of the city seemed to grow less after Marjorie had left and finally dulled into boredom. Her hotel room was too small, the streets were too hot, she was too much alone among crowds. There was something else, too. Perhaps it was the heat, or the freedom from worry about him that made her think such a lot about John Fall. She capitulated at midday on Friday. She was waiting to cross at the lights on 98th and 103rd when she accepted her need. Danger or no, she was hungry for him. She saw him so strongly. He comes, she thought, walking to me with that wonder, bringing wonder to me, the wonder of man. And I love it.

She turned around and went straight back to the hotel, where she paid her account and then drove out to the reserve. There was a question which occurred to her on the way—how will I get over this need when he is no longer available to me? She pushed it out of her mind, it lacked the urgency of her immediate need.

During the late evening she searched for him, wandering from deserted saw-mill to the lakeside, and walked many paths before dusk came down to end her efforts. The classroom lights shone a message into the night but it was not answered. There was no visitor to rise, ghost-like, from the darkness of the stairs and drag her into that well-known darkness. The scents of the night came to her, the moth-needing flowers, the breathing forest, the inevitable tinge of smoke. She listened to its stories, screech, clink of can, sudden barking to west and farther west, the incessant throbble, the honk of a startled duck, the loneliness of a distant drum.

Ayee–a! Ayee–a!

She lay, clad in white froth on clean, candy strips, alien in this night yet knowing it, wanting it. But the man who would have brought it with himself did not come. There was never a tap, never a scratch on the screen.

On the following morning Ruth drove to Upcreek to get the mail. Since the trouble about Julie and Marjorie's father she had not been to the store, but now she found that she had to go there if she wanted the mail, because it was here that a temporary post office had been set up. So she went, and watched the owl-eyes blinking through the embarrassed moment and saw the thick fingers tighten on the counter. Then, 'Oh, the mail . . . uh, sure. Right away I get it.'

She waited while he shuffled the letters and parcels, dropping some and bending to pick them up, bending so that the bulges almost hid the belt. She thought of Julie lying underneath that mountain of sagging flesh and being sought by that mouth, and she felt repelled, disgusted by the waste of the girl's beauty. He pushed the mail towards her and she thought: you are what they mean when they talk about dirty old men. What is it that makes old men so? You males are all the same, men or animals, you won't hand over to your young. Why is this so? Why are you so desperate?

Then she felt a quick sadness for him. He must have been magnificent once, he must have been sought after. Then his time had come but he had not been able to accept it. 'Who will you go after now?' she asked silently, and as if in answer she heard a familiar voice say, 'Miss Lancaster,' and turning, saw John Fall.

'Hullo, John.'

God, she thought. How can I be so calm! How can I be so bloody calm?

She got some things; had them put into a box and paid for them. Then she looked again at him. 'I am going back to the reserve if you would like a ride,' she said. He sure would. He walked behind her and carried her box and they were so smooth about it that they deceived even that old deceiver behind the counter.

In the comparative seclusion of the reserve road he put his hands on her. 'Not here, John,' she said. 'I won't be able to drive.'

'We could stop the car. Take a walk.'

'Into there?'

'Sure!'

'No, John. I don't want to do that. But tonight. Can you come tonight?'

'Sure. It's a good thing I seen you. I was goin' away in the mornin'.'

'You're going away? Where to?'

'Huntin'. Don't I have to get you a pelt? Didn't I promise?'

'The beaver.'

'That's right. It's time to go get those guys. I got it all fixed for the mornin'. Goin' up there with George. That's my brother, you know.'

'I know he's your brother.'

186

She thought quickly. He was going away. It might be for a long time, there was no telling how long it would be before he returned once he got deep into the bush. It could even become weeks. She thought quickly, but the trail was approaching its end and she was pushed into a reckless decision. Marjorie was away, so was Flanagan. She asked, 'Could you stay all night?'

'That's kind of crazy, ain't it? All night? Some guy could walk in on us. Matt could walk in on us.'

'Matt won't be here. And he doesn't walk into my bedroom.'

'You mean we're gonna stop in there?'

'Where else?'

'Jeez!'

'Would she ask where you were staying?'

'Anna?'

'Yes.'

'No. I don't guess she would. Long as I come back with a fist full of pelts she's not gonna say nothin'. I don't know about it though. It could be crazy. If I get catched in there.'

'I'm the one to worry about that. Make your mind up, John, I'm not begging you, but make your mind up, we'll be at the school in a minute.'

'I'll come.'

'And stay?'

'Sure.'

'We'll have a party,' she promised. 'I'll get some beer and we'll have a party.' He whistled and she laughed and said, 'Then I'll show you my room. It's got the bonniest bed.'

'Christ!' he swore.

'And then you can go and catch my pelt.'

'I sure as hell will. I'm gonna bring you the best goddam pelt you ever seen. If I got to kill every beaver in them damn rivers, I sure will, but I'll get it. The best you ever seen.' In his enthusiasm he reached out and put his hand on her leg.

She said, 'Don't!'

'Please, Ruth.'

'Not now.'

'Just a little touch.'

She stopped the car and said, 'Out you get. Or you'll spoil it for tonight.' He grumbled but she insisted and he obeyed. She laughed through the window at his rueful face and said, 'It will be worth waiting for, John, I promise you.'

She drove past the school without stopping and went on through the reserve to the highway. At Smallhill she collected two crates of beer and some steaks. During the remainder of the afternoon she anticipated the coming night. She stripped her bed and changed the sheets, brought in another pillow and a chair. She set out the table in the kitchen and prepared a supper. There was a lot of pleasure in this. She could have been planning a party, a going-away party, a staying-away party too, she thought. Our days are numbered, John, and they count up to this one night. She went often to the bedroom, to stand and lean against the doorpost and look down on the two pillows. She knew that he would be in some near-by shack, watching a clock or taking time checks from a radio.

At one minute to nine, the arranged time, she went to the bathroom and ran the water for a bath. When John arrived a few minutes later he entered the kitchen, and not finding her, walked through the house. She was pouring salts into the steaming water. 'You gonna take a bath?' he asked.

'I've had mine. This is for you.'

'Me! Jeez, I don't want no bath, not now I don't.'

'Well, you're going to have one. Yes, John. I want you to. It's important, it's part of the night.'

He went into the corridor and she came after him to the doorway. 'It's crazy,' he said. 'I want to do somethin' else, not takin' a bath, you know that.'

'Please, John. Come on. What are you frightened of?' She went back to the bathroom and dried her hands on a towel. Then she turned, and as she had hoped, he had followed her. 'Stand still,' she said, and began to unbutton his shirt. She pulled it free from his slacks. 'Please let me do it,' she asked when he would have stopped her. Later, as she knelt over him, soaping his chest, she said, 'This is not the first time. I've seen you before, John. I saw your three beards long ago.' He looked blankly at her and she added, 'At the creek. One day last year. You were swimming. Don't you remember?'

'I remember. And you was there?'

'Yes. Turn over!'

'That makes you a proper peeper, for sure.'

'For sure. How do you feel now?'

'Like real good. You gettin' in here with me?'

She laughed at him. I have seen you before, she thought, but I have never had you like this. When I marry, this is what I shall want to do. To have, to see and to minister to. That will be my loving.

'No,' she answered. 'I have work to do. I'm going to start

188

supper. Stay here until I call, then come to the kitchen. I have put a big towel out for you to wrap yourself in if you want to. Would you like a bottle of beer now?'

'I sure would. Ho, Gee!'

She went out taking his clothes with her. She put them in the washer and set it in motion. When she gave him the beer he asked about his clothes and what she had done with them. 'You don't need to worry,' she told him. 'I have locked the doors. There will be no one to see you except me.'

Nor was there.

Drums from somewhere.

Boom! Boo-boom!

And other things. Sinatra for a while but who wanted that smooth pretender when nakedness was rough and almost cruel, and painted, and scented sweet or salty. Food. Wine drunk from a navel. Things such as these, on and on and on, because neither wanted to hurry.

But no one else.

Ruth was awakened by piercing cramps in her arm. She eased it free from the weight of the sleeping head. He turned and snuggled down against her, but she slid from him and got out of bed. She crossed to the window and looked out. It was still early, light but not sunny. She untied the braiding from her waist and put it on to the dressing table, then she went into the main room where she saw the debris of the previous night scattered across the floor, her own clothes, empty bottles, cushions. 'White tail,' he had called her. 'Like them deer. They got white ass like you.'

'You men, you must use names like that for us. I had a man once who called me a name like that.'

'What was it he called you?'

'It doesn't matter. You have the tail here, not me. And it isn't white.' She was sorry the moment she had said it but he hadn't noticed. 'White tail.' Another name for her to remember.

She picked up the cushions and put them in place again and then went into the kitchen. I suckled him like a child, she thought as she filled the coffee pot. What a quiet morning it is out there. Quiet in here, too. The storm is over, the violence is ended. It is a good time to return him to his bush. And about time, too! God, I've been lucky to get away with this.

While she waited for the coffee she pressed his clothes. She put on his shirt and buttoned it. It reached almost to her knees. Then she went in to waken him. She stopped to look at herself in the mirror, caught a stray wisp of hair and then sat on the bed. He was still sleeping and she drew back the sheet, slowly so as not to disturb him. She saw and looked at him, at the deep brown chest and the pale lower body, at the strong sinews, relaxed now but capable of such tension. The uncovering had disturbed him and he stirred, lifted a knee. She thought of his strength when he had carried her into this room and then she thought of his weakness, of his sad dream of escape, his hopeless plans. She remembered the description 'people without a tomorrow.' Here was one, building a tomorrow around himself, sleeping on it, perhaps dreaming about it, not knowing that he had just helped end it. She reached out a finger and stroked him with its tip and his eyes opened.

'It is time, John.'

He sat up and reached for her, but she moved away. 'Not now. Breakfast is ready and going cold. You must eat before you leave and you can't stay too long.' She slipped out of his shirt and threw it to him and then wrapped herself in a dressing gown. She sat on the bed while he dressed. Then he came to her and knelt with his arms around her.

'Jeez! I don't want to go!'

'You must. You have to go a long way.'

'I don't want to go there neither. I don't want to go up there no more. I want to quit that bush, I want to get the hell out with you. I'm all finish with this place, and the bush and all that. I want it nice, like we got it here. We can do that, Ruth, can't we? This summer, uh?'

'Yes, John. Later this summer.'

'You gonna go with me then?'

'I'm thinking about it.'

'You know what I think right now? I think, to hell with goin' up there today. I think I'm gonna stay on the reserve until you quit school.'

'What about my skin?'

'It's sure nice, that skin. Gimme a peek, Ruth.'

'My pelt, John. What about this lovely pelt you've promised so often?'

'Oh, sure. That pelt. Say, what for you want that pelt anyways? You never told me. One pelt no good for nothin'.'

'I'd keep it right here. Next to my bed, so that I'd have something nice and warm to stand on every morning.'

'Jeez! I'm wishin' I'm that pelt, too.'

'Why, John?'

'What I see when I look up there. Man!'

He tried one more trick before he left. It was hard for her not to smile when he made the suggestion. 'Say, Ruth. When I bring back that pelt—what you gonna give me for that?'

'Whatever you ask. Twenty dollars, ten dollars.'

'I don't want no money.'

'What do you want?'

He pretended to think and she restrained her smile. Then he said, 'I'll tell you. If that's a real premium pelt I get for you, then you go in the bush with me for one time. How's that, uh? Jeez! We'd really have a good time in there.'

'Bring the beaver first, then I'll tell you what I think it's worth.'

'We'll make a party up there. You and me and nobody else in that bush, Jesus!'

After his departure she went into the bush and walked some of its trails again. It was in full growth, light now and airy and full of life. She went in quite deep, following a trail that she had taken in the Fall, and came in time to the stretch of moss that she had lain on that day. She sat there again now and the sounds and the scents which surrounded her, filled her with nostalgia for those early days.

It was John Blood then, she thought. John Blood and his poor dead Julie. But that was before John Fall. This is where he would like to bring me, here where I could not control him. He would stretch me here, and there would be no mercy for me then. He would have his way. She felt the moss springing beneath her, the bush bed he would use without sheet or pillows. Then she got up and returned to the lake and followed its shore until she found a grassy shelf overhanging its water. She seated herself there and began to day-dream.

Sun diamonds sparkled in the water. A school of tiny fishes hovered and changed direction and depth with perfect precision. Their shadows stroked the golden mud beneath. A bug trailed a fine ladder across the silken surface and she watched it approach her reflection. She pulled a grass stem to use as a teasing wand, but as she reached it towards the bug something came fast from the farther gloom. There was a flash of white and a swirl of water and the bug was gone.

Even here, in this peaceful moment of sun warmth and silence, savagery lurked and nothing was safe from it, however small or harmless. Wherever there is beating blood, she thought, violence sleeps, and at that moment a shot sounded and was followed by a chorus of shouts.

She got to her feet and saw a crowd of young boys running towards her. One of them held something in his hand and as she watched she saw him strike at it with his clenched fist; again and again he struck. She realized that the thing he held was a duck and that it was not dead. She ran at him and seized and shook him. 'Stop it, you little beast! Stop it!' she shouted.

The boy's mouth opened wide and the lips were turned away from the teeth. She glared into the dark eyes and saw at first only blankness. Then came bewilderment and a loosening of the lips and jaw. She calmed a little and began to plead a case for the fluttering bundle in his hand. As she did so, bewilderment gave way to suspicion and then to scorn and insolence.

'Let it go!' she said.

'It's my duck. My dad shot him. It's mine. You can't have him. I'm gonna bang his head on a rock so he's dead and we can eat him.'

'Let it go.'

'No! He's mine!'

She sought desperately for a way out of her involvement, one that would spare herself but would also prevent further hurt to the creature. Money! she thought. Money! She was about to offer this, when suddenly Bruchk, of all people, was there, one big hand on the boy's shoulder and the other taking the duck.

'Give it to me, boy. That's right.' He examined the duck and said, 'It's a gonner.' Then he swung his arm and the bird made its last flight and plummeted into the water. 'You get your dog, boy. He'll fetch it for you and it will be dead for sure. Go on! Beat it!'

The boy nodded and grinned and ran with his friends. She said, 'Thank you, Bill. I didn't know what the devil to do. He was hitting the poor thing.'

'I guess he would. They're born with that, it's huntin' you know. Once they've put their mark on it, it belongs to them. They can do what they like with it, and don't bother about what anybody says. Like the weasels that way, same kind of hunters.' He looked across the water and added, 'Best way to finish it off. That's how they got to go in the end.' They turned from the lake and its spreading rings and she saw the grader, still and silent on the road.

'Did you hear me shout?' she asked.

'No. Can't hear anythin' up there, that old man makes too much noise for me to hear anythin'. No, I didn't hear, but I saw you.'

'I screamed like a squaw.'

'You couldn't never be no squaw.'

'You didn't hear me.'

'Is Matt back yet?'

'No. I'm all alone.'

'Would you like to come over and visit? Christine's home for the day.' The suggestion appealed to her. It would cut into the long day that she must spend before either Flanagan or Marjorie arrived. There would be company, she could see the farm and its animals.

'Yes. I'd like that, Bill. What time should I come?'

'Any time. Right now, if that's okay.'

'Give me an hour.'

'Sure! I should be home by then myself.'

In the early afternoon she drove through Upcreek. It presented, beneath its brooding elevators, a picture of a town easy-going about its business. She saw two farmers leaning against a pick-up outside the store; caught a glimpse of movement in the dark maw of the garage; saw two boys pitching ball on the lot watched by a group of girls—elbows on knees, hands lost in hair, heads lost in dreams. An old lady slept in a chair in the sun.

Arthur McKenzie drove past, sitting high behind the steering wheel and wearing a jacket and tie. She thought he smiled, and she responded half-heartedly in case she was mistaken. A cat ran from a doorway and scuttled around a corner. Then the town was behind her, an experienced town, with a serenity born of the sufferings and acceptance of the bruises of time and weather. A town tolerant of dust and flies, patient under the paint-peeling sun and the harshness of winter. It would survive many things and, although she had walked its streets, when she left it would scarcely notice her departure.

The tall farmer said, 'She sure does bounce that little buggy around some, that English girl. Wouldn't care for her to be out in my Chev!'

'Nor me!' the fat farmer answered and carried on with his interrupted story. 'So I get the vet and he gives the cow those needles, try to get the goddam thing to vomit, but she cain't.'

'She cain't vomit at all?'

'No, she cain't. She got something in there all blocking her up. For five days she don't eat nothing'. I try everything. I even lie her down and punch her in the gut but it's no use, she cain't throw up.'

'So?'

'So I sent her and they did her. Know what she gotten in there?'

'What she gotten in there, Tom?'

'She got one them goddam, plasticated bags in there. Couldn't digest the goddam thing. I lose me a good cow for hamburger meat.'

'Jeez! That'd make me goddam sore.'

'Me, too, it made sore.'

'How you figure that gotten in there, that bag?'

'Well, I figure this; maybe this cow gone down by the pool for drinkin', and maybe those goddam picnic guys, they threw this bag down there and she pick up this lump, and that's how it happened.'

'I guess they come around there all the time, uh? It's good fishin' and their kids running around, and then they make a picnic.'

'No more they won't! I figure I beat out that deal. I trucked over a load of horse-shit, tipped it close by there. Man! You should see those flies—inch-long they are!'

'Oh Jeez, don't they bite, too!'

'They sure do. No, I reckon I fixed that one good.'

'Howdy, Mr McKenzie!'

'Hi there, Mr McKenzie!' they called as the elevator manager drove slowly past, giving them a nod of recognition.

Ivor Jones stumped by on his way to the store. He wore a high, white straw hat to keep the sun off his face during the crossing of the street, and he had suspenders over the striped, collarless shirt. His pants were an inch higher than the tops of his laced-up boots, and they had the extra precaution of a thick belt, decorated with old brasses. The farmers saluted him also, again in unison.

'Hi Ivor! How're you doin' there?'

'Goddam hot, uh?'

'For sure!'

'Don't he got that Helmut by the short hairs though?'

'He sure has. He's a mean old sod for sure, that Ivor.'

'They say he's been around tellin' all those Indians to switch their allowances before next pay-out, so Helmut won't get his hands on the money they owe him.'

'Is that right?'

'Yeah, anybody owes money to Helmut, good luck to that guy is what I say.'

'For sure.'

Little Moise, returning to his work after the quick reconnaissance, wiped his fingers through the thick dust, leaving a shiny streak along the fender. Bet she's a honey, that one—a real honey. Them quiet ones like her, I'll bet they're real honies underneath. Jeez, I'll bet they're good, those quiet women. 'Cept it would take for ever to get her going.

Then Arthur McKenzie drove his car in, slowly, carefully, two feet clear on either side of the door post.

'Usual service, Mr McKenzie?' He asked brightly, wiping his hands on a rag, prior to opening the door for him.

'Yes, please, Moise . . . don't forget the spare.'

'Nossir, I won't. Do I bring it over when she's ready?'

'Yes, please—I would have had it over this morning but Joan wasn't feeling too well.'

'Gee I'm sorry about that, Mr McKenzie.'

'Oh, it's nothing. It's the heat, I expect.'

But Little Moise knew that it wasn't the heat. Joan McKenzie hadn't been to the garage since picnic day. He knew that she would never come there again. He knew it wasn't the heat to blame.

Down the street a fly stroked clean his tarsals and took to wing, soaring, dipping and circling, and dropped on to the cheek of the sleeping old lady. She woke with a start and struck at the offender. 'Git to hell, you dratted thing! Ain't no peace, no place!'

It was a quiet town and the afternoon sun was warm. The dust Ruth had caused was already settling back on its street.

2

I guess the men will be out for beaver right now. Lots of pelts, lots of money, lots of eats, lots of wine. God bless those little beavers, too.

For the first time Bruchk had her to himself. The sun aided him, making the afternoon lazy with its heat—their progress was leisurely, and she saw the riches of his work, the golden wealth of his land. They walked together around the farm and through the uncleared thickets. They went without hurry and stopped often to sit upon a rail or smell the sweeter air in the shadow of a spruce. He spoke freely now that he was on familiar ground, showing her his life though he spoke of his work and his livestock.

They walked by Johnnie Walker's Slough where there was still timber and he told her of the different wood and the use for each. 'Spruce, that's for building. It's the best timber we have for that. That's willow, we take it for pickets. Pickets? Fencing, you know. Shape the end into a spike and drive it into the ground, then you string them with wire, like over there. That is tamrack, it's for line poles, it don't rot in the ground. There's a lot of money in this timber, it's been real good for me; it built my house and got me into the hogs. I'd hate for it all to go. I like to keep a little, you know.'

'How long will it be, Bill, before you've cleared the rest of this land and have crops growing on it?'

'Gee, I don't know for sure. It's slow. It took me years to do what I have already. There's a lot of muskeg in the basins . . . you know, that's peat land, but first it's got to be drained and then burned, I guess, though now they do say that it's better not burned. It'll need lime too, I'll have to think about that. Then there's a lot of bush. That's got to go. Could I get a cat in there, buy one I mean, I'd get it done faster. I think I could finance one if I hired it out; down on the Beach, lots of cottagers want roads putting in. I could do a lot of work if I had a cat. All the time I could be using it here, too.'

'What! And do the grading as well? How can you manage all that work?'

'Days are long. There's time . . . I see my crops spreading more.'

'Yes. I suppose that is a reward—to see the land in use and know you caused it. It must be! There's creation in it.'

'I like to see the earth come all over green. For so long it's white; then it's black; and then the first green comes. I like that.'

Yes, she thought, you would. You are a gentle man, a kind man. You are a man of the land. I hope your land is good to you.

She followed him from the grain to the buildings and they inspected the hogs, the young litters in their compartmented sty. They watched the older piglets in their enclosures running loose in the sun; listened to the scolding hens, and then walked across to the pasture, to the long-backed sows whose lines of dugs flapped along their bellies. A hairy one caught her eye and she said, 'Look at that one, isn't she huge?' and saw immediately that Bruchk was embarrassed, and then realised why. She had pointed out a boar, and now that gentleman, as if he had heard her remark and felt the insult keenly, scattered the females that surrounded him and stalked away, uttering great, straw-blowing snorts from his gaping nostrils.

'Isn't he handsome?' she said, but the farmer had moved on. She watched the boar trampling at the earth, and she stared, she could not help herself, at his enormous swinging testicles. Then realizing that Bruchk was waiting for her she went to him. 'You have only one boar, do you, for all those pigs?'

'Just the one.'

'He's a grand old man. I'll bet he's spoiled. I bet they all fight over him.' But Bruchk didn't answer; he was working the long handle of the pump and the streak of water scattered the inquisitive hens.

'This is the only water we got,' he told her. 'But I could get a pump rigged up and run a pipe into the house.' It was said almost as an offer, and she knew that though it was not intentional on his part, everything was being offered to her along with himself. He was wooing her with his pride for and love of his land. She could not let him continue. She said, 'I'm going home, Bill.'

'Home?' Puzzlement knitted his brow. 'But Christine's makin' supper for us.'

'No, Bill. I mean to England. I'm going home when school ends.'

'You're not. Not really?'

'Yes.'

'Don't you like it here?'

'I love it, Bill.'

'Then . . . why?'

'You wouldn't understand. I couldn't explain—I don't really know myself. I want to go. I have to go.'

'Will it be for good?'

'I don't know. I'm not sure about that. I could come back.'

'I sure hope you do. Jeez, we're gonna miss you, me and Christine both. You know best, I guess. I sure hope you do come back. Maybe you will, Ruth.'

'Yes. It depends.'

'Could we do something? Maybe you've been too lonely down there. You don't have to be lonely, you should visit more. We'd be happy if you'd come to us more often.'

'You have been very good, Bill. You couldn't have been kinder, you and Matt and Marjorie. I'm so grateful to all of you.'

'I guess we couldn't persuade you then. To stop here, I mean.'

'You can try, Bill. But not just now. We'll talk about it again, should we? Let's go and help Christine.'

After supper they played checkers and Christine beat both of them so they called her 'Champ' and they each gave her a dime. When it was time for to go, Bruchk went out to the car with her. They saw sparks in the deepening dusk. 'They are fire flies,' Bruckh told her. 'You don't have those in the Old Country?'

'No, Bill. We don't have fireflies.'

The heat was gone from the air leaving it to the scents and the flickering mites. In the growing darkness his face was a pale blur. Beyond him, in the tree behind the barn, a squirrel chattered and there was an answering movement in the pens. He said, 'Goodnight, Ruth,' but she waited. Then he put his hands on her arms and she raised her face to his. As she had expected his was a timid kiss, there was no forcing, no breaching of her mouth.

She drove back to the reserve and seeing a light in Flanagan's house went there and called to him, 'Can I come in?'

'Sure. Is Marjorie with you?'

'No. She went to Redville on Thursday. I got back here yesterday. I've spent the day at Bill's place.'

'How is that walking spruce?'

'Bill?'

'Uhuh!'

'He's fine. He doesn't change—not in a week anyway.'

'Tell you somethin' about that guy. These roads are gettin' the best gradin' they ever did get. I doubt there's a hole between here and Upcreek.'

'What is that supposed to mean?'

'Nothin'. You had supper, I guess.'

'Yes.'

'Then you won't want a beer?'

'Show it to me.'

'Out of the neck, uh?'

'Out of the neck.'

'Are you going to marry that guy?'

'I was wondering how long it would be before someone asked me that. But I expected it would be Marjorie.'

'Then you're going to.'

'I'm going home.'

That silenced him for a moment. Then he asked, 'When?'

'As soon as school ends. I've booked a flight in July.'

'Well, I'm sorry, real sorry. And you know what, I never thought I'd say that. But it's right. I'm goddam sorry. There's one thing for sure.'

'And what is that?'

'You'll be back.' There was a wish as well as the thought in his words. She sensed this and it pleased her, she felt a sudden shaft of regret at the loss of this relationship with him and with Marjorie. She realized that tears were very close and she said, 'My bottle's empty.'

'Judas Priest! So is mine. We'll fix that. I got a dozen in back.'

'I have some too.'

'You makin' into a secret drinker?'

'Just a drinker, an out-of-the-neck drinker.'

Later she asked, 'Did you know that Ivor has given up the post office?'

'Yeah! I heard that. One of the Indians told me about it. They're all busy switchin' their allowances before old man Goldin' gets hold of them.'

'That's not very honest, is it?'

'I don't suppose! I don't see any store tradin' with Indians out of love. Golding's after what he can make, same as the rest. They know once he gets their cheques that's it. So they're pullin' out fast. He's gonna have to do some chasin' to collect what he's owed.'

'Everything concerned with these people, everything that touches them becomes complicated and difficult.'

'Haven't you worked out the answers yet?'

'How can I? Everybody tells me what is wrong with them and how it could be put right. But they all have different ideas. I've had so many opinions, I feel like a computer. So much has been fed in the right answer is bound to come out if I wait long enough.'

'I told you already. We poison them.'

'I don't accept that. They lead a hard life, there's too much cruelty in it. You said once about their being everybody's rabbits.

They will be as long as they live in these places, they are too cut off from the rest of us. Marjorie is right about that. They won't live until this bush is cleared away. That's where the cruelty is.'

'Look, we're havin' a party, right? And what's the best way to foul up a party? Start talkin' politics or religion. To me, Indians are politics, I guess they're my religion too. So, why don't we stop talkin' about them for just this time, uh? Why don't you tell me somethin' about that old country of yours that I used to hate the guts of.'

'Matt! You don't hate the guts of anything.'

John Fall lifted his head from his hands which were spread flat on the strip of canvas. He stared through the screen of reeds into the mist over the water, hoping for a movement, a swirling—not caused by the drifting air currents. Although he could not see the dam he could smell the decaying greenery, trapped and rotting in its branches. The smell was dank and heavy and strong, held low by the weight of the mists, and the cold was getting into him now, even through the canvas. He had been here for some hours after creeping in during the night, coming against the breeze and keeping out of the shallow water in the creek bed.

He had chosen the spot carefully, after scouting the area from the far bank days ago. There was a log lying there, beaver-cut and abandoned, and around it grew many young shoots, tempting feeding close to the water. To reach them the animals would have to leave the deeper, safer water above the dam—they would be more easily seen in the shallows, their trails would show more, there would be no sudden head emerging at the very bank. There was another advantage; he could get into there at night without being seen or smelled or heard if he was careful enough. The wind, blowing down creek from the dam, would cover the smell and some of the noise; he wouldn't have to be noisy at all. If he could get into there and if the beaver did take it into their heads to go down that way to chew on these shoots, and if the Old Man was the one . . . then!

On three nights he had come in from the north of the dam, moving slowly, a few yards at a time, becoming one of the shadows, finally sliding forward the strip of canvas and stretching himself along it, the ·22 next to him. From this place he had watched three mornings lighten up the waters, brighten the bushes and set everything to calling. Three times, and for many hours the sun had tormented him and countless mosquitoes had landed and sucked and departed, bloated and unsquashed, because he had to remain part of the unmoving bush. And only once in all that time did he hear the gurgle of disturbed water on this lower level. But that had been yesterday!

Each day he had finally retreated, silently and as slowly as he had come—not as a white man, standing and swearing and trampling—but as an Indian, knowing that an animal learns from all things. And so he waited to uncock the gun until he was well away, and waited even more, before he lit the cigarette. For days he had known this animal; his behaviour during these hours would determine the outcome of the scant second during which it would know him.

He had to get the Old Man.

When he saw him the first time—shining, on the top of the lodge in mid-stream—yes right then! he knew right then that this was her pelt. Even if he had to go in there with an axe and then cut into the lodge he'd do it. This one he had to get. He was so big, that son-of-a-gun beaver!

On the first sighting he watched the animal slide down from the lodge into the waiting water, causing scarcely a splash, and immediately became the hunter. Although by now his quarry was deep below the surface, perhaps even in the safety of the inner roads and passages of the lodge, the Indian did not move. He thought and studied, his eyes inspecting every inch of the creek sides, choosing the places for his traps and the best approaches to them. After a long time he went silently from this creek and detoured to take in another on which he already had traps set. He collected these, finding one sprung and holding a dead she; he carried them and the dead animal to his trapline cabin.

Twice he set traps, hoping to get the Old Man and at the second caught a small beaver, but it had not sprung properly and the animal had struggled fiercely. This was bad. It would put the Old Man on guard; he would be scared and would keep away from the creek sides for a while, hide out in the lodge. So John Fall scouted around some more, and that was when he saw the good feeding below the dam, and thought that maybe the Old Man would be smart enough to go down there. But he would be trap-scared. The Indian decided to try to shoot him.

He told George about the big beaver, and George laughed and fooled him some. 'You sure you don't have a big old bear down that creek?'

'Jeez, that's a good animal. I'm gonna get him for sure. He's a helluva big fellow, that guy; you see for sure when I fetch him. He'll stretch clear over that door.'

'You don't even fetch him, I bet.'

'Five bucks say I get him.'

So there was a bet in this, but five bucks was nothing—already he had seventy, eighty dollars in pelts. The bet was nothing, except that he'd like to beat out on George. He wanted the pelt for Ruth. When he took that fat hide, black and shiny thick—what would she say then, when she got that? Nobody could get a better pelt than he could. She'd know that for sure. If he had to take the axe and wade out there. She'd know that. And then he'd take her in the bush like she'd promised. Then she'd know something else, for sure.

He imagined the fur, a round, black circle on the water and rising from it, white like smoke, swirling with the mist, he saw the woman. The picture was so vivid that he could almost smell her scented body and as his nostrils widened in anticipation, something crept into them; something from somewhere near; from something unmoving, waiting like himself, unseen but smelt. He made no movement, not a quiver that might spread his own scent beyond his clothes. Then a slight breeze crept over the water, a dank, cold breeze that fluttered the heavy heads of the reeds and lifted and carried away his own breath, and brought to his waiting nostrils that other smell, the unmistakable smell of a hairy thing.

Still he waited, and then, scarcely feet away, the water reeds parted and their shadow became a shape. And John Fall looked into the eyes of the Old Man.

This was the danger time, the time for the warning smells to burst from his body as the blood burned beneath his skin, but he forced a quietness; allowed the lids to lower slowly over his eyes; put his mind to the white figure standing on the pelt; saw the smooth shining stomach, the nutted breasts and the hair. Then he saw the stomach again, but now it was swollen, bulging from the child within, the dark child, his child. He opened his eyes and there the Old One was, balancing on his hind feet and flat tail in the reeds, and pawing and sniffing the air. The Indian raised the gun barrel and the Old Man, turning, dived. He would have escaped except for a patch of mud that threw one of his feet into a slide, and the Indian shot him through the neck. Even now the animal thrashed through the reeds and fell into the water, but John jumped in after it and flung himself on the beaver. He seized fists full of hair and forced it down below the surface. Blood swirled up towards his face as the animal kicked and jerked, and mud came too, from the bottom, thickening the water until he could no longer see the black fur, but he could feel. Feel the shaking body; feel the cold, flat tail between his legs.

Feel.

And his rage was high that it should try to escape him. He felt so great that he began to shout and shout and shout.

'That's the best goddam pelt I ever seen,' George said. The store-keeper where they did the trading thought so too, but he wasn't going to say that. 'I'll give you twenty-two for that one. This, twenty. Okay? These two, they're kinda smaller, worth seventeen, eighteen. Tell you, I'll make it thirty-five the two, how's that? That makes up seventy-five.'

'Seventy-seven, I think.'

'Sure! That's right, seventy-seven bucks. Say, you tradin' that one?'

'Not this. I'm keepin' this.'

'Can I see it?'

'Sure.'

'That's pretty good, too. Yes, that's a nice pelt you got. And you don't want to sell it?'

'No, I'm keepin' it.'

'Could let you have another twenty-two.'

'I ain't sellin' it.'

'Tell you what, I'll go to twenty-four. Christ! I'll make it twenty-five, cain't go higher than that.'

'I got me a buyer already for this.'

When they got out of the store George was mad as hell at him. 'You're crazy, man! Twenty-five bucks! Sure that's a good pelt. Twenty-five bucks, that's good too. Me, I'd take the money. Who's gonna give you more, anyways?'

'I don't like that guy. He was for cheatin' me, George, you seen that. I'll keep the pelt, try some other place, Golding maybe.'

'Let's get some beer then. We got the money now. We can have us a beer drink, uh?'

They went to the back door of the store, where the storekeeper's son sold them two crates of beer at ten dollars the box. It was three times beer parlour price, but they were Indians buying at a bush store. They paid and took the boxes out to their cabin, where they started a party. It was a good party. They had beaver meat to help along the store ham and they ate both without embellishment and drank until their swollen abdomens and overworked kidneys drove them to the door. They sang and they danced together, holding each other by the shoulders and shouting:

'Ho! Ho! Ho!'

'Ayee! Ayee! Ayeeyah!'

They didn't fight at all, but eventually fell to the floor and slept in fuddled unawareness on the ungiving earth. John woke to a burning in his belly that could only be quenched by more beer. George still slept and he left him, going from the cabin and along the road to the store. The storekeeper saw him enter and noted his appearance, unkempt and red-eyed and he said to his son, 'No more for that guy, Willie.'

'Can I see you round back?' the Indian asked.

'I'm pretty busy. You got that pelt with you?'

'I ain't sellin' that.'

'You see Willie then. I'm too busy. Willie! Go 'round will you? See what this guy wants.'

John Fall went to the back door, where he found that the white man could not or would not accommodate him.

'You got the last yesterday. We don't have no more any place. Can't give you the goddam stuff if we don't have it, can we?'

'I give you ten bucks, didn't I? I paid you, uh?'

'Sure you paid. An' we sold it, didn't we? You know what the cops would do if they knowed what we done for you. Anyways, we don't have no more, so that's it.'

'I'll pay. See, I got the money right here. I got plenty of money.'

'I told you! We don't have none!'

'A couple of bottles, that's all. Jesus! I'm all burnin'. I gotta have me a drink.'

'You'll have to get it some place else.'

John's thirst increased with every yard of the walk back to the cabin. George had gone off somewhere, in any event he was staying for several more days. But John was in a hurry to get back to the reserve. He had the pelt and she had promised. He swore to himself that she had promised. He had only to put the pelt in her hands, let her see the shine of it, let her feel the thickness of it. She'd know then that no man ever took a better pelt and no woman neither. She'd go for sure. She'd go right away with him and she wouldn't get out so quick. By God, she wouldn't once he got her in there. She wouldn't get out so quick neither. And when she did come out she wouldn't be like she was when she went in. It would be there, right inside her and waiting for her to fatten it up. She would be okay too, once she knowed what she was carrying around. Once she felt that inside her she would go like all the other women, she would think about nothin' but that kid. Their kid!

Then south with her, and to hell with the Big Fish. And everybody would know that she was his woman. He gathered his few possessions, his knife and mittens and his coat. He rolled the pelt and tied it across his back. Then he began the walk, and as the hours passed the aches grew—he did not know which he needed most, liquor or Ruth Lancaster.

He walked a lot and he caught a couple of rides, and when he dropped off on Upcreek's street, noon was gone for that day. Little Moise would not hire, the McKenzie car was in his garage and hope had been reborn; that morning he had seen Joan McKenzie again. He would not leave the garage until the car had been collected. So John was forced to look elsewhere. He was standing on the sidewalk when Dan Blood, brother of John the breed came up to him. Dan's shack was this side of the lake, a mile behind Upcreek, and he had a boat. He used it for fishing and sometimes to ferry Indians across to the reserve. He also supplied them with liquor, some of which he bought and the rest he made. A useful man, in short, and especially now to John Fall. Dan said 'Hi, John! How's it going?'

'Pretty good, I guess. 'Cept that I got real thirsty. I only now come down from the traplines.'

'How was it up there?'

'Oh, it was not so bad. I got me three, four pelts. Say, look at this. How you like this one?'

'Jeez! That's sure a honey!'

'It sure is, I'm keepin' this for a special deal I got.'

'George up there, too.'

'Yeah! He's there. He's stoppin' up there yet. He don't do so good as me. Say, you got any beer at your place?'

'I got a little, yeah. You wan' come and get some?'

'I'd sure like that. We had us a beer drink, me an' George. Man! That gives a thirst, don't it?'

'It does for sure. You got to have another to get shut of the first. You got the dough, I guess.'

'I got the dough. After I get a drink maybe you'll take me across, uh?'

'Sure, John. I'll give you a little ride over there. Maybe we could play a little cards too. John, he's down there, and some of the reserve guys.'

Tom Henry Littleleaf and his brother were at the shack—their team nibbled at the grass on the house corner—and already they were drinking. John Blood shuffled a pack of cards and flipped them out, practising-fashion, on to a blanket spread on the floor. The Bloods brought out many bottles of beer and these they all drank, bottle by bottle, until none remained. Then they began on

Dan's own making, brewed out of many bases, a liquor of imagination and improvisation that burned in the throat and fought to come back, so that it had to be held down, a liquid that burned, but not in the throats of the Blood brothers.

John Fall drank deeply. His body needed it, his throat needed it, his head needed it most of all. He drank deeply and the others accompanied him and when their money was gone he stood for them. They played poker too and the hours slipped away along with his dollars. He reached for more, missed a last note and thought all was gone. 'Christ!' he swore.

'What's wrong, John?'

'Jeez, I dunno. My goddam head. She's crackin' open.'

'I guess you're flat, uh?'

'I don't know. Lots, I got me. Say! Look at this goddam skin, uh. Ain't it, she's premium, uh—ain't it?'

'You want to sell it, John?'

'Sell! I ain't sellin' that one; this ain't—no I ain't—sellin'. No.'

'I figure you need the dough. I'll give you ten.'

'You go to hell! Ten bucks! This pelt, not for a hundred, man!'

'A hundred! You crazy or somethin'? You guys, did you hear what he said? He's got a hundred-dollar skin, he says. Are you crazy, John?'

'Ain't crazy—you don't get it, anyways—I got him for special— I did.'

'Tell you, I'll give you fifteen bucks man, how's that, uh? Fifteen bucks 'cause you're my friend, John. That's why I give it.'

'No. This—this—I don't sell this.'

'What for, John, you won't sell it? What is it you're gonna do anyways? I think you're a goddam liar myself. You tell us what for then, if you don't sell him.'

'I can tell you. Sure I can—because you guys—you don't get what I get. You don't get it you guys—I gets it.'

'What you get, John? Ain't nothin' you get, what I can't get the same. Not except that Treaty money, everything else I can get it, me.'

'Not this, you can't.'

'Everything!'

'No!'

'Yes, for sure!'

'Not her, you don't get. Not a white woman like that.'

'White woman! Christ! I had me a dozen!'

'Not this one! No! I got her, nobody else. You don't—I got this one. Me, I'm gonna put a little baby—in this one.'

'Hear that, you guys! John, he got himself a white girl. You got a white girl, uh? Is she better with it than the wife? How she look when you got her peeled off? You got no white girl, you don't fool us none. Your babies gonna be all Indians. Like you an' me and these other guys. All Indians!'

John got to his feet. The pains in his head hurt too much for him to think. He held on to the door post as the black waves pressed behind his eyes. He staggered and his feet crushed the cards.

'Hey! Watch it, you crazy guy!'

'Gimme ride home.'

'Me, I ain't givin' you no ride. That boat, she's all broke anyways. You're gonna have to walk, else you don't wait around and catch a ride with Tom Henry.'

'I don't wait none. I got to see. I got to get over there, me. I got to get there quick.'

'Then you can goddam swim across.'

'Jeez, I can swim too. Who's better? None of you guys can't for sure. You guys go to hell!'

As he stumbled from the cabin Dan Blood called after him, 'You change your mind about that pelt I'll buy him. Ten bucks! That crazy guy, him and his white girl. Like that with her I guess.' He made a sign with his hands and they all laughed. Then John Blood collected the cards and began to arrange them, face upward on the blanket.

Two of the breed's sons were playing near the boat. They watched the Indian's unsteady approach with interest and giggled to each other. When John was quite near they moved back a few paces and stood watching. 'You drunk man!' one shouted and the other also, 'You drunk!'

'Drunk guy!'

'Catch me, drunk guy!'

'Say! Come on, you guys! Give me a ride, uh? See I pay you guys, take me over—there.'

'Drunk man!'

'You give me a ride, you kids.'

'Nossir!'

Somebody called out from the hut and John turned. He shouted to the group in the doorway, 'Dan! You get off your ass. I want—go over there.'

'Get the hell away from that boat, you kids. Don't you touch it, you hear!' The boys grinned and ducked their heads. 'He's drunk man, daddy.'

'Sure he's drunk. Leave him be!'

'You see me then. By God, I swim over there. Holy Christ, I swim that. You see me, you guys. I'm the best, you bet!'

He couldn't think very well. The aches were like trapped lightning inside his head. He could not get his boots off. He had to keep kicking to get rid of them. He threw down his coat but he took the pelt. Though thought was hard, he knew by instinct what would happen to the pelt if he left it. Besides he had to put it into her hands. He pulled open his shirt and stuffed the pelt inside, wrapping it around his body.

'Crazy drunk man,' one boy shouted, and threw a handful of mud against his back. The men at the hut laughed, and their taunts reached between the pains in his head. 'I come up there, smash you guys. I break your goddam place to pieces.' They fell silent. He was too big and too crazy to provoke further, and so they contented themselves with watching.

He approached the water barefoot and he cursed as stones bit into his flesh. Then he saw the buildings across the lake, white buildings, shining in the sun. White buildings and inside them, white woman and white sheets. He had a sudden longing to lie on those white sheets, just to lie there. 'I'm comin',' he said, and his words were a mumble, unintelligible to his audience. 'You get ready, Ruth. This guy's comin' over. Right now he comin' for you.' Water splashed up over the dry end of the boat stage as he belly-flopped into the lake, and the little boys screamed and hopped with glee.

'Drunk man! Drunk man!'

The water was cold. Its shock drove into him, thrust into his mind, pushed out much of the stupidity. He struck out against the cold. This was a crossing that he had made often, though not during recent years. And now one thought came, that he was being watched from the far side; that Ruth was there, at the school watching him coming through the water. He could see her face so clearly. He could see her eyes looking at him and he pushed out his arms and kicked with his legs. Soon his feet would touch mud and she would see him walk out, maybe she would even come down there.

He made good progress, but the water remained cold—cold as its first shock. The chill, left by the departed winter, came up at him, reached into his legs and into his stomach. It felt as if something down there was pulling at him. Sudden pains knifed into his calves and reached upwards to lock his knees. He thrashed his arms and tried to kick his legs free of the torment, but they refused to obey. He tried to get over on his back but the pelt encumbered him. He tore at his shirt, trying to rid himself of his burden but his numbed fingers were too thick. The buttons defied him. He tore and tore at the shirt but it would not open.

'Jesus!' he screamed into the unhearing water.

'Jesus! Ruth!' Twisting and turning, he sank and screamed, 'Ruth!'

SUMMER

1

They say death's got to come in threes. There was Julie and now there's John. Who is the other poor Indian that's gonna die then?

The death of John Fall hit Ruth very hard. She remembered her decision to free herself from him as a betrayal and became sick with herself. She played the game of 'if only,' put her mind back to their last days together and had herself not persuade him to go for beaver. But it was useless and she knew it. The man was dead, ended. Face, mouth, arms, everything ended. Words ended and wants, and little grunts and teased gasps. There was no more of him. There was a basement he had sat in, and a bed on which he had lain, and a creek with dark pool, and empty beer bottles in the kitchen cupboard, but there was no John Fall and there was never again going to be a John Fall.

Fear brought her out of her melancholy. Her senses told her that no man could die like he had without everything concerning him being brought out into the light. It was not possible for him to have kept such a secret, the man in him would need to make a boast of it. He must have boasted. She asked herself how he could possibly have kept such a thing to himself. He must have told of his other woman, said that she was not an Indian. His people were shrewd about such things, he would not have had to name her, they would go through the names of all the women available to him. There were not many. They would come to her. And then it would pass from mouth to mouth and eventually from Indian mouth to white. He might have named her. She waited for exposure, and while she waited she prepared her excuses and her alibis. But no one came to point a finger. Those who might have guessed and become dangerous preferred to keep silent. The Bloods knew nothing, had heard nothing, had seen nothing.

John Blood had brought the body to land. Though she had left the group of watchers as soon as the men in the boat shouted their discovery, she learned later that it was he. The children told her, they were her main source of information about what had happened.

'All that mud came out of his mouth, Teacher.'

'John Blood, he got him, Teacher.'

John Blood of all people. The man whose hands had started the whole thing for her now finished it with those same hands. And she had almost forgotten him!

Julie Redstone and John Fall. Both alive and lovely beings when she had come here, now both destroyed and in such hard ways. And the other thing that they had in common, both had tasted Flanagan's poison.

'No!' she told herself. 'I gave him everything he asked for. I gave him everything he needed. Nobody, no woman could have given him more than I have done. I risked myself for him. I didn't poison him, I made him a better man. He had pride after he got me, he wanted to get away from all this, he wanted to make a way in our world. That's what I did for him. And he didn't know that there was no hope for us, I kept that from him, I let him have his dream.'

Poor John! she thought. Poor man! No more in the creek naked, in the bed naked. No more the raging bull at the edge of my teasing. No more on the lakeside among the spruce needles. No more walking the tyre ridges, no sniffing in the bush and swift striking. No more talk of giving me a child. No more touching me. No more following of the she. No more the man, sodden bundle on the earth with mud in in the mouth.

She stood with Marjorie when he was buried. They were too far away to hear the visiting Minister's words but she heard the women singing. She listened to their wailing sadness, as the men shovelled at the heaped earth, sending it spade by spade upon him, and she felt the heaviness of her own sadness. At last there was no more hole to fill and a little hill rose above the grass, a betraying little mound. And only with the last spadeful of earth had the singing ceased.

A dog scratched at the new-turned soil and one of the men kicked it so that it fled howling. Then rain began and sent them all away. It was still raining on the following day, when she walked after school to the Fall cabin. She could not have driven, the trails were already sodden and treacherous and she would not risk them. She needed the walk in any event, she could think much better and the rain helped, it kept people away from her. She did not know what she would say when she met Anna. She had thought of a score of phrases and would probably use none of them. She could pretend an accidental discovery of the shack and go from there, ask about the children and so on.

Two things had sent her on this visit. She had to see Anna and not only to talk to her and assure herself that the widow knew nothing. And she had to get the pelt. She had heard that John still had it when they found him. The pelt was hers, promised to her, hunted out and skinned and brought back to her. It was John's gift and she wanted it. She had fifty dollars in bills in her picket; she would talk to Anna first, and then bargain with her for the pelt.

The shack was surrounded by a curtain of leaves, all wet, all dripping, each with its tiny drop of clinging water. Beneath the leaves and around the shack and in the yard in front of it, the pools shivered and broke to every falling tear, and there were so many. There was no need for her to announce herself, the children ran out to her—Paulie, son of John, and his sister whose eyes reached just above the classroom table. They escorted her across the yard to their mother who was waiting at the door. It was the first time that Ruth had seen her since the picnic, and she would not have recognized the woman from that day. John had told her that his wife was pregnant but she had not anticipated the physical change. Now that Anna was in front of her she could see how advanced her state was, the woman's time was very near.

There was a flatness about her face that contrasted strongly with the swollen body beneath. Her mouth was kept open and she was breathing through it, long breaths that ended in a dropping of the upper torso. They faced each other and Ruth was lost for words. She had to speak at last because the Indian woman made no effort to.

'How are you, Anna?'

'Okay.'

'I was very sorry about John.'

'Sure. It was bad, that.'

'Is there anything that I can do? I'd like to help you if there is anything. Is there?'

The woman shook her head. There was another silence.

'Well if there isn't anything.' She began to feel foolish and was about to go when Anna said,

'I got something for you.' She pushed open the door and went into the house. While she was away Ruth talked to the boy. 'You've got to be a good boy now, Paulie. You've got to be extra good, haven't you?' She looked for signs of his parentage in his face, but he was like all the reserve boys, black mop of hair, high dimples and thick nose. The looks and body of John Fall would not be his for a long time, and she herself would never see them. Then Anna came back out. She carried a parcel which she handed to Ruth, and Ruth knew immediately what it contained.

'That's for you.'

'For me? Why is it for me?'

'It's for you. It's yours.'

'Why is it mine?'

Anna didn't answer. There was no point in asking the other question. The woman knew. John had talked, and to her. They stood with the parcel between them, his wife and his woman, and Anna had made this so, with her statement. Ruth took out the money and offered it and Anna accepted the bills, and without counting them put them inside her blouse. There was no bargaining, she was paying a woman for the loan of her husband. She said, 'Goodbye, Anna,' but the woman turned and went into the house.

The children followed Ruth for a long time and then let her go on alone, and she returned to the school. Marjorie said, 'You must sure love that rain to go out in it.'

'It washes things away,' she answered.

But that was not quite true. That night she awoke in fear. She had been dreaming of snow, of great walls and skies of snow; and there were dark shapes rolling and fighting, and blood began to creep from them. It flowed and flowed, turning the snow red. Everything became red, running red, flowing up to, and around, and over her. When she woke she was covered in sweat. Her body was wet with it, even under the single sheet. She got out of bed and went to the window. Rain was still falling, heavy rain, running and dripping, running through the soil, filtering down to where John was lying; who had touched her here, and here; who had watched her white tail. She knelt on the dark round of fur and buried her fingers in it. They were white sticks in its darkness. White sticks!

Wherever there is hunting there must be hurt, and sadness for the hunter, she thought. What matters it now who was hunter and who hunted? She felt cold and got back into bed, but she took the pelt with her, held it tightly against her body and remembered; I'm wishin' I'm that beaver.

'I'll step softly, John,' she promised. 'I'll step softly on the beaver.' Then she wept for him.

That night's rainfall was the last for many weeks, and as the land dried into dust its people suffered equally. Sweat rash was general, in the toes, in the crotch, and in the bristly neck region. Tempers grew short and beer parlours flourished; so did the coke stands in the drug stores. Most conversations began with a grumble at the heat and ended with a hope for rain. As the arid days succeeded each other and the drought worsened, the farmers grew morose.

The lack of rain brought a host of problems in its wake. Fire regulations were called into force and the parks were closed to visitors. But in spite of constant precautions fires broke out—often these were caused by shafts of lightning that touched off the dry tree-tops; sometimes by campers, sometimes by a cigarette butt carelessly flipped from a car window.

There were other problems. The Argot brothers and their friends, meeting as they crossed the road, took up stance in the centre of Redville's wide street and discussed these. They spoke first of the caterpillars that were infesting the eastern side of the province.

'Fella I met, said them goddam things fallin' off the trees in goddam millions. Crawlin' over the goddam roads every place. Highway's greasy as hell, he said. Can you beat that, uh?'

'They're big bastards, those!'

'Too right! They're goddam monsters.'

'Don't they eat too.'

'Worse'n hoppers.'

'Oh no! Oh no! Nothin's worse any place than hoppers.'

'Hell no!'

'Then fires bad, too.'

'Sure. Say, I heard on the radio—they closed down roads everywhere. Fires jumpin' out all over.'

'This goddam province ain't gonna grow nothin' 'cept fireweed if this keeps.'

'It's so goddam hot!'

A spiral of dust rose in the air a few feet away and veered towards them and one of the Argots spat through it as it passed.

'You save that, you're gonna need it.'

'It don't rain no more.'

'No. It don't look that way either.' They looked at the sky. They gave it the searching gaze, squinty and hopeful, as if even now a puff of white—or grey—might bounce up over the I.G.A. roof.

'Who's gonna be a farmer?' one of them asked.

'Who's gonna be a farmer? Hoppers, beetles, cutworms, caterpillars . . . what those goddam things don't take then the hail, it's gonna come and smash it down.'

'You forget them salesmen too.'

'Oh Christ! Them!'

'Wish it'd rain.'

A pick-up drove past, perilously close to the little group and its grinning driver leaned out to shout to them, 'Get off the road, you French bastards! Get off the road!'

'Aw shit!'

'He's a real boy, that one!'

'Sold him a horse once, that guy. Best sellin' I ever did make. It got killed the same day, hit by lightning.'

'Is that right?'

'Sure is. Man, she was a pretty little horse! She could put her foot in a beer glass, she was so little and pretty.'

'I'm gonna put my mouth into one right now.'

'Me too.'

'Wish to Heaven it would rain.'

The people of the Big Fish were living in tents now. There was a village of scattered white blocks above the lake and a dozen fires burned there, or smoked beneath any flesh that could be found, fish, fowl or bush rabbit. Card games began that would endure day and night through the summer, and in which much money would change hands—and also shirts and hats and guns. Some families, like the Willie Falltimes and Joey Birds stayed in their huts because they did not own tents, or because they preferred to live away from the rest. When it got too hot, Joey Bird took a stick and knocked the glass out of the windows. And still it didn't rain, not even enough to shine the head of a bird.

There were so many things to do in those last weeks, as the school time that remained dwindled away, and vacations grew from sun-dozing day-dreams into an imminent and exciting prospect. There was the school picnic taken at the Beach—eating and races and splashing in the water; and then a six-innings ball game up the hill, with Bruchk helping out as umpire. Afterwards Marjorie passed around ice cones and they sat under the trees, sheltered a little from the sun, and listened to the chattering of show-off boys and added their laughs to the audience of girls.

'Me, one time I pulled a little boy out of the water. He was drowning when I got to him. His dad watched me do that. I got lotsa Coke that day.'

'Did you get drunk then?'

'I got sick.'

'Why don't teachers get sick once in a while?'

'They don't ever, uh?'

'They must love us kids.'

There was great laughter at this, the boy carried it on. 'They like school more than we do, I guess.'

'They don't do the work, that's because.'

Flanagan said, 'Lots of work I've got for you guys in the morning.'

'Me, I guess I'm gonna be maybe a little sick.'

'If you're not in school I'll come by your place, pull you out.'

'Aw gee! School, that's all prickles, no berries!'

'You got short legs, long tongue.'

'Jump back on the coyote, little flea.'

When they left the Beach, Flanagan and Marjorie walked away first, leaving her to follow with Bruchk. They did this always now, and she knew that the two men had arranged it so. It gave Bill a chance to take her hand and walk with her. They met on most nights, either in a group at Smallhill or just the two of them on the farm. It was too hot to do more than sit and sip in silence, and smile at each other when their glances touched. He always kissed her when they parted but never before then. Once only had he touched her, his hand trembled on her and was removed before her breast could answer.

She promised him nothing and they never spoke of her coming departure, but when she was alone and sleep would not come she thought of him.

'I could come back,' she told herself. 'I could make the trip a holiday, a final goodbye. I could come back to Bill and his farm. There would be peace in that, and a kind of contentment. I could help in the building of the farm and the man. I have much to give to him and it is time for me to give, I have been too long without that, without giving. And there would be purpose for me.' Then she would remember John Fall and she would sweat with horror at what he could have done to Bruchk. 'Thank God that is finished,' she said, time and again. 'It is over, it can never be used to hurt Bill.'

She could almost be glad then, not that John was dead, but that he was no more.

And so her last weeks on the Big Fish were peaceful, but she would remember afterwards that behind the peace there had always been the heat. There was always the headache just a touch away. There was always the overlying oppression. It was there, all the time, only she had been blind to it.

Big Fish, here I come!

June was almost over. Only two days remained after this Friday and the school would close and its families scatter. Some were already gone, on premature release to work with their parents on root-picking contracts. The rest were itching to be away, to see that big door close on another year, eager like all children, to spend their lives as quickly as possible.

And still the heat clung, not relaxing its grip day or night, and winter had been cooked right out of mind.

'Damn the heat!'

'And the flies!'

'And the dust!'

'And the heat again! Damn it twice over and send a little rain.'

Ruth had arranged to visit the farm. She went early, the sun was still high and the air was stifling. It's hot enough to start a riot, she thought, and so dry. The ditches had long been robbed of their spring water, and the undergrowth that had crept after the disappearing moisture, was yellowish and short of leaf. A patch of red scrub caught her eye and she was looking at this while trying to keep the car on the narrow trail, when she realized, quite suddenly, that a man stood behind it. She slowed, expecting him to wave her down and ask for a ride into Upcreek, but he made no sign and she drove on. He was not one of the men whom she knew and she forgot about him before she was off the reserve. She was hoping that Christine had fixed up to go out, so that she and Bill could drive somewhere. He had never been in this car with her; for her to drive him would be something new for them both. She looked forward to a quiet hour, sipping cold beer and watching the people in the beer parlour. There might be opportunity then for her to resolve her problems—in one week she would be thousands of miles away. The thought was not easily acceptable. She was filled with such indecision that mental drifting was becoming a habit. If he took hold of me tonight, he could decide for me, she thought. If only he would do that, if only he would be a John Fall for one hour.

When her car had disappeared the man came from out of the bush and stood in the road. He began to walk after the dust and it came down to settle on his hair and his shoulders. He walked easily, but his strides were long and he covered ground quickly. When he reached the turn to the creek he took it, and came to the bridge. He slid down the bank and scrambled through the scrub. Here too, the water had dwindled until it was possible to walk across, using an exposed piece of timber as a platform. The man squatted on this in the centre of the stream. He stared into the water, and after a few moments he reached down a hand and groped. The hand was full of mud when he brought it back, thick, slimy mud. He looked at the hand and its mud. Then he stared back into the water. He sat on the board for a long time and the mud dried on his hand and began to crack.

He was Martin Crow and he was looking for Julie. He knew that she should be here because she had gone away here. In the little part of his mind that gave him pictures, he kept seeing her here. But each time he saw her, her face was spread with this mud. She had gone into the mud. When she came back to him, to take him to the shack again, she would be like that. She would come back out of it. She would be covered over like his hand.

At last he rose and stepped across to the far side. He would have gone up its bank and lost himself in the bush if the sun had not moved into the space between the willow heads. It searched the creek and found sparkle. And Martin saw the sparkle and went into the water to catch it. He came out with a pair of spectacles.

He sat on the bridge and put the spectacles between his feet. He had to look at them for a long time before the picture that he sought found its way to him. He had to wait until the spectacles were not on the boards, but were where he had seen them before, on the face of Helmut Golding. He knew then that the storekeeper had sent Julie away. He wanted Julie; he would have to ask the man to bring her back.

There was a large leaf close by, he took it and wrapped the spectacles in it. Then he set off for Upcreek. It was late when he reached the store, not dark, but late as store time goes, and he caught Golding at the end of his sweeping. He went in quietly so that Golding, looking up to find him in the worsening light, was startled.

'It's time! You can't have nothin'. Not now.'

Martin went to the corner and put his hand on it. The storekeeper repeated, 'Didn't you hear, boy? The store's finished, yet. I done for today. You can't have nothin'.' He stopped talking because the boy was unrolling the leaf. He moved in, curious and leaning on the broom. Then he saw the last cover come away and his own spectacles stared up at him. His heart leapt—he felt it, it was almost a pain to breathe for a moment.

Martin said, 'Julie,' and he made a question out of the name.

'Where did you get those, boy?'

Martin grabbed the spectacles and fell back a step. The store-keeper followed, crowding him against the counter. 'Them's mine, boy. You better give me, give me quick.' The boy shook his head. He was afraid, he did not want to be shouted at. He was scared and needed help, and so he said, 'Julie,' as if by calling he could bring her.

'You get a couple of bucks for finding. Now give them me. Give me the goddam things!' By this time Golding had hold of the boy's shirt. He pulled and Martin fell to his knees. Golding's fear became rage and he began to beat the boy with the broom. Then he saw the white flash of Ivor Jones's straw beyond the window, and he knew that within seconds the Welshman would be entering, on his usual delaying spree. He had no time to waste; he dragged the boy along the floor to the back of the store and through the door there. He let him fall on the cinders and kicked him.

'Goddam Indian bastard! You don't come here no more. I bust your goddam neck if you do. Now get the hell out of this town or I put the cops on you. Go on! Git!' Martin crawled around the side of the store and Golding went back inside the building.

'Hello then, Ivor,' he said. 'I didn't hear you come in.' The little Welshman grumbled, 'Where in Chrissake you been?' and Golding knew that he had seen nothing. It had been a very close thing, and the big man began to sweat, and wonder how he could keep Jones in the store until the Indian boy had gone. But he need not have worried, Ivor Jones had no intention of hurrying. He stumped all around the store and the minutes went by, enough of them for Martin to drag himself along to the back of the ball pitch.

The usual crop of teenagers were going through the usual pitch, hit and catch drill, and gave him no more than a passing glance. 'That crazy Indian. He's been on the hooch again.' The boy crouched and watched them for a while and then he went away. He walked along the ditches of the reserve road, going slowly and limping, because he had an ache in the hip where the store-keeper's boot had struck. Long after dark he emerged from the shadows cast by the fires along Muskrat Lake, and stood behind the card players. Nobody paid any attention to him. He pulled the arm of his uncle and showed him the glasses, but his uncle said,

'Go 'way, Martin! Go 'way, boy!' So the boy went, but as he

passed between the tents he saw a large jug in one and knew that it contained wine. He reached inside and picked up the jug and carried it away, unaware that in doing this, he was robbing Tom Henry Littleleaf.

He took the jug to the Painted Rock's shack where he had been living for some months. He went in and picked up his shotgun and put a few cartridges in his pocket. Then he took the trail to the creek. As he crossed the bridge he tossed the spectacles into the water. Then he turned into the bush and was soon swallowed up in its darkness. At last he came to the shack—to Julie's hiding place. But there was no Julie to go in with him and it was dark in there.

He needed Julie. He wanted her bad. He stood the gun against an outside wall and went to the centre of the bare patch, where he squatted on the earth. The moon was high and he could see its light flash from inside the bottle. He lifted this and bit out its cork and began to drink. Some of the time he held himself where Julie had held him. Sometimes he stuck things into Golding's face in the earth. Some of the time he sang.

Francis Littleleaf came over the crest to what for him was the right side of Top Hills. He sang a little, talked a lot and shouted at times—all to himself. He was reclaiming that which was his, every wrist-wide branch, each rock, the earth and its covering sky. He did so each time he returned to the Big Fish, which was his heart and his stomach and his feet and whatever lay behind his eyes. But this day was more than just a returning, it was a pilgrimage. Other guys brought offerings when they came back, meat maybe, or pelts. He had a piece of paper. Right with him in this bag. The best piece of paper that ever had writing on it. What was it the Principal had said? 'Here's your passport to life, Francis. Use it!'

'Oh man! This is a good land.'

'Hey up there, Johnnie Painted Rock's house. How is Johnnie treatin' you then?'

'Hi, Good Lake!'

'Hi, Bad Lake!'

'Shake up those fish, you lazy guys. Leave go of that sun and shake up those fish.'

He whistled at a bird and shouted at a squirrel, and when he heard a following peep from the far side of the hills he imitated it. 'Peep-a-deep.' Then the object of his mockery came into view and slowed, as it caught up with him. 'Say, we're going to get us a ride, Mr Littleleaf.'

'Hi, Marjorie! You got yourself a new car then?'

'Hi, Francis! No, it isn't mine. It's Ruth's. You know her, Miss Lancaster?'

'Sure, I know her; it's neat, uh?'

'Sure is! Throw those things in back. Are you right?'

'I'm right!'

'Then here we go!'

'You okay then, Marjorie?'

'Yes. And you?'

'Same.'

'I'll be better next week. You get that, don't you?'

'That's for sure, Marjorie.' He waited for her to ask him the important thing. She would pretty soon, as soon as she remembered that High School had ended for him.

'I guess it was hot walking?'

'It always is, Saturdays. Didn't you know that? Old Sun grows hotter on Saturdays, it's for sure.'

'Francis! That city doesn't make you any better!' Then she did remember and began to ask him, but a boy walked out of the bush and stood in the road, right in front of the car. She changed her sentence, 'Hey, what does he want?'

'Watch it! He's Martin Crow. You'd better stop, could be he won't move.'

'He'd better! Damn him!' She put on the brakes. The car skidded and shuddered to a stop, only feet short of the waiting youth. She put an elbow out of the window and leaned to shout at him. 'What do you think you're at, Martin? You can get yourself all killed that way.' The boy came round the side of the car. Before she could move he jerked at the door and she fell out as it opened. Even then, while she fought to straighten herself, her strongest emotion was disgust at the stench of liquor that came from him. It was appalling, it was enough to make her sick.

'Come,' Martin ordered, bending over her. He seized her shirt and began to drag her from the car repeating that one word time after time.

'No!' she shouted. 'No, Martin!'

And she heard Francis Littleleaf call to him telling him he was crazy and to leave her be. Then right by her ear sounded the loudest noise she had ever heard. Her brain shivered under it. She began to shiver through all her body and still she was being dragged and her legs were out of the car now. She looked upwards and saw Francis's face leaning over the edge of the seat and at that second his eyes rolled away from her. A trickle of blood found its way down the side of the seat and dripped on to her.

She screamed and Martin stepped back. Then pushed down with the gun barrel against her mouth.

'Golding,' he shouted. 'Golding come! Come!' She got to her feet and cowered against the car. 'Please, Martin,' she begged and began to weep, 'Oh please, please, Martin.' He struck her on the shoulder, and struck her again. 'You've hurt Francis,' she told him but he was not hearing anything that she said. He got hold of the front of her shirt and ran and she was dragged with him, down into the ditch and up its other side. She was not going quickly enough for him and he came behind her and beat her across the back and she fled, lost one shoe, then the other but did not stop. He drove her through thickets and across meadows. She fell, was dragged up and forced on. She ran beyond pain because terror of Martin gave her strength, but her soft body was taken over by a multitude of aches. She had never been farther than a few steps into the bush in her life, now she was lost in it, scrambling over dried creek beds, crossing trails, going deeper and deeper. Then Martin stopped. She dare not look at him, she stood with sagging head, trying to drag breath into her lungs. And Martin came for her and took her by the collar and turned her and she saw the creek and its bridge. He pointed his gun to the water and pushed, and she stumbled down to it. Then he threw the shotgun to the ground and came after her.

'No, Martin,' she begged but he forced her, first to her knees and then full length, her face to the mud.

The little boy who brought the news to the school, trickled out his information like he would sand through lazy fingers. He sat below Ruth on the porch steps and played with his toes, and then moved up a little higher so that she took notice of him. Then he said, 'That car, she's all stopped, Teacher.'

'It's stopped, you mean.'

'It's all stopped.'

'You don't need to say all. Say, "it's stopped".'

'It's stopped, Teacher.'

'Which car are you speaking about?'

'That white one, it's stopped.'

'Which white one?'

'That teacher's car. It's all stopped.'

'White car? Do you mean mine? Do you mean my car?'

'That's him, teacher. That white one. It's all stopped up there.'

She breathed deeply and patiently. 'Did Miss Golding send you? Is she having trouble with the car?'

'Miss Goldin', he's not there. That car, she's up on the road.'

'Has she had a breakdown? Where is the car?'

'He's up there on the road.' The boy used his chin, then added, 'He's all dead, too.'

'It won't go?'

'He's all dead, teacher. I see'd him.' He held up a palm; it was very dirty. She stared at it and thought, trust a boy to find mud, even during a drought. Then the boy said, 'I touch him, Teacher. He's all blood. See!'

They took the boy with them, to where he had seen the car, and before they reached it they knew that there was truth in his words, from the group of Indians who were standing around it. Flanagan was out of the Pontiac almost before the engine stopped running. Ruth watched him push through the Indians to the car. He stood there for a few moments, and then came back to the Pontiac and leaned on both arms over its hood.

She opened her door and got out. 'What is it, Matt?' she asked. He shook his head, he would not look up but she saw the grey colour of his face and thought he was going to be sick. Then he said,

'It's Francis Littleleaf. His throat's shot away.'

She stared at her little white Beetle, unable to believe that it contained such a burden. Marjorie had only borrowed it for an hour.

'Matt! Where is Marjorie?'

'How in Christ's name do I know?'

'She isn't in the back, is she? Did you look there?'

He replied, 'I looked,' but he returned to the car and this time stared through the passenger window. Then he turned to her and shook his head. He went round the car and opened the trunk. When he came back into sight he shook his head again. He shouted to the Indians, and his words broke them free of the spell this death had cast upon them. 'Get lookin' in them goddam ditches! See can you find anythin'. Quick, for Christ's sake! Get lookin'!'

They made a hurried search of the immediate neighbourhood, but it revealed nothing and they gathered again around the Pontiac.

She asked, 'Do you think she can have been thrown out somewhere? It could have happened, couldn't it?'

'Why should it?'

'I don't know. I don't know, Matt.'

'It could though. Any goddam thing could have happened. She's got to be some place. We'll go back up the road and look. Get in!'

226

'Matt, should we leave him like that, with those children there?'
'No! We shouldn't. George! Can you get a sack, a bit of cloth or something. Cover Francis up from those kids. Keep them away from there till we get back.'

He spoke once only, during the drive. 'Do you think she could have done that?'

'Marjorie? No! She could not!'

'You're right! Could she hell!'

They drove slowly and watched carefully, but found no sign of the missing girl. They held another conference when they reached the highway. Flanagan stated, 'I'm going back down there and I'll get those guys out lookin' some more. She's got to be some place, and that car is the nearest we can get to where she was. 'Less he stole it. He could have. Sounds crazy, and I don't think he will have but we'd better check. Then again, she could have lent it to him, but where would that leave her? They were comin' from the highway, I don't see where she could have got to. 'Less she took off in there. You take this car. Go on through to Upcreek. Try her folks, and if they know where she is come back fast and work the horn. We'll hear it. And you'd better call the cops, too. Yeah, you'd better do that.'

The gathering by the Volkswagen had become a Band Meeting. Groups of men were standing near the car or sitting on the lips of the ditches. There were several teams of horses, heads bent and tails flicking. Flanagan got out of the car and said, 'I'll get these bums working. Good luck!'

She drove away, and as she went, she realized that she was going to have to tell the Goldings what had happened. She began to think of phrases she could use.

Oh God! Marjorie thought. Oh God! It is going to happen to me. It's so sunny. It's so nice. Not to me, God. Please not to me. Help me, God! Help me!

She waited for Martin to turn her, she had sunk into the mud and it was difficult to keep her mouth clear of it but she pressed downwards. She was terrified of being rolled over and having to face him. She waited and then something cold touched her neck and she tensed at the shock. She shivered beneath a knife that began to tear and slice through her shirt. She saw his shadow move in the mud beside her face as he worked. He cut and ripped and tugged until her shirt and jeans, all her clothing was torn from her and tossed away. Then his hands came against her back and they were cold and slithery and wet. Her breath fled. She thought, he is spreading dirt over me—that is what he is doing—wet dirt.

Then she was rolled and looked up not at his face but into the sky above his shoulder. She watched the sky all the time he was working until the mud came over her face and then she closed her eyes. When he had finished and she was covered with the slime, he went from her to the bridge and came back with a piece of rope. He knelt and pushed it beneath her and knotted it round her waist. Then he stood up and pulled, and she rose and he led her away.

They walked until she was so tired that she could hardly move her legs, and then at last came a time when she was no longer moving. She raised her head and saw an old shack; it was a shamed wreck, its abandoned bones as white as driftwood. Its door was a gap from which splintered bits of wood still hung, and it was towards this that Martin dragged her. He forced her inside and came after her. She retreated into a far corner, until protruding logs stopped her. But he still came and put his hands on her. She was too afraid to resist and she began to cry as he fondled her and squeezed and pushed at her.

'Julie,' he kept saying.

'Good, Julie? Is that good?'

After it had gone dark he took her out of the cabin and made her lie on the ground. Then he sat near to her and began to drink from a glass jug. Later still he started to sing, a strange, low-pitched monotony of sounds without words. It went on and on. She crept away a little at a time, until she reached some scrub, and here she curled herself.

Sometimes she slept. More often the mosquitoes kept her awake—and his singing. The mosquitoes were greedy for her, they seemed to drop from the trees; they searched her as he had done, seeking any tiny opening on her mud-caked flesh.

Whenever she woke she thought she heard him singing.

It seemed as if all of Upcreek had parked their vehicles outside the school and were trying to fit themselves into Flanagan's house. Except for Helmut Golding; he was still outside in his car—he had been there since before dark, long before the search party had begun to straggle in.

There was plenty of talk going on inside there—theorizing, suggesting tactics, making guesses as to why and how. But nobody knew where, that was the trouble. There was bush enough on the Big Fish to lose an army. And if she was hiding in there, that wouldn't make it any easier either. But she couldn't hide for ever, she'd have to come out and eat some time.

It didn't seem to have got any cooler after sundrop, and thanks to all those hot bodies, and the smoking and the breathing too, the atmosphere was getting a little too much for Ruth. She sought the sweeter air outside. But even that was sultry. She heard a voice say,

'A man daren't hardly light a cigarette, 'case he sets the air burnin'.' He is right, she thought, it is too dry to sweat. Then she saw the flicker of flames under the nearest trees. She saw a group of grotesque silhouettes crouching over a fire there. She wondered why they should want a fire on such a night, when the heat of the day lay heavy over the land. Perhaps it was a psychological need. In times of stress it took the place of the white man's cup of tea— the Indians lit a fire, and sat, and watched it smoke, together.

She was thinking this when there was a sudden commotion over there. A burst of talk was followed by a mass movement. The fire watchers approached in a group, and as they drew near she saw that they were escorting a woman, and the woman was holding a girl by the hand. From the light of the house she recognized Lily Falltime, daughter of George. The group went past her and crowded into the doorway of the house. She followed, curious as to what this meant, and she squeezed into the room. She heard the Chief say,

'You tell the Police here what you seen, girl.'

There was no reply. From where she stood Ruth could not see the girl, but she could imagine her, cowering and terrified by all these men and especially the policeman. She heard Flanagan say, 'For Christ's sake, you're scarin' her. Get back a bit.'

'Yeah! Get back. Quit shovin'.'

'Kid's scared. Let her be!'

Ruth pushed through to the central group. The men gave way when they saw who she was and she was able to reach Lily. She knelt on one knee and put an arm around the girl. 'What is it, Lily? Tell me. Tell me what you saw, dear.'

The girl's tears ceased. 'Teacher, I see'd them.'

'Who did you see, Lily?'

'I see the teacher. I seed Miss Golding. She was with that Martin guy.'

'Hey! She was with a fella!' a man shouted. Flanagan turned on him. 'For Christ's sake, shut up!'

'Tell me again, Lily. Who was she with?'

'That Martin. Martin Crow. He's that crazy guy. She was with Martin.'

'Where did you see them, Lily?'

'I see'd them—they was by the creek. They was over there. I see'd them over there.'

'Which creek was it?'

'That one, over there from Devil's Lake.'

'When was this? When did you see them?'

'It was long time.'

'This morning or this afternoon?'

'Yes.'

'Which, Lily?'

'I don't know, Teacher. It was a long time.'

'What were they doing? Were they walking?'

'They was walkin'. Martin, he's huntin' too.'

'He had a gun?'

The girl ducked her head. Then she giggled. Ruth asked, 'What is it, Lily? Why are you laughing?'

'That teacher, she don't have no clothes on.'

Somebody said, 'Jesus!' Other than that, there was silence. Then the police officer told the child, 'Thank you, Lily. You can go home now. You've been a good girl, you've helped a lot.' When she had gone he said, 'So now we know where she went and why she won't come out. She can't. She's got to be found quick. This Martin, Chief? What do you know about him?'

'He's Pete's boy. Pete Crow.'

'The girl said he was crazy. What did she mean by that?'

'He's crazy.'

'How? Is he violent? Has he ever got into fights? Does he go for any of the reserve girls?' The Indians conferred. Then the Chief shook his head.

'So there's no pattern to it. Could be the heat. It's caused this kind of thing before. This creek, Chief, where is it from here?'

'West. 'Round the lake. You take the Upcreek road and you come to a turn off.'

'They weren't on that road. The car is north of there, towards the highway.'

'They must have walked some.'

'What is your guess, Chief? If you had to find him, where would you look?'

'He's some place north of the creek.'

'How would you look for him?'

'I guess—maybe I'd go up from the creek with some guys. Some other guys'd have to come down from the highway. He can't cross that Devil's Lake. They should get him between them some place in there.'

'Then we've got some lookin' to do. We're goin' to have to go right up through that bush, and we want a party comin' down from the north. But we aren't goin' to do any good chasin' around in the dark. We'll go in there first thing, soon as we can see. And we go in careful. No shoutin'. No noise. We might be lucky. We might catch this kid sleepin'. We don't want to scare him, or there's no tellin' what he'll do.'

'What do we do now?' Flanagan asked.

'Make up a couple of parties. Those guys who are comin' down from the north will have to get up there in plenty of time. They'd better pull out of here no later than three. The boys goin' up from the creek could leave at half-past. I'll be with that gang. And by the way, all this armour, leave it. You won't need it. We're makin' a search, not a war. Leave it.'

A man ventured, 'That kid is armed. Already he's killed a guy. I'd say we'd be better keepin' these, in case.'

'Would you shoot him?'

The man didn't answer. The policeman said, 'We don't know for sure that he shot anybody. Leave the guns.'

The men began to drift out to their autos and make themselves as comfortable as they could for the remainder of the night. Ruth sat on the steps to her porch and listened to the crackling of the fire. There was no point in going to bed, she knew that she would not sleep. She was too disturbed. The peace of the last few weeks was gone, and there was a constant undercurrent of excitement behind the fear she felt for Marjorie. The quiet nights at Smallhill might never have been; here was the story of the bush again, sudden and savage, and the smoke from the Indian fire was a fitting accompaniment. She sat and brooded.

Two men walked across and stood beside her. She looked up and saw Flanagan and Bruchk. Flanagan began,

'I brought that kid here. I talked her down here.'

'She wouldn't have come, Matt, if she hadn't wanted to,' she answered.

'She had to work some place,' Bruchk said. 'Nobody figured on this happening.'

'I let her come into it, Bill. I should never have done that.'

'You couldn't have stopped her, Matt,' Ruth told him. 'She would go anywhere to be with you. If you haven't seen that by now, then you must be blind. She's in love with you, Matt, and when we find her, you'll have to do something about it.' She began to climb the steps, then added, 'And I'm going to bed. Good night.'

'Wait a minute! Who told you that? Did she tell it you?'

'It has never needed telling. Good night, Bill!'

'Ruth! Is that why she came to live down here?'

'She came to live down here because she caught her father in bed with Julie Redstone.'

And Ruth went in to the house and left them to their silence.

The Chief had gone from the house back to the fire with the other Indians. He smoked through a cigarette and then asked, 'Where is that Pete Crow these days?'

'Last I see'd him, he was stayin' by Old Lady Fall's house.'

'John's place?'

'That's right. He's livin' with Anna now.'

The Chief looked around the group and chose a young man.

'Simon, you go up there, quick. Tell Pete I want to see him. Tell him Chief said to come now.'

'Okay, Chief.'

Within the hour, Pete Crow, sometimes known as Twisted Eyes, came out of the bush and seated himself at the fire. The men moved to give him room and the Chief reached across. The two men gripped hands. The Chief said, 'I didn't see you long times, Pete.'

The half-breed nodded.

'You been okay?'

Again the man nodded. 'I been okay.'

'You heard about that Martin?'

'I heard that.'

'He's your boy, Pete.'

The man nodded a third time. He did not speak. Somebody passed him a cigarette and he picked up a glowing twig to light it. He smoked until it was half gone and then passed it to a waiting hand. The Chief continued, 'The cops is here.'

He let that sentence rest for a moment; the other men were silent listeners behind the fire smoke. They heard and knew. The Chief was smart. He was a good Chief. He took his time, spreading his sentences:

'When they get hold of Martin, they put him in the Fort.' 'They're gonna tie a rope around his neck.' 'They pull down on that boy's legs. They choke the hell out of him.' 'He don't come out of that Fort, once they got him. They make a hole for him in there. That's what they do if they catch your boy.'

This time the silence was longer. Then the Chief continued:

'Pete, you had a place up there, north of the creek. You lived up there one time, when Martin was a little kid.' For the first time the half-breed answered, 'That's right!'

'I thought you did.'

Somebody threw another log on to the fire. Sparks flew, and there was a quick flame. The Chief coughed and spat into the fire and Pete Crow got up and went away. The Chief turned away from the fire, took off his hat and put it on the ground. Then he curled himself so that his head was on his hat. There was a general movement towards the horizontal and soon all were sleeping.

3

The mosquitoes were a nuisance in spite of the repellent. Ruth's shirt sleeves were buttoned down and she had tied a piece of chiffon high on the neck, but still they found openings; there was a constant humming as they homed in on her. She was a lone woman in a silent, cigarette-smoking group. They were silent because there had been enough talking during the night. Now each was isolated in his own private world, pondering in the pause before action.

Ruth had Bill Bruchk on her mind. She could not bring herself to think about Marjorie being somewhere in there beyond the trees, with a man who might kill her at any moment. She pushed these thoughts away. She thought of Bruchk and his farm and after him, of this land, hot now but with its great periods of bitter cold. It had come to dominate her so much, it was hard to accept that in two days it would affect her no more. Bruchk was in the party to the north. He had gone off very early, before she was called by Flanagan. She knew that he would be thinking about her. She considered him once again; it was becoming a continuing pre-occupation, this reconsideration of Bill Bruchk. He was a strong man, she thought. He does not blaze like Flanagan, his friend, but he is strong. He might bend before the elements but they will never break him. She knew that if she took him, this would be a part of their life together, this battle against the elements. She would have to be strong enough to stand with him. And she would not have to look for excitement. He was not a man to provide excitement.

'That is what I would have to give,' she told herself. 'I would have to furnish that.'

She looked for Flanagan and saw that the men were no longer movements only, but were now distinguishable. And the trees too—she could see individual branches in the thickets. The awaited dawn had stolen up on them. The men began to move about. One said, 'Last time I was up all night was when the wife first pupped.' She heard Flanagan say,

'Let's quit the talk and get goin'. What the hell are we waitin' for?' Then someone down the line raised an arm and they began to move forward.

Ruth was to one side of Flanagan, an Indian was on her left and beyond him an Upcreek man. They walked purposefully, a thin straggling line, over-aware at first of every clump of bush, each dip or hole. As they came to impenetrable sectors the line divided, and soon it lost its form. There were too many breakings and some of the younger men were too eager to be at the front. She kept close to Flanagan; he was striding out to her right, stooping slightly forward. She saw a flash of colour at his hip, and knew that it was part of the ripped shirt they had found in the creek. What a moment that had been, grovelling in the water, putting hands in the water, searching in the wet darkness and fearing the touch of cold skin. Then somebody had found a rag and the collection of Marjorie's clothing had begun. Lily Falltime had been right. Wherever the poor girl might be she was naked.

As I would have been if John Fall had taken me in here. She couldn't drive this thought from her mind. She ran to catch up to Flanagan, and all the time she could see that patch of cloth.

They came to a small slough and skirted to its left to search the reed beds. These were isolated growths in a cake of mud and they snapped as she strode over them. She searched and found nothing and then looked for Flanagan but did not see him. She knew a moment of panic—we are all being swallowed up, the bush is devouring us. Then she heard voices and ran in their direction. She came through a screen of poplars and saw him with two Indians. She went up to him and he said, 'There's nothing on either side of us. We'd best go on. We're fallin' behind. The goddam line's all to hell.'

'How far have we come?'

'Two miles maybe. No more!'

Suddenly the quiet of the bush was broken. A shot sounded, and immediately, as an echo of the first there came a second explosion. The group broke, the Indians were first away, silent runners, but Flanagan was on their heels as they entered the far bush.

'Wait!' Ruth shouted, but no one listened. She could not match their speed and after a while did not bother to try.

Something ran across Marjorie's face. It was a light, feathery, scratching of the skin, hardly discernible, but it startled her out of a fitful sleep, and she lifted herself from the ground. Pains swept through her numbed legs. She got to her feet and she hopped in agony, as the livening blood circulation needled a thousand pricks into her flesh. She rubbed her calves and the mud crumbled away into dust in her fingers.

Dawn had come to end the long night and she could see the

squat shape of the shack, its propped-up decadence, its flaking mortar and the dark holes in its roof. She could see the framing bush—blue in the pale light—high over the roof and level on either side with the window top, and creeping around, up to, and into, the dark entrance.

Martin Crow lay between her and the shack. He sprawled on the bare earth, his face turned in her direction, and his knees tucked in almost to his chin. Beyond him, towards the hut, lay his hat, and nearer to the hut, his shotgun.

For the first time in all the hours since she had left the car, she thought of escape. But she was afraid. She did not know where to go. If he awakened and came after her he would be enraged, he would do things to her again. And she thought that she would die if that happened. She couldn't last through that again. So she crept a little way into the bush and hid. She worked to free the rope that still hung on her. She was doing this when a quick rustle in the grass startled her. When she dared to look she saw the tiny furred figure of a chipmunk. He made several darting runs and she sat quite still until he passed by her and scooted up a tree. She watched, and as he stopped he faced about so that they stared at each other, the chipmunk bright-berry-eyed, inquisitive about this new arrival. Then, in a sudden flash of fur he was gone. She turned her head to see what had scared him. A man stood in the small clearing. He had made no sound to herald his appearance; there had been no shout, no breaking of bush. Something about his silent approach kept her from calling to him. She watched from her hiding place as he stood over Martin. She saw him reach the gun towards the sleeping figure and thought, he is going to waken him.

She would have fled then. She would have run anywhere, once Martin got up. She was tensed to do so, when smoke leapt from the mouth of the gun. She stared, unable to believe, at Martin's body as it jumped about on the earth. She saw the dust rise as he kicked. Then a second shot put an end to his threshing.

She pressed herself down, gripping the grass with her hands to get herself lower. But she still watched and saw the man take Martin's arms and drag him towards the shack. They disappeared into its darkness, and now it seemed that the whole bush was silent and waiting like herself, until the man came out. He walked towards her and she crouched again, but he stopped to pick up the boy's gun and his cap and took these back to the doorway. He flung them inside and then walked around the side of the hut, pushed his way into the bushes and was gone.

The disturbed dust began to settle, but Marjorie saw a new

haze forming between herself and the shack. It hung around the doorway and thickened and began to swirl upwards. She watched the cloud grow and become tawny where it poured from the top of the doorway, or seeped out of the sacking at the windows. It thickened in the clearing, until the shack was hidden from her, but it couldn't hide the blaze as the tinder-dry roof exploded into the branches.

There was a roaring now, and the crackle and scream of dying bush and trees. But there was shouting also, and there were men. They burst into the clearing and she saw them run through the smoke, trying to get to the hut. And Matt was there! She saw him run at the hut and then fall back before the heat. She screamed to him to stop and he heard and turned to her. Then she remembered her nakedness and began to cry again, as she crouched and tried to cover herself.

He came to her and he knelt and put his hands on her shoulders. She watched his mouth as he spoke, but she could not take in his words. Then he unbuttoned his shirt and pulled it off his shoulders. He wrapped it around her and fastened its collar and buttoned each hole, talking to her all the time. The smoke swirled around, blocking out the sky, and men were everywhere, stamping and beating at the flames. 'Get the hell out!' somebody shouted, and a man staggered past, coughing and rubbing his eyes. Another figure appeared from the gloom and leaned over them. He shouted, 'Are you hurt any?' She shook her head and he said, 'Well, that's something! Where is the boy? Is he in there?'

She nodded and he said, 'That's it! Get her out of here, Flanagan!'

Matt lifted her, and another shirt was given to him. He tied its arms around her. Then he ordered, 'Get on my back.' She was still weeping. She said, 'You can't carry me, Matt.'

'Do as I tell you. Get on!'

He carried her from the clearing and as they went, others passed them, retreating from the fire. They staggered on through the sunlight towards Ruth and a waiting truck, and behind them at the shack the friendly chipmunk died, and the mice, and sawflies, and fleeing squirrels. Birds choked and fell through the clouds to the flames below.

A monster had been loosened and was running wild. It was branching in all directions, pulling in oxygen and making its own winds, leaving a strange world in its wake, a spreading grey desert, out of which smoking spikes poked, all that remained of trees that had begun the day in glory. Along the fire-fronts dying

237

trees passed the torch to neighbours, and a second tier of flames spread in their tops, as ravenous as the one below. Sometimes the fire ran towards a tree, rushed the trunk and climbed till the foliage burst like a fired gusher, and when this happened, the smoke that belched into the whirling fog was blacker, more funereal than the rest.

And so the forest began to die, yard by yard, and acre by acre, but it was not a quiet passing. There was a roaring, like surf against a beach; there was the scream of sap and the snapping and crashing of branches; there was the all-at-once crackling of thousands of shrivelled leaves, and often there were squeaks and screeches.

A dozen shacks burnt out in those first hours. Many had already been deserted—hostages to the heat of summer, others had long been abandoned to the spiders and the mice. But some were occupied and their inhabitants reacted to the danger, each in his own fashion, answering to his fibre.

Joey Bird and his two sons left their home and stalked the fringe of the fire and Joey shot the fleeing, frightened rabbits as they staggered from the bush; his boys grabbed them, and if they still kicked, they held the rear legs and battered the heads against the trees. Only when they could carry no more did he cease to shoot, and then, burdened, they fled and other rabbits came about them and fled with them. The flames torched the toilet frame, and then the house, and then the tyres on the upturned wreck in the yard and the melting rubber dripped to the earth and poured forth foul blackness.

John Shortleg and Lucy, his wife, smelled the fire and saw the sky grow darker. John brought his team to the open door of his shack, and then he knocked the pipe away from the stove and tied a rope to one of its feet. He fixed the rope to the team board and whipped up the horses. The great stove lurched and began to move across the floor, leaving gouges in the boards. The horses dragged the stove out into the open, to a place where the earth showed all round and no grass grew. Then he ran the horses to his wagon, and hitched them and led them again to the house. Lucy, who had been piling things at the door, started throwing them up into the wagon—clothes, shoes, guns, traps, nets, cans of tomatoes, bread, flour, hides. Only when the fire winds were moaning and the ash was dropping on them, did they climb into the wagon, and whip the leather across the rumps of the team.

And Willie Henry Falltime sent his wife and the girls down to the slough with the horses while he and his boys waited with soaked rags at the far end of his tiny pound. When the first flames appeared they were quickly beaten out, and the boys shouted their delight as they swung the wet sacks and won out again and again. But the flames ran freely on the flanks of the pasture where the bush lay thick—and the air grew so hot and the smoke grew so thick. Their legs were tired now from running between the buckets and the fires, and sparks flew over them and caught in the dry grasses that lay between them and the house. The man dropped his rags and called to his sons and they fled. As he passed the cabin, Willie Henry reached out his hand and slapped the logs, once, twice. When they reached the slough they found Maggie and the girls having trouble keeping the horses quiet, and the little ones were crying. Willie Henry flung himself on the head of the nearest horse and dragged it down into the water, and he took off his cap and held it over the horse's eyes. The boys pulled at the other one and got that down as well.

'Get down, all of youse. Get in the water,' Willie Henry shouted, and then, 'Wet them up, Maggie! Wet those guys up! Wet 'em up good!'

They lay in the green-scummed water and they heard the fire take their home, and they heard the screaming of the forgotten dog.

And the fire swept down on them and around them until they were ringed with flames, and the burning air made their insides heave and they coughed themselves sick. But they stayed alive.

Ruth went out on to the porch. It was noon. The sky was brown as if it, too, had been plastered with mud. There was a roaring, a constant surge of noise, the rushing of winds as they passed the school on a dash into the bush. She could hear the complaining of countless disturbed leaves and wondered how long they would remain alive to complain. She watched their green fluttering and saw how pale they were against the sky. Then she walked down the steps and set off across the diamond. At the edge of the lake she turned and saw the extent of the fire. It stretched across the whole northern horizon, a great line of smoke patterns, sometimes still and heavy, but drifting in places and streaked with flame. It was a horizon of anger, of sullen belches and leaping lights, and growing over all was the gathering mushroom of ash.

'Let it burn,' she said. 'Let the whole rotten jungle burn and burn! Let there be an end to its evil and its cruelty! Burn it and destroy it! Let in the light so that these people can live. I hope not a stick of it is left.'

She walked back across the pasture and in the half-light she saw the leaning post, white and pointing. She turned her head away from it as she went on into the house. She looked in on Marjorie. Flanagan and the girl both slept, he in an armchair, his feet on the end of the bed. He had carried Marjorie in and bathed her, washing off the mud and the blood from the scratches. Then he had smothered her with oil and cream—all Ruth could find. They had slept that way ever since.

She closed the door and went along to her own room.

The ash rose. Throughout the afternoon it climbed, so that when night came it brought no stars. Ruth woke to a dark room. She lay for a while and listened. Somebody was speaking at the front of the house. The voices were raised, they were insistent. She thought, they will waken Marjorie. The thought nagged and eventually she got up. She went to the front and found Smythe arguing with several other men. She heard their words before she saw them.

'We've got to talk to those guys. We've got to talk to that dame.'

'No!'

'Aw, come on, Mister.'

'You can't see anybody. You can't talk to anybody. You'd as well go home.'

'Mister, if we go home without seein' this kid, we've got no job, we've got no home!'

'Good night!'

Night, she thought. It is night again. Then the men saw her and she saw the greed appear on their faces.

'Hey! Is that the dame? Was it her that was all night in the raw?'

She turned without speaking and went back into the house. She was glad that Smythe was there to handle the reporters: Flanagan would have murdered them. She went back to bed and immediate sleep. Only a few minutes after this, Bruchk came to the school. He walked through the school, missed Smythe and the reporters and found her sleeping. He sat for a long time beside her bed and then he went out. The reporters had gone and Smythe was talking to Flanagan. Bruchk said, 'Ask Ruth to come over when she can, Matt,' and went out to his pick-up.

Smythe confided, 'It's a hell of a mess, Matt. I'd give a lot for it not to have happened.'

'It's gonna knock hell out of your Redville deal.'

'I meant more than that.'

'Sure you did.'

'Can I see her?'

'No!'

'Tell her I'm sorry.'

'Who isn't?'

'You're wrong, Matt. You've been wrong all along about this question of schooling.'

'This kills it dead!'

'It doesn't. That boy wasn't an Indian.'

'He was as Indian as the Chief.'

'He wasn't Treaty.'

'Judas Priest!' Flanagan turned from him and looked across towards the distant tents. Over there, where grass was still green and juicy, the card-players leaned closer around the blanket. It was hard to see the spots and they had to peer. So did the without-money watchers—they all had eyes only for the Kings and Devils, and never for the flashes to north and west, where the Band riches were turning to ash.

He could not see the Indians, but he saw the pin-pricks of their fires. 'God help them,' he commented.

'What did you say?' Smythe asked.

'God help them. They lost their Jesus yesterday, and the poor bastards don't even know it.'

4

Ruth was wakened the second time by bumping in the corridor. She listened for a few minutes and then got up to investigate. She found Flanagan taking stuff out to his car. She asked, 'What is going on here, Matt?'

'We're pulling out. There's been a bunch of newspaper fellows over here. Smythe shifted them, but they'll be back. We aren't waitin'. We're takin' off soon as I can get loaded.'

'How is Marjorie?'

'She's rough. But she'll be better when we get the hell out of here. I've fixed the back so she'll be okay in there.'

'Where will you go?'

'Christ knows! South first, to my folk's place. After that, any place, it doesn't matter. But where we go, it's together. Does that suit you?'

'Yes. Can I help?'

'Go in to Marjorie. She wants to see you. So does Bill. He was here a while back, but you were asleep. He asked me to tell you to go over there, soon as you can.'

'Was he in with me?'

'He must have been, he came out of your room. I don't know how long he was there, it must have been a hell of a time. You're gonna have to marry the guy after that.'

'I'll talk to him about it, Matt.'

'You do that, and say, keep in touch, uh? Through Bill. I guess we can write to you there.'

'I guess. They're going to miss you, these people.'

'Are they? I don't know. I guess I don't know that.'

'What about the police, Matt? Won't they want to see Marjorie?'

'You know what they can do. They want us, they can damn well come lookin'.'

She smiled at that. He was the old Flanagan, he would take trouble with him wherever he went. He would find someone to fight down south or out west. She touched his arm and went in to Marjorie.

After they had left, she went to bed again but she had recovered from her fatigue. The smoke was thick in the room, it would be strong over wide areas; it would be eaten and drunk and breathed for many square miles. But in this room it was a constant reminder of the violence, so near by. Ruth thought of that violence, connected it with the darkness of the night and the black smoke she had seen over the forest. Over and over again, to her mind came Marjorie's mumbled words. The story of what had happened inside that hut. And always with them came the thought—it could have been me . . . it would have been me.

The idea of Bill watching her while she slept was a warming and happy thing. She remembered how she had looked down on the sleeping John Fall. 'It should have been me watching Bill,' she told herself. 'It could be like that. I want to share life. I need to. I will dry up if I don't. I will dry up into a withered bag. Oh God! I don't want to do that. I need tenderness and he is giving it to me. I want to be discovered, there is more to me than sex. He could find out what I am and show me myself. He could do that. I don't want to wither. Don't let me wither, Bill.' She began to weep and after a bout of this, swore at herself, 'Don't be so bloody stupid!' And the thought leaped into her mind—you can always look for another John Fall.

She got out of bed and washed her face, then she went outside. Not long ago, at a similar hour, the bush had spoken to her. Its message of awakening day had been alive. Now it stank and was silent and she turned from it. In the park, the white post beckoned.

She left as soon as Little Moise brought the cleaned car back. She had burned the last of her papers and given away anything that she did not want to take. Now she had only to say goodbye to the school and its swings, to Muskrat and its people. This was soon done, a slow circling and a silent thought, there was need for no more than that. She got into the car and switched on the engine.

Little Moise held out a notebook. He said, 'I found this down the seat here. It must have been that kid's. Do you want it?' She took the book. Its soft cover was creased down the centre from much folding. Its late owner's name was on the front cover, written three times and with decorations:

Francis Littleleaf.
F. Littleleaf.
Francis Littleleaf. Private.

She opened the book and read the first line:

When the kids go back to school it's goodbye Summer.

She turned to the last few pages and found a verse:

Did you hear the noise, John
Of the rope on your coffin?
That's a deep hole you can't climb from,
Deepest on earth.

Ruth closed the book. She asked, 'Have you read this?'

'Nope. Didn't find it till just now. Under there it was, got pushed down there, I guess. You know—when he fell over.'

'Yes.' She was glad that this man with the dirty eyes had not read the verse.

She was wearing a white dress. It was a deliberate choice, she had prepared herself carefully—for Bruchk rather than the flight. She would not mind if he marked the dress, there was a matching sweater in her travelling bag. But she would give him the opportunity, it would be a simple thing to take his big hands in hers and put them to her. Then her breast could answer him; it would do all her speaking for her and he would know. He would feel her, he would be reassured.

They drove through a cleared area from which she could see grain high in the fields and a distant elevator. The sky there was clear of ash and cumulus climbed. It will rain tonight, she thought, it will rain on my land tonight.

It was only a brief flash, in a moment they were back in scrub country and she saw burned patches—here, south of the reserve. She was surprised and asked, 'Has the fire been here?'

'Sure. Didn't you know? Came through by the lake end, under the moss they reckon. Jumped out close by Upcreek. We damned near got burned out, we did. If the tender didn't come from Redville, we'd had it sure. Man! That was a scare.'

'When was it?'

'Late on. She really burned. Me, I don't think I've seen a worser fire. Us guys were tryin' to keep it back.'

'Was anybody hurt?'

'No. 'Cept a kid. They were on the roofs, splashin' water. He fell off, broke his leg too. But nobody else wasn't hurt.'

'I'm glad of it.'

'And Bruchk. They say it got into him.'

The car slowed. 'What did you say about Bruchk?'

'It got into his place. Burned a little, I guess.'

'Is he all right?'

'Sure, he's okay. Lost a cabin, they say, but he's okay. The tender was there too. It saved his house.'

Suddenly the car seemed to fly, so often were its wheels clear of the ground. He clutched his seat and held tightly. He forgot all about her knees and her close legs, he remembered that this was a death car and he clung to his seat and prayed.

Ruth could not wait to be rid of him. She left him scratching his head on the street until he started to run after her.

'Hey! You didn't pay yet! You didn't pay!'

She drove along the track to the farm and all the way now was following an ash-strewn trail. The ditches were cleared of growth and black-whispered, the dust in the road was grey. All life was gone, shrivelled into the earth. The trail led to the farm and she saw the buildings. A cabin, Little Moise had said, but it was more than a cabin. Bruchk's main sty, his hog-house, was reduced to smouldering debris; remnants of its insulation floated in the pool of filth in the yard. The house itself was undamaged apart from the dirtying of its face. There was evidence everywhere of the fight that had taken place here while she slept.

She got out of the car, stepping carefully to avoid the wet ash. Its stench was sickening, more than straw and wood had burned. Wisps of smoke rose on all sides, to flatten into a layer that hovered above her head; it stretched from her to the house and beyond. The smell would be in the house. It would remain in its wood and its clothing for weeks.

It was a desolate scene, the destruction of order, the driving out of all heart. I don't have to go now, she thought, there is work for me here. He couldn't do it alone. She knew how hard this would have hit the man and she knew what value she would be to him. For he would need rebuilding also. He had loved what this had been.

She could not approach any nearer to the house and so she called out for him. There was no response and she sounded the car horn. This brought movement, but it was from behind the barn. She shouted again and a man walked round the corner. He was carrying a board but let it drop when he saw her and cleaned his hands along his jeans. She looked from the hands to his face.

John Blood said, 'Hi then!'

She answered, 'I want Bill.'

'He ain't here.'

She was very conscious that this was the first time she had spoken to him and yet she had used him so often before John Fall came to her, she had put so many words into his mouth and had wished so many deeds from those hands that she did not speak to him as a stranger.

She asked, 'Where is he?' and a tremble began at her knees. It was slight but it was there, and it was a cause for wonder and then for worry that he might see it. She looked at him and saw the darkness and the grin and the wide shoulders and the foolish trembling continued.

'He ain't here. He's took the hogs down to the meadows. We're pennin' 'em there so we can get to this.' His arm swept across the buildings. Woodsmoke, once the harbinger of the man, stretched like a curtain over their heads. He had walked through pools of ash, it was smeared on his clothing. She stared at his face; she dare not take her eyes away from his or they would be at her, they would go for her legs, they would see the shaking knees.

'Is Christine home?'

'Nobody's home.'

He came a little closer and then he did look her over and she had to stand and suffer his search because her legs seemed to have lost their power to move. He looked and he laughed and he said, 'Why don't you come in then?' She shook her head.

'You can wait for Bill. He'll come by.'

She objected, 'It's too dirty.'

'Jeez! that's nothing. I could tote you over that.' She looked immediately at his hands and then wished that she hadn't but it was too late. He said, 'See, I clean 'em for you,' and he rubbed his palms against his rump. She shook her head. If he takes one more step I'll go, she thought. I don't have to stop here. If he takes one more step.

'I don't think you're gonna be all that heavy neither.' He began to walk through the black slush and all the time he was grinning and she could not stop from looking at his face. If he puts a hand on me, she swore, I will scream the bloody place down. Then he was standing right in front of her and she had to look up he was so tall and this was a hard man, she could see that now, he was hard no matter how much he showed his teeth. He was John Fall but stronger. He was John Blood.

'If you don't want me to tote you it's okay,' he remarked. 'Me, I don't care neither.' He waited and when she did not answer he continued, 'No guy's gonna see you. There's nobody round here. There's only you and me. Jeez, though, I didn't know you was as nice as that, honest to God I didn't!'

She still did not speak and he took her as the other John had once done, his arms around her thighs and he brought her body against his, 'Jeez,' he said again, 'You're real sweet!'

She smelled the familiar odour as strongly as if there was no competing stench surrounding them. She put her hands to his shoulders as he began to walk.

246

'You're heavy too,' he told her. 'You've got meat where it don't show.' At these words something strong and unburnable rose from the dark bush of her own being. It swept away all thought, all reason, all plans and hopes. It swept away everything except now and being gripped, and smell, and man. It drove out her stiffness and she relaxed on to him and knew that he would surely halt before they were clear of the filth. When he did stop she closed her eyes. She felt one arm take a firmer grip of her and the free hand stretch itself across her buttock and begin its caress. She let her head rest on his shoulder. She opened her eyes and the sinew of his neck was close, taut and shining with sweat. She moved her lips until they touched his skin and then pressed them and worked them against the firm muscle. And his hand continued to stroke her as he might stroke his horse and extended its range and suddenly forced its way between her buttocks.

'You got a sweet ass too!' he said.

And then she hit him. She whimpered with fury at herself and struck at him, beating his head and face so hard that he had to let her fall. She staggered at first and then turning, fled through the dirt to her car. She paused there and looked back. John Blood had not moved. Amazement showed on his face, but it turned into humour and laughter as she watched. He bent under the laughter, slapping himself with those hands. He howled with it, put his head back and howled. She shouted to him. He stopped laughing to catch her words and she repeated them. Then she got into the car and reversed it and drove away. She saw him for one moment in her rear mirror and he was laughing again.

When she was out of sight and he could hear her no more John Blood picked up his boards and set off for the meadow. 'Jeez, that was a crazy one!' he told himself. 'She was enjoying that. Come on so quick, too, and who would have guessed that. Jeez, I was nearly there with that one! I bet she never had it proper, that's why she come over scared. I shouldn't have let her go like that. I should have toted her right into the house. She's gonna be harder now for the next guy. Shoutin' that too. What does she mean by that? How in hell is a guy ever gonna get poisoned that way? Not me! I ain't ever. Nossir!'

Far down the highway, Ruth Lancaster pulled off the road and stopped. She stared at the massed grain until it began to shimmer, then she wept. Much later, she started the car and drove on to the city.

Joey Bird spread the cards on the blanket and Annie Littleleaf cut them. Her fat fingers squeezed and bent the chosen half. The other players crouched closer as the cards began to flip through the air, and the watchers also. A boy threw a handful of green spikes and cones on to the fire and a puff of smoke rose upwards towards the hanging rabbits, scattering the flies from the open guts so that they came instead around the bowed heads.

Behind the group the lake flashed.